TREMOR

INFECTIOUS RHYTHM SERIES, BOOK 6

TONYA PLANK

ISBN paperback: 978-1-942289-16-6

ISBN eBook: 978-1-942289-17-3

Library of Congress Control Number: 2019914625

Edited by Rebecca Pruner Kimmel, The Writing Refinery

Cover design by Marisa-rose Wesley, Cover Me Darling

Cover photo from istockphoto.com

Author photo by Bruce Heinsius

For all of my wonderful readers, and for everyone who loves ballroom dance.

INTRODUCTION

After losing her husband and dance partner to a motorcycle accident, ballroom showdance champion Arabelle has developed a hand tremor, making it impossible to perform the beautiful balletic feats she is known for. In her devastation, she's lost her love of dance anyway. But when she meets Jett, a theatrical dancer specializing in daredevil aerial stunts, Arabelle feels a double tremor – one producing trepidation, the other pulsing excitement, as he evokes the bad boy ways of her husband that had so enthralled her but had also resulted in his tragedy. Can Jett help Arabelle overcome the pain of her loss, cure her trembling body, and reinvigorate her passion for dance and life? And can Arabelle tame Jett's reckless ways before they result in his own misfortune?

Tremor is the sixth book in the *Infectious Rhythm* ballroom romance series.

Arabelle

"**A**nd now, Ladies and Gentlemen..." The emcee's voice boomed over the microphone, and was followed by a drumroll. "I introduce to you, Tarzan, King of the Jungle! And his sweetheart, Jane!" Loud applause, filled with lots of whoops and hoots, echoed throughout the theater, along with a good deal of whispers.

"Oh this is it, this is them," my friend Lucia squealed, squeezing my shoulder. The drumroll intensified as the lights dimmed. Lucia rocked back and forth, her butt knocking into mine on the padded bench seats. The percussive sequence ended with a loud clang of a steel drum, which made me jump in my seat. I was definitely used to live performances, but not of the circus-like thriller variety. I'd been—well, I still was—a showdance ballroom dancer. We did our share of stunts, but not death-defying, airborne acrobatics like the ones here.

The spotlight shone across the stage, revealing a young woman. She was standing on a precipice that was made to resemble a very thick tree branch. She was wearing a teensy-tiny loincloth around her crotch and an even teensier bra. Yes, very Vegas.

"That's her! That's Mandi!" Lucia beamed. I shot her a sweet smile. She was so proud of her little sister for getting this gig. I was happy she was proud, even if it was in a super risky show in Vegas.

The "tree branch" was shaking and Mandi looked on the verge of falling. She had fear in her eyes, though I'm sure it was acting. I took a deep breath. I didn't think watching such a show would make me so nervous.

The music swelled into an old Hollywood movie-style crescendo. The spotlight on Mandi faded, and another shone across the stage. We all followed the light up, up, up—Lord knows how many feet high— to where a man stood. He had sexily messed-about dirty blonde hair, was well-built, very tan, and wearing only a skin-toned loincloth that made him look naked. I gasped, literally. I would have been embarrassed but the room was filled with gasps. There was no way a soul heard me, including Lucia. He was beautiful. He was also perched on a tiny stick of a beam, though I couldn't tell how wide it was since he was up so high. He was holding onto the bar of a swing, about to take a step off the perch.

Suddenly, Bonnie Raitt's "Holding Out for a Hero" began to blast. He took off, flying across the stage on that swing. He was stunning. His upper body was generally lean, like the majority of dancers—you can't stretch muscle if you build it too bulky—but still more muscular than most. His face was a mix of classic matinee-idol and strong he-man, with a square jaw, prominent nose and solid cheekbones. His large eyes held an intense gaze that was visible despite the distance. He was like a cross between Tarzan and an old time movie star.

He swung back and forth through the air a few times like a well-seasoned gymnast, making gorgeously perfect lines with his legs. His attention to form revealed a ballet background. And his strength was insane, both in his arms and legs. He propelled himself up and over the bar, doing a handstand at the top. He held his legs upright before doing a straddle split. He held the position for a while, showing a great deal of strength. He then flew across stage, propelling himself with just a single hand. The theater was so full of cheers the music was barely audible.

He swung through the air several more times, now showing the strength of his legs by supporting his weight with his feet and ankles. On one swing across, he flexed his foot over the bar and flew upside down, supporting his entire weight on the top of one foot. But it wasn't solely about strength. He also made a variety of shapes with his upper body, some beautiful, some funny. He flexed his muscles as if he were a body builder, then made a kind of male model pose with arms folded in front of him and a handsome smile. Finally, he stretched toward the other side of the room, his arms outward, as if he were reaching for a long-lost love. I was getting so wrapped up in the amazement of it all, that I almost forgot there was another dancer on the other side of the stage.

Now another spotlight shone on Mandi. My right hand began to shake. Crap. The tremor. I gave it a little smack. I wasn't even dancing. *Why was it shaking now?* I was sick to death of it. I looked up at her again. The trembling grew more intense. I looked away. But then I suddenly felt a shadow over me. I looked straight up and saw him—the male dancer—reaching down toward me. Of course, he was way above me and couldn't possibly reach me, nor could he see me with the bright lights. I was a performer; I knew how bright lights blinded you from seeing anything in the audience, no matter how much it seemed from the audience perspective the performer was looking right at you. It's

3

something we dancers call presence. And this guy had it in absolute spades. But still, it was completely surreal how it seemed like he was reaching right down to me, as if to pull me up, pull me out of myself and toward him, toward the light.

I had a brief flash of Willem, my husband. No. I mean, my former husband and dance partner. My now-deceased husband and partner. A quick wave of heat crested over me, before turning into a shiver. I tried to shake it off.

"Are you okay, honey?" Lucia patted my knee.

I sat up straight, took a deep breath, and nodded.

The light was back on Mandi.

"Oooh," Lucia squealed again.

Mandi now had a smirk on her face. She looked at her Tarzan while he flew across the stage in a variety of crazy poses, shaking her head as if he were such a show-off. It was meant to be funny, and it was. The guy *was* a major show-off, to put it mildly. This so-called duet was far more about him than her. But it seemed like the performers were going with it. The audience laughed along with her. As he went back toward her, he did the same stunt as before, holding himself by the tops of his feet and folding his arms in front of him, flashing her—and us—his handsome male model smile. I smiled, noticing my tremor had abated. *Thankfully.*

He perched atop his own little tree branch again, right as she wobbled on hers and seemed poised to fall. He beat his chest as a Tarzan call sounded over the microphones. Funny again. But then he swung over to her again, the spotlight highlighting his stunning physique, making him look like a Rodin statue in motion. He reached out for her, and she jumped into his arms. Or rather, his one arm. He held her around her waist with that one arm as he gripped the swinging bar with the other. They flew together back across the stage.

It was a spectacular stunt. But thrilling as it was, I couldn't help thinking how wrong it could have gone, ending in a serious calamity for her—if not for both of them. The audience didn't seem to share my worries, instead going wild with applause. The pair continued swinging back and forth across the stage from perch to perch, doing all kinds of miraculous holds and making a multitude of beautiful shapes with their bodies wrapped around each other. I felt my trembling start again. I looked away, annoyed with the choreographer for creating something so death-defying. But when they passed over us I felt that weird sensation again, like his eyes were shining down on me, like he was compelling me to look up at him, to see him.

And when I did look up, it was impossible to take my eyes away. The choreographer had arranged their swings back and forth to resemble the development of a relationship, each rotation illustrating a different stage. First, she hung below him, holding his feet with her hands while he let go of the bar with one hand, as if they'd just met. Then they tumbled about each other playfully, exemplifying the fun, flirty stage of their relationship. Then, they did things that looked more sexual—this was a show for eighteen-plus, after all. She spread her legs into a wide split, then wrapped them around him, which, completely ludicrously, made me feel a pang of jealousy. *What was that about?* Then they grew into love, embracing each other in a variety of poses that were simultaneously risky and extremely difficult, yet immensely beautiful. In their last pose, they looked like another Rodin sculpture in the air. Okay—the choreography *was* amazing, though still nerve-wracking.

The audience went completely wild at the end of their number. His face oozed boyish charm as he took a bow with her far, far above us. Lucia raised her hands above her head as she clapped, chanting Mandi's name. But all I could think was how much he outshone her. Hot as he was, he really was the definition of show-off. I'd been in the ballet world before I switched to ballroom and I knew so many of these kinds of men. They all wanted to be Baryshnikov, stealing the spotlight for themselves with no regard to their partner. Cocky male bravura asses. I emulated Lucia, raising my hands high above my head and screaming, "Mandi! Mandi! Woo!"

2

Jett

As much as I loved this show, as much as I loved highly theatrical, stunt-based dancing, as much as I loved Vegas, I was getting kind of tired of these after-show receptions where I had to spend hours meeting audience members with backstage passes. They all—both women and men—always seemed to hover around me the most. Yeah, I know that sounds cocky. And I understood why, with the routine and the Tarzan character and all. I admit, at first when I was new to Vegas, it was a blast, getting all fawned over. But it got old; setting boundaries, toeing the delicate line between pissing someone off with a rejection and letting them touch you practically wherever they wanted, incurring the wraths of their husbands or boyfriends.

I'd taken to staying out of the limelight as much as possible. So, at this party I stood in the corner with my dance partner, Mandi, and two other dancers in the show, Max and

Rosy, eating sushi and drinking sake at the table in the back. As guests arrived, a few spotted us. Friendly chatter and handshaking ensued.

And then, my more typical encounter occurred.

"Oh, what a true hero you were!" an older woman said to me, raising her brows, as she pawed at my chest. She was dressed to the nines and her crimson lipstick matched her hair color and the little red hearts on her inch-long fingernails.

"Thank you, ma'am." I laughed.

"You were just totally sexy and amazing, with all those feats and those legs and big man-arms," she went on. The man beside her looked away. He wore beige shorts and a stained t-shirt. He looked dressed for a day on the beach, and she for a fancy cocktail party.

"Thank you, again," I said.

"Where are you from?" She reached under my suit jacket and ran her long fingernail down the buttons of my shirt.

I backed away a little, not liking where those nails were headed.

And then I saw her. This holy beauty. She was standing on the opposite side of the room, next to another girl. She was looking all around, her eyes big and a soulful gray-blue, taking everything in. She was simply radiant. She had light blonde hair that hung nearly to her waist, like a ballerina's. She stood with feet turned slightly out in third position, her long, luscious arms held gracefully out in front of her in an oblong pattern, as if she were subconsciously making a ballet-perfect port de bras. She was tall and thin, and her long legs had the fine musculature of a dancer. Definitely a ballerina, either now or in the past. Her face was heart-shaped and doll-like, with inquisitive eyes and full, pink lips that I wanted to kiss immediately without even knowing her.

Okay, who the hell was this creature to cast such a spell on me? She had perfect posture and looked out on the world with an air that was somehow simultaneously regal and humble. She wore a pink, silky sundress that hit a couple of inches above her knees, and high-heeled white sandals. She had a long strand of white pearls around her neck. She was the definition of grace and elegance.

She wasn't the type who came to these parties. She wasn't really the type I'd often seen in Vegas, in general. She didn't look like she was here to let loose and have fun; she looked serious and, actually, a bit sad. She was totally out of her element, but beautifully, intriguingly so.

And she didn't look the least bit interested in me or in meeting any of the cast.

"Um, oh, originally New York," I said to the woman running her finger down my chest as she cocked her head at me, making me realize I hadn't answered her. "But I've lived here for a long time now. Several years," I added, wanting to distance myself from New York and my father, and everything there that I didn't want to be part of.

Hard as I tried to focus on the woman in front of me, I couldn't take my eyes off the beauty who'd just entered my world.

"Ooh, Lucy!" Mandi squealed. To my immense delight, Mandi started waving madly at the girl who was standing next to my lady. The friend had dark brown shoulder-length hair and wore tight jeans, a low-cut V-neck shirt, and high-heeled ankle booties. Now this was more the typical Vegas girl. They were friends? And she knew Mandi?

The brown-haired girl waved back madly, and Mandi ran over to her. *No, no, no, you come over here*, I thought. Right then, the beatific blonde turned her eyes to me and our gazes connected. My heart pounded and shot a rush of blood downward to my groin. Geez, what was wrong with me? She literally gasped, and looked away immediately, focusing on Mandi. Did I do something wrong? Well, I'd just have to find out.

"Please excuse me for a moment," I said to the woman whose fingernail had now rested right above the top button of my jeans. "I see an old friend." She shot me a look of disappointment but I didn't have time to deal with it. I gave her a polite smile and pat on the shoulder and walked toward Mandi and the beauty.

As I approached, the blonde's gaze connected with mine again. She peered down at her drink, as if suddenly entranced by the bubbles at its surface. Though they stayed focused on the glass, I could see her eyes widening as I approached. Long, long lashes covered dreamy blue irises. She swallowed and looked off in the distance, as if searching for something. I couldn't tell if she was shy or aloof. Or maybe she just didn't notice me, and there really was something interesting out there. She shifted her weight as if she were uncomfortable in my presence, then blinked and focused on the brunette, who was chatting animatedly with a very excited Mandi.

"Hey, aren't you going to introduce me to your friends?" I said to Mandi, after clearing my throat.

"Oh, sorry. Yes, Jett, this is my big sister, Lucia. Lucia, Jett, my partner," she said, her hands gesticulating wildly, in typical Mandi mode.

"So awesome to meet you!" Lucia extended her hand.

"Nice to meet you, too," I echoed, taking her hand, with a nod and a smile while looking back and forth between her and the blonde. The blonde held her head slightly downward, but looked up at me over the tops of those long-lashed lids. Long as those lashes were, I noticed they didn't seem to bear a lot of mascara, only a smidgeon. She didn't wear a whole lot of makeup, another un-Vegas thing about her. She didn't need to; she was naturally beautiful. "And who's your friend here?" I asked.

"Oh, this is my good friend Arabelle. She's a dancer in L.A. I brought her here to help her celebrate her twenty-fifth birthday!" Lucia chirped. "And I thought this most amazing show would be a perfect way to do that!"

"You thought right." I extended my hand to Arabelle. "I'm Jett. Pleased to meet you."

She didn't smile but her cheeks began to redden. Was that a blush? I thought so, but then she looked at my hand as if unsure of whether she should take it. I didn't get it. Did she think I was poisonous? After a hesitation, she clasped my hand and gave me a single shake.

"Nice to meet you too." Her voice was so soft I had to strain to hear her. Her eye contact lasted all of a tenth of a second. Now it seemed like she was trying hard to be polite. Cocky as it sounds, I hadn't often been given the cold shoulder. Not here, anyway. I noticed her free hand was gripping the stem of her champagne glass as if for dear life. My presence made her very ill at ease, to put it mildly.

"Jett?" called a woman's flirty voice behind me. I turned to see the waitress—one of my many so-called friends with benefits here—holding a tray of champagne glasses. "Wouldn't you like to partake?" She shot me a very sexually-laced lift of the brow. I glanced back at Arabelle. She continued looking off in the distance, searching for whatever. Shit, Cassandra's timing would normally be just dandy, but not now. "Sure. Thanks, Cassie." I politely took a glass from her, making sure my voice contained no sexual innuendo at all.

"Happy twenty-fifth," I said, holding my glass up to Arabelle. Despite her cold treatment, I couldn't help myself. I was too intrigued, and needed to know what was up with her.

Finally, she cracked an ever so slight smile. I extended my glass to hers and gave it a light clink.

"Thanks, I appreciate it." Again, her voice was nearly a whisper. She lifted her eyes but still didn't look directly into mine.

"Mandi loves the show. Loves performing with you. She says you're the best partner a new girl could ever hope for," Lucia squealed.

"Well, thank you. That's what I've been told." A slight frown crossed Arabelle's beautiful face and I realized how cocky I sounded. "I mean, I haven't dropped a girl yet." Arabelle's frown deepened. No, that wasn't right either. What was wrong with me? I was usually pretty suave. Lucia and Mandi cracked up into a fit of giggles apparently at my mess-ups. Arabelle's mouth turned into a thin, flat line. Once again, she looked into her champagne glass as if for help.

I cleared my throat. "Well, here's to a great show, a great partnership, and a fantastic quarter of a century." I raised my glass. Everyone clinked but Arabelle.

Normally I would have given up by now, but something about this girl just wasn't letting me. "So, you're a dancer in L.A.?" I tried again.

She considered the question, and after a few seconds, gave a slight nod and glanced up at me, her irises finally connecting with mine.

"Ha! She's so modest!" Lucia laughed. "She's a champion ballroom dancer. She placed in the finals last year at Blackpool!"

"Blackpool?" I asked. I hadn't heard of it.

"The most prestigious ballroom championship in the world!" Lucia hooted. "In England. And she's a favorite for the first-place championship at the U.S. Nationals this year!"

Arabelle pursed her lips and looked once again into her champagne. Her expression was unreadable, but she certainly didn't look happy. She looked quite sad actually. Why? Lucia looked at her friend, reading her the same way as I did. "Oh come on, honey. You're doing awesome. Own it!" She wrapped her arm around Arabelle and side hugged her.

The edges of Arabelle's lips curved up, ever so slightly. But she still looked sad. She nodded and closed her eyes.

"I was a ballet dancer," she began, eyes still closed. "Then a showdancer. And then..." She took a breath, opened her eyes and continued. "I switched to regular competitive ballroom. Latin. Which I like a lot." She nodded rapidly, as if trying to convince herself.

"It sounds like it if you're doing so well," I said. "I mean, I have to admit, I know next to nothing about Blackpool and these ballroom competitions." I laughed and shrugged. "But you said you were a showgirl? In L.A.?" I didn't think they had showgirls in L.A., but I really didn't know. And I was surprised. She didn't seem the type.

A frown slowly overtook her face. "What?" she said, now looking at me square in the eye. Her tone was a combination of bewildered and accusing.

"Didn't you say you were a showgirl?"

"No!" both Arabelle and Lucia said at once.

"Okay, sorry, I misheard." I held my hands up in surrender and chuckled nervously.

"I was a showdance champion at Blackpool," Arabelle said, her words like small barbs. I'd really insulted her. "Showdance is the central part of a ballroom competition."

"Oh. Okay. Cool." But apparently my confusion was obvious.

"Instead of, like, the regular ballroom dancing competitions where everyone's dancing on the floor at once, they're showcased individually because the routines are a performance in themselves," Lucia explained, realizing her friend wasn't going to. "They're like a combination of ballroom dancing with ballet, with lots of lifts and beautiful things you can't do during the regular competitions. They're a lot more fun to watch than regular ballroom, in my humble opinion," she finished. But then she looked at her friend. "Oh, I mean, now I love the regular ballroom competitions! Especially the Latin. Latin's so rhythmic. It's awesome!" Lucia was now jabbering a mile a second, obviously nervous about saying the wrong thing to her friend. Arabelle seemed quite fragile.

Just then, Bobbi, a friend of mine—really, another friend with whom I'd enjoyed many "benefits"—passed by. "Hey sweets," she said, giving me a peck on the cheek. She *was* a showgirl, and wore a matching rhinestone-studded, candy-red lacey bra and a G-string, black fishnet hose, and high-heeled red dance shoes. "Awesome job out there, honey." She cupped my chin with her hand.

"Thanks, Bobs." I chuckled.

"Keep it up!" She raised her eyebrow and turned to Arabelle, whom she eyed up and down. "Hello, dear," she said to Arabelle in a low voice.

Arabelle gave her the same judgmental up and down, then raised her chin and looked away.

"Okay then!" Bobbi laughed, patted me on the shoulder, and walked off.

Now this girl was starting to piss me off. Bobbi was a nice person. Who did she think she was? God's gift to the dance world? So she'd been a ballerina and was now some ballroom star, whatever that was. I'd been a ballet dancer too, back in New York, before I came here. And I was with a good company. All that classical shit? Please. This was so much more thrilling, and far more fulfilling. I'd met more than my share of ballerinas who thought they were superior because ballet was supposedly the hardest dance. Well, this was a hell of a lot harder. Screw that pompous shit.

"Hey, are you Tarzan?" I turned to see an attractive, well-groomed older woman smiling at me in wonderment. I was tired of this haughty girl. And ready for someone who appreciated real dance.

"That would be me." I flashed her my usual sexy smile.

"Oh my God, you were brilliant! You were just amazing!" she squealed. "You took my breath away!"

I turned back to elitist Arabelle. "Excuse me," I said to her. Her eyes widened and her face reddened again. She didn't smile. She simply looked back into her champagne glass. I walked away with the excited woman.

But as I stood in the center of the room—where I belonged as the star of the show after all—I was increasingly surrounded by appreciative women. But I couldn't stop looking back at Arabelle. She was participating in a conversation with Mandi and Lucia but she didn't seem completely engaged. Her eyes kept wandering. At one point—well, several points—our gazes connected. She'd blink and swallow, and look back into her glass.

At one point, she actually brought the glass to her lips and took a sip. Or, tried to take a sip. When the rim reached her mouth, the glass began shaking. I looked at her hand holding the stem and noticed it was trembling. She pulled the glass from her lips and took a breath. But the glass continued to shake. The tremble seemed uncontrollable. She took her other hand and clasped it over the trembling one, trying to still it. That managed to stop the quaking. She sighed, momentarily looking relieved. Then she took her attention away from her wrist and looked back up, connecting with my gaze immediately. She gasped, blinked hard, and looked away. She looked both embarrassed and horrified that I'd caught her.

As I returned to my conversation with the show's female fans, I thought about that shaking. There was no way you could do difficult lifts and tricks with that kind of tremor. There was no way you could even hold a line. It would be so noticeable. Especially in ballet. She was a broken ballerina. That's why she'd introduced herself as a former showdancer.

Arabelle

For the rest of the night I couldn't get that pompous ass, Jett, out of my mind. What a jerk. "Yeah, I hear that a lot," he'd said when Mandi told him he's good partner. Who says something like that? And "I haven't dropped a girl yet?" He'd have killed her if he had. How nonchalant could you be over something like that? And then, those two women who passed by offering him drinks – that cocktail waitress and that showgirl? They'd obviously slept with him. They'd made that more than clear. Definitely a ladies man, and not afraid to show it.

And then he'd seen my tremor. How embarrassing. At least, I think he did. But he's so into himself and so into all the attention he gets from his female fans, he probably didn't even notice me. *Yeah, what am I thinking? It's just my imagination that he was even looking at me. And why do I even care?*

I pulled the plush covers up and tried to sleep. It was hard. I was really wound up. Lucia had meant well when she invited me to come with her to Vegas for the weekend. It was my twenty-fifth birthday and she knew I'd spend it at home, alone, if she didn't drag me out.

But it also happened to be our third wedding anniversary. Or what would have been, anyway. Willem passed away almost two years ago now. Motorcycle accident. He was only twenty-three. My best friend and soul mate. We were childhood friends, together since ballet school. Our partnership started very young. We'd begun competing together in junior ballet championships, and then went on to the showdance circuit. We ended up doing very well. We were champions, many years in a row. Anyway, suffice it to say, my birthdays were no longer reason for celebration.

I was also in the middle of training for the Blackpool Latin ballroom championships with my partner, Drew. After Willem passed, I couldn't do showdance anymore. I tried to find another partner, but I just couldn't dance what had been *our* dance with anyone else. Then I developed the nervous tremor. That made showdance all but impossible. There were too many dangerous lifts where our connection, our balance, would have been destroyed by my shaking wrist.

When I first developed the tremor, I was terrified, thinking it was some horrible disease or neurological disorder. But after several tests, my doctor said it was a psychosomatic—a physical manifestation of a psychological state. She believed it was likely caused by anxiety. Made perfect sense. The severe stress of losing the love of my life. But how to overcome it? That, the doc didn't know. She sent me to a therapist, who was helping, but slowly. And she was hard to afford on my salary.

Dance was my life. And I wasn't rich; I had to support myself. I couldn't mourn forever. Because I couldn't dance showdance, I switched to Latin ballroom. It was fun, and a good change for me. At least, it had been. Lately, it wasn't going so well. My tremor had begun rearing its ugly head, causing problems again. Even if it didn't present the danger it did for showdance, it still wreaked havoc on my Latin dancing. There were lots of stops and poses, and I couldn't hold the line out well. Plus, Drew would feel it in my connection and it would mess him up. Drew was so nice that he denied sensing it, but I knew he could. And it was throwing off our balance.

I think the tremor had returned because of my accident last year at Blackpool. Drew and I were dancing in the last round, having made the final cuts. Someone meant to sabotage another dance couple, so they actually threw a water balloon out onto the floor, expecting it to explode and make the other dancer fall. But it was during a Paso Doble, a traveling dance. The idiot didn't realize the dancer he was trying to hit was first-rate Sasha. That man moved so fast, seemingly at the speed of light. He was the current champ for obvious reasons, and by the time the jerk's water grenade landed, Sasha was far from the spot he'd aimed at. It hit me instead, right in the face, and then burst on the floor right where I was doing a difficult back arch. I slipped on the water and fell, and ended up splitting my lip and busting my nose. Fortunately, nothing was broken, but I certainly felt like it was. And I had to dance the rest of the competition with a lovely bloody face. The judges may very well have placed us so high because they felt sorry for us.

The more serious damage was emotional. Every time we rehearsed Paso, I'd think about something hitting me in the face, slipping and twisting, and the sound of my face hitting the ground. My hand would start to shake. Soon, it happened with the other four dances too. I was getting the tremor all the time when I was dancing. Then it began to come on even when I wasn't dancing, just at odd times. It happened when I was reaching into my bag for something, when I was typing on the computer, or even like last night, when I was simply holding the stem of a champagne glass.

The fall wasn't at all Drew's fault, of course. And they did catch and punish the culprit, thankfully. But I couldn't help but think if I was dancing with Willem he never would have let it happen. He would have saved me. I knew that wasn't true; Willem was human after all, and vulnerable. His motorcycle accident was proof.

So here I was in Vegas trying not to think about these things, trying to get away from them. And I hadn't had the tremor from the time we got in the car to drive through the desert until last night. Until I met Jett.

I got no sleep. I kept being awakened by strange dreams. I was at the show sitting next to Lucia when Jett flew down from the ceiling via that bar. Except it wasn't Jett. It was Willem. He swung back and forth from Mandi to our side performing the same tricks as Jett, and every time he flew back to our side, he'd look at me. He smiled serenely. I smiled back. On his next rotation back he blew me a kiss. It was totally normal in the dream, like nothing was off at all. It was like he was still alive.

Then suddenly the show changed. It was now a ballet performance, like something I'd see in New York on a regular proscenium stage. There were ballerinas all in light blue tulle tutus, bourré-ing on their toes across the floor. It was very angelic, very sweet. Then suddenly, the roar of a motorcycle engine sounded. I remembered seeing something similar in a ballet movie I couldn't remember the name of. Suddenly, fog encompassed the stage and when it evaporated, the motorcycle was center stage, all the ballerinas surrounding it. On the motorcycle was Willem. But then it was Jett. And then Willem again. It was actually the same person. You know how in a dream sometimes things that can never happen in real life are completely possible? And normal? Somehow the motorcyclist was both of them at once.

Then the motorcyclist stopped revving the engine and climbed off of the vehicle, stepping away. He did a crazy series of pirouettes, with some whipped turn fouettés thrown in. Then he began doing these great big bravura jetés all around the floor. The ballerinas swooned over him, and he'd take them one by one and twirl them into a frenzy. He was a show-off and a womanizing flirt. That's what Jett was for sure, and now that I remembered, what Willem had been before meeting me. But between each woman, the Willem/Jett character always looked out at me, eyes connecting with mine in the audience, giving me that devilish smile that made me tingle from head to toe. After the final spin with the last ballerina, he looked out at me, and reached toward me, saying, "Belle…" I couldn't hear the rest. The fog began encompassing the stage again. It was beautiful and dreamy, but suddenly became something haunting and horrible. I had a sense that something awful was about to happen. The engine started again, and then there was a bright burst of light.

I awoke in a sweat. I sat up in bed, ripped off the lavender eye mask I wore to help me sleep. I was shivering and shaking all over, not just my hand. After my eyes adjusted to the bright lights outside, I got up and walked to the bathroom where I splashed ice cold water on my face. Several times. The water was so cold and the splash so harsh that it began to hurt. But it also felt good. I needed to forget that dream.

"Honey, you okay?" Lucia was standing in the doorway of our suite.

I took a breath, then nodded. "Yeah, just a bad dream."

"Oh no, not again, hon. You want to talk about it?"

"No, this one was different. It started out good. It was…

weird. Totally nonsensical." I didn't really want to explain. I just wanted to go back to my bed and get under the covers. "But I'm okay. You go back to sleep."

"You sure?"

"Totally. I'm fine now."

* * *

I TRIED to go back to sleep but couldn't. So I got up and showered and dressed, all by 7:00am. I tried to be quiet for Lucia. We had one more full day here before we headed back to L.A. Vegas had to be the noisiest, least relaxing place on earth. So, even though it was supposed to be a vacation, I was looking forward to going back and maybe winding down at the beach. The beach was always nice in winter.

Vegas in the early morning wasn't too bad. Especially in winter, when it was quite cool. It was actually nice to walk along the Strip. I sauntered around the pond in front of our hotel, Caesar's Palace, and up to Serendipity, the ice cream parlor. I bought a small latte at their outside stand, and then crossed the street to the Flamingo, the hotel with all the history. I walked around inside, looking at the black and white pictures of old time Vegas.

I walked outside to the pond behind the hotel where the pink flamingos danced about. I found myself a vacant bench—most were empty at this hour—and sat and watched. The birds were so elegant, so graceful, and without a care in the world. They walked around pecking at the ground and each other; not in a nasty way, but as if this was their way of communicating. Their lives seemed so simple. They didn't have to worry about how they were going to support themselves if their chosen career was no longer an option if they, for example, developed a physical problem like a tremor and could no longer dance. They didn't have to wonder what was to become of them now that their life plans had been so violently altered. But surely they felt pain over losing a loved one, just as we do. All living beings do. I allowed myself to get completely lost in my thoughts as I watched the graceful creatures just exist, just be.

I closed my eyes and breathed in the fresh air. I smelled the scent of breakfast being prepared not too far away. And I began to hear the voices of children. *It must be from the outdoor restaurant around the other side of the hotel*, I thought.

Soon, more people were milling about. I took out my cell phone to text Lucia. When I did so, I realized I'd been there nearly two hours. There was already a text from her.

U OK, hon? U were gone by the time I got up.
I'm fine. Sorry. I texted back.
No worries. Where r u?
At the Flamingo, in the back, watching the birds.
OK. I'm going shopping in the Venetian. Want 2 join?
No thx. It's peaceful here.
OK. Will see u 4 lunch at 12. Right?
Yes. Where?
Restaurant is in the Venetian. Will text u.
Sounds good.

I put my phone back in my bag and closed my eyes. It still wasn't that crowded, and it was just so peaceful.

Suddenly, I felt a presence beside me. I automatically grabbed my bag. The strap was crossed over my shoulder and body anyway, and my hand placed over the flap, but I pulled it closer. I opened my eyes, and needed a moment to adjust to the bright sunlight. It was much more crowded than before, and the sunlight was making it a bit warmer. I took my wrap off my shoulders. I must have finally fallen asleep.

"That's a good idea," a male voice said. It was a voice I recognized but couldn't immediately place. Then it hit me.

Jett. "This is the quintessential tourist trap after all," he said. "You don't know how many thieves are about out here."

I sat up and looked away, back toward the birds. It appeared I wouldn't finish my morning in peace.

"I...must have fallen asleep. I didn't sleep well." I was immediately annoyed at myself for feeling defensive enough to have to explain my choices to him. "What about you? Isn't it early for you to be up? I mean, aren't you Mr. Late Night Partier?" I added before he had the chance to make any commentary about my sleeping habits.

"Okay!" He laughed. "I guess that's maybe about one fiftieth of who I am."

What was I saying? I didn't know him at all. That was a total assumption. I would have apologized if he wasn't such a pompous ass. But when I looked at him, he wore a wide grin, not seeming offended in the least. His blonde hair was mussed about and he had a five o'clock shadow, having obviously not yet shaven. I had to admit he looked quite attractive. He wore jeans and a denim jacket over a white tank top, through which I could see very well defined pecs. He smelled like fresh beach air, even though we were nowhere near the ocean. I found myself breathing him in.

His dark sunglasses had covered his deep brown eyes, but when he took them off and I looked into them, the dream / nightmare from last night came back. I flinched in my seat. His grin grew more lopsided and cocky, like he thought his eyes had sent a chill down my spine. *Ha, hardly!* I thought.

But then I heard a motorcycle engine gunning. Maybe my dream hadn't entirely been a dream. At any rate, my right hand—the one clutching my bag—began shaking. *Oh jeez.* I pulled it away, and placed it behind the bag, so he couldn't see.

But his eyes followed the path of my hand. He'd seen it. It began trembling more, and I had to actually sit on it a bit to get it to stop, the blasted thing. His eyes became very serious, his smile gone. Great. I didn't want to have to explain it to him, especially since I didn't even really know what it was about.

"I love watching the birds. They relax me," I said instead. "But that was earlier. Now it's getting crowded." I scanned the crowd of people leaning on the bars, children throwing breadcrumbs and squealing. My thoughts momentarily went to the children Willem and I would never have. I really needed to stop going here every time I heard the sound of children. I took a deep breath and steadied myself.

"Yeah, it is." Jett followed my gaze.

I felt my hand relax. I used it to push myself up. "So…it was nice running into you," I said, not knowing what else to say.

"Yeah." He rose along with me, putting his sunglasses back on. "So, tonight's dark in the theater. I have the whole day off. If you want someone to show you around Vegas, I'm your man." That cocksure laugh again. He held his arms out to his sides as if presenting his spectacular body. This guy was the embodiment of cocky! And was he for real wanting to spend part of his day off with me? I felt something catch in my chest, as if my heart skipped a literal beat. I felt a slight bit faint. What did this man want? Didn't he have, like, several dozen women to lay? At least.

"Um, I'm supposed to meet Lucia in the Venetian."

"Okay. Why don't I walk you over there?"

Would I ever be rid of this guy? I shrugged. "Sure."

It had become unbelievably crowded in the couple hours since I'd dozed off. I had to admit, I was glad he woke me up. As he led me through the throng, I took out my cell phone. No text yet from Lucia on where we were meeting. It still wasn't for a while, anyway.

Where are you? I texted her.

I stared at my screen waiting for her response. *Wham!* A serious bump almost sent the cell phone flying out of my hand. I looked up. So many people, I had no idea who just ran into me.

"Dude! Seriously! Watch where you're going!" Jett yelled behind me.

"Fuck off," came the disembodied response.

"Typical tourist asshole." Jett gently touched my shoulder. It felt nice—both the shoulder touch, and him standing up for me.

"I guess it's not the best idea to be staring at my cell phone while walking through a crowd." I managed a little laugh. He chuckled with me.

After Lucia didn't respond for several minutes, I put the phone away so I could focus on wending my way through the people. Crowds had never bothered me before. I hoped this wasn't another new anxiety thing. I seriously didn't need any more.

There were already club girls standing around outside, even though it wasn't even noon. We passed a trio of young women wearing nothing up top but strategically placed body paint. It seemed cold for that, even in Vegas. I half expected one of them to call out Jett's name, but not only did he apparently not know any of them, he passed them right by without so much as a glance.

We made our way up to the escalator of the Venetian. We had to go single file since it was so narrow. He extended his arm toward me, indicating I should go first. I gave him a slight smile and passed in front. I felt self-conscious with him right in back of me.

"You really don't have to escort me all the way," I said over my shoulder. Though, I had to admit, he wasn't really bothering me.

"I'm here now, so I might as well," he said.

I turned back, trying to take in all the surroundings. Vegas was just so huge. Everything about it was extra sized. Not like L.A. at all, which was, despite everyone thinking it was all phony, was more real to me.

Jett held the huge glass door open for me and politely nodded. As I passed under his arm, he shot me an ever-so-slight devilish grin that sent a little bolt of electricity down my spine that I immediately tried to kill. Ugh. I was not going to be attracted to Mr. Womanizer.

Once inside, he removed his sunglasses again and ran his hand over his hair as if trying to smooth out his unruly waves. If he wasn't so pompous, he really would be quite attractive.

I looked around. The inside was vast. I needed to find a quiet spot to text Lucia and find out where we were meeting.

"Okay, thanks for—"

"Oh, come on. You're not getting rid of me that quickly." His smile was punctuated by two dimples that caused his whole face to ooze boyish charm. Again, I felt that tingle flitter down my back. Wow. These were like my first pangs of attraction for Willem. I was just a teenager then. "Come on, let's go find Lucia." He held his hand toward me as he walked. Weirdly, he seemed to have direction, like he knew where I was meeting her.

I stopped. "Where are we going?"

"You said you were meeting your friend. I'm just...helping you get there. Since you're new here and all."

"But how do you know where I'm supposed to meet her? There are a bazillion restaurants here."

His loopy smile and cocked eyebrow were at odds with his shrug. Lucia had wanted me to come on this trip with her. She'd been insisting ad nauseam for the past six months or so that I needed to get on with the task of living. That's what Willem would have wanted me to do. Now I was beginning to sense this was a set up. But I'd agreed to go on a short vacation with her, not to be set up with anyone, let alone Mr. Cocky.

I looked at my reflection in the water. We were right by one of the canal passages. I'd been to Vegas before with Willem. I'd been in this same hotel. But it was years ago. He'd had a student who wanted to compete in a competition held at the Rio. The studio was paying, so we went as well, and took the opportunity to compete ourselves. We'd done Blackpool so many times it was almost too simple for us. But we did it anyway. We won easily. I'd found the canal kind of cheesy, but also kind of nice. We'd actually taken a gondolier ride.

Just then two happy tourists canoed past.

"You want to take a ride in the gondolier?" Jett asked, his voice piercing my memory and taking me out of my sweet reverie. He looked at his watch. "We have time. I mean, I have all day." He even knew what time I was supposed to meet Lucia.

My annoyance flared. How dare she set me up with someone behind my back? And how dare he ask me to do something I'd only ever done before with the only man I'd loved? Not that he knew that.

I found myself backing away from him. He frowned and cocked his head even more, looking thoroughly confused. This man was not used to rejection. But before he could react, high-pitched squealing female voices from behind me interrupted.

"Oh my God, are you Tarzan?" said one. Jett smiled. Of course he did.

"It *is* him. I told you!" chirped another.

"We saw you two nights ago. You were so awesome!"

I turned toward them. They were both young, maybe just a little older than I was, and pretty. Both were heavily made up and dressed in sandals and sundresses despite the still-cool air.

"Thank you. I really appreciate that," Jett said, politely but surprisingly not flirtatiously.

"Can we get a picture with you?" They giggled.

And then a completely bizarre thing happened. Jett actually looked at me as if for permission. They now looked pleadingly at me as well. I suddenly felt very bitchy. They were sweet. Whatever issues I had with this man, they deserved a photo with him. His performance was impressive, if you're into that hyper-risky overly theatrical kind of stuff.

I smiled at the one closest to me. "I can take it."

"Oh, awesome! Thank you!"

The two girls flanked Jett, and he placed one arm around each of them. They both smiled as if posing with Brad Pitt. When I looked through the cell phone's camera window, that boyish dimpled grin returned. Again, it sent flashes of heat straight to my nether regions. *Shit, why was he having this effect?* I felt my hand waver a bit.

"Let me just take one more," I said, placing my left hand atop the right—the one with the tremor—to steady it. I concentrated on the women this time, not him, and clicked again. This one was good. No shakes. "Okay, I think that one's good." I handed the phone back.

"It's awesome! Thank you again!" As they walked away, I overheard their whispers.

"At first I thought his girlfriend was bitchy, but she was really nice."

"It figures he'd be with such a pretty girl."

"They're a cute couple."

When I returned my eyes to Jett, it was clear he'd heard their conversation too. His entire face was covered in his cockiest grin yet.

"Are you in line?" asked a man behind us. He held the

hand of a woman. They were a nice middle-aged couple who looked excited about the ride.

"Come on. It's going to get busy and the line's soon going to be snaking all around the hotel. Carpe diem?" Jett extended his arm to me. "I saw the way you were looking at the water. I know you want to. Don't worry, I promise to let you have your peace." He smiled, this time sans cockiness. He seemed to have the ability to be genuine.

"Yes, we are," Jett said to the man behind us, before I had a chance to respond.

"Hey, Jett," the gondolier called out, pulling up. "How's it going, man?" I should have known they knew each other. Jett probably brought girls here all the time. It was too late to turn back now. The gondolier held his hand out to me. "Miss," he said with a polite nod. When I saw him from afar I'd thought he was an older Italian man, but now that I saw him up close I realized he was just made up to look that way. Under his fake moustache and greyed hair, the skin of his face was actually quite smooth, like a young man's. He was probably not past twenty-five.

Jett wasn't lying about letting me have my peace. He didn't encroach on my space and rested his hand on the bench beside me, rather than touching me. We floated through the waterways, passing tourists. The canal-side restaurants were filling up. I looked up at the buildings, made up to look like rustic houses aligning the banks of the canals in the actual Venice. They really had put a lot of work in to making this hotel look authentic.

There was a man dressed as a clown doing a pantomime performance for a group of onlookers. It reminded me of George Balanchine's "Harlequinade," which I'd had a supporting role in before leaving the world of ballet. My thoughts returned to my life with Willem, as they often did. I'd landed an apprenticeship with my dream company, New

York City Ballet. Willem was an apprentice too. Things were going well for me. I was getting lots of small roles. But then my mom got cancer. After she passed I had a hard time regaining my ability to focus. Willem helped me get myself back together. The company gave me a reprieve, offering me boarding so long as my aunt in upstate New York acted as my guardian. I improved. But the company didn't like Willem as well and ended up letting him go. He got a job at a small ballet company in Connecticut. I followed him, and got a job there too. But the way my beloved New York company treated the love of my life made me lose my passion for ballet.

I saw an advertisement for a ballroom competition. I was curious and talked Willem into going with me. We had a blast. Ballroom dancing was fun and you could make far better money as a teacher than as a ballet dancer in Willem's company. I was really smitten with the showdance performances. They were a perfect mix of ballet and ballroom. Willem and I trained together and soon we were competing on the open circuit.

I looked at the children, mesmerized by the performers. Willem and I competed at several international competitions, but we'd never gone to Italy. I wondered what the real Venice was like. I felt tears well in my eyes, but I breathed deeply and blinked the sadness away.

"Hey, birthday girl!" a female voice called out, making me aware how lost in my thoughts I'd been. My leg twitched and my knee hit Jett's thigh. He shifted his weight, but still kept his hand next to me on the bench.

"Over there." He pointed to his left. I turned to see Lucia and Mandi hanging over the side of one of the balconies waving. "We got a great table for four! Come up when you're done!" Table for four? Yep, I was right. This had been planned.

4

Jett

When Mandi called me late last night and invited me to Arabelle's birthday party, I really didn't want to go. It was clear this girl wasn't into me and was, in fact, annoyed by me. And, as intriguing as I found her, I just wasn't in to forcing myself on someone who didn't want me. Again, not to sound obnoxious, but I had a lot of women who did want me. Why would I need that crap? But Mandi begged, insisting it would make Arabelle happy even if she didn't want to admit it. Mandi said she was trying to recover from something, but wouldn't tell me what. She really needed companionship. Fine, I thought. I'll do it for Mandi. Not good to have your main dance partner pissed off at you.

So it was funny when I actually ran into her this morning without trying. I often walk around the Flamingo early in the morning. It's so peaceful there, and one of the only times it's quiet anywhere around the Strip. I was a little surprised when I saw Arabelle asleep. Early as it was, thieves abounded here. With all the unsuspecting tourists, it was a pickpocket's paradise. And I did spot a guy kind of looking at her quizzically, a greedy look in his eye. I walked over and sat down next to her. I gave him the eye and he sauntered away. Asshole. As soon as he was gone, I got my coffee at the kiosk while watching her, sat back down next to her, and watched the birds. That girl really needed sleep. She snoozed all the way through the initial rush of tourists.

When she was all lost in her thoughts during the gondola ride, I knew she had a heck of a lot going on inside that pretty head. I knew she needed to think, so I was true to my word and let her have her peace.

Truth though, even if she came off as a superior ballerina princess up front, I knew there was more to her. Especially when I saw that tremor in her hand. Something serious was going on, and that drew me to her, made me want to know more. Maybe even help her. If she'd let me. So, yeah, even though I knew Arabelle wasn't that into me, I was happy when Mandi invited me to her birthday lunch.

"Just keep it a secret so we can surprise her," Mandi had said. So I did. Or tried to. I kind of tripped up when Arabelle asked how I knew to take her to the Venetian. Now, with Lucia and Mandi hanging over the balcony waving down at us, the little secret was up. I could feel Arabelle tense even though we weren't touching. Tension between dance partners can travel, even when you're not touching each other. And even though we weren't dance partners, it was happening now.

We got out of the canoe and I handed Mike a big tip.

"Thanks, man," he said. I always tried to be as generous as possible. Most of the entertainers here didn't make a whole lot. Everyone knew I came from money. As long as I didn't feel like people were taking advantage of it, I tried to spread the wealth around. Especially since my dad was such an asshole, looking down on performers as he did. Well, dirty lowlife dancers though they were, he was tipping them nicely —giving them the money he should be giving waiters and the like back in New York, which I knew he never did.

I kept a low profile at lunch and chose a seat at the back of the table so that Arabelle could sit closest to the balcony, where she could look out on the crowd and lose herself in her thoughts, which, judging by the gondola ride, I knew she wanted to do right now. I didn't really want to be seen. It would just interrupt lunch to have girls I knew coming up and chatting.

I was right about Arabelle. She kept her face to the crowd the whole time, peering over the balcony at the canal. Not like she was trying to ignore anyone, just that she was lost in her thoughts. Throughout the meal, she wore a light smile that never reached her eyes, and said little except that the wine and food were good, that Vegas entertainment was quite different from L.A., and that she had amazing friends to treat her to such a nice lunch. Lucia and Mandi kept giving each other worried smiles. Under other circumstances, the awkwardness would have annoyed me to the point I would have found a way to leave politely and get myself the hell out of there. But I was so intrigued by this girl that somehow, I was content just to watch it all.

"We were thinking of checking out the high roller," Lucia said as the waiter took our dessert plates. "You want to come with us?" she asked me, raising her eyebrows in encouragement for me to accept.

"Me? I have the rest of the day off, as I told Arabelle. So, sure."

"Awesome!" she answered. "I mean, that's okay, Belle? The more the merrier?"

Arabelle, still looking down at the canal, said nothing.

"You know, I totally don't mean to intrude," I said.

Now it was getting awkward. Mandi widened her eyes at me, as if to say, *come on, don't bail out now!* I caught Lucia shooting Arabelle a similar wide-eyed look, her eyes motioning to me in the classic, *come on, go for it*, look. When Lucia made eye contact with me she immediately looked away, her face flushing red. Arabelle rolled her eyes. Okay, this was getting ridiculous. I really didn't need to spend my time with someone so hard to convince I was worth being around for a few hours. Mandi would have to understand. She'd forgive me. I was just about to get up and excuse myself when Arabelle finally spoke.

"No, it's not you." She laughed nervously. "I'm just, I'm not sure if I want to go up there. It always looks like the line is so long to get in and it's just an over-large Ferris wheel anyway, isn't it."

"No, it's actually really cool." Some friends were instrumental in creating it and I was really in to promoting it, not just because of them, but because I really did think it was a cool addition to Vegas. "It goes up really high, and you can see all over the city. And I know people. I can get us to the front of the line."

Lucia raised her eyebrows at Arabelle. Arabelle harrumphed. "Okay, I guess," she said after a sigh. As if she had to force herself to be nice to me. This girl. Who was she? And why did I care?

While the girls went together to the bathroom, as women are wont to do, I called my friend Red and got us tickets. Of course he was happy to oblige.

"Hey Jett," I heard a familiar voice call out while I was waiting outside. I turned to see another of my friends-with-benefits approaching.

"Hey there!"

Gwen, a backup dancer in one of the shows down the Strip, sashayed up, looking me up and down with hungry eyes. I looked around to make sure Arabella and Lucia weren't around, then flashed her my usual wicked grin.

She laughed devilishly. "What's up? What are you doing here this early?"

"Showing some friends around town. And it's two o'clock in the afternoon."

"That's what I mean! Seriously, I know you, you know!" She play punched me in the ribs.

She did. We'd spent more than a few nights together. Up way late, hitting the clubs, drinking ourselves into a frenzy, having sex all night and into the following morning. Okay, into the following afternoon. I had to blink and look away thinking about it. She was really hot. Legs that went on forever, long red hair that was actually real, and well built up top. Plus, she knew some nasty moves. Tempting. Very tempting. But then I heard Arabelle's voice in the distance.

"I know, I know. I just…need time." Her voice was soft, light, feathery, delicate, like her; a sharp contrast to Gwen.

I smiled at Gwen again, this time sans devilish grin. "Here come my friends. It was really good seeing you."

She gave me a bemused frown in return, as if not understanding my sudden lack of flirtation.

Arabelle and the girls emerged from the restaurant and walked up behind me.

Gwen did an up and down of Arabelle, then smirked. "Okay, well, have a good day off and call me when you want to get together, all right?" The way she said 'get together' was dripping with sex. She might as well have licked her lips and winked. She giggled and was off, swaying her sexy-as-hell ass side to side as she went. Totally overdoing it. It occurred to me I was rude not to introduce them. I looked back at Arabelle. She narrowed her eyes at me. She clearly thought I was a man-whore. Well, she wasn't really wrong. I'm a fun-loving guy. That's why I live here. What's wrong with that?

"I made the reservations. We're in," I said to all three, not taking my eyes off of Arabelle. I held my hand out to her and she looked at it like it was a snake.

"Awesome! Thank you, partna!" Mandi squealed.

* * *

ONCE WE WERE INSIDE and seated, Arabelle looked a little pale.

"Don't worry, it goes really slow. It's not like a roller coaster or anything," I said.

"I'm okay," she responded, again rejecting my snake-arm. She looked outside, toward the window, her gaze lost again.

"Ooooh," Lucia squeeked as we began to move higher.

"It's so cool. You can see everything from up here," Mandi chirped.

But Arabelle was inhaling and exhaling deeply. And I noticed she had her middle finger of each hand pressed to her thumbs as if in meditation, as if she was trying to calm herself. Her head was turned away from me, so I tapped gently on her arm to ask if she was okay. She flinched at the touch.

"I'm sorry. Just making sure you're all right. Some people have gotten sick up here. You wouldn't be the first." I joked.

"I'm not going to get sick," she said, emphasizing the 'not.' She glared. But her eyes belied her fear.

"Yep, she's the flying queen, Jett!" Mandi said.

"Been known to ask how high a chandelier way, way up on the high ceiling was before she'd take the floor!" Lucia added. But when she realized her friend wasn't taking well to the compliments, she toned down. "There's plenty of steel supporting us. Don't worry, hun, this is totally safe. Right Jett?"

"Absolutely. I wouldn't have brought you guys up here if it wasn't."

"I'm not scared," Arabelle reiterated. "But I think it's now you who's the flying queen." She smiled at Mandi. "Seriously, you were really gorgeous out there last night."

"Oh, you're so sweet. That means so much coming from you, Belle."

Arabelle's lips curved up into another of her smiles that didn't reach her eyes, and she looked straight out the window. I saw a tiny bit of water pooling at the edge of her eye. She blinked it away.

From that point on, Arabelle made the same oohs and aaahs as the other two, but I noticed she often closed her eyes. I didn't know whether it was to keep fear or tears away. So, she'd once been a fearless dancer like Mandi and me before this tremor thing set in. I sure hoped it wasn't permanent. I figured not, since it wasn't constant. I wondered what caused it. I'd have to look it up. Anyway, I could only imagine how gorgeous she must have been.

"So how are you girls going to spend your last night in Vegas?" I asked while walking them back to Caesar's Palace.

"Well, Mandi's going to take me clubbing, right?"

Mandi nodded rapidly. "Oh yeah. We're gonna go to Dre's!"

"Excellent choice," I said. "I know one of the bartenders. Actually two. Kid and Mack. You see either one of them, tell them I sent you and they'll give you a free drink. Or two."

"Okay!" Lucia had an impressed grin. "You know everyone!"

"He really does," Arabelle echoed, her tone indicating she meant it in a bad way.

"I get around, I guess." I shrugged, realizing I was making myself into Arabelle's imagined man-whore. But I was starting not to care how it sounded. "I've been here a while. I go out a lot."

Mandi and Lucia cracked up laughing. I joined them. I could laugh at myself. The only one not laughing was Arabelle.

"Well, we were gonna ask if you wanna come with us, you know!" Mandi said.

"Me?" I sounded ridiculous. Of course they meant me. But I just envisioned walking through Dre's, meeting half the girls I'd hooked up with here. Well, maybe a quarter. Okay, maybe a tenth. Regardless, it would be real fun trying to avert all of them around Arabelle.

"Of course you, you dork." Mandi laughed.

"I'm always game. You know that," I said. "What time you want me to pick you all up?"

"You mean Mandi and Lucia. I'm not a clubber," Arabelle said.

"Oh come on, honey. It'll be fun!" Lucia play whined.

"You know that's not me, Lucia."

"Just for a while! What else are you going to do?"

"I'm really tired. I didn't get any sleep last night."

"Oh come on. You can't just go back to the room and sleep. This is your last night here! It's your birthday night. You gotta do something."

Arabelle took a deep breath. "Lucia, I just really don't want to go, okay?" Her voice was getting angry. She stopped walking and turned toward her friend. "I know you brought me here for my birthday and I'm grateful, I really am. But I just...I just don't want to do the clubbing thing, okay? I did everything else you wanted." Her voice was blunt, as if she was reaching a breaking point.

"If you want," I began, trying to stifle the tension. "I can keep you company, and we can do something mellow. There's a really nice French restaurant inside the Paris. I mean, I'd love to…take you there." Everyone was looking at me. Mandi looked hopeful, but Lucia still looked a bit stung from Arabelle's sudden anger. I couldn't believe I was offering to take her out to the best, most expensive restaurant in town. Now I had to spend one-on-one time with this girl who clearly didn't like me. *What was I doing?*

"Wow. That sounds really nice, Jett. That's more your style, right, hon?" Lucia said.

Arabelle looked down, glanced at me, then faced Lucia. "Luce, I'm really sorry for snapping. I didn't mean to. And, yeah, I can do the French restaurant."

"It's okay, hon." Lucia put her arm around Arabelle's shoulder and they continued walking arm in arm. Everyone was feeling better but me. 'I can do the French restaurant,' she'd said. Talk about feeling reduced to a major Plan B.

I agreed to pick her up at seven, and called to make the reservation. Of course the restaurant was full. But my friend Wynn, who was actually a nice, married young woman and not a friend-with-benefits, said she'd manage to find a little private corner table for us.

I went back to my house, not too far from the Strip. I walked my black lab, on older guy named Ranger, whom I'd gotten from the shelter when I first moved here. I had a Heineken and watched the last two episodes of *Banshee* on Cinemax on Demand. Then I took a shower, and dressed in a dark grey suit with a black t-shirt underneath—instead of a pressed shirt—to make it more casual. I slicked my hair slightly back with a little gel so I wouldn't look like a surfer dude, and hopped into my red convertible BMW to head over to Caesar's.

5

Arabelle

Ugh, why had I agreed to go out with this guy? I knew why. Because I'd felt badly about snapping at Lucia, especially in front of the others. She was only trying to help me out of my depression, which had been going on for a ridiculously long time. And she'd organized such a nice weekend. I was being pissy and needed to stop. So, fine, I'd be game for what she wanted. Then when we got home I'd go back to my life, my cat, my training with Drew, my teaching, to my life without Willem—which was admittedly not great, but was perfectly fine.

I guess if I thought about it, Jett wasn't really that bad. He was definitely a major womanizer, and very cocky. He was a total name-dropper, and a show-off onstage. But he wasn't all bad. He was pretty nice to set things up for Mandi and her friends, to give them free tickets and all, and he gave me distance when I made clear I needed it.

I looked out the window. We had a view of one of the pools. Everyone looked so happy in their skimpy bikinis, chatting and laughing and sipping champagne from plastic flutes. I did really want to get this weight of sadness off of me, to be happy like them, to be part of that world again.

Lucia slept while I dressed. It was going to be a late night for her, so I didn't wake her to ask her what she thought of my outfit. Not that it mattered, because I couldn't have cared less what this guy thought of me. I wore a black strapless sundress with an opaque sheath covered by a lacey, see-through outer layer. It wouldn't be too cold with my long wrap. Plus, we'd be inside most of the time. The opaque part was substantially shorter than the lacey diaphanous layer, so I was covered—but it was still sexy. Not that I cared to be sexy for him; I just didn't want to attract stares from all of his so-called friends and fans, some of whom, judging by the way they looked at me, clearly thought I was too virginal.

I finished off the look with a pair of peep-toed patent leather kitten heels. I tied my hair up into a chiffon, then decided it looked better down. I put on a light but classy coat of makeup, mainly light pink lips and blush, with just a smidgeon of mascara and a hint of sky blue lining my upper lid.

"It's Jett," he called, knocking on the door. I looked at the alarm clock. Right on time. A couple minutes early, even. Hmmm, impressive.

When I opened the door, I had to admit—he looked hot. He was wearing a dark suit that made him look professional, but with a t-shirt underneath that gave it a more playful, casual look. And his shoes were black, with the squared toe that was so in style and very expensive-looking. His blonde hair was slicked back, contributing to the more professional look and also making him appear a bit ballroom dancer-ish, since that's how they all wore their hair. I wondered briefly if he'd meant to evoke that, then answered my own question. *Of course not.* He knew nothing about ballroom dancing; he'd admitted as much. He was trying to impress other women, not me.

"Good evening. You look lovely." That damn dimpled grin made him ooze boyish charm all over again.

"Thank you," I managed. I peered around the corner to Lucia's bed, but her head was under the covers. I grabbed my purse and closed the door behind me.

"How was your nap?" he asked as we walked out through the vast lobby into the Vegas twilight.

"Pretty good. How about you?"

He shook his head. "I don't need that much sleep."

Of course not, I thought. You're Mr. Perfect. This guy, no matter what he said, it just seemed to rub me the wrong way. He seemed to sense my annoyance.

"I just went back home and watched some TV, took the dog for a walk, you know, stuff like that."

"You have a dog?"

"Yep."

"What type?"

"A black lab. Ranger."

"Oh." I nodded. For some reason that changed my perception of him. Slightly. He took care of an animal. He couldn't be completely self-centered.

"What about you? You have any pets?"

"A cat. A little white cat."

"Sweet," he said, and I wondered if he meant it. Usually dog people hated cats. Especially people with big manly dogs, like labs. "What's her name?"

"Arabesque," I said under my breath.

"Arabelle?"

I looked at him. "What? No, no, Arabesque," I enunciated.

"Oh, I was going to say. You named your cat after yourself?" He laughed. "Arabesque is a cute, dancer-y name."

For the first time, I laughed with him. Of course he got it.

He's a dancer. "The way she stretches, she elongates one leg way behind the other and points her little toes. Her body is so lithe and her legs are so long, it looks like she's doing an arabesque."

"Well, it sounds fitting then. Just funny that it's so close to your name."

"Yeah. Well that was part of it. She's white, blue-eyed, and small-boned, and she's part Siamese. And, well, my husband, when he saw her at the shelter, he thought she reminded him of me. So…" My voice faltered at the memory of Willem bringing her home in one of those cardboard containers they give people who decided last minute to adopt. I swallowed.

I pulled myself out of it and looked at him, realizing he was staring at me wide-eyed. "I'm sorry. Your husband?" His sunglasses were on, as it was still light out, but I could see him eyeing my hand. I'd finally taken off the ring about six months ago. Oh, of course he was confused.

"I mean my form– I'm widowed." I was still uncomfortable saying it.

"Oh, God. I'm sorry," he said, nearly backing away from me. "I…I didn't know."

"It's okay. It's not your fault." I knew people didn't mean they were taking the blame for his death when they offered me their condolences, but the way he backed away from me —as if I were diseased—made me defensive.

"No, I mean…" He shook his head and put his hands in his back pockets, seeming not to know what to do with them. He didn't seem to know how to react. This was the first time since I'd met him that words evaded him. I wished I could see his eyes to better interpret what he was thinking. "I just mean, I'm sorry to hear about something like that. So tragic. I mean, so young. How'd it happen? I mean, if you don't mind my asking."

I paused.

"Only if you want to talk about it, of course."

"Accident." I surprised myself by enunciating as well as I had when I'd repeated the name of my cat. "Motorcycle."

"Holy shit," he said. He looked around for a few moments, then returned his gaze to me. "How old was he?"

"Twenty-three. Same age as me. I mean, as we were back then." It still seemed like it happened yesterday.

"Wow," he said after taking it in. "That's just…that's horrible."

I nodded. People always said things like that, but he genuinely seemed to take it to heart, as if it somehow personally affected him.

"Oh, we're here already." My eyes followed his to the giant, festive hot air balloon that marked the entrance to the Paris.

We walked down the long walkway to the entrance. It took a while to get there because the walkway wended along the valet area, which was quite substantial; it was one of the most popular hotels on the Strip. I'd never been inside before, but when Jett opened the door and we walked in, I had to say I was kind of smitten, feeling transported to another world. The ground-level floor housed the casino, and they'd made it up to look like it was night and you were surrounded by twinkling stars. I'd always thought so much about Vegas was cheesy, but this was actually really cool. I then noticed the base of the Eiffel Tower. My mind went back to when Willem and I took a brief trip to France. We'd won our fourth Blackpool in a row and he'd insisted we treat ourselves. So, we stayed in Europe a few extra days and took a little puddle hopper over to the Continent. It was my first time in Paris—well, my only time since I'd never been back—and I was just infatuated with everything. Our last night there, we bought ourselves a mini-picnic and camped out underneath the base of the Tower as the daylight turned to dusk. So beautiful.

"It's beautiful, huh?" Jett's voice brought me sharply back to reality. I was not in Paris, I was in Vegas. I was not with Willem. I was with this…this other guy. Albeit, a rather handsome one who was, at least for now, not being a jerk. I blinked hard, willing away any tears that might be on their way, nodded, and swallowed.

"It's my favorite hotel on the Strip," he continued. "The most authentic, I feel. Sometimes I just like to come here and chill out, you know?" I nodded again. I would come here to chill out as well if I lived here. "Ready to eat?" He looked at his watch—a very expensive-looking one, I might add. "The restaurant's over here." He extended his hand to a corner of the huge room. I don't think I would have even noticed if it hadn't been pointed out to me. Which, I guess, was part of the attraction.

"Right this way, Mr. Ridley," an elegantly-dressed young woman said. She seemed to know Jett, but her tone indicated it wasn't in a sexual way—surprisingly. Unless she was hiding it? I don't know why she would have, since no one else here did.

Ever the gentleman, he pulled my chair out, giving me the seat looking out onto the restaurant, while he took the seat facing me.

"Thank you," I said.

"You're welcome."

One look at the menu verified that this was an extremely pricey place. I was mortified, in fact. Entrees were $50 and up, the cheapest glass of wine was $25. Even appetizers were $30 or more. This guy was a dancer. Dancers didn't make that much. Not unless you were a famous ballet superstar who performed all over the world or a hugely in-demand ballroom dancer, like Sasha Zakharov, with whom I had a rather amusingly short-lived partnership before Drew. I wondered if Vegas dancers made a lot more. He was the star of this particular show. But, I mean, he wasn't Britney Spears. Was he just trying to impress me and was this going to make him go broke? Or was someone else paying?

"You okay?" he asked, his glasses now off. His chocolate brown eyes were dreamy. He looked sincere. My thoughts were getting away from me. I needed to stop worrying and making ridiculous assumptions. It wasn't like I was marrying the guy. Why did I care how much money he spent?

"Yes, I'm fine." I nodded and smiled.

The waiter brought a basket of bread so warm and fresh I could see steam coming from under the cloth napkin, poured olive oil onto a saucer, and sprinkled some kind of herb over it.

"Do you have any questions about the menu?"

Jett looked at me. I shook my head.

"I know what I want," I said.

"To drink, still or sparkling water, Madam?" the waiter asked.

"Just tap," I said.

"Well, how about Evian. If you want still, I mean?" Jett said.

I shrugged. "Fine with me." *This guy!* I thought. *We can't even have regular water!*

"Should we have a bottle of champagne to celebrate your birthday?" Jett's face was now one excited smile. Like the proverbial boy in a candy store.

"Ah…" I wasn't sure what to say. Champagne seemed a little formal and festive, not to mention expensive, for someone you just met.

"Yeah, we'll do that," he said, nodding. "The Veuve Clicquot."

"Certainly, Mr. Ridley," the waiter said.

I didn't even have to look at the menu to know that was the most expensive one.

Jett sat back in his chair, looking satisfied with himself. I gave him a polite smile. I wondered how many women he'd brought here. How many he'd ordered the Veuve Clicquot for. Clearly both the waiter and the hostess knew him.

"Well," Jett said, uncovering the bread. "I'm pretty hungry. I fed the dog at home but not myself." He laughed. "Ladies first." He motioned for me to take a thick slice. It did look delicious. I broke off a piece and dipped it in the oil mix. The bread was warm and spongey and melted in my mouth.

"I know, it's really good, huh?" Jett said.

I nodded vigorously, mouth full.

The waiter returned with an ice bucket and our champagne just as a busboy set two chilled glasses and a large bottle of Evian on the table. He popped the cork of the champagne and poured a taste for Jett.

"Perfecto," he pronounced.

The waiter served the champagne in two long-stemmed glasses while we ordered. I went with a plate of gnocchi and a dandelion salad, and Jett ordered the ribeye. "Black caviar as a starter to share?" Jett asked me. "It's superb. The best you'll ever have, I promise." His eyebrows shot up. Again, the boy in the candy store. Albeit, a super expensive candy store.

"Um…" I was becoming a bit overwhelmed. How much money did this guy have, seriously? I managed to nod and smile politely.

"Cool," he said, giving the waiter a thumbs up. "So, here's to a beautiful girl celebrating her first quarter of a century on this crazy planet. May there be four more equally beautiful quarters to come!" He began raising his glass. "At least. Five, even!" he added when I hesitated.

I laughed and raised my glass.

"Ah, finally I get a little laugh out of her!"

But the second I'd clinked his glass, it returned. My stupid tremor. Why did it have to do this to me now, while the glass was on its way to my lips? I took a breath but it only got worse. The glass was too full. I was going to spill it if my stupid hand didn't stop shaking. And I didn't want to do that with such expensive champagne. It was so ridiculous that I couldn't control this. I was right-handed but I transferred the glass to my left. No such luck. That hand trembled too. And my left hand wasn't as strong as my right, making spillage even more likely. Ridiculously, I placed both hands on the cup, then moved my head forward, over the table, and took a sip. Just like a child drinking soup, using both hands to hold the bowl. I immediately set the glass down, so thankful it was out of my hands that I couldn't enjoy the contents at all.

The tremor was so obvious. Jett totally noticed. There was no way he couldn't. He looked right at my hands, then into my eyes, a worried look.

I laughed nervously, but felt like crying. I was such a mess. I really hoped he wouldn't make me explain. I *so* didn't want to go into my problems now.

"So, I wasn't clear on what type of dance you do? Ballroom or ballet-style showdances, or both?" He put his glass down as well. Oh good, he was going to ignore my obvious issue.

"Ballroom. Latin ballroom. Rumba, Cha Cha, Samba, Paso Doble, and Jive," I added when he looked confused.

"Oh wow." He raised his eyebrows. "Sexy." His lips curved up into a devilish grin that, for some ridiculous reason, sent blood shooting straight to my lower belly. I squirmed. "I just assumed you did, like, the Waltz and all that."

I nodded. "I did that before. That's what I started with when I began teaching. It kind of has the same look as ballet, the same straight frame and all."

"Right." He went to pick up his champagne glass again,

then decided to leave it. I wanted to tell him not to avoid drinking because I couldn't handle picking up my blasted glass. But I didn't know how to say that.

"Then I saw some showdancers perform at the studio I was teaching at and knew I needed to do that. It brought me back…well, I'd loved ballet, so it made sense."

"Why'd you stop ballet? Boring?"

"What? No!" *How could anyone find ballet boring?* I thought. "I just…" But I didn't want to go into my mother dying of cancer and all. "Do you find it boring?"

He frowned, then shrugged. "Well, yeah. I mean, there was just so much emphasis on perfection of technique and classical dance with what I felt was a limited vocabulary, there just wasn't… I don't know… I felt like there just wasn't that much to it. I felt like we were never going to really learn how to perform, how to wow an audience." He certainly excelled at that now. "I wanted to learn more, do more, branch out."

But his words "limited vocabulary" kind of sent my back up. "Limited? It's the basis of all dance."

"Well, I mean, not all dance. Not hip hop or popping and locking, and I mean, the dances you now do. Ballet is French. Swing originated out of African dance and Samba is from Afro-Cuban—" We locked eyes. Mine must have been sending daggers because he looked away momentarily and adjusted his posture, along with his line of reasoning.

"I mean, ballet is extremely helpful for developing solid dance technique, for, you know, the kind of dance that's performed on a proscenium stage. Don't get me wrong."

"You've certainly used your ballet background. Your form was excellent," I nearly yelled, the anger spiking my tone humorously at odds with my words.

"Well, thank you for noticing." He laughed. And now that sly, cocky smile was back. That damn smile! Another wave of electricity went down my spine and ended in the same place as last time. What the hell was that about? I squirmed again.

The waiter arrived with our salads and the little bowl of caviar, which came with a plate of golden crackers topped with a smidgeon of cream.

"Mmm." He moaned, the wicked smile still on his lips. He motioned for me to take a cracker. I took one, and, with the small porcelain spoon, topped it with a tiny bit of the black pearls. Of course the second my fingers touched the spoon, the stupid tremor was back. I made sure I didn't take much caviar, so as not to spill any. Way, way too expensive. Again, I had to eat two-handed, placing one hand under my fingers clutching the cracker, bringing both to my mouth. Again, I had to lean my head over the table so I wouldn't spill. Not that I'd ever spilt anything before; it was more the fear of doing so. Particularly now, when everything was so expensive.

Again, he looked worried but didn't say anything.

"So, seems like you loved it so much. What made you leave it?"

By now I was so consumed with the effort it was taking me not to spill anything, I had to think back to what we'd been talking about.

"Ballet." He read my mind and reminded me. "What made you leave ballet?"

"Oh, right. Um…" I suddenly realized I'd never actually talked about this before. About myself, or my past. I never really dated, if that's what this even was. And it wasn't! Willem and I pretty much grew up together from classes onward, so we never had that period of explaining ourselves to each other.

"I mean, we don't have to talk about anything you don't want to. No worries," he said, apparently sensing my appre-hension.

51

But I was being ridiculous. "No, it's okay. I just…well, I'd gotten a scholarship to the School of American Ballet in New York—"

"Wow. Prestigious," he said.

I nodded. He definitely knew the ballet world. But it also made me sad. That had been my dream, and I did have a prestigious start. And then …it slipped away. "Then my mom got sick," I continued. "I really missed her and didn't want to be away from her."

"Where did she live?"

"San Pedro, in Southern California."

He nodded. "I know it. That's where you're from?"

I nodded. "It was obviously really far away. And, well, I just didn't want to be that far from her."

"Totally understandable. Who would, when you're so young. I hope your mom is okay?" He said the last part with hesitation.

I shook my head. "She had a form of fast-growing cancer, so…so, she passed before I could even make a decision to return. Before I really could think."

"Jeez. Shit." He shook his head. His lips were twisted into a grimace. "You've lost two people and you're only twenty-five. Man." I knew he was trying to be sensitive, understanding, express shock. But somehow he was making me feel I was tainted.

"Yeah, well… what can you do?" I shrugged. "Life hands you what it hands you, you know?"

"I guess."

I didn't know what else to say, so I tried eating another bite of caviar. Now that it was so obvious I was having a problem, I was hyper-conscious of the tremor. I barely got it to my mouth this time.

"So, did you end up going back to California?"

"No. I stayed in New York. That's where Willem was. And

he'd helped me through things. He was my family by then."

"Willem?"

"My husband. My…"

He nodded. "Wow. So you met him in ballet school." It looked like he was counting years in his head.

"Yeah, I kind of grew up with him."

I took a few bites of salad. My hand shook a bit, but the tremor was far less pronounced than with the caviar spoon and champagne glass. Maybe it was easier because I was using a fork, or maybe because I wasn't as worried about spilling something expensive. I was happy I could do something without it being an ordeal.

"Anyway, so what about you?" I said, wanting badly to change the subject. Don't most guys like talking about themselves anyway?

"Me. Oh, I came out here three years ago."

"From where?"

"New York."

"Oh, you were in New York too. What were you doing there?"

"I was an apprentice with the American Ballet Theatre."

Now I did drop my fork. But not because of the tremor. He'd just named the top ballet company in the United States. Arguably in the world. Holy crap! My eyes revealed my obvious shock, because he laughed.

"Yep, believe it or not. ABT."

"What happened?" I picked up my fork again. Fortunately, it had only fallen on my plate. My tremor was gone.

"Beauty in Motion—the company I'm with now—was on tour out there and I was totally impressed. I auditioned, and…well, the rest is history." He extended his arms out.

"So, you left ABT to come here?"

"Yep," he said, smugly.

I truly couldn't understand how someone could do that.

"But, I mean, that's the most prestigious company in the world—or at least, in the U.S."

He shook his head. "I was just bored. It was all classical ballet, as I said. And I was an apprentice, not even on their payroll. No indication I ever would be. They offered me the starring role here. And this stuff was fun!" He looked at me like I was off my nut.

"But—"

"And, I told you. I just wanted more out of life, out of a dance life, than ballet," he snapped. The way he said the word ballet was so derogatory. "And now I have it." Again, smug.

He excused himself to go to the restroom. I took the opportunity to down a few more crackers, along with the rest of my glass of champagne. The champagne truly was splendid, so smooth and rich, like liquid gold. Okay, I was secretly glad he'd spent this much on me. I poured myself another glass, then spooned a huge dollop of caviar over a cracker. My hand shook, but less so. I wasn't as worried about spilling because without Jett there, I could just look like an ass and spoon it all from the tablecloth. I could cover up any spilled champagne with my plate. *Mmmm!* It felt like the ocean exploding in my mouth. By the time Jett returned to the table, I'd downed my half of the bowl. Scrumptious. And I never did spill.

"So, you do like the caviar!" Another full-face dimpled grin. He was giddy, like a schoolboy who'd just showed an uber-cool secret hideout to his bestie.

"Delicious," I admitted.

"And the champagne." He laughed, noticing the bottle.

"Mmhmm." Downing a glass all at once had made me a bit tipsy.

The waiter exchanged our salads for entrees. They looked heavenly. The buttery gnocchi melted in my mouth, the same as the caviar.

"So, enough about dance. How do you like L.A.?" he said. "Is it true what they say about the traffic?"

"What do they say?"

"Oh, come on. That it's horrible and makes you feel like your life is stuck because you can't get anywhere, and when you finally manage to, you just have to turn around and go back because there's nowhere to park."

I felt put on the defensive. Truth was, I lived near the studio and didn't drive all that much in L.A. "It's easier than on the Strip." I shrugged.

He looked toward the door as if thinking about outside. Then he gave his head a little shake and emitted a light laugh, turning his attention back to his food. "Okay," he said after another bite.

I took another swig of the champagne, figuring if I hadn't spilt yet, I likely wouldn't. He eyed my jittery hand when I did so. Now more confident—likely due to the alcohol—I shot him a *don't even think about bringing it up* look, and he didn't.

We finished our meal with pleasant conversation. I told him what it was like to work in Hollywood and about the studio's clientele, and he told me stories—some, rather funny —about some of the Las Vegas characters he'd met. If we kept the conversation light, he could be an okay guy. Okay, a really hot okay guy who kept sending liquid heat to my nether regions. But I couldn't get it out of my head that he'd given up ABT because he was supposedly bored by it and preferred to be here. He was a womanizing show-off who thought he was too good for the greatest dance company in the world.

Then the check came. I knew as a modern woman, I should pay half. But I also knew there was no way I could afford to. I grabbed my purse by its strap, from the back of the chair.

"Don't be ridiculous," he said, seeing what I was doing. "I invited you here."

Made sense. He knew how expensive this place was and hadn't told me. I smiled and thanked him. But the way he threw a credit card down as if it was nothing unnerved me. Throwing around money like that? He was definitely careless. I thought about him flying through the air, well above the ground—with no net to catch him—using only the tops of his feet to support himself. Yes, reckless was definitely the word. Careless with his bank account, careless with his life. I felt a bit sick thinking about it.

I told him he didn't have to walk me all the way to my room once we were in the lobby of my hotel.

"You sure?"

"Yes," I said. His brown eyes really were dreamy. I hadn't looked into them all that much.

"Well, thank you for joining me for dinner. I loved getting to know about you and Hollywood and the world of ballroom dancing, and all. I had a really nice time."

It was sweet, even though we'd gotten off to a rocky start and never entirely left it. "Yes, me too. Thank you for inviting me."

"You're most welcome." He took my hand, reaching into his pocket with the other, and withdrawing a business card. "If you're ever in Vegas again, don't hesitate to give me a call," he said. He pressed the card into my palm, and held my hand warmly between his palms. The heat radiated throughout my body. He looked me in the eye, flashing that smile that oozed boyish charm, melting me with those baby browns. He gave my hand one final squeeze, turned away, and then turned back. When he did so, he caught me still looking at him. "I'm serious. If and when you're in Vegas again, I want to hear from you." He gave me a wink and was off.

I rubbed the card with my fingers. 'I want to hear from

you.' *Yeah, so I can be another one of your fuck buddies.* Ugh. I felt like tossing the card in the trash. But I didn't.

* * *

"COME ON, tell me all about it!" Lucia nudged me on the ride home.

"Not much to tell." I shrugged. It still gnawed at me that they tried so hard to set me up. Lucia had been asking me ad nauseam over the past six months when I was going to start dating again. I'd told her repeatedly I didn't know, but I'd know when I was ready.

She'd sigh and say, "Belle, you know he'd want you to go back to living. He knows you love him. He knows you've mourned him. Look at how he lived life to the extreme."

And I'd get annoyed and wonder who she was to tell me when I was ready to date again. And more, to tell me who Willem was. No one knew Willem more than I did, of course. And even though I knew in my heart of hearts she was right about him, I never said anything. I needed to be in control of my grief, of my pain, of my decision to let go of it all. I'd let it grate on my nerves for too long without speaking up. And maybe now that she'd gone behind my back to arrange this thing with Jett, I was on the verge of letting loose.

"It went horribly," I spat.

"No! Really?"

"He's a total pompous ass, not to mention a man-whore."

"Belle!"

"I'm serious. He totally looks down on ballet dancers, dissing the biggest ballet company in the world because 'It was boring,' he said. I would have killed for an apprentice-ship there. And just so he could come out here and be a total show-off. He tosses around money like it's dirt. He bought the most expensive champagne, and ordered the most expensive appetizer and entree on the entire menu."

"But, Belle, he spent all that money on you! Doesn't that tell you something? Like, he cares about you?"

"No. It tells me he likes to show off. The same way he dances for himself and doesn't take care of his partner at all."

"Mandi says that's all an act. That he's actually a really good partner."

Oh right. I blew that right off. "And he flirted with just about every woman we encountered. And it was more than obvious he'd slept with at least half of them. He's a man-whore, Luce."

"Okay, okay, stop. This isn't helping my hangover." Lucia held her palm toward me. But there was lightness in her voice. Then she laughed.

"What?"

"It just seems like you're trying way too hard to hate him. I've never seen you so worked up over anyone, Belle."

"What do you mean trying way too hard?"

"Please." She laughed again. "Ouch, headache. Can't laugh right now."

"What's so funny, anyway?"

"The way your face totally lights up, the way you squirm in your seat like your pants are on fire when you talk about him, and then the way you insist to high hell he's a total jerk. The way you take pains to insist he's a jerk."

My face lights up when I talk about him? Because I'm fuming red with anger, that's why! Argh. It wasn't worth talking about this with her. I sighed. It's not like I'd be in Vegas again for a while. I'd never see him again, anyway.

6

Arabelle

W hen I got home, Arabesque met me, circling my feet with her angora-like soft fur and sweet, cold, wet nose. I was so glad we'd gotten her; she was part of what kept Willem's presence alive for me.

"Hey Bessie." I parked my Pullman in the foyer and set my handbag on the table, then sat down on the sofa and patted the cushion next to me. Like a puppy, she jumped right up, found a place on my lap, and began kneading my tummy. Her purr vibrated throughout my body, the proverbial music to my ears. After enough of a cuddle-fest for my abdomen to feel like a porcupine had had its way with me, I picked her up and placed her on her cat bed, put a small can of tuna into her little sky-blue kitty dish, and made myself some chamomile tea. I was semi-hungry but it wasn't yet dinner time, so I made myself a bowl of strawberries, grabbed the mail, and sat back down on the couch where I flipped on the TV.

I didn't have much in the way of mail; mostly bills and

junk. My heart didn't stop this time, as it used to, but merely threw in one extra beat when I saw a piece of junk mail addressed to Willem from an animal rescue wanting donations. After he'd died I'd moved out of our old one-bedroom into a small studio. I'd had a hard time affording it, especially after I took the dance hiatus, but it was harder dealing with the constant reminder of his absence. And yet I still received mail for him at the new address, even though the new apartment was registered in my name only. *Los Angeles post offices are odd.* Anyway, I tossed it into the trash, as I did with a coupon for a new hair salon, an advertisement for a new dental practice in Beverly Hills, and a take-out menu for a local pizza joint.

And then I saw it. The piece of junk mail that actually did make heart did stop. For a split second, anyway. I noticed the front image first. It was of a near naked man flying through the air on a swing, way the hell above the audience, their heads tilted far upward. I recognized the body right away: the taut, defined muscles of the chest, the long legs, the narrow waist, and the strong biceps. The, yes, perfect balletic line he made with his body. The image was focused on the body, not the face. But I knew right away it was Jett. I read the flier. Yep, Beauty in Motion, same company we saw in Vegas. Apparently it was touring and would be at a Hollywood theater for an entire month. I examined the flier closely. It didn't give the names of any of the dancers; only said the company's main base was Las Vegas. Why hadn't Jett said anything to me about it? Was he going to be here? I'd told him where I lived. The theater he'd be at was just down the street. Well, not all dancers toured. He was so happy sleeping with half of Vegas, he'd probably want to stay put. Why on earth was my heart pounding so?

I tossed the flier into the trash along with the other junk mail.

* * *

I MET DREW, my Latin dance partner, the following night after my last class. We were training to compete at Blackpool, several months away. The studio gave us full use of the main practice area to rehearse after all the teachers' private lessons were over.

Drew was the perfect partner for me. I'd initially trained to dance with Sasha, the current reigning Latin ballroom champion. He was a gorgeous dancer, but man, was he difficult to partner with. Can you say "perfectionist?" He ended up with partnering with the love of his life, Rory. They won Blackpool together last year, and are now married. I partnered with Drew, a soft, gentle, gay guy who was perfect for me. I did so much better with him. He was attentive and caring, always asking me my opinions about the choreography, and whether anything felt too harsh. He insisted he couldn't feel my tremor at all. But I knew he told me that in large part to keep my anxiety at bay and my confidence up. I loved him for his little white lies.

At the last Blackpool, we'd placed third; it was amazing since we were a new partnership. But I often wondered if that was partly because the judges felt sorry for me – both for losing my husband and partner the prior year, and because of the nasty fall I took. Drew assured me it wasn't pity the judges felt. If anything, it was a reward for powering through despite the pain I felt all over my body after that spill. Well, even if the judges had given us accolades for our resilience, would it be enough to do well this year too?

"Happy belated birthday, dear!" Greta, our coach, wrapped her long swan arms around me with all the grace of the queen she was as a ten-time Latin Blackpool champion.

"Thank you," I said.

"How was Vegas?" Drew followed her in.

"It was good." I nodded. "It was…interesting." Ridiculously, my mind shot immediately to Jett, as if he was the only thing that happened to me during the whole trip. I mentally chastised myself for not thinking more immediately of Lucia or the lovely lunch she and Mandi treated me to, or even the fun show itself—sans pompous ass.

"Interesting?" Drew raised his brows, his voice rising at the end as if I'd laced the word with some kind of sexual innuendo. "As in, hot guy interesting?" Drew, fabulously gay but as-yet unspoken for, was always on the prowl and always asking me to keep a lookout for a cute male dancer who might swing his way.

"I…no, I mean not that I met," I lied.

"That you saw then? Come on, any good shows?"

I took a breath, not really knowing what to say.

"You did, and you don't want to say! Come on, where did they take you for your birthday? Thunder From Down Under? Men of Experience? Chippendale's?" His face looked orgasmic.

"No! They didn't take me to any of those!" I laughed. "No, no, no, we just went to see Lucia's sister's show."

Drew's eyebrows were raised practically to his hairline. I could feel my face redden. What was wrong with me?

"And this show was called…" He would not let up. I should have known.

"I can't even remember," I said, dismissively, waving my arm about.

"Oh come on, Lucia's not going to like that."

"Okay, it was called 'Look of Love.'"

"I've heard of that. Some aerial show, huh? It got great reviews."

I nodded. My cheeks just kept getting hotter and hotter. I must have looked like a tomato.

"So, did you actually meet this guy you saw dance in it?" Drew could read me better than I knew myself.

"We just all had drinks together," I lied again. "Wait, I mean, what guy?" Greta and Drew cracked up. I was ridiculous.

"Don't worry, I won't ask, honey. What happens in Vegas…well, you know the rest." Drew held his palms up toward me.

"Nothing happened in Vegas!" I stomped my foot. "I'm not kidding. There is no guy." I was getting perturbed.

"Okay, seriously guys. I think it's time to start." Greta, thankfully, eyed the clock. "Let's do the rumba routine."

Our music started and we began with a nice, slow, seductive basic, with Drew holding me close in his arms. Then, he swung me out into a series of spins, and pulled me back in. I was a little out of practice from the long weekend, but the steps were in my muscle memory. We did a pretty spiral, followed by our first beautiful trick. He lunged toward me, lowering himself to one knee. I pulled away from him, and lifted one leg high in back of me. I was flexible thanks to ballet, and had developed long, sinewy limbs, so it was a good look for us. But the second I had my leg high in the air, the tremor in my hand returned. I was standing in a split position on the ball of one foot, so maintaining my balance meant leaning on Drew's hand and him returning that force. My shakiness sabotaged that. Still, Drew was strong enough that he managed to keep me in balance. I lowered my leg in time with the music.

I spiraled out and walked away from him, doing slow sensual rumba walks. Drew followed me. I held my arms out and moved them in line with the walks, and, as I did, I felt my right hand tremble again. I glanced at myself in the mirror, which I hated doing. You do that in ballet—fixate on yourself—to the point that it can drive you crazy. Sometimes literally. I closed my eyes and looked inwardly instead. I felt the music, the beat, my movement, the mood of our dance, its story, and Drew's body approaching mine from behind, catching me, spinning me into him again. When he reached me and took my hand in his, my jitters were still there. So badly my whole arm began to shake. How unsexy could that be to an audience? I could feel that Drew felt it. I could sense his nervous energy resulting from mine. This had to stop.

We finished the dance. I didn't even want to look at Drew. He was a wonderful partner, as I said. But this was making even me nuts.

I looked at Greta. She cocked her head thoughtfully, raised one eyebrow, and twisted her lips as if she didn't like what she was about to say. "I mean, you've got the steps down," she began, trying to start out with the positive, like a helpful coach. She took a beat to consider what to say next. "I think you're just getting back into the flow of things after a long weekend. I think you need to practice a few more times. I don't think it's fair of me to judge you at all on this first try. Let's do it again." Gracious, I thought.

We did, and had the same problems. Now it was worse because I was shaking the whole way through. My nerves had definitely gotten the better of me.

"I'm sorry," I said. "I don't know what's...I'm trying." I needed to stop saying I didn't know what was wrong with me. I didn't, but that was no excuse. I was seeing a shrink, though probably not as often as I should. Insurance only reimbursed me for half, and she was expensive. I don't even know that she was helping all that much. But she'd suggested the tremor was a way of preventing myself from doing the same kind of dance I did with Willem. It was my mind's way protecting myself from the pain that may come from feeling like I was replacing Willem with another partner. But that didn't explain why was it still happening long after I switched dance styles. "I'm trying hard to get it under control," I said.

"I know you are," Greta said. "But, even apart from that... Well, it's hard to separate that from the rest of your dancing, actually." She scratched her head, took a breath, and paced.

"It's really okay," Drew said. "I mean, I can still support her even when her arm shakes. It's not like we're doing any dangerous lifts or anything."

"It's not just about lifts," Greta said. "The nerves affect the whole body. They radiate out through the arms, during port de bras, through your legs when you take a simple step. Those walks need to be earth-shatteringly gorgeous. They're your chance to show the judges you're a master at this dance, at the technique, and that you can use your artistry to bring something extra special that makes the onlooker's mouth water. Instead, I see you and I get nervous."

Her words hit me hard. As I knew deep down, the tremor didn't just affect my hand, but my whole being.

"Really? You think? I mean, it doesn't feel that way to me," Drew insisted.

"I know, but you're not watching," Greta said sharply.

I sensed Drew's eyes on me. I looked down. I was sabotaging us. He walked over to me and wrapped his arm around my back.

"I don't mean to attack you," Greta said. "I'm your coach and it's my duty to tell you what I see that's wrong and how I feel the judges are going to react to it." She took another breath, and paced for a few moments. "Okay, let's just keep going through the other dances. We'll choreograph the other routines and we'll just keep working on them, and hopefully you'll either overcome it, or you'll get so good you can find a way to hide it."

I looked at her. She held her arms out and nodded, as if convincing herself it could happen. That would definitely be an alternative. Since I wasn't sure I could control whether I trembled, I could aim to control how visible it was and how much of myself and my weaknesses I'd actually reveal to the audience. I could hide it. I would try damn hard.

Drew and I nodded in unison.

"Sounds do-able," he said, shooting me a brave smile. I could tell he was worried, but he was trying to hide it.

"Gud," Greta said, dusting her hands as if she'd solved the problem, cleared it away. This was the only word where her German accent was so noticeable, and I liked it. Willem's mother was German. Though they looked nothing alike, there was something about Greta that reminded me of her. It was soothing and took me out of myself, and made me realize how vast the world was that two completely different people who'd never met were so alike.

7

Jett

I couldn't put my finger on what intrigued me about this girl so much. On the surface she was all superior and distant, but there was something substantive beneath all that. Like she wasn't really that way; it was all an act she was putting on for some reason. She obviously missed her husband, but it had been two years. And that tremor. What was up with that? Was it medical, or psychological? I'd known people with anxiety issues before and sometimes they manifested in similar ways. Hopefully it was just that, something that could be overcome. Funny how I even cared so much to be hopeful for her.

I wondered if she'd been that way for long. I found myself at a store specializing in all things ballroom dance in Vegas. When I walked in and the clerk asked me how she could help me I realized I didn't know Arabelle's last name.

"Just looking for some DVDs of this girl I just met who's a, uh, Latin dancer finalist in big competitions, and, uh, supposedly a former showdance champion?" I sounded ridiculous. I made no sense to myself, but maybe I made sense to her.

The clerk was in her mid-twenties and had long, auburn hair. She had a dancer's physique, and was petite with long limbs. She shot me a cutely cocked smile that immediately made me want to take her in the back room. *Stop it*, I told myself. *Control, you asshole. Control.* Suddenly, her face blossomed with recognition. Oh good, I thought. She knows who I'm talking about.

"Hey, aren't you Tarzan on the Strip?"

I laughed. She was a dancer; of course she'd recognize me. "I am."

"You're awesome." She gushed. "I've been to the show six times."

"Wow, you're a regular. So, you dance yourself?" I always enjoyed a compliment, and I always enjoyed connecting with other dancers. But, as interesting as I'm sure this girl's dance life was, I really wanted to find out more about Arabelle.

"Yep. I'm in the corps at Las Vegas Ballet."

"Oh, cool."

"Yeah, and I also do ballroom so I can teach and stuff, you know?"

I nodded. I did know. That was Arabelle's story too. And, having been a ballet dancer myself, I knew how much harder it is for girls to get jobs than us. They have far more competition than the guys because there are so many more of them. And most never advance out of the corps, where you make hardly enough money to live on. Some girls end up stripping to make ends meet. That could be dangerous; one woman I knew had been assaulted, and her friend even kidnapped. I felt relieved Arabelle had chosen a less dangerous side gig. Again, I found myself caring about a girl I hardly knew.

"So, anyway, back to why you're here," she continued. "Are you talking about Arabelle Fonseca?"

"Oh, hey, yeah, that's her name!" I was so excited I must have sounded like a schoolboy. "I didn't get her last name when I met her."

She laughed. "Yeah, she and her husband used to do show dances at Blackpool and some of the other big competitions. Since I'm a ballet dancer, I used to really like them. Then he died, and she stopped and suddenly changed to Latin. She and her new partner competed in Blackpool in Latin, not showdance, and they made third place. Drew and Arabelle are okay. But they're nothing compared to Willem and Arabelle."

My heart sank a little for her.

"Wow, I'm impressed. I met her and you know way more than I do," I said.

She giggled. "Yeah, well, you know, that's what they pay me for. So, you wanna check out some of her videos? We have most of the DVDs of when she and Willem danced at Blackpool in the showdances. And we just got last year's Blackpool Latin of her and Drew."

Okay, what the hell was happening to me? My heart was pounding nearly out of my chest at the thought of sitting home tonight, on my night off, and watching videos of Arabelle. "Everything you have," I said.

She disappeared into the back room, and returned with an armful.

"Cool. I'll take them all." I whipped out my credit card.

"What's she like?" the girl said, ringing me up.

"Oh, ah, really nice. Shy and soft-spoken, sweet." I lied, leaving out the haughtiness—and the tremor of course, wondering if it had been visible to this girl too.

"She seems all of those things, just from watching her dance."

I nodded and eyed the girl's tag. "Listen, Nancy." I reached into my back pocket, where I kept what everyone who knew

69

me called the 'fuck forms.' "Here's a backstage pass with a code for a free ticket. Check the roster to make sure I'm dancing, and I'd love to treat you to a drink and a little backstage tour." As the words came out of my mouth I wondered what the hell I was doing. This was totally out of habit. I really wasn't interested in Nancy, though she was pretty and certainly fuck-worthy. What the hell was wrong with me?

She giggled and snatched the pass from my hand.

* * *

I HAD TO ADMIT, it was nice to spend an evening in. Just Ranger and me. It was a rarity, but one that was starting to become more frequent and that I was beginning to enjoy.

And this was the best evening I'd ever spent in alone. Arabelle was simply breathtaking. Judging by the way he cocked his head at the screen, I believe Ranger agreed. And I don't just mean the way she looked. I mean the way she moved, the way she worked with her husband. He did these really gorgeous lifts with her, holding her high above his head. She'd make these beautiful, beatific lines, looking heavenly, like an angel. She was feathery and weightless in his arms. He was so clearly her hero—both in the act and in real life. The lifts were stunning but weren't presented as such. They told a story, the story of their romance, with him lifting her up to the heavens. Hell, how horrible the guy went so young. But watching him made me really want to be him. To hold her, lift her like that.

And, really, I could do anything he could. I could lift her, hold her high above my head, make her soar high above me. I could balance her on one hand, hell, on one finger! She knew what I was capable of after what she saw during the show. There was no tremor whatsoever throughout any of her dances with Willem. It had probably resulted from his death.

So, it was likely psychological. Maybe I could help her overcome it.

But I had to agree with Nancy about the Latin dance. Arabelle was too lyrical a dancer for all that sexy booty shaking. She didn't really have the rhythm in her body. She didn't really have the sexed up-ness of it all. Above all, she just didn't have the passion for it. I could tell. She was a ballerina, a show dancer. I know she'd quit because of her husband's death, but that's where her heart was. It was crystal clear.

And that spill she took at the end of the Latin competition was really awful. In the semi-finals round, some asshole threw a water bomb down into the crowd. It just barely missed this hot Latin couple, a Russian guy named Sasha and his partner, Rory, who the crowd really went nuts for. Now *they* had a passion for Latin, and for each other. They were by far the favorite of the crowd, and someone obviously wanted to sabotage them. But they totally missed Rory, and struck poor Arabelle. She went crashing to the ground, landing on her face, then slipped and slid halfway across the floor. When Rory helped her up, Arabelle's face was all bloody.

Drew carried her offstage. But then she and Drew returned for the finals. She wore a big bandage across her nose and her beautiful eyes now bore dark bruises underneath. Still, she was a damn trooper. She really went for the gold, more determined than ever. The finals were their best round. Even if her will to kill it was more out of anger and struggle to overcome than passion for the dance, she really did have a damn good comeback. Shows major fortitude.

That resilience, that beautiful artistry, that passion for showdance, that lack of passion for what she was doing now and who she was with...I could help. I could take her back to her roots, and help her return to stardom, to doing what the world needed her to be doing. I knew I could. If she'd let me.

I knew Beauty in Motion's tour was coming up. Not to sound like a bombastic ass, but I was rather famous in Vegas —at least in the dance world, if I do say so myself. Well, I was well known anyway. A lot of local women wanted me. A lot of tourist women, and men, admired me when they saw me dance. They wanted to meet me, and some wanted to be me. I had a good thing going here in Vegas. The touring sub-company was never quite as good a deal. You were only in other places for a short time, and didn't develop enough roots there to get a reputation. Travel could be interesting, but I'd already been to most of the cities the tour was going to, most of all L.A.

But given that Arabelle lived and worked there, that presented a whole new aspect to touring L.A. I had been in Vegas for a while. I had to admit, every night I grew more sick of the after-parties and of always having to entertain people long after the show ended. Maybe it was time for something new.

* * *

"I WANT to be Tarzan in L.A." I told Veronique, the company director, the next day.

"Sorry, what?" She peeked up at me from the mountain of paperwork currently creating a little volcano on her desk.

"I want to go on the tour. At least to L.A."

"Why in the world would you want to do that?" She laughed, tossing her brown curls about. "You're a star here. People come just to see you."

"Don't be ridiculous," I said, shrugging off her compliment.

"I'm not! Didn't you read the early reviews, when the show first premiered?"

I had. Of course. They mentioned me by name. Maybe

Arabelle would look that up, like I looked her up. Yeah, not likely. I nodded. "So then, that will draw people in L.A. to the show. And come on, it's not that crazy here in the winter."

She threw up her hands. "Jett, it's always crazy here. You know that. And it's a different crowd. You know that, too. Those audiences don't know the local stars; they just want to see tricks. They'll be happy with anyone who can do them. Like Buck, for example."

"But that's just it. No one can do them better than I can."

She snickered. I shrugged. She knew I was right.

"They won't appreciate you like you're appreciated here. L.A. is totally different. You know Hollywood. People there are snobs. Do I really have to tell you this? You've never asked to tour before."

"I really want to branch out. I really want to try L.A. Give me a chance, Ver. Maybe they'll give us a longer tour, more staying power. Maybe we can open a franchise or something." I didn't know where all I was going with this. I was blabbering. I knew she'd let me go. But I wanted to make as good a case as I could.

Her mouth hung open. "You mean you want to stay permanently?"

"No, no, no. I'm just thinking big, Ver. I'm not making any plans. If we get a solid start in other cities, we really could extend the franchise. Become a way bigger company. Like Cirque du Soleil."

She shook her head. "That's kind of what I was trying to gauge with this initial tour. I just can't lose my Vegas star."

"Okay, then how about if I come back on weekends. Maybe do the Friday and Saturday night shows here, and the Tuesday, Wednesday and Thursday ones there?"

She laughed. "That's a lot of traveling."

"No it's not. Vegas and L.A. are a forty-five minute flight apart from each other."

She lowered her head and looked at me over the tops of her eyelids. "Jett, is this about a girl? I mean, you're going to a lot of trouble for her."

"What?" I laughed. "I'm sorry, not to be obnoxious Ver, but do you know how many girls I have here? What would I need with one there?"

"You're right. That *is* obnoxious." She rolled her eyes, shot me her cocky smile. I knew she'd had a thing for me. She'd even so much as told me one evening, when both of us had had a few too many, that if I wasn't her employee she'd want nothing more than to get me in the sack and screw my brains out. I knew how she felt. The attraction was mutual. Or it had been, anyway.

"Come on, give me a chance, Ver. Let me prove to you what I can do for you. For this company."

She shook her head and raised her palms to the air in a 'what can I do' gesture. "Let me think about it."

"Thanks, Ver. You rock." I kissed her hand.

8

Arabelle

Saturday night was the monthly party at Infectious Rhythm, my studio. Most of the teachers usually did a showcase, and the advanced students who were training for competition performed with their teachers. Infectious Rhythm boasted a large number of pros who did very well at the big competitions—including Sasha and Rory, the current Latin Blackpool champions, Mitsi and her partner Billy, Hustle champions, Pepe and his partner Jose, top same-sex national mambo champions, and now Drew and me, third place Blackpool finalists. Alessia, the studio head and a former champ herself, encouraged all of us to perform at the parties. It helped draw new students to the studio and kept the returning ones happy and entertained. So, Drew and I decided to show our now finished rumba routine, which we'd dance in competition soon at Blackpool.

Pepe and Jose danced first. They were always a huge crowd pleaser. Pepe was such a fun, sexy, fantabulous gay man, and he really knew how to ham it up with all the booty-swinging and super sharp hip twists. He and Jose danced to "Mambo Italiano." Predictably, everyone went wild at the end as Pepe placed a big sloppy kiss on his partner and boyfriend's lips.

We were next. Since our costumes were nowhere near ready, I wore a light blue practice dress made of a leotard with a diaphanous blue tulle skirt. It was soft and pretty, and nice for lyrical dance. Rumba wasn't really lyrical, but it was close.

"Ladies and gentlemen," Alessia boomed over the mike, "This next couple needs no introduction for those of you who have been with Infectious Rhythm for a while. But for newcomers, this amazing pair competed for the very first time at Blackpool in May. Though they're a new partnership, they actually placed third in the entire competition!"

Everyone cheered loudly.

"Belle Arabelle," some students chanted. That was my nickname, the name that audience members who knew me would often call out when I danced. It began after Willem died. I think everyone felt sorry for me, or for the former us. I think it was their way of saying I was still a beautiful dancer, that I still moved everyone, and that they still wanted me to dance. It was very sweet of them, and I appreciated it immensely. But at the same time, I didn't want people to feel sorry for me, to see me and think, 'there's the tragic girl who lost her partner and life-long love.' As time went on, I didn't want people to be moved by my dancing just because of what I'd lost, or who we were. I wanted them to be moved and entertained by my dancing with my new partner, in my new style. Yet, whenever I had that thought, I felt like I was being unfair to Willem and to his memory. Like I was being selfish for wanting it to be about me, the new me.

After watching Pepe and Jose I really longed to do a fun dance like theirs. I regretted not doing a cha cha or a samba instead of rumba. But everyone—including Alessia—knew I was best at rumba, and that's what they expected from me. It was the soft, pretty dance closest to ballet.

"They're going to be competing at Blackpool again in not too long," Alessia continued, to the increasingly raucous cheers.

"Yes, Arabelle and Drew! Go, Arabelle, Belle Arabelle! Go Drew!" people chanted.

Alessia smiled. She ate this up, like she was reliving her earlier days when she reigned supreme in the ballroom world. "Yes, go Belle and Drew! Here, to give you a sneak preview—you're the very first audience to glimpse it—of the rumba routine they'll use to compete... Ladies and gentlemen, Drew Charles and Arabelle Fonseca!"

The students graciously cheered so loudly and so long, we had to wait a few seconds to cue the deejay to start our music. I stood center stage, blushing. Applause just often did that to me. But suddenly, a split second before the music began, I felt something. I don't know how to explain it, but I felt a presence. A strong presence. I'd always told myself Willem was in the audience, watching me. But now I really felt it. I gasped as our music began. Drew shot me an 'Are you okay?' look and I nodded a silent response.

We danced to a lyrical, wordless instrumental that was very soft and balletic. I tried hard throughout the opening sensual sequence to focus on Drew, on the movement, and not on the strange sensation that I was being watched by a strong power. The choreography got more complicated as Drew led me into a slow, romantic underarm turn, then pulled me quickly in to him before whipping me out into a series of spins. I was good at spins thanks to my background and I rose to my toes and did the lightning fast chaîné turns I knew the audience would love. And love them, they did. Drew abruptly stopped me and pulled me into him again, lunging as I hovered over him, almost angel-like, my arms up and back arched. My back was flexible and I could go far back. I made it look as if I was soaring.

The audience oohed and aahed. And that's when it happened. That stupid twitch. I felt it in one wrist, growing stronger and stronger, and finally beginning to trickle all the way up my arm to my shoulder. Talk about ruining the beauty of the shape, of the bird image it evoked. A fluttering bird maybe. *The Dying Swan*. Not what we were going for. The audience slowly grew quiet and I knew they could see.

Drew released me, pushing me back into an upright position on my feet. We did a couple more basics, and now I could feel the tremor snaking its way through our entire connection. I felt it flow from my shoulder through my fingertips straight into his and all the way up his shoulder. I could tell he was trying hard to steady me, to steady both of us.

Drew held his arm up so I could do several spirals. It meant my shaking hand was up high above for everyone to see. Still, applause returned. I was good at spins. About halfway through the turns, which were supposed to extend across the stage, Drew had to briefly let go of me. My trembling was so bad I had to steady myself by holding my wrist as strong, and therefore, inflexible, as possible. The quick continuous turns meant our connection had to be as light as possible; if he was holding me too strongly, he could damage my wrist by keeping it from turning with the rest of me. I'm not completely sure what happened, but I could feel my wrist straining. Seeming to know he was going to hurt me—or I was going to hurt myself—Drew let go. It was so embarrassing. Fortunately, my dance skills enabled me to continue with the spins by myself, not needing him for balance. But it was such an obvious mistake.

After the spin sequence, he lunged again, this time on one

knee as if proposing. This was one of the most beautiful moves. I was supposed to look down, hold my hands in prayer, then slowly open my palms and press them into his, while standing on one leg, and lifting the other up and back in a beautiful arabesque penchée. Done right, the move was absolutely beautiful. But of course my tremor mucked it up. I pressed my palms into his with my shaking hands—both of them were vibrating now—and he pressed back. But our connection was so tenuous, so literally shaky, that I could have fallen again. Good balance skills prevented that. But I definitely wavered.

The rest of the dance didn't contain any difficult tricks or evocative shapes, thankfully, but every line I tried to make was messed up my jittery limbs. I was a madly shaking mess. I couldn't wait until the dance was over. I knew the audience could see not only my foibles, but my emotions too. It was only too obvious how horrible I felt we looked. People still clapped, but it was definitely a polite cheering. As we took our bows, the chants slowly began again, the "Belle Arabelle's" and "you are the bests," and all. But I looked into Drew's eyes, which were as deeply worried as mine. We would be in trouble if I didn't get this figured out soon.

I finally stopped trembling after we sat down and Alessia announced Mitsi and Billy. As they took the center room, I had that eerie sensation again; that someone was here who hadn't been here in a while. That I was being watched, or watched over. That someone could see deeply within me, knowing not only that I had a problem but how badly I felt about it. That I believed I was letting Drew down, and Willem too. Though the tremor had abated, my heart now raced. Was this what paranoia felt like, I wondered? Had I developed that now too?

Alessia announced Sasha and Rory last.

"Before they perform for you, they have a little announcement to make," Alessia said.

"Well, I don't know how little it is," Sasha said, taking the mic. "Ladies and gentlemen, we are announcing that we will not be competing in Blackpool this year."

Gasps filled the room. The audience disappointment was palpable. Disappointment and shock. They were the current champions. Why were they not performing?

"We will be taking a year off. Because we are…" Sasha wrapped his arm around Rory. Her face was radiant. There was a good reason they were taking a year off. And I knew what it was. The whole audience did before he announced, "We are expecting a baby!"

Now all the gasps turned to squeals and the room filled with applause. This was our star couple and they had been through so much together. There was no way to not feel their joy.

For a moment, I felt a bit sick. How I'd wanted to make that announcement some day for myself and Willem. I closed my eyes, trying to keep back tears. I wanted to get up and run out of the room, but I couldn't. It would be too obvious what I was feeling. And I shouldn't be having these feelings anymore, anyway. It had been long enough. I needed to be happy for this wonderful couple, who deserved the world. And I was. I opened my eyes, blinked away the wetness, and raised my arms in the air, hooting and cheering along with everyone else.

I took a deep breath as they began their routine. They performed a rumba as well. Their Blackpool-winning rumba. It was simply mouthwatering. They were so in love. And they were both such spectacular dancers and performers. She was a diva. And he was her support, her man, her strength. Far from being shaky, Rory radiated confidence and steadiness, steadfastness, and constancy. She was brilliant. I wanted so badly to be like her right now, to dance rumba like her, to be the consummate Latin dancer like her. And right then, I knew I never would be. I felt my stomach sink all over again. For everything I would never be. Again, I forced my pain away. This was ridiculous. I could never be Willem's wife or mother to his children, but I could be a great Latin dancer. I just needed huge amounts of practice. And the key to ending my tremor.

And then my stomach took its last—and biggest—nose-dive of the night.

"Ladies and gentlemen," Alessia began. "We now have a special surprise for you. We have a temporary instructor who will be spending the next couple of weeks with us teaching contemporary dance, specializing in lifts and other tricks. He's a big star with a company called Beauty in Motion in Las Vegas and he's currently in L.A. on tour, performing just up the street at the Hollywood theater. He and his partner in the show will be doing a contemporary show dance for you tonight. Ladies and gentlemen, please give a warm welcome to Jett Ridley and his partner, Belinda Baxter!"

What, what, what? This had to be my Jett. But who was Belinda? Mandi was his partner. And why hadn't he told me he was coming to L.A.? It had only been two weeks since I saw him. He had to have known then. And why was he at my studio? Did he even know this was my studio? Of course; it would be too much of a coincidence otherwise. My blood began to boil so I felt my whole body redden.

The audience clapped excitedly, people now regarding each other with inquisitive looks. The lights dimmed until the room was completely black. A few seconds later, a spot-light slowly lit up the center of the room.

A very pretty young woman with long brown hair, wearing a light pink dress stood center stage. She looked down at the ground sadly, clasping her hands together, as if remembering something. Then, Jessica Simpson's version of the song "Take My Breath Away" began. Jett slowly walked up behind her. Yes, it was my Jett, as I knew it would be. I mean, of course not mine, but the one I knew.

He circled her a few times, doing rumba steps around her, which I had to admit, were very sexy. He knew how to move and seemed to have a natural instinct with Latin. Damn him. He caught her attention. At first, she looked away, but then she couldn't stop looking at him. It was like she was smitten. Of course that would be their story: sexy guy, smitten girl. He convinced her to take his hand. And then his touch appeared to work magic, as he twirled her around him, at first slowly, and then speeding up, way up, making her dizzy with lust.

When the lyrics swelled into the song's title and Jessica's voice carried throughout the room, he swept her off her feet. Turning around and around, he held her up, looking straight into her eyes, neither of them spotting as they turned. The audience went wild with applause. Of course, the lack of spotting was a good trick.

Then came a stunning sequence of lifts that literally took my breath away, in both a good and horrifying way. He went straight from that waist-high lift, to raising her over his head. When she got there, she took a bird-like position, like the lift made famous in *Dirty Dancing*. But it was harder for both of them because she started from a still position without using the momentum from the movie where Jennifer Grey ran up to Patrick Swayze and jumped into his arms. As she soared above his head, the music swelled again.

What nearly made me choke was that I recognized the whole sequence, from the pedestal to the bird lift. It was choreography Willem and I had done, many times at Blackpool. The first time we did it, it drove the audience into crazed cheers. The second time, it had the same effect. The audience began to expect it. It became our signature move. I'd soar above Willem in his big strong arms. But, unlike Belinda, I'd arch back and bring my legs up so that I could grab the back of my foot. She didn't do that; perhaps she didn't have the flexibility. But everything else was the same. The idea of transcendence, of being able to soar from someone's love. The bird lift was nothing new of course, but the sequence was, and I wondered how he knew it. The memory of performing it so many times, and of feeling so secure and free in Willem's arms, made me queasy.

Jett brought Belinda back down into a waist-high lift, swinging her around him, first in front of him, then behind his back, her feet never touching the ground. I had to admit it was spectacular, and the man must have major abdominal strength. When her feet did finally touch the floor, she swung back, lifting her arms high above her in joy—but a kind of joy that made her lose her sense of footing. She almost fell but he ran toward her and threw his arms around her right before she hit the ground.

Again, my stomach did a nosedive. This was another one of our moves, Willem and mine. From Blackpool, again. I knew what he was going to do now before he did it. He swept her up into his arm, again overhead but this time only briefly, before placing her back down. As soon as her feet hit the ground, he knelt, as if proposing. She placed her hands on her chest, in prayer, and then he lifted her from a sitting position, raising her above his head. She took her hands of out prayer and again extended them forward, bird-like. Like she was soaring. This time, he slowly stood up, still holding her. Once standing, he took one of his arms down and lifted her only with one hand. It was extremely hard to do. The woman had to make herself extremely light, basically holding herself up in the air through her muscles alone, and the man had to be very strong and extremely centered. Willem and I ended that lift with him taking one foot off the floor, then going on demi-pointe, balancing only on the ball of one foot and holding me only with one arm. But Jett didn't do this. It was smart of him, as it was damn hard and very risky. He could so easily have dropped her. And the floors were solid here; there were no springs because dangerous lifts weren't often done at the studio.

I could swear he made brief eye contact with me for one instant. I know the lights were bright and I was very probably mistaken, but I could have sworn it. He'd seen me dance, and he knew where I was sitting. Now I felt as if he were saying that he knew Willem had done that lift and he wanted to do it too, but Belinda wasn't me and he wasn't Willem, so he didn't dare go there. That's what I sensed anyway—but I sensed it strongly.

He brought her back down, rolling her along the way, dropping her into what's called a fish dive, holding her almost upside down, her arms and head nearly at the ground, her legs in the air up above his head. Yep, exactly how we ended one of our lifts sequences. Damn him! He had to have watched recordings of the Blackpool dances. I felt violated.

Jett went so far as to end the lift the same as us. Or at least, he tried to. He took Belinda all the way down into the dive, then wrapped her back leg around his body. He was supposed to let go of her, let her support herself in the air using only the strength of her leg and her back. That's what I did. But she didn't seem strong enough to do it. He didn't let go. Again, I felt him look at me, as if to say, *I could do it with you.*

The audience went wild anyway. The music ended, and they got a standing ovation. There were so many people around me standing and clapping, hands held high above their heads. I couldn't join them. I just couldn't. I couldn't help but feel the memory of Willem, of Willem and me, had been violated. It made me sick. The room became chaotic by all the applause, so I was sure no one saw me slip out the back door.

I ran down stairs, into the locker room. I fumbled with my lock—my whole body was shaking now, not just my hand —and finally got the damn combination after about four tries. I grabbed my bag and ran to the large bathroom stall to change back into my street clothes. I normally changed in the general room, but I didn't want anyone to see me right now.

Tears streamed down my face as I was brought back to our final Blackpool, to our last dance—although of course we didn't know it then. The way he held me in the air. His solidity, his strength. The breathtaking, risk-taking lifts we did that made everyone ooh and ah. But I knew he'd never ever drop me. He was the only one who could ever hold me like that, who I'd ever dance with like that. He was the only one I'd ever trust.

Jittery as I was, I managed to text Lucia, telling her about Jett and Belinda and asking what happened to Mandi. She didn't text back right away. I took a deep breath, and left.

On my way out, one of the students, a popular, advanced girl named Kendra, stopped me. "Aw, no, you're leaving already? We wanted you to dance more!"

I had to catch my breath to answer her. But I couldn't. I could only shake my head.

"Hey, are you all right?" She frowned and gently touched my arms.

I nodded, finally able to speak. "Yes, thank you, honey. I'm just not feeling well." At that point, I seriously felt like I might throw up.

"You sure?"

I patted her on the shoulder and nodded, whispering "thank you," my voice gone again.

I jogged down the street. I lived close by so I often walked to the studio. When I rounded the corner of my block, I had a text from Drew. *What happened? Kendra said you didn't look well.*

Yeah, sorry, I don't feel well. Suddenly came on. Going home. It took me about ten minutes to type those three partial sentences because I was shaking so much. I stood at my corner, held onto a light pole, breathing deeply. I closed my eyes, placed my jittery fingers in meditation mode, and tried to focus on my breathing. I really needed to go back to meditation.

My phone sounded, indicating I had another text. I had two actually. One from Drew telling me he hoped I was okay and to call if I needed anything, and the other from Lucia.

Yeah, weird thing, he...oh never mind, I'm calling.

The phone ringtone sounded just then, like clockwork. Lucia's name popped up.

"Hey," I muttered, trying to regain my voice.

"Hey, it's me. So, yeah, weird thing. All of a sudden he wanted to go on tour. He gave Mandi like, a week's notice to get comfortable working with a new partner since she's just getting used to Vegas and doesn't want to tour yet. But I think he's still supposed to go back to Vegas every other weekend or something, and he'll be her partner then. What's he doing at Infectious Rhythm though? I texted Mandi. She didn't know anything about that. She thinks he's after you!" She said this with an inflection at the end as if it was a good thing. "Honey? You there?"

I breathed, still having a bit of a hard time catching my breath. "Yeah," I finally made out.

"Hey. You okay?"

Another breath. "Yeah, just a little freaked out by every-thing." I began walking again.

"By what?" she asked.

"You know, by seeing him…with Belinda…dance…"

She laughed. "What? You're so freaked out about seeing Jett in L.A. you can hardly talk? Hon, I don't get it?"

"They just…did a performance that was…really similar to one Willem and I did at Blackpool. Many times. Like he…like he saw the routine and totally…copied the choreography. I'm just…weirded out." *Inhale, exhale*, I reminded myself. I was almost home.

"Holy shit. Wow. I can't believe he did that. The tremor must be horrible."

"I'm shaking so much I can't even feel my usual tremor." I made myself laugh, which actually felt good. My *usual* tremor. How ridiculous.

"I'm coming over."

"No!" I nearly shouted. "I mean, I'm sorry, I think I just need to be alone tonight. I mean with Arabesque." The last sentence made tears well again in my throat. Dancer cat, Willem's cat.

"Oh Belle! Gosh, you're really worked up."

"I know."

"Promise you'll call if you need anything. I'm not far away." Joke of the century, that you'd probably have to be an Angeleno to get. She lived in Studio City, just a few miles north of Hollywood. But on a Saturday night in L.A. it would take well over an hour.

"I will," I said. "Thanks Luce."

"Oh honey, any time."

I was thankful for good friends who cared about me so much. But tonight, I really needed to be alone with my thoughts.

When I got home, I made myself jasmine tea, turned on the TV and DVD player and got out all my old Blackpool videos, watching them well into the night with Arabesque curled up at my side.

9

Jett

Our L.A. premiere was excellent. My traveling partner was Belinda and we worked fantastically together. Opening night was a total blast. No hitches. Everything went smoothly—better than smoothly. The theater was perfect; it was more than spacious enough, and the audience was full and very appreciative. They gave us a standing O that went on for quite some time. Belinda and I totally ate it up. And afterwards, people actually waited outside the stage door to meet us and get autographs. It was amazing. I signed for well over an hour.

We got the reviews the next day. The critic was totally enchanted. She pronounced me a "hero for our times. The way he swung in as Tarzan, picked up his girl into his big brawny arms, and really took care of her exhibited great artistry and theatrics simultaneously. It takes a seasoned dancer to do that." And she also said my ballet technique was enormous and my lines and form just as stunning as the feats. Better review than anything I'd ever received in Vegas!

After our practices indicated we had everything under control and all the glitches worked out, I ventured out looking for other studios. I'd found a house to rent in the Hollywood Hills. It had a nice backyard for Ranger and it wasn't far from all the studios, many of them in Hollywood. I wanted to see what L.A. had to offer dance-wise. It didn't take much research and asking around to find out that Infectious Rhythm in Hollywood was the ballroom studio with the most teachers who were champion ballroom dancers. Was it any surprise it was also Arabelle's studio?

I honestly didn't originally plan to teach at her studio. But when I learned it had the best and brightest pro dancers—which attracted the best students—I couldn't help but want to be part of that one. I checked their roster of classes and saw that they had no showdance classes. Arabelle was teaching Latin only. Showdance was a part of ballroom, so I thought I'd mosey in and talk to the owner about maybe teaching a class in theater dance that included aerials and tricks and the like.

The owner was this pretty cool chick named Alessia. I explained who I was and said I just wanted to watch some classes and maybe teach a short one for the time I was here, if they had use for someone of my talents. I gave her a little CV I had of the shows I'd starred in, along with some of the clips of reviews I'd received. I told her she could definitely look me up on the Beauty in Motion website, as well as YouTube, if she wanted to see my work.

"Very impressive," she said, watching the videos. "We used to have a showdance teacher and champion here. Well we still do, but she's switched to Latin and she seems to want nothing to do with showdance anymore."

I almost instinctively nodded, and had to stop myself. "Oh really?"

"Do you know what showdance is, in the ballroom context I mean?" She looked dubious.

"Yeah. I had a friend in Las Vegas who was really into ballroom and wanted to go into showdance. I went with her to performances." Okay, this was a little white lie. But I'd really learned a great deal from watching Arabelle.

"Well then, I think you'd be great to take over Belle's old class for a month! I'll get the syllabus to you and find a time that doesn't conflict with your performance schedule."

I nodded. "I just want to make sure I'm not taking over someone else's thing though. I mean, if this belongs to her, I'd never want—"

"No, no, as I said she's done with all that. She's one of our Latin teachers. Wants nothing to do with showdance now. Damn shame, too." Alessia looked out the window.

"Really? Why?" I figured I knew the answer, but wanted someone else's perspective.

"She was a beautiful dancer. Her husband died—that's who she danced with—and I think she may think she's not honoring him if she dances with someone else. It would be too painful." She looked me up and down again. "You and she would make quite the couple, now that I think of it."

"Really?" I hoped I didn't sound too over-eager.

"Yeah. You're a tough, manly guy. And she's this sweet little thing. I can totally see you guys together." Alessia sounded like she was lost in a dream. "But, you know, she'd never go for it," she added, shaking her head, shaking off the thought. "And it's too bad."

Yeah, you can say that again, I thought.

Before starting classes, Alessia wanted me to perform at the first student party of the month so she could introduce me. I talked Belinda into doing a routine with me. It was really fun choreographing. I knew Arabelle would be there, so I took some of the tricks I'd loved watching her do and put them into our routine. Of course, I meant to entice her back into doing them, to show her I knew how to do the man's end of it. Belinda couldn't do all the tricks full out, which was fine. It would show Arabelle that she could do the woman's end. That I'd look way better with her. She was too great a showdancer. She had to come back to it, leave Latin behind.

Those feelings were again confirmed at the party when I watched her dance with Drew. As I'd noticed in the Blackpool videos, she was good; she was beautiful "Belle Arabelle" with a ballerina body and nearly perfect technique. But there wasn't that extra zing that she had when she danced showdance. Her body was naturally more geared to lyrical, not rhythm. But most importantly, you could tell her heart wasn't really in it.

And then that tremor thing happened again. Poor thing. It started not at the very beginning of the dance, but pretty soon after. It was right after they'd done this series of turns, she just started shaking. First the wrist, then the whole hand, then from the elbow down, and eventually all the way up from the shoulder. At first it was only apparent whenever she held her arm out. But then you could see her shaking while she was holding onto him, when she was trying to do a balance against him. It had to be hard to maintain control, for both of them. It totally destroyed the line, her concentration, their connection, and the whole beautiful, carefree image. I felt so badly for her, for both of them. And yet I noticed the shaking wasn't always there. It wasn't there at the start of this dance, and it wasn't there when I first met her, or at lunch, or on the High Roller. It couldn't be a disease, like Parkinson's or something permanent. It had to be anxiety-related.

And then we were on. I'd seen Arabelle take a seat in the audience after her dance ended. She'd be watching us. I'd taught Belinda the whole two and a half minute routine in only two days. She'd gotten it down right away. I showed her the DVDs too, so she'd know what it was supposed to look like. Belinda wasn't the natural ballet beauty that Arabelle was; she wasn't quite as flexible and her limbs weren't as long so as to make the mouthwatering lines. And she didn't have the same weightless feathery look Arabelle naturally had. And, as I said, she couldn't do all the fancy tricks Arabelle could. But we did everything with proper technique and conviction and made it look flashy and sexy and romantic all at once. My trademark, if I may say so myself.

The audience was definitely into us. They cheered like crazy and gave us a standing ovation. I couldn't tell what Arabelle thought. I couldn't look at her while we were dancing; with some of the tricks we were doing it would have been dangerous to take my eyes off my partner. But I caught her gaze at the end, very briefly. She looked away the second our eyes connected. But they connected. People were standing and clapping, their hands raised in the air. I led Belinda to take bows in all different directions, as was the cordial thing to do. By the time we returned to Arabelle's side of the room, she was no longer in her seat. I looked all around but didn't see her.

I wanted to find her, but several people wanted to talk to me. They asked me about the Beauty in Motion show, where they could get tickets, and wanted to find out more about my class at the studio. You have to be super cordial with people, with your fans. That's what it means to be a true professional. So, I gave up looking for Arabelle to chat with everyone. Before I left, I found Drew, complimented him on their routine, and asked him if his partner was still around. He thanked me, but told me she'd gone home feeling sick and that he was worried about her. He didn't know me, and his feelings seemed genuine. Immediately, I liked this guy.

I was worried too, but didn't want to bother her. Now that she knew I was at her studio, she could come to me.

The students who signed up for my class were an awesome bunch. There were about twenty people. There were more women than men so we'd have to rotate partners. Most of the men—and a few of the women—said they'd seen me perform with Belinda at the party and were just interested in watching. They didn't know if they were ready to learn lifts yet.

The other half of the class was ready for anything—my kind of people. My favorite from the get-go was a lesbian pair, Kendra and Josie. I like those two and a woman named Paulina, who had a deep voice and whom I figured to be transgender. She was one of the ones who'd said she was smitten with me, and therefore curious about showdance, but just wanted to watch for now.

"I'm a lead and I'm strong, sir," Kendra announced, flexing her bicep. "I can do anything. Just lay it on me, sir."

My kind of girl!

"I'm not sure you can do anything with me, dear!" Paulina called out from the back, with a laugh. "But don't worry, I'm just watching for now."

"Bet you I can, Paulina. Bet you I can!" Kendra pumped her fist in the air again.

"You know what, I bet ya you can too, girl," Paulina chirped. Everyone laughed.

"Well, let's wait until we're a little farther along in class and everyone knows the basics." I chuckled.

"Mr. Ridley, we compete in the amateur Latin competitions," Josie piped up, her voice much softer than Kendra's. "We're thinking of changing to showdance. I know teachers usually rotate students in class, but we kind of wanted to work together, if that's okay."

It was perfect actually. I took note of Josie's size; she was much smaller than Kendra. They should do well together. If Kendra partnered with more muscular women, it might be harder on her. In addition to Paulina's humorous little outburst, I had seen several female open mouths and raised eyebrows when Kendra had announced she was a leader and could do anything. So I was glad they wanted to remain together.

"Excellent choice," I said. "The world needs more show-dancers."

And the following is why Kendra and Paulina easily became two of my favorites.

"Sure does, sir. We need Arabelle back, is what we need," Kendra shouted loudly enough for the entire building to hear.

"Second that one! Belle, Arabelle," Paulina hooted, clapping.

At the mention of Arabelle's name, I felt my face redden a bit. *Was that a blush? From me?* Crap. I hoped the class hadn't seen.

I spent the first class basically teaching people how to not get hurt. I started by teaching the men not to try anything too crazy on someone you just met, and to get a feel for the woman first and see what all she could do before you went doing some deep dip or mini lift, or the like. And to always check the dance floor to make sure it wasn't too crowded and you had the room.

Then we talked about how women held themselves up from their center and therefore helped support some of their own weight during a lift to make it easier on the guy. And I taught the guys how to lift using legs and thighs, not back muscles. Never, ever back muscles. It's the worst and easiest place to get hurt badly. I led them in an exercise where we felt each other's weight, kind of like in the game of trust, where one person falls onto another relying on them to catch you. We talked about how lifts and tricks depended so much on trust, as did all partner dancing. At the end, I showed them a couple of easy, basic dips and we took turns practicing with each other.

It was a great class. The students who danced seemed into having fun but being serious at the same time.

After class, I gathered my things and was just about to head down to the lounge when Kendra and Josie approached me.

"We decided we want to compete in showdance," Kendra said confidently.

Josie nodded.

I raised my eyebrows and felt a big grin spread across my face. "That was quick. You liked the class that much?"

"We did, sir," Kendra said.

"So, we'd like to sign up for private lessons," Josie said.

Private lessons. I hadn't asked Alessia if I could teach those. Flattered, I told them I'd ask her and get back to them.

* * *

"ARE YOU SERIOUS?" Alessia laughed. "One group class in, and you already have private lesson students!"

I shrugged and shot her my loopy smile.

She laughed again. "We can always use more private lesson students. They're the bread and butter of the studio, you know. If you can fit it into your schedule, it would really be amazing."

I thought about it. Belinda and I were already well rehearsed for the show. I only had performances five nights a week. I had my days free. If need be, I could call Veronique and tell her I wanted to stay in L.A. full time. I was doing well here; critics and audiences both liked me, so she shouldn't mind that. I nodded. "Yep, I can fit it in."

"Excellent. Let me show you the private lesson room."

Alessia led me up two flights of stairs to the third floor, and into this enormous room lit by several chandeliers. The space, which looked to be nearly 5,000 feet, was enclosed by mirrors on all four sides, with side track white Christmas lights around the bottom and top perimeters. It looked like Heaven up there.

And that it was indeed Heaven was confirmed the moment I spotted her. Arabelle was in a back corner with Drew and an older woman with a very chic asymmetrical platinum bob that made a dazzling wave whenever she shook her head "no" in a correction. Definitely a former pro, now presumably a coach.

The second I saw her, Arabelle's big blue eyes met mine. Her mouth opened as if she had to catch her breath. She blinked, those gorgeous black lashes covering her beautiful irises for a slight second. Then she immediately looked away, seeming determined not to make eye contact with me again. Drew paid close attention to the blonde woman, but the blonde seemed to know Arabelle's concentration had been momentarily taken away, and she looked right at me. Her eyes connected with mine, and she gave me a full up and down, followed by pronounced raised eyebrows. Her lips curled up into a slight smile. I wondered if she'd seen me dance Saturday night at the party, or at the theater. I didn't remember her from Saturday night. She turned back to Arabelle, who wouldn't even slightly turn her head my way. She didn't seem happy I was there. Why? The blonde, however, kept looking back at me, that smile curling up a little more every time she did. Maybe Arabelle was mad I'd encroached on her studio. Well, fine then. I'd leave her be.

I'd made the lesson with Kendra and Josie for two days later. But the next day, Alessia called me to ask me if I could take another couple as well. Apparently word had spread fast that I was available for privates. I said sure thing, of course.

My first private lesson was this couple who was on a mambo team at the school. They wanted to branch out and compete on their own. They were very advanced mambo dancers but wanted to know how to do the "cool stuff" that would really wow the crowd, as the guy put it. They weren't in the class but had seen me at the party and thought I could help. Paolo was a muscular Latin guy and Judy a tiny-boned, dark-haired beauty. They looked good together. I was working with them on a pot stir—a cool-looking but difficult move where the guy stands over the girl and spins her while she's seated, and he keeps turning her while she slowly comes to a standing position.

About halfway through our lesson, she walked into the room. I was concentrating on helping Judy spin without getting dizzy when I saw her out of the corner of my eye. Arabelle took one look in our direction, huffed, then stood looking at me, hand on her hip. When Judy finished the spin sequence and took a breather, I turned to Arabelle. She immediately removed the hand from her hip and looked up and away, as if she wasn't really looking at me in the first place, before stalking off. She marched to the very back of the room, nearly walking into a mirror. But the mirror was actually a door leading into another room. After she walked in, a light came on. I could see her inside. The endlessness of this place really impressed me. But, geez, why was Arabelle so mad?

By the end of the lesson, Judy was clutching her stomach, announcing she was on the verge of losing everything she'd had to eat that day. But she assured me I'd given her solid skills for learning how to turn fast without spotting, which she'd need to go so fast.

"It just takes practice," I assured her. "Practice, practice,

practice."

We scheduled a lesson for the following week, and I told her to contact me before then if she had any questions or problems.

I didn't have to be at the theater for several hours so I decided to practice some of my own turns. I hadn't done much floor dancing in a while and I could use some practice to up my game for teaching here.

I found myself an ideal piece of real estate, a corner area surrounded by three mirrors ideal for scrutinizing my technique. Drew walked through the main practice area to the back, followed by the blonde-haired coach from before.

I decided to practice a series of pirouettes. It had been a while since I'd done those. I held my arms out to my sides and swung myself around with as much force as I could muster. I made four the first time, which was pathetic. I was really out of practice, ballet-wise. I tried again and made five. Then six. But I couldn't go past that. Damn. I used to be able to do twelve. Ten on a bad day.

I wondered how I'd do at whipping fouetté turns. I held my arms out to my sides, wound myself up, and gave it a go. *Crap, only four?* I was sucking at those, too. And I hadn't before. I really hadn't. I was way out of practice. I was determined to get back to where I'd been while at ABT, dammit. I could nail these. I whipped myself around and had another go at it.

Suddenly I spotted the blonde coach looking right at me. Her eyes could really pierce you. I couldn't tell if she was annoyed or intrigued. *Well, whatever.* I turned back to myself, started back to the fouettés. Better. Seven in a row. I tried again, holding my leg out like Baryshnikov for a few of them. Not as good, but fair. I put them together, throwing a pirouette or two in between the fouettés. Yeah, I was clearly out of it. But I'd be back in shape in no time.

Soon I realized I had a small audience. Several people in the room had stopped what they were doing to focus on me. I glanced to the back room. Sure enough, the coach's eyes were still on me. Or one eye anyway. She seemed to have a way of looking at me and Drew and Arabelle simultaneously.

I caught Arabelle looking at Drew, rolling her eyes. Drew looked right at me. He smiled and waved. I waved back. But Arabelle wouldn't look at me.

I felt a tap on my shoulder. I turned to see a tall, thin woman who looked as if she'd had some plastic surgery done. Her face was a blank stare.

"Oh, hello," I said.

"You need to reserve practice space with reception downstairs. Even teachers."

"Oh, I'm sorry, I didn't—"

But she'd already stomped off. Wow, who was this woman? Alessia's little minion when Alessia didn't want to be the bad guy maybe? I looked around the room. It wasn't crowded at all. I couldn't have been bothering anyone. I guess rules were rules. I took my things and began my way downstairs to check with Alessia.

"I see you just met everyone's favorite studio biatch," a voice I recognized called out on my way out the door. I turned to see Paulina from my class who was practicing a Waltz with a partner.

"Oh, hey, Paulina." I chuckled. "I was wondering what I did."

"Uh-uh. Nothing. That's Luna, aka, the Wicked Witch of the West, honey. Pay her no mind. She hates everyone here and everyone pretty much hates her. But they pretend to give her a little smidgeon of power, because…you know." At this she rubbed the fingers of one hand together, the universal sign for money, indicating the woman was loaded.

"Ah," I said with a nod, now a little glad I didn't teach here permanently. Studio politics… well, I could definitely live without those. "Thanks for letting me know."

"Sure thing, hon. We don't want her sending any excellent new teachers running in the opposite direction now."

I smiled. "Don't worry. She won't."

"I'm going to your show next Tuesday. Can't wait!"

"Paulina, get ready, our music's next," her teacher said, taking her into closed beginning ballroom position.

"Thank you again," I said. "I hope you enjoy the show."

"Honey, I know we will!"

Her music started. It was a sweeping Viennese Waltz. I watched as she and her partner flew over the dance floor. Wow, she was very advanced. She was a little larger than her partner, but once they took off they looked perfect together. She was so light on her feet. She knew her stuff, that was for sure. Maybe I could convince her to dance in class.

"Ooh," she mouthed at me as she whisked by. She averted her eyes to someone behind me. I turned to see Arabelle and Drew walking toward the front door, bags in hand. As she flew by me again, Paulina shot me a raised eyebrow. I smiled. This woman was on the same page as me, for sure.

I followed Drew and Arabelle downstairs. I wanted to talk to Arabelle. It seemed she was mad at me and I wanted to make things right, to explain why I was here. But they were fast. Drew ducked into the men's room on the first floor.

"Arabelle," I called out. But she disappeared behind the door on the opposite side. I jumped into the men's locker room, changed into my street shoes, and threw on my sweats above my Latin pants as quickly as I possibly could so I wouldn't miss her.

Just as I was about to run out, I heard someone call out behind me.

"Hey, quite impressive." I turned to see Drew.

"Oh, hey, thanks."

"Yeah, you sure wowed the women. Especially Greta."

"Greta?"

"Our coach. She trains lots of people here, including Belle and me. She's a former longtime Latin champ and she's wicked good. You impressed the queen of ballroom."

I laughed. "Yeah, I mean, she looks like it." I badly wanted to know how he knew I'd wowed the other woman in the back room as well. "You know how long Arabelle will be here? I just wanted to say hi since I missed her the other night."

"You know each other?" He seemed surprised, so she obviously hadn't talked too much about me.

"We just met briefly in Vegas."

"Oh," he said. Then, his eyes seemed to dart up and to the right, as if he was thinking of something. "Ohhh," he said, now apparently putting two and two together.

"Ohhh, what?" I said.

"Oh? Ah, nothing. I just, my mind wanders sometimes! Anyway, it looks like I'll be seeing you around!" He patted my back, somewhat awkwardly, as if he'd been caught in something and wanted to escape the situation, then fled out the door. I left the men's room and stood in the hallway, across from the ladies' room door. Damn, where was she? I waited five more minutes, then ten, then decided to call it a day. Drew was right, I'd be seeing plenty more of them.

Oh my way out, I approached the receptionist, a very pretty brunette. She blushed when she looked up at me.

"Hey," I said, somewhat flirtatiously, before mentally kicking myself. Why was this always my first approach with women?

"Hey yourself," she said, more flirtatiously.

"Ah, I was practicing on my own after my private lesson and someone came up and told me I needed to reserve space on the practice floor. It was pretty empty up there, being morning and all, so…"

She laughed. "Luna? Yeah, she's a nutter. I mean, you're supposed to, but, you know, we don't always enforce the rules on the pros. Especially during quiet hours." One eyebrow was impressively raised and she had a sly smile.

"I see. Thanks for letting me know. But since I'm new here, I'd like to play by the rules."

"Okay, that always works," she said. "Sooo, you want me to book something for you?" She said this with the same tone as you might say, *so, want me to do you?* Ugh, I could really kick myself now. I'd started this with my flirtatious tone. Not that she wouldn't be quite fun to hang with. But I didn't want Arabelle thinking I was a total man-whore. And, I don't know, for some reason I just couldn't get my mind on anyone but her. Even though she wasn't being so cool to me right now. Maybe that's what made me long for her more.

"Yeah, can I, uh, see a schedule?" I tried to be nice without sounding like I wanted to fuck her. That was always a hard balance to find for me.

"I have it right here. You want to come over?" She faced the computer, and motioned to the seat beside her.

"Sure." I walked over to her side, looked down at the screen. It had all the rehearsal times of everyone who'd booked the private room for the week. I saw Arabelle and Drew had lots of standing reservations, early morning and afternoons. I made a mental note of when I could catch her.

"Cool, so can you put me in for tomorrow from two to three?"

"Of course."

"Cool. See you then," I said before realizing what it sounded like. I did not know how to not flirt. I just didn't.

She giggled again and I waved and walked out.

Arabelle

I met Drew and Greta in the practice room at Infectious Rhythm for our regular one to three practice time. For the first hour we had the back room. Things went the same as they had been for a while. I was still getting the tremor. Okay, it was actually getting worse. I needed to book another session with the therapist. I just had to work in a few more private lessons before I could afford it. Insurance paid very little for mental health—which this was classified as— since I'd had all the medical tests my primary care doctor ordered and they'd all come back negative. That left only anxiety, she'd said. I felt like I could conquer it if it was only mental. But I was beginning to think mental disorders were the hardest to overcome, because it's like you're playing mind games with yourself and you don't know how to stop the game. I just had to pinpoint what was causing it, and eliminate that.

That was really our main problem as a partnership. It was hard to maintain a good solid connection with Drew. I felt my nerves radiate from my body to his. It was getting so I didn't even want to touch him for fear of making him all shaky, like me.

It was also affecting my concentration. I knew the steps of our choreography backward and forward, but it was now the shaking that was making me more nervous. So I was forgetting simple things. My technique was solid since I'd been dancing so long, but Greta was adding all this fancy styling and it was hard to focus on making that as brilliant as she wanted it when most of my attention was on this ridiculous tremble.

"I'm sorry," I heard myself say over and over again.

"You shouldn't say that, because it's not your fault. It's not something you can control," Greta said. "Really. Just try to concentrate and not think about it. I know it's hard but you've got to put it out of your mind. Sweetie," she added, trying to make her tone sound less harsh.

For the second hour of coaching, we used the main room since one of the wealthy students had booked the back room for a private lesson. I hated being out in the open room for all to see. And I hated feeling that way because I'd performed in front of large audiences so many times before. I didn't want to be scared of people watching me. What was wrong with me?

The second we got settled in the main room, guess who waltzed in? Out of all the studios in L.A., he had to walk into mine. I'd noticed him yesterday out in the main room with this same pair of students. Unbelievable. He already had private lesson bookings and had only been at the studio for a few days. He caught me looking at him. He smiled and even waved. I looked away. I was still fuming about him stealing our choreography and doing it so obviously, and right in front of me. But I didn't care to say anything to him. It might seem petty, though it wasn't to me. My choreography with Willem was everything to me, the most important thing I still retained of him. But he didn't need to know that, or that he'd upset me. I'd just ignore him.

"Okay, with that little drama over, can we continue with our lesson?" Greta said to me, one eyebrow raised to her hairline. What? Drama? Drew looked like he was about to crack up, which at first seemed inappropriate until I looked at Greta again and noticed her cocked smile. She was ribbing me about something. What? "You and this guy seem to have a little something from the past, no?"

Greta, being German, sometimes didn't get her words completely perfect in English. I had no idea what she was talking about.

"You know, Mr. What Happens in Vegas Stays in Vegas." Drew pointed toward Jett.

"Or not, apparently," Greta cackled. "You met him in Vegas?"

Ugh. Were they serious? I was totally ignoring Jett. "No. Nothing at all. I don't know him at all."

At this, it was Drew's turn to cackle. Greta turned her cocked smile and raised eyebrow toward him.

"Ah." Greta raised a palm to both of us. "Yes, it should stay in Vegas then. I do not need to know."

"Nothing happened. We just met. Nothing happened," I repeated more adamantly.

"Well, he is a good dancer. Very good. We saw yesterday. That is all I have to say about him. Anyway, let's continue." Greta waved her long, graceful, swan-wing-like arm at us.

We continued, picking up where we left off with the rumba routine. But now my stupid shaking was even worse, being in the direct line of vision of Jett. Would he steal this choreography too? Greta would be pissed. And then he'd have to deal with her wrath. He shouldn't be watching me since he had students of his own. But this guy didn't seem like the type to respect rules.

"It's okay, shake it off. Do you need a moment?" Greta asked after my trembling was so bad, from elbow to wrist, I had to use my other hand to quiet it. I shook my head no.

"Yeah, that's gonna look so cool if you end on no hands fish. That's such an awesome step, and totally in line with the music. Wham!" Jett said, smacking his hands together excitedly.

Was he out of his mind, I thought? A no hands fish is a popular ballet trick but it takes a very advanced student. Both the male and female have to have a great deal of strength and coordination. The woman needs to be able to hold herself up by her back for a solid several seconds. That's not easy. And she has to have very strong legs to hold herself around him by wrapping one leg around his back. The students were all amateurs.

"Earth to Arabelle?" Greta sang out. I whiplashed back to her.

"I'm fine," I said. I took several deep breaths, pretending I'd merely been regrouping and catching my breath and not completely engaged in another teacher's private lesson. Especially that other teacher's.

"Okay, are we ready to try again?" she said. I nodded. We repeated the routine. My shaking was intense but I tried hard as I could to ignore it, along with the increasingly loud laughter and animated talking coming from across the room. They were having a damn lot of fun trying to kill themselves.

"You got it, you got it!" Jett shouted. "I mean, I think. I mean, wait, how's that gonna..." The student was trying to wrap her leg around the poor guy with the damn Latin stiletto on. She was going to drill a hole right in his back with that thing. She needed to take it off and try it bare-foot. I'd never seen anyone do that trick in heels, only in ballet shoes. "Ah…" Jett looked at the heel and then up at me for this first time since he began his lesson. Then he glanced at Greta. He quickly looked away and I wondered whether she'd given him a little glare for being too loud. When I returned my attention to Greta, she was looking right at me with the raised brow. "It seems like he could use your help, Ms. Showdance Diva." She nodded toward Jett.

Ugh. I was kind of busy myself. "We don't—"

"It's okay with me if it's okay with Drew," she said.

He nodded. "Yeah, why don't you take a little break from this. Maybe that's what you need. Just for, you know, five or ten minutes. I can stay a little late."

No one seemed to realize I didn't want to help Mr. Jett the Jackass. I turned back to him. He seemed to have heard the whole discussion from all the way across the room. "No, no, no, I'm totally not bothering you while you're at work. I can…I'll talk to you about it later, and you can give me pointers, Arabelle. Seriously. Thanks but, really, go back to your work."

"He needs your help. That girl is about to ice pick her guy right in the back and he doesn't even know it, poor dude," Drew said. "Just take five, Belle. Come on. Do it for the guy. Not Vegas guy, I mean the other one."

He was right. The male student needed help. Because he wasn't getting it from this teacher.

"I'll only be a second," I said to Greta, then hurried over to Jett. Jett shook his head but I cut him off. "I only have a second, but you can't do that with the heels on. At least not for now. She needs to practice and get the strength in her back first so she can hold herself up or he's going to drop her straight to the ground when he lets go of her torso. And he *will* freak out and drop her once he feels that stiletto ice-picking his back."

"Ice pick?" the male student said. Jett's mouth fell open. But for once Mr. Pompous had no words.

"Seriously, let her down so she can take off her shoes."

The student looked at Jett, who nodded. "Lady knows her stuff. She's the world showdance champion five years in a row." I didn't remember telling him that. I had no idea he knew.

"Yes, we know." The woman giggled.

"This is Paolo and Judy," Jett said to me. "And, I guess you already know her, but if you haven't officially met, this is the amazing Arabelle Fonseca, world showdance champion." It was sweet how he was lauding me so, but I kind of wanted to slap him since I was a *former* champion, and only with Willem. Now I was a Latin finalist. And I knew he knew that, since he apparently knew everything else about me.

Judy giggled again and Paolo offered his hand with a polite and grateful nod. I took it. He was strong. "Honored to meet you," he said as we shook. I couldn't help but blush. How'd Jett land such nice students?

"Well, thank you. And same here. You're on the mambo team. I've seen you dance. You're both very good."

"Ooh," Judy squealed.

"You don't know how much that means coming from you," Paolo said.

Another blush.

"Thanks so much for helping, Belle. But, I mean, I don't want to take too much of your time right now. I know you were practicing."

Belle? That was what Willem had called me. Then my dearest friends. How dare he just start using that nickname! I seethed, but only inwardly. Judy and Paolo were too sweet. And any blowup right now would be totally unprofessional. I looked back at Drew. He was practicing the routine with Greta and she was giving him corrections and advice. They were working. I was glad they weren't stopping the lesson for me.

"Okay, so you will need to take your shoes off," I said to Judy. "I've never seen anyone do this in Latin heels, or in any kind of heels."

She looked deflated. "But I need to wear the heels for our performance."

I understood, but seriously didn't know if they could do this move if she wore them. But I wasn't going to say that right now. They'd figure it out later. "That could end up being okay. But definitely not when you're learning. You need to hold yourself up wrapping your leg around his back, and your heel could get stuck somewhere bad. Let's just try it without first."

He held his arms out for her as she kicked her shoes aside. I shook my head again. "No, you're not ready to do it together. Judy needs to make sure she has the strength in her back first. Here, get down on the ground. Like me." I sat down, then laid on my stomach. She laughed and did the same.

"Good, now raise your legs and your arms, like me."

She imitated me.

"Good, now arch your back up as high as you can, like me."

She did so, but her arch was way too low.

"Come on, higher. You can do it."

She took a deep breath and lifted, for all of three seconds.

I stayed arched for a few more seconds and then let myself down, out of breath as well. But it felt good to work muscles I hadn't worked in a while. "See, you have to work up that flexibility and strength in your back. If you're not arched way up, when you're at his waist level and he bends down, your head's going to hit the floor. You have to arch way up to avoid falling into the ground. And you'll have to hold it for longer than that."

"Ooh, wow," she said, her expression indicating it was finally sinking in just how hard this trick was.

"It's a lovely trick, though. If you really want to do it, you can. You're a good dancer, Judy. You just have to practice these arches. Do them every day. Build up the strength and flexibility in your back. Your legs are important too, but your back is the most important in terms of this move. Hold yourself up for two seconds, then five seconds, then ten, not letting your back down at all. Once you have that down, we can move on. I mean, you can move on," I quickly corrected myself. She wasn't my student. I wasn't Jett's assistant. What was wrong with me?

"Okay, I'll do it! I will!" she chirped. "Thank you so much, Arabelle!"

"You're very welcome." I nodded, then looked back at Drew and Greta. They were still immersed in the routine. For a split second, and I mean one tiny fraction of a second, I wanted to stay with Jett and teach Judy and Paolo no hands fish dives and other tricks, and leave Drew to Greta. But then reality returned to me, thankfully. And I brushed off the silly thought. I turned and went back to my Latin people, not looking again at Jett.

"Thanks, Belle." I heard him call out behind me, annoying me all over again with use of my nickname. I didn't turn back.

The second I took over Greta's place in our rumba, my shaky hand returned. I then realized I hadn't shaken while demonstrating the fish dive. Well, that was about a five-second period of time. Of course I didn't shake. It meant nothing.

"I'll get this under control," I whispered to Drew. "I will. I promise." Judy's determination inspired me. She was so adamant about learning to do something for a student competition. I desperately needed to get rid of a problem for Blackpool that could very well keep my partner and me from winning the gold. And I would, dammit. Whatever it took.

We finished our coaching at the same time as Jett finished his private with Judy and Paolo. The room was still fairly unoccupied, so after I said goodbye to Drew and Greta, I sat on a bench and changed into my street shoes. I needed to go out and get an early dinner before starting my evening set of group classes.

"Hey, I can't tell you how much I appreciated that." *Ugh, really?* Jett sat down beside me. Without my invitation, of course. I'd managed to escape him yesterday, but it didn't look like I was going to be so lucky today. "That was seriously so helpful, and so amazing of you. I totally owe you."

"No, you really don't," I said immediately.

"No, come on. Let me treat you to a little dinner."

Eating was my time to relax before evening classes.

"You going out to get something now?" he asked.

I tried quickly to make something up. I was raised not to be rude. Or to lie. Even telling white lies could come back to bite you in the ass. I *was* on my way to get a bite to eat. If I told him otherwise, he might see me at Tender Greens, where I often went. I'd have to think of another place to go, and then he might see me there. And I had to be fairly quick so I could be back for classes in time. Looked like I wasn't going to be escaping this.

"Come on," he insisted. "Tell me your favorite. Let me treat." Like the big fancy dinner in Vegas, I thought. The pomposity. I didn't need his money. "Come on, please bestow on me the pleasure of your company," he said reading my mind and changing tacks. "I'm new here, you know." I looked at him, at his boyish dimples and those soft dark eyes.

I sighed. "Okay, but I don't have a lot of time."

"Awesome. Where to?"

"I usually go to Tender Greens." I immediately regretted telling him where he could almost always find me between classes.

"What a coincidence. My favorite!"

I rolled my eyes. "You've been here for all of two minutes. How can you have a favorite?"

"More like two weeks." He laughed.

* * *

HE HELD the restaurant's door open as I passed under his arm. He smelled of oak and musk. He just smelled expensive. How do some people do that? We walked to the counter, where I ordered the vegan salad and an iced green tea, and he a falafel plate, with a Red Bull. "I gotta have energy. I'm performing tonight," he said, showing those boyish dimples again, which were killing me.

He let me choose the table. I walked to one with a window view. It somehow felt more open, like I could escape him if he really made me mad.

"So, how's the show going?" I asked once we were seated.

"It's going very well. Thank you." This one had all the confidence in the world. And he had that natural charm, as always. I would not be conned into being nice to him. Not after the stunt he pulled at the party—imitating us, copying us.

"Good," I replied brusquely.

"Yeah, theater's great, crowds are great, critics are great. The critics are awesome, as a matter of fact," he said with a cocky laugh and a sly raise of his eyebrows that sent an electric volt straight down my spine. That again? I sat up in my chair, so he couldn't see me squirming.

"I'm glad you're enjoying *my* city so much," I said,

emphasis on the possessive. I looked down at my salad, and gathered a forkful. When I glanced back up he was looking me straight on.

"It was really last minute, when Veronique asked me to come. I wasn't supposed to. I definitely would have told you in Vegas if I'd known then," he said, giving me an explanation I didn't really ask for, though I guess I did hint at. I lowered my eyes again, not really knowing what to say. If I made it obvious I was annoyed with him for not telling me, it would look like I wanted him to, like I was interested in him. So, I focused on my fork.

When I looked up, I saw he was focusing on my fork too. He made eye contact with me, a look in his eyes that was somehow concerned, relieved, and curious all at the same time. I blinked, not sure what to make of his gaze. Did he not approve of the way I ate?

He cleared his throat and diverted his attention, seeming embarrassed for having gotten caught at something. "Anyway," he began. "So you and your partner are getting ready for Blackpool?"

I nodded.

"Oh. Well, you guys look…like you're working hard."

I almost wanted to laugh. From the way he hesitated, it was obvious he couldn't tell me we looked good together and be honest about it. If I was being honest with myself, I knew we didn't. I should have admired him for his genuineness. But I was pissed. Because I suddenly felt like he'd violated some kind of privacy.

"How did you find my studio anyway?" I said, somewhat snappishly. "I mean, I would think a general dance studio would suit you better."

He shook his head. "Believe it or not, there really aren't any studios that want to offer trapeze lessons," he said, sticking an entire falafel ball in his mouth. I must have glared because as soon as he swallowed, he said, "that was supposed to be funny."

I forced myself to nod, though I didn't join in his laughter.

"Okay, after I met you, I just thought about what a ballroom studio must be like. You intrigued me. So, I came and observed a few classes, and I really thought it looked fun. I thought maybe I could get a part time gig teaching—"

"But I thought you've never danced ballroom," I said.

"I haven't. But I noticed that a lot of the students like to compete and perform and I definitely know theater dance, so I thought I could teach, you know, some lifts and dips and tricks and just general performance quality dance."

"That's showdance," I said. "You just described showdance."

"I guess I did," he said with a cocky smile and seductive raise of the eyebrows that would have looked sexy if his attitude didn't make me want to kill him.

"That's what I do," I said before realizing it wasn't what I did—not anymore.

The cockiness in his smile disappeared and his grin spread across his face, creating the cute boyish dimple thing again. "It *is* what you do."

"No, it's not," I snapped.

"Ah…" He shot me a bemused look. "I believe you just said—"

"It's what I did. Not now. Not anymore." My last performance with Willem flashed through my mind and for a brief second, I felt like I might cry. I looked down at my salad and took a bite, swallowing it along with the tears. When I looked up, I caught Jett glancing at my fork again. What? I wasn't shaking at all? Unless I was doing so unconsciously. I followed his gaze. Nope, the fork was still.

"Understood," he said, now looking at me. "You're a Latin dancer now."

"I am."

"I know you don't dance showdance anymore. But why don't you teach it anymore?"

I shook my head. "Because it just wouldn't make sense. And most of my old students either went to another studio or switched to Latin with me." It suddenly occurred to me he may want to steal my old students. He seemed to be into stealing. Well, it wouldn't be stealing if I wasn't teaching them anymore. But what if I wanted them back? I didn't though. That was my world with Willem, over now. Who was this guy making me so internally confused?

"Okay. 'Cause I was just thinking..." His voice edged up at the end as if he wanted me to consider something but was being hesitant. "I mean, you were really helpful today with Judy and Paolo, and...ah...I was going to maybe ask them if they'd like to take a lesson once in a while with both of us. We could co-teach."

What was he on? I used to do that with Willem. Who did this guy think he was? I felt my heart start to flutter, and then the shaking began. *Oh, great.*

I shook my head rapidly, my heart rate speeding up even more.

"It's okay, you can just think about it. No need to give me an answer now. Just putting it out there." He put his hands up, seeming to know my blood pressure was rising. "You're just... I mean, you're a brilliant dancer. Showdancer. Were, I mean. And the students all seem to...know you and really like you."

I looked at him straight on. Was he making fun of me? But one look in his eyes made me realize he wasn't. He seemed truly nervous and babbling, unable to get his words out right.

"How would you know I was a brilliant show dancer?" I asked, though I full-well knew. He'd filched steps straight from our routines for his studio party performance, so he'd obviously watched our dancing.

"Well, I actually...there's a little ballroom store in Vegas and I went there and just bought a couple of DVDs of you dancing."

I swallowed, then took a breath. I'd assumed he just looked some videos up on YouTube. Had he really gone to a store and bought whole DVDs?

"Which ones?"

"Ah, Blackpool for, ah, the last two years, and okay, maybe it was three. Four?" He shrugged his shoulders and those dimples returned, though the full grin didn't. He looked like a little boy caught with his hand in the cookie jar.

I glared at him, not sure whether to be flattered he'd watched so many videos of me, or scared he was exhibiting somewhat stalker-ish behavior. I still felt a bit violated that he'd taken from our routines. "I knew you watched some of them," I said after a long pause. "Because you borrowed *liberally* from the choreography in them for your party performance."

Now his full, dimpled grin returned, his cheeks reddening a bit. "What can I say? You deeply impressed me. You totally wowed me. You...you took my breath away." That was a reference to one of the songs Willem and I had danced to, that he'd stolen for his routine Saturday night.

"Yes, you stole our song, you stole several of our moves, you practically stole our entire routine. I could sue you, you know." I spit out.

He laughed. "Oh come on. That was Jessica Simpson's song. And we borrowed, as you said. And it was just for a showcase at a school, not a professional performance we

116

charged people money to see. There was hardly a copyright violation."

Now he was turning into a lawyer, dismissing my supposedly ridiculous claim with the wave of his hand. It was our song, our routine, our lifts, our choreography. It was ours together—Willem's and mine. I took a breath and gathered my thoughts. "I know you weren't making money off of our choreography. But it was ours. We created it together. It's my…memory." My voice was very close to breaking.

"Oh come on, Belle," he said, now reaching across the table and placing his hands over mine. "I didn't mean any harm. I'm sorry if I upset you. It's just that you're such a breathtaking dancer. You…inspire me to dance as well as I can, to dance as well as you do. And, I guess I just wanted you to see that I could."

I caught my breath. His arrogance kept my tears over my memories at bay. He wanted to show me he could watch our routines once and then do them as well as we did, with no practice?

"I mean, not that I could do as well as you. That came out wrong." He corrected himself. "You own the world of show-dance. Obviously. The judges have spoken on that many times. I mean, I wanted you to see, I guess, that I could be a good partner too. I mean, if you ever—"

Suddenly I felt sick. I'd only eaten half of my dinner, but I was done. I freed my hands from his clutching palms, and scooted out my chair.

"Oh no, don't leave. I totally didn't mean to offend you, Belle." He reached out to me.

I shook my head. "No, you didn't. I just don't feel well. I'm sorry, I just have to go." And I was off. I picked up my bag and jacket, and walked out, not looking back.

I made my way back to the studio on unsteady legs. As much of an ass as he could be, I didn't like leaving him all there alone at the table. But the thought of someone ever replacing Willem made me so sick to my stomach I felt like I may need to lie down for a moment, especially if I was going to be teaching a full load of classes tonight.

I made it to the studio, ran into the ladies lounge, found a bench, and lay down. Fortunately it wasn't too crowded yet, and I still had over an hour until my first group class of the night. I set the alarm on my cell phone to give myself plenty of time to get up and get ready, then tried to sleep. But all I could think about was Jett dancing at the studio party, and about how good a dancer he really was. And how thinking of him sent a tingle down my spine, and ache in my belly. A good ache, not a stomach ache.

11

Jett

Shit. I totally made her mad at dinner. She said she didn't feel well, but I know it was me. I came on too strong. I shouldn't have hinted that I wanted to partner with her.

Or was it that she felt she was so far above me, she couldn't deign to dance with me? I couldn't figure out what was going on in this girl's head.

I don't know what I was thinking anyway, wanting so badly to dance with her. My life was in theater dance, in aerials, in performing on a proscenium stage for a large Vegas audience, not on a ballroom dance floor for a ballroom competition crowd. That was her world.

Yet something inside of me made me so badly want to perform with her, to take her back to all that, to all that she excelled at, where it was so obvious her passions lay. I don't know what the hell I wanted. I just wanted her. I wanted to lift her high above my head. I wanted to kiss her beautiful lips. And I wanted to do more—a lot more.

The truth is, regarding my private lesson with Judy and Paolo, I knew that a no hands fish would look killer in their routine. And I knew it was damn hard, but I really thought they could do it. And I knew Arabelle could help us. We both had high-level dance skills obviously, but she had way more experience teaching, and I knew she could figure out better how to show them the lift. So when I saw Arabelle and Drew rehearsing, I knew it was wrong of me to take up her time, but I knew she'd see us and help. I wouldn't let that happen again. I could—and would—teach my own lessons. If she did think herself superior to me dance-wise, I didn't need her thinking the same of herself as an instructor.

The next day, I had a lesson with Kendra and Josie. Drew and Arabelle were practicing in the main room. And I knew they would be, because they were always practicing during the day in the main room since they were training so hard for competition. It would be nearly impossible to book a day lesson without running into them. I took pains to pay them no mind.

Kendra turned out to be quite a hoot, as I knew from class she would be. She was a skilled dancer, as was Josie, and, as she'd indicated in class, they were determined to do every lift every male/female partnership did. Kendra insisted she could lift Josie in every way possible, and I believed her.

But what Kendra told me that I hadn't known was that Sasha, the star dancer here, was the subject of some kind of dance documentary and the star of an upcoming movie. There would be film crews all over the studio in a couple weeks. Josie, an actress, was also in the movie. She and Kendra were to do a dance routine for it. And it needed to look very sophisticated, very theatrical, and full of crazy-ass stunts. I was to put this together for them. They were also planning to use this routine to compete in showdance, if the championship competitions would allow same sex couples. They were going to be the first same sex pair for showdance, which was very cool in my opinion.

"After watching you perform, sir, we feel there's no one who could ever do this better than you." Kendra cracked me up with the "sir's."

I realized very soon that this studio was like a quintessential small town. Though it only happened yesterday afternoon, Kendra already knew that I was teaching Judy and Paolo the hands-free fish dive. Now, of course, she and Josie just had to do it as well.

"Everyone's saying it's the coolest thing ever, sir. Bring it on!" She bent over like a quarterback and waved her arms toward her.

I laughed, trying to remember who all was in the room during Judy and Paolo's lesson. Probably about ten people other than Arabelle and her crew, and she certainly wouldn't have been the one to talk. The walls apparently had eyes.

"Well," I began, hesitantly. This was a crazy hard lift. Josie needed strength and Kendra needed more. "Each of you needs a great deal of strength in your own center and back, and Kendra, you need substantial upper body strength to lift Josie into the waist-high fish first. Waist lifts are hard. Even if they don't seem as difficult as over the head, they are."

"Dude, I can totally do it! And I totally want to take her over my head later in the routine. Waist high is nothing. Man, I'm strong." Kendra clenched her fist.

Over her head? I couldn't remember ever seeing a woman do an overhead lift with an adult. Josie had to weigh at least 115 or 120 pounds.

I said nothing, but the look on my face must have thoroughly revealed my thoughts.

"Dude, you don't understand. I bench press at the gym."

I looked over at Josie. She nodded. She didn't seem the least bit dubious or scared.

I accidentally looked toward the back room where Arabelle was, thinking maybe she could explain how hard this was and how much work they needed before trying. The coach's eyes met mine the second I glanced that way. I liked this coach. She saw everything that was going on in the room, not just what was right before her. Yet, she didn't seem the least bit distracted. Arabelle and Drew were in the middle of a routine. They were concentrating. My idea was a bad one—I wasn't going to bother Arabelle anymore.

"Yeah, she's the best showdancer on the planet. Seriously, sir. I wish we could take lessons with both of you," Kendra said.

I'd had my head turned to Arabelle for all of a split second. When I turned back to Kendra, she had a cock-eyed smile and one raised eyebrow. She seemed to know I had a thing for Arabelle. I guess I was obvious.

I shrugged and chuckled. "Hey, what about me? You doubting I'm enough for you?"

"Of course not, sir. But she helped you with Paolo and Judy."

Yep, the gossip mill. "Well, unfortunately it looks like she's busy right now."

"I know, but in the future, it would be fun to book a lesson with the both of you. Just sayin'." At that I noticed Arabelle's gaze in my periphery. Kendra naturally had a loud voice but I think she was making it louder on purpose. Arabelle put her hands on her hips and shifted her weight, giving me a scowl. I shrugged and shook my head, indicating I had nothing to do with the suggestion.

"What would that run us?" Kendra said, all business. "When you guys start teaching together? Is that going to be double the cost, for two teachers? Because I don't know if we have that kind of money, sir." I was loving this girl. And her booming voice. Arabelle shook her head, closed her eyes, and turned back to Drew.

"I...I haven't even thought of that," I said to Kendra. "That would be a lot to pay for two teachers. We'd have to ask Alessia. But I mean, I don't know if..." I looked back at Arabelle. Her face was now red, with anger I assumed, not embarrassment.

"Okay, well in the meantime, you'll have to do," Kendra said. "Now come on, help us get into this lift."

I took a deep breath. "Okay, but I don't want you getting hurt. Take off your shoes first, Josie." That much I now knew. "You both need strength in your back, so I want you both on the floor—"

"Sir, we've been doing that," Kendra said, and waving me off.

I shook my head. What was she talking about? Did she already know about the exercises before? Or did someone give her very specific details about my private lesson with Judy and Paolo? That was only yesterday. "For how long?" I asked.

"Let's show him what we've got so far, Jose," she said without answering my question. She swung Josie out fast and pulled her back in. Josie rolled herself into Kendra, then lifted her arms out and raised one leg behind her, while standing on the tip-toe of the other foot. Kendra held one arm under Josie's stomach, the other under the thigh of the still lifted leg, and, without bending her legs, began to arch her back and raise her arms with Josie underneath. In other words, lifting with her back not her legs, which was a huge no-no.

"Okay, I'm ready, hon," she said to Josie.

"Here I go." Josie lifted her standing foot and spread her

legs out into a split, one high in back of the other. Kendra was still bent back, her back arching at a bad angle.

"No, no, no!" I said, in a panic. "You're totally lifting with your back. You're going to hurt yourself." My voice was loud, as it often was when I was worried about someone getting hurt.

"No, it's really not that bad. I can do it, I got it. I got you, babe," Kendra said, in a huff. But she didn't have her at all. Josie was falling, Kendra was bending over more. Josie was going to hit the ground and Kendra was going to throw out her back if they didn't stop.

"Seriously, put her down. You're both going to get hurt!" I shouted.

"No, no, n—" Now Josie's head was pointing toward the ground, as were her feet. She looked like an airplane trying to make a dangerous landing. The whole shape looked ludicrous, and would have been funny if it wasn't so dangerous.

"There's an easier way," Arabelle said. I hadn't even seen her approaching. She gave me the evil eye. Big time. "Seriously, put her down and I'll show you."

"Okee-doke," Kendra said, doing exactly as Arabelle asked. What the hell? She listens to Arabelle, who's not even her teacher? Josie pulled her feet toward the floor and tried to straighten herself.

"Okay, I'm down," she said to Kendra.

"Okay, letting go."

Once Josie had both feet on the ground and was fully upright, and Kendra had taken a few breaths, everyone looked at Arabelle.

"You need some water?" she asked Kendra.

"Nope, totally good, totally good." She held her arms up and out in front of her, clutching the air with her fists, then lunged to one side, then the next, as if she was working out some kinks in her body. This chick had more bravado than any guy I knew.

"Okay then." Arabelle brushed her hands together as if ready to get down to business. "You need to plié with your standing leg so you can kind of jump into Kendra's arms, so that she doesn't have to bend over and get you," she said to Josie. Josie nodded. "And then, while you place your arms out, you should put one arm around her back, all the way to the other shoulder." Arabelle demonstrated. Kendra tried to pick her up but Belle stopped her. "No, not yet. Let me just give the directions first."

"Sure thing, sweetheart," Kendra said.

I chuckled but Belle just smiled. She looked more relaxed. Hopefully her anger at me was dissipating. *Thank you, Kendra*, I thought.

"Okay, so you wrap your arm around her back, and drape it over her far shoulder," she told Josie. "I like this little trick because it looks pretty, like you're hugging her, like you've got your arm around her, but it's also functional because it gives Kendra support. So, you press down and pull yourself up from your center. Pressing down on her shoulder will actually help you to hold your own weight in the air, using the muscles of your abdomen as well. Capiche?"

Josie nodded. Both women looked at Belle like she was a goddess. And yeah, she was.

"Okay, so I'll try it."

Kendra nodded.

Kendra and Belle started the move the same way Kendra had with Josie, making me realize Arabelle had been watching the whole thing to begin with. Kendra swung Belle out, brought her in, and then wrapped Belle in her arms.

"Now I plié," Belle said as she bent her standing leg slightly, and gave enough of a jump that Kendra didn't have to bend down at all. "Now I wrap my arm around Kendra's shoulder and then I can help hold myself up," she said, lifting her gorgeous leg up in the back, toe pointed deliciously. She extended her other arm out.

"Whoa! Awesome!" Kendra said turning around several times, Belle fully lifted, fully centered in her arms. It did look really beautiful.

"Okay, okay," said Arabelle, apparently feeling Kendra start to get dizzy and waffle. "Now we come down, just as gently as we went up. This needs to be as elegant. The dancing is not just the tricks but in the in-between points just as much, if not more so. So, I point my toe toward the floor, feeling for it, and you can just bend a bit, with your knees not your back, Kendra. And, voilá." Belle put the other foot down, ever so elegantly, then twirled back out of Kendra's arms.

We heard clapping and looked up. The coach and Drew were watching and applauding.

"Wow," Josie said. "That was beautiful."

"It felt that way!" Kendra said.

"Breathtaking," I echoed.

Arabelle shot me another scowl, then began to walk away.

"Hey, wait," Kendra called out. "Now we need to learn the no hands fish dive!"

Arabelle's mouth opened, and I knew she was going to dash Kendra's plans on that one.

"Let's practice this one until you've got it totally down," I said.

"Okay," Kendra said, but to Arabelle. "Can you demonstrate my part now, with Josie?"

Arabelle looked at me, then Drew and Greta, mouth still open. I didn't know if she'd ever lifted someone before, even waist high. Likely not, since she'd only danced with a man. And if she got the tremor, it could be bad.

"It's okay. I can demo with Josie," I said. "I've got that from here."

Arabelle nodded at me. "Call me if you need help, but, yeah, you can trust him," she said to Kendra flatly, without looking at me this time.

Okay, if that was my vote of approval from her, I guess I'd have to take it.

I supervised Kendra as she lifted Josie. It wasn't as graceful and carefree as it was with Belle, but Kendra didn't look like she was about to drop over in pain. Practice made it better and better.

"Seriously, though, I really want to work on the no hands," Kendra said as she was packing up. "And maybe we can work something out so we can have Arabelle for maybe half the session or something. To make it semi-affordable?" I saw Arabelle glance our way in my periphery. I didn't look at her full on this time; I didn't need to know how she felt about that.

* * *

"I THOUGHT we'd put together a little routine made up of tricks and dips and very easy lifts that we can set to music. That okay with you all?" I asked at my next group class.

"Yeah, as long as they include the no hands fish dive!" Kendra yelled out.

I rolled my eyes. "Now, now, we're not doing those in group class. I don't want anyone throwing out their back or crashing to the ground. This parquet floor is not that forgiving."

"Oh come on Mr. R, we can do it. There are no wusses in here." Kendra threw up her arms and looked around the room.

Now I was Mr. R? This chick cracked me up. "At the end

of the course we may—emphasis on may—throw in a regular fish, with hands," I said. "But that's it. Nothing hands-free."

Now she rolled her eyes.

"And that's just for people who want to do them."

"All right, Mr. R. And maybe for people who want to do more, they can do the no hands version," she said more than asked, as if she were running the class. She was too sweet to get angry at though. Not to mention, too enthusiastic. I was beginning to realize there's nothing a teacher appreciates more than a student who wants so badly to learn.

"What's a hands-free fish dive?" asked Eduardo, this fifty-something social dancer by night, engineer by day, whose favorite dance was the Hustle and who'd introduced himself on the first day as wanting to do "really cool disco moves."

"They're awesomely hot," Paolo piped up.

I sighed and threw my hands up. "Okay, for people who really want to take that risk."

"Woo hoo!" Kendra hooted.

"And I may make you sign waivers because, seriously, they are hard—as you know," I said, partially as a joke.

"Whatevs, R. Maybe Rory can make up the forms."

"Rory, Sasha's partner?" I asked, a bit confused.

"Yep. She's an attorney by day, Blackpool champion by night!"

Every single person in class either clapped or giggled at this.

"She just started here last year and easily became Sasha's fave, after, you know, he dumped Arabelle," Kendra said.

Dumped? Arabelle danced with Sasha and was dumped? This was news to me.

"Kendra! Dumped is about five thousand times too harsh!" Josie said, play-smacking her girlfriend.

"Yes, it is," a very good Russian student named Svetlana,

agreed. "They broke up because Sasha only had eyes for Rory. They were…how do you say? Destined."

"Argh, Josie and Sveta are total Sasha and Rory groupies!" Kendra rolled her eyes. "But yeah, I sometimes get carried away. Dumped is too harsh. They just didn't work out. Anyway, my point is just that she can write up these legal docs you want."

I heard some heavy harrumphing in the corner. I looked over to see Luna, the one who'd kicked me out of the practice room, tapping her perfectly pedicured foot on the floor. I hadn't noticed her in the room before. I guess she was one of the watcher students. Her gestures made it clear she wanted me to get on with class.

"I was kidding about that. I'll have to ask Alessia. Anyway, let's get going. Let's start with the rag doll. It's not a fish dive, but it's still fun, and cool."

I explained the move to them, that the guy dips the woman and then kind of rolls her around and pulls her up quickly. I knew Judy's body weight because I'd worked with her and knew she had some dance skills already, so I called on her to demonstrate. I pulled her into me, then held her close by the waist and told her to bend backward, doing the deepest arch she could. As she did so, I told her to be as loose as possible. At this everyone laughed.

"Come on, you guys. I mean with your muscles." I laughed. "Tensed muscles are easier to tear for everyone. And the looser the ladies are, the easier it is for the man to lead." More laughter. I rolled my eyes. Judy did as I instructed and I circled her body around. She could arch pretty well.

"Excellent," I said. Everyone clapped. "Okay, let's try it. Everyone take a partner."

Of course the first time we went to do it, many of them nearly fell, the guy headfirst, the woman back first. I hadn't told the men to lean back. I guess it looked like they were supposed to lean into the woman.

A chorus of exclamations rang around the room. Amazingly, no one actually fell but several guys rocked back on their heels so quickly they ended up taking several steps back and the girls ended up lunging toward them.

"Okay, sorry. I should have made clear to the men that you all have to lean back to stabilize the couple's center of gravity. If you lean toward her, the laws of physics—"

"Um." Kendra cleared her throat loudly, commanding my attention. Wow, Josie was in a deep rag doll, her long arms nearly grazing the floor, and Kendra was weighted back, holding her up perfectly.

I nodded. "Very impressive. But just bend your knees a slight bit so that you're lifting from your leg muscles, and not your lower back."

"Oh yeah, that makes sense," Kendra said, obeying me. "Yep, that's a lot better on the old lower back, Mr. R."

"That's what I'm here for," I said.

We practiced it several more times, with everyone doing as I instructed. And miraculously, it worked much better. Everyone looked pretty good. I realized though that my teaching skills were lacking, which wasn't surprising given this was my first time actually teaching. I had to remember to tell the students exactly how to do things. Simply having them watch me wasn't enough. These weren't professional dancers, and they were used to learning through words, not visuals.

"You guys are quick learners," I said, truly impressed. This was going to be a fun class and a fun routine, so long as I learned how to teach.

"Hey, if we get this routine done by the end of the month, maybe we can perform it at the next student teacher showcase," Kendra said.

A chorus of cheers filled the room. I was growing to love this girl. She was performance oriented, like me. But we only had one class per week. We'd have to get Alessia to turn it into a longer class, or add more nights.

"If you guys are willing to work hard, I think that's an awesome idea," I said. "I just think it's going to take more than four classes. If you guys are willing to double- or triple-up on classes, I'll check with Alessia."

"Of course we are, R!" Kendra shouted. Now I had become simply "R." I looked around. Not a single person in the class was shaking his or her head, or doing anything but nodding and smiling.

"I mean, we could even create a team, like the mambo team?" Paolo suggested.

"The mambo team rocks. I'd be totally into that!" This was a guy of Indian origin named Rajiv. "My girlfriend would totally go for that too. She's good friends with Rory, and she always wanted to be on the mambo team when Rory was. But now that Rory's no longer on it, I think she'd like this just as well."

"Um, okay…" I had no idea what this mambo team was. But a performance team was totally up my alley.

"Of course things would go more quickly if another showdance pro could join and co-teach?" Kendra said, raising her eyebrows seductively.

"Yes! You guys could lead the team. You'd make everyone else want to watch us!" Judy echoed.

I put my hands on my hips and squinted at both of them. I knew from the private lessons that they both adored Arabelle.

"It would be nice to have Arabelle back teaching show-dance," Svetlana added.

Everyone nodded. Arabelle was definitely a star here.

"I don't know if she's going to go for that…" I began.

"Oh boo, hiss. You have to make her!" Kendra shouted.

"We'll petition her," Josie said.

I chuckled. *It's going to take quite a petition to get her to dance with me*, I thought. "Let me run it by Alessia. And Arabelle." But I knew this was going to be near impossible.

12

Arabelle

When I arrived at the studio, I had a message in my box that Alessia wanted to talk to me. At first, I panicked, wondering what I'd done. I'd been a bit out of it lately, thinking about Willem and being annoyed with Jett, but I didn't think I had forgotten about any private lessons or anything.

I knocked on her office door. It was already open, but she was hard at work on her computer so I didn't want to startle her by just walking in.

"Oh hi, Belle," she said looking up. "Would one o'clock be okay? I'm a little busy with something now."

I had one eleven o'clock private lesson with Jones, a retired older man. And then nothing until my coaching with Drew and Greta at two. "If it's not going to take a long time. I have a coaching with Drew at two."

"It definitely shouldn't take that long," she said with a smile.

"Okay, see you then."

I changed and walked upstairs to the private lesson room. I had about a half an hour until Jones arrived, so I used the barre in the back studio to stretch and practice my Latin basics. Drew wasn't even around—no one was this early— and still, my hand began to tremble. I had to get over this. I had to get in to see the doctor again. My student base was beginning to dwindle. Almost all the male Latin students were with either Bronislava, the other Latin teacher, or had transferred to another studio to take private lessons with Xenia, a Blackpool finalist. It was a lot harder generally for female teachers to attract students, because not as many men took dance classes as women—and certainly not private lessons. But it was doubly hard for me as a Latin dance teacher since there were a plethora of others in this city, and I'd lost all of my old showdance students who didn't want to dance Latin. I needed to figure something else out, because I couldn't make ends meet for much longer on only group classes and the few performances Drew and I did during the year. We were still a new couple so we didn't get many well-paying gigs. With Rory and Sasha not competing at Blackpool this year, if we won or came in second, it would help our status immensely. But that wasn't going to happen with my tremor.

Jones came storming through the door early, as usual.

"Hey sweetheart, how ya doing?" he said, giving me a cheeky kiss with way too much tongue and patting me on the shoulder, quite close to my breast. I knew he wanted to be more than teacher/student, and I was very thankful to Alessia for implementing the non-fraternizing policy at the school. It was mainly to protect people—often female teachers—from the likes of male students—particularly the rich and powerful, like Jones—who wanted to take advantage of them.

"Fine, thank you. And you?"

"Always so polite. That's what I love about you, hon." He squeezed my arm and this time his finger did gently press against my right breast.

Jones had always been a little this way but after Willem passed, he got worse, and was really starting to make me feel uncomfortable. I didn't want to be a whiner, so I didn't say anything to Alessia. Plus, I really needed students. And, of course, he took a lot of lessons and brought a lot of money into the studio.

We were training for an upcoming local competition. We never placed that well, since he often spent our lessons trying to touch me "accidentally" in various places instead of listening to my instruction. But he was an older man with a lot of money to burn, so I guess he didn't care that much. I wondered briefly if that was what Alessia wanted to talk to me about.

Still, I tried my hardest to teach him. We began, and he placed his hand very close to my behind, instead of on my back shoulder blade. I moved his hand up, reminding him, once again, that the judges would count down for that. He cackled, as usual.

From the get-go, my tremor was ridiculous with him.

"Honey, honey, honey, do I do that to you?" he said at one point, grabbing my arm, gently but firmly, and holding it still. It didn't stop the trembling at all, but made it more internal, like it was speeding through my insides now, aiming toward my heart.

"I'm sorry," I said, shaking my arm free.

"Don't be sorry, baby. I just want to know how to help you."

"I think I'm still just nervous because of Blackpool, you know," I said, trying to laugh it off.

"I know, but, darling, that mishap was a while ago now.

And it's not getting any better. You want me to get you in to see my doctor? I'll pay. I know they don't pay you too well here."

"No, no, no thank you. That's kind of you, but I have my own." That's all I needed—something I'd owe him for.

"Well, he's not helping you too much." He snickered.

I swallowed and tried to smile. "She said it'll just take some time. That I have to be patient. So I ask that you be, too. I'm working on it." I tried to sound as assured as I could.

He reached for my hand, pulled it up to him, and kissed the back of it. It would have been a nice gesture if it wasn't from him. My hand now shook worse than ever, and he dropped it gently, laughing and shaking his head.

I WALKED to Alessia's office, half wondering if that was going to be what this was about, that students were complaining that I couldn't get my act together with the tremor. The door was open. But when I entered, I saw none other than Jett sitting in one of the chairs facing hers. What was he doing here?

"Hi Belle, come in," Alessia said, warmly, extending her hand toward the vacant chair next to Jett.

I eyed him as I sat down. He smiled up at me, dimples pronounced, with a kind of puppy dog pleading in his eyes. "Hey, Belle."

I made a mental note to correct him. Only my very good friends and my boss called me that. I hardly knew him. And I certainly didn't consider him a very good friend. But I didn't want to get pissy in front of Alessia.

"Actually, before you sit, can you close the door? I'm sorry, I should have told you right after you walked in."

"No problem," I said. Why did we need privacy? What in the world was going on here?

I sat again, taking a deep breath.

"It's nothing bad, Belle." Alessia laughed. "It's good, all good. I promise!"

I swallowed and forced myself to smile. Both my hands were shaking now though. I placed them between my knees hoping they wouldn't be as noticeable that way.

"So, Jett has a proposal he wants to make," Alessia said. "He made it to me earlier today, but I needed to have you here, because it involves you."

What? I looked at him. He gave me a loopy, pleading smile. More puppy dog eyes.

"Why don't you tell her, Jett." Alessia gushed at him. Of course he'd won her over. He won over every female he ever looked at. Except for me.

"Well, here's the thing. I'm teaching this group class, a performance arts class..." His chocolaty brown eyes lit up with excitement. He sat up in his chair, making Alessia outright bounce in hers. "They're such dedicated students!"

I know, I wanted to say. *They were once mine.* But I said nothing. Instead I just looked down. He had what I'd had; what I no longer had, and no longer wanted.

"And they're so dedicated, they want to start a performance team. Like, there's some kind of mambo team here, apparently? I don't know since I'm new—"

Yes, you are new and you don't know anything, I wanted to say but, again, didn't.

"And they want to form a similar team but for showdance, which will perform for the studio and maybe some nearby competitions!"

I couldn't look straight at him now but I knew his face was about to burst with excitement. I could hear it in his voice. I knew he wanted me to co-coach and I wanted to smack him.

"I don't understand," I lied.

"What…don't you understand?"

"I'm happy for you, Jett. But what does this have to do with me?"

"Oh, that's the thing. They all love you; they think you're a goddess. And they want you to co-lead the team, and dance on the team, as…my partner."

I closed my eyes.

"I haven't figured all the numbers out yet," Alessia said. "But of course they would pay the team rate instead of the class rate, which, since there are performances involved, is much higher. And you'd also get paid the class rate if you helped with the regular class. You'd also get paid extra for each performance. Jett mentioned he has some private lesson students who'd like to work with both of you. If that happens, you'd get paid the private lesson rate as well. So, this would be a lot more money for you, Belle. A lot. How does all of that sound?"

Her voice, in contrast to Jett's, was all business, all seriousness. She was trying to entice me with money. And I *did* need the money. I really did. But I so didn't want to return to showdance. I didn't know if I could. I really didn't. My hands were shaking so badly, I literally had to lift myself off my seat and slide them underneath my thighs.

I glanced at Jett. By the look in his eyes, you'd think he was asking me to save his very life.

I didn't even know if I could do this with someone I liked, let alone him.

"Just think about it, Belle, okay? Please," he said. "I know Belinda would be willing to do it too."

"But of course they want you, Belle," Alessia said.

"And I do too," Jett said softly. I could see him out of the corner of my eye glancing at my hands.

"Why?" I shot out. *You know I'm a freak right now*, I wanted to say.

"Because you're the best!" Alessia laughed.

I blinked again and looked back at Alessia. "Well, what do you say?"

No, is what I meant to say, but somehow I heard the words, "I'll think about it," coming out of my mouth instead.

They both interpreted this in the affirmative though. "Excellent!" Alessia said.

"Oh thank you." Jett reached for my hands, which I didn't give to him.

If I danced with Jett as the team's centerpiece, I couldn't do any difficult tricks with the tremor. That was for sure. Not to mention, I couldn't do any serious showdancing with anyone other than Willem. It would be like cheating on him in death. Alessia knew that's why I switched to Latin. At least I thought she did. Maybe she'd honestly never noticed the tremor. If I did this—and it was a big if—I couldn't dance a regular show-dance. It would be a student performance piece. That would be okay. That wasn't dishonoring Willem, and easier on-the-floor moves wouldn't be problematic with the tremor.

* * *

AS I PRACTICED WITH DREW, I forced myself to ignore the shaking and proceed as if it wasn't happening. Drew and Greta did the same. Jett was having a private lesson with Judy and Paolo. I could see out of the corner of my eye he wore a huge smile, as if he'd won something. He glanced at me a few times. I guess I'd basically given him and Alessia the go-ahead on the team.

I forced myself to ignore them when they began practicing fish dives again. I was determined not to help them this time, at least right now. But I couldn't help but notice in my periphery how wrong they looked, how much better I could make them, how well I could do the trick my frigging self—or could have, at one point in my life. And I couldn't stop thinking how much I needed the money.

13

Jett

I knew Arabelle would go for the team idea. I had my worries after lunch but I knew deep down she wanted it, and needed it. Alessia's little speech had made clear how much she needed the money. But I knew she needed more than just money. She needed to regain her passion again, to do what she excelled at like no one else, and what she loved with all her heart.

So, the next day when I had Kendra and Josie again for a private, we eyed her repeatedly while she worked with Drew and the coach. I'd let on to them that the team was probably going to be a go, though I didn't say Arabelle would be involved. I couldn't help it; I was too excited, as were they. It really impressed me how hard those two were working— Kendra and Josie, I mean. Josie could already hold her back up for several seconds while lying on the floor. They'd learned to practice that only a few days ago. Kendra had been working out with large weights, bending her knees to lift so she'd have lifting with her legs, not her back, in her muscle memory. She even showed me. I commended them as loudly as I could on how awesome they and the team were going to be with all the effort everyone was putting into it.

"It's just a shame you can't dance on the team yourself and lead us with a great team captain," Kendra boomed, her voice likely echoing all the way down to the Ethiopian restaurant on the first floor.

"Yeah, like the best show dancer in the world," Josie echoed, her voice not as loud as Kendra's but still bellowing throughout the entire room.

Okay, you guys, now we're overdoing it a bit, I thought. I glanced at Arabelle. Drew was grinning, as was the coach. Arabelle was the only one who looked pissed, her mouth a straight line. She pretended not to notice me and didn't glance back. She just kept on doing her routine with Drew, albeit with very bad trembling.

After I was finished with Kendra and Josie, I turned back to Arabelle before leaving the room. She was looking right at me, hands on hips. She pointed to the clock and held up three fingers, then pointed down, as if toward Alessia's office. Amazing that I totally understood what she was saying. I nodded, and couldn't help but grin broadly. I knew I'd won.

* * *

AND I WAS RIGHT. I walked into Alessia's office at three on the dot. Arabelle wasn't there yet.

"Sit down." Alessia held her hand toward the chair closest to her.

"So?" I said, sitting.

"I don't know yet. I guess we'll find out."

Arabelle sauntered in about three minutes after three. "Sorry. Kind of lost track of time while practicing with

Drew." She enunciated Drew's name, as if to indicate he was her real partner.

"No worries." Alessia extended her hand out to the seat next to me. Arabelle looked at me as if I were diseased, then sat very hesitantly.

Sheesh.

"Well?" Alessia asked when no one spoke.

"Okay, I'll do it," Arabelle said after a several-second pause. "But only with a couple conditions. First, I'm not doing anything too risky. I'm done with that. No crazy over-head lifts or anything. I don't think the students are ready for that, and it makes me too nervous to try things on them that I...don't want to do myself. I'm just...not into that anymore."

She breathed deeply after this, as if that was really hard to get out. Alessia and I looked at each other. I nodded slowly. It sounded like she was considering dancing herself, if we promised not to do anything she "didn't want to do herself," as she'd put it.

Of course, I knew it would be the best if we could do just such lifts, making the choreography as theatrical as we could. It would be good for both scores *and* pleasing and chal-lenging the students. Well, Arabelle may need some working on to come around. The tremor was obviously holding her back. But I had plans to help her in that regard—hopefully, cure her.

"Also," Arabelle continued, after another breath. "I will dance with Jett but only as the centerpiece of the team, and only if my first demand is met. I most certainly will *not* dance with him outside of the team." She looked not at me, but at the floor.

"Totally understood," Alessia said. "I think this is going to be very popular, go very far. Just to make sure, you will commit for three hours a week with the group, and if individual students want more of you and Jett together, you're available, right, Arabelle?"

Still looking down, she nodded. "If it's for the team, then yes."

"Great!"Alessia said. "I really think this is going to be a wonderful thing for the studio, you guys. Thank you so much for trying! I've been thinking about competitions. There's one coming up in Orange County that the studio always goes to and they take showdance entries. And there's one in Las Vegas—"

I could sense nervous energy coming at me from Arabelle's chair.

"Yeah, we'll really think it over and plan," I piped up, cutting Alessia off. "Hopefully the team will be up for all that soon. I really think they will be with the progress I see the individual students making in my class, and in my private lessons."

"Excellent. For now, you'll commit to performing at the next studio party," Alessia said, more than asked. I had to admire her for that—just telling you what she wanted instead of asking. Just like Veronique. "You know, to get them used to being before an audience, and, you know, let the other students know about it in case they want to join."

I nodded. "We'll get something together, even if it's rudimentary."

Arabelle looked down, but nodded.

"Excellent," Alessia said. "I'll let your students know, and will put the word out in case anyone else wants to join."

Arabelle got up to leave, still looking down.

"Arabelle?" Alessia said before she left. Arabelle turned to her. "Thank you, honey. I really appreciate your effort." Alessia's wide, serious eyes indicated she wholly meant it. Arabelle stared hard for a few seconds then blinked. When she opened her eyes again I could see some tears in the crevices. She took a breath, nodded again, and was out.

"Thank you," I said to Alessia, then ran after Arabelle.

"Hey, hey!" I called out to her.

She turned around, squinting at me. "I meant what I said. This is it. Only for the team. Nothing more," she spat and turned back around.

"Yes, I know."

She turned to me again. "Oh, and one more thing. No one calls me Belle except close friends. I'm Arabelle to everyone else. Including you."

Ah, okay. Ouch. But my ego wasn't really bruised. She was just trying to set boundaries after I got my way with the team —boundaries that wouldn't last for long. At least I hoped not. "Okay, Arabelle," I said, enunciating the first syllable. "Belle Arabelle. By which, I just mean pretty Arabelle. Just like all of your other fans."

She opened her mouth but no words came out. Then she shook her head and walked off. I could see a tiny smile brightening the corners of her face though.

14

Arabelle

Wen I walked into the room where the first team class was being held, everyone stood and clapped loudly. Oh geez. This was followed by several very loud whoops that the diners two floors down in the Ethiopian restaurant likely heard. I rolled my eyes and shook my head, trying hard not to blush. Jett smiled and lifted his hands, clapping high above his head.

I waved them down. "Okay, okay. Thank you, you all. I, uh, really appreciate it." Now I was blushing.

"Are you kidding? You are the queen of showdance!" Kendra boomed, which brought about another round of hoots.

"Well, thank you for that. I used to be, anyway," I said, now looking away, out the far window.

"A queen never retires," Kendra insisted.

I laughed. *No, but she does abdicate her throne sometimes. If she needs to.*

"So, looks like the team is comprised mainly of the more serious students in my group class," Jett said, looking around. "Give or take a few new members."

"Damn right we're the most serious!" Kendra pumped her fist in the air.

Jett laughed. "So, let me show you what we've done so far in group class that we can use for the team." His face was one huge dimpled grin. He motioned Judy over. "So, we start out in closed position, then swing the lady out, then pull her in with two spins—you can do three, Arabelle—and then into a low, down and dirty rag doll."

Everyone cheered. Judy was very good. He was definitely right about this group being hard working and enthusiastic.

"So, yeah, come on everyone, let's do it all together!"

Everyone lined up in three rows, with two couples each row, leaving Jett and me in the center. I don't think I'd seen students organize themselves so quickly, and so perfectly.

"Okay, ready," he said, holding his arms out to me, inviting me into closed position. As he did this, he raised his eyebrows in a way that sent a bolt of electricity down my spine. Not that again. It had to stop. He could tell what I'd felt, I knew he could. Because now a twisted smile began brewing on his face. *No sir*, I said to myself.

"Ready, sir!" Kendra sang.

I stepped into Jett's extended arms. His biceps were solid muscle, his embrace all-enveloping in a way that momentarily made me feel protected and cocooned, his hold both firm and gentle. With his left hand he held my right; his long fingers gently laced though mine. He placed his right hand on my back, fingers gently but firmly cupping my back shoulder blade, exactly where they needed to be for proper lead. He pulled me in a bit. He was right to do so, as much as I didn't want to admit it; I was too far from him for a proper ballroom hold. He smelled like musk, like night—like a starry, moonlit night. Like in the Paris in Vegas.

Suddenly, it was too much. I backed out of his embrace. I gasped and caught my breath. He wasn't like Drew at all. Or Sasha. Sasha was way too intense to ever develop any kind of attraction to. For me at least. No, something about Jett was very...very Willem-esque. It unnerved me. I swallowed hard and took another breath.

The whole class looked at me with wide eyes.

"You okay?" Jett asked.

"I'm sorry," I said. "I don't...I...I'm just sorry." I forced myself to laugh, and returned quickly to Jett's arms. I placed myself in his hold this time, looking not into his eyes but off and to the left, right behind his left ear. I could still smell him, still feel him, but I forced myself to block it all out. He was just another man. He wasn't anyone or anything special. Just a dance partner, nothing more, nothing less.

"Okay now?" Jett whispered, sending more chills down my back, which I tried hard to ignore.

I nodded.

"Yep, yep," Kendra chirped.

"Okay, here we go." He began counting out the beats, and the steps. One, two, three, four were a basic social rumba in closed hold. Then on five, he whisked me out away from him. It felt good to not be in such close hold with him. And it felt like we were now doing a run of the mill dance routine. He raised his arm. "Okay, three underarm turns back toward the man. One, two, three, four." He pulled me in, and I rose to the balls of my feet and turned three times. He held his hand lightly above mine, his grip so light but still there, to give me maximum freedom in making my own turns, my own flourishes, my own speed—and my own number of spins, I realized, as everyone around me started giggling. I stopped when I got back into Jett's arms.

"Whoa, dizzy!" Judy squealed.

"Oh shit. I mean, crap. Sorry. Sorry," Jett said. "I didn't mean for everyone to turn as many times as Arabelle."

"You should definitely apologize about the cursing. No one ever does that around here," Kendra said, gruffly. Everyone laughed. I'd heard more than a few potty words coming out of her mouth in my time here.

Jett laughed too. "Okay, well shit then. But I meant to say two turns. I was talking to Belle, ah, Arabelle when I said three. So, you know what? Do however many you're comfortable with for now. We'll decide whether to officially change it or not later."

"Coolness," Kendra said. "Now, let's do the lowdown, dirty ragdoll!"

Everyone laughed again. This was a fun group. Jett pulled me into him again, this time quite close, and I got a very good feel of those pecs and abs. The man had muscle. He aligned my body with his, my pelvis at his hip, his crotch right on my hip. I breathed deeply. I was a professional dancer. And all I could feel was big solid man.

He brought my waist toward him, propelling me to stand high on the balls of my feet again so he could lift me ever so slightly, pulling my pelvis right into his. My lower abdominal area filled with liquid heat. I willed it to stop. We were torso to torso, our nipples touching.

"Feel free to let go of my shoulders when I dip you and arch your back to your fullest extent. I got you," he added with a wink that nearly melted me. Right. The rag doll. I was supposed to let go of him and arch back.

"Yes, of course." My full extent was quite full. I let go of him and let myself fall straight back, trusting him not to let me fall. I arched back as far as I could, really stretching myself out, really feeling it, letting my hands fly behind me like a bird, grazing the floor when I bent all the way. I lifted my left leg up ever so slightly so that I'd have more leeway, and pointed my toe. It felt so good. Like nothing had since I last showdanced.

Jett swung me around in a semi-circle, holding me up just as he said he would, just has I knew he would. It's funny how ridiculously risky I'd thought he was when I first saw him perform, and again when I witnessed him with his students —but how I was totally trusting him anyway. Not that it would be a horrible fall that I couldn't right in time before my head hit the floor, but still. I knew now I could lose myself and he'd be there completely.

And of course the nanosecond that thought passed through my brain, that I was trusting someone besides Willem, and especially this crazy-ass bravado trapeze artist, it came back. The tremor. It started slowly, in my fingertips, then made its evil way up my arm, to the elbow. Jett seemed to sense it because next thing I knew he was bringing me up, and quite quickly.

After he'd whisked me up and pulled me into him again, closed position, crotch to crotch, abs to abs, small breast with rock hard nipple to big solid pec, everyone hooted and clapped like they'd never seen anything like it before. *What?*

"Man was that a badass arch. W-T-F, Arabelle!" Kendra shouted, actually using the letters of the acronym. Now I really blushed. I felt my whole face turn flaming red, completely matching how my heated insides felt. I didn't know whether to be more thankful that people obviously hadn't noticed the tremor, or that Jett had momentarily made me feel a tremor of a completely different kind. *What was wrong with me?* This man was so not for me. I should not have enjoyed any part of dancing with him. This was purely monetary, I reminded myself. Nothing more.

Jett seemed to know I needed my space right now. He had the students go on and do the routine again thus far, this time without modeling the moves on me. He walked around, helping to improve their connections, their styling, and their technique. I followed his lead and did the same, re-centering people, helping to make their connections more solid.

"That's a gloriously deep dip," he told one couple. But just then the man leaned toward his partner, probably to dip her even further.

"Eeek," she screeched, nearly falling backward.

"No, no, see? He needs to be centered," I said to Jett. Then, realizing how much I hated it when people talked about me when I was right there, I turned to the man and explained the same to him. "You have to be centered in order to hold her up. So you have to weight yourself backwards, onto your heels. I know it seems like you should lean forward to allow her to dip more, but it's actually the opposite."

He seemed embarrassed and his raced reddened substantially.

"It's okay, your partner is okay," I said.

"I am!" She laughed. But her laughter was of the nervous sort.

"I'd taught them that in the group class, but this is one of the new couples. So they weren't there for my instruction," Jett said.

I nodded. "It's all okay. Just something to remember for next time. Which I'm sure you will."

"Yeah, I'm not into dropping my partner!" the man said.

After class, Jett took me aside. I wondered if he was annoyed with my instruction to his student.

"You okay?" he asked, a serious look in his eye.

His question took me aback. I looked at my arm. I wasn't shaking. I hadn't shaken since the initial rag doll at the very beginning of class. Did he think that was my normal state of being?

"I'm fine," I snapped, more than I'd meant to, out of confusion.

He held his hands up. "Okay, okay."

"I do think we have different teaching styles though."

"What do you mean?"

"I mean, I would have made clear from the beginning of class to all of the new couples that the man needed to lean back on the rag doll or the woman may fall."

He sighed. "I told you, I taught them that in class."

"But you'd forgotten there were new students."

"I had. But there were only a few, Arabelle."

"And they don't matter?"

He sighed more deeply. "Of course they do. I just forgot."

"I would have taken that opportunity to remind everyone again. I mean, people could get hurt."

He sighed again, then chuckled. "Okay, Arabelle. In the future, I will remind the students repeatedly of every potential problem they may encounter."

Now he was being sarcastic, and deeply annoying. As I'd known, this man was all about the flash. I couldn't believe he was being so reckless. Women could get hurt. Men could hurt their backs as well. "You could open the studio up to liability."

"Oh good lord, it wasn't that big of a deal. No one was really going to get hurt."

"They could have. And what about the harder moves, Jett?" I didn't turn to look at him. I could hear his deep breaths of annoyance.

"Like I said, I'll remind everyone all the time of potential issues," he said, and walked off.

"These are students, not professionals, Jett," I called out. "They don't know what they're doing. It's our job to teach it to them."

He turned around, widening his eyes. "I think you worry too much."

Worry too much. Words I couldn't hate more. I worried the second Willem got that motorcycle, how he sped on that thing. Maybe other people needed to worry more.

15

Jett

I hadn't realized how much of a worry-wart Arabelle was. That was probably where her anxiety disorder had come from. I mean, it was just a dip. The woman could right herself easily if she felt herself falling backwards. Certainly no one was going to break a neck. I mean, it would be possible, I guess, but one of those crazy, unforeseeable things. Like her slip at Blackpool. It made me wonder how hard it was going to be to work with her when we started doing more difficult stunts. I did want to put a few lifts in there. Would she fight me all the way?

That night when I performed with Beauty in Motion, I let myself soar more than ever. I took every risk in the book. I did a one-handed fly on the way to Belinda, instead of two-handed. I did three somersaults in the air at one point instead of two, and I overextended my splits, which I could tell thrilled the crowd more than anything else I'd done. I almost did a one-footed hang-down from the trapeze, but decided against it. I hadn't practiced it with the trampoline underneath. I didn't want to do something that risky that I hadn't even practiced. Okay, even I had my limits. But I made a mental note to practice it. I couldn't let Arabelle's freaky weirdness kill too much of my mojo.

Mind you, I didn't take any chances with my partner. Only myself. So, I guess Arabelle had rubbed off on me a little. Funny how I couldn't get her out of my head the entire time I performed.

* * *

"OKAY," I began at our next team meet. "Before we learn any more moves, I think we should think about the performance and what type of basic ballroom dance we want to do. Because that will determine what kind of showdance tricks we want to focus on."

Arabelle inhaled deeply and folded her arms across her chest.

What? I thought this would make her more at ease and give her an artistic focus so that the students—like Kendra—wouldn't have as much license to ask to learn any crazy hard thing they wanted. She opened her mouth but no words came out. She simply shook her head.

"Do you have a suggestion?" I asked her.

"No, no, just go on," she answered with a flick of her hand. There was no tremor.

"Okay, well, does anyone have any thoughts? I've researched the different styles of dance the performance teams have done at the competitions in California and Las Vegas and Atlanta—all the places where they have prestigious team comps—and they're mainly focused on popular social dance styles like salsa and west coast swing and even disco." In my periphery I saw Arabelle frown.

"But we can always add a slower, rumba section in the

middle and do some pretty lyrical stuff," I added. Her eyes grew big. And she shook her head. This woman. What did she want? She didn't want fast, but she didn't want slow.

"I like the idea of fast and fun, and then ooooh-so-slow-and-sultry woven in between, Mr. R," Kendra said lifting her eyebrows flirtatiously. I chuckled. I was Mr. R again now.

"We've already done salsa on the mambo team," Judy noted. "I mean, salsa is a form of mambo. It is a fun dance obviously. But so is disco."

"But disco is so seventies," Josie said.

"Not necessarily," said a woman new to the group named Samantha. "I mean, we can make it more modern with samba steps, since it's the same beat. And we can add some salsa, too. You can do a lot with disco music."

Kendra shrugged. "Well, I guess it depends on the music."

"Yeah, I mean, we're if we're going with retro like Abba or the Beegees, we'll have to make the whole thing retro, and have it be like a fun period piece," Judy said.

I loved how the women were totally making all the decisions. Other than Arabelle. She looked like she was thinking hard though.

"But for something contemporary, there's always Donna Summer. We could do a little tribute since she passed away not long ago," Samantha said.

"Or Gloria Estefan, if we wanted to add Latin dances," Judy said.

"Whatev, but I think something mainly fast but with a slow lyrical section would be most awesome," Kendra said.

"What about "Last Dance?" It starts out slow. Or "Proud Mary" by Tina Turner?" This was suggested by a woman named Charlene, also new to the team.

I couldn't read the thoughts behind Arabelle's eyes. Her gaze was now focused on the window. It didn't look like she was looking at anything in particular, just thinking.

Then I got an idea. "You know, there's a Donna Summer song that's really cool. Fast and fun for the most part, but with lots of slower sections and very emotional. And a lot of people don't even know it's Donna Summer. It's called "Con Te Partiro" and it's her upbeat remake of the Andrea Botticelli song." I'd seen some ballroom dancers perform to in Las Vegas once and I'd thought the song was perfect for fast fun moves combined with beautiful, slower lyrical sections. I took out my iPod and flipped through till I found the song. "Here, listen."

It started out slow and then built up. Everyone's eyes lit up.

"I love all the different instruments. And how it builds to a crescendo. And the words! So much passion! I can't even believe it's Donna Summer!" Kendra chirped.

Nods spread around the room. Everyone seemed to agree.

"Arabelle?" I called out, hoping she'd heard at least some of it. She was still looking out the window, seemingly lost in thought.

"Yes," she said, her focus still off on something in the distance. "The music has a nice melody with different contrasts. And the beat of the song is fun while the words are passionate. She's telling her lover, she'll go with him to the ends of the earth. To be together forever and ev..." Her voice began to falter, but then returned clearly. "But it's still high charged musically, so the words...they don't really necessarily dominate."

She seemed to like the song, albeit for reasons I didn't fully understand, but she was clearly approving. Yes, our first meeting of the minds!

"Awesome. We'll start choreographing to this then."

I played the song a couple more times and thought about different moves we could do. We could still fit what we'd done so far in the beginning. We'd just need to take a little more time with it, and we could easily do so by having the guys—or leaders, in the case of Kendra—start out already onstage, and have the followers walk out to them, each to her partner. That would make the rag doll happen right before the first swell of music.

"Okay, so after the rag doll, the leader brings the follower back up, close to him, and then the follower does, let's say, three spins out away from her leader. We'll turn left and then the guy—I mean the leader—will follow her, catch up, and do a long lunge while holding her from behind around the waist. She can fall back into him and lift her right leg up, développé it up into the air. And then she'll—I mean the follower...damn." I had to keep reminding myself we had a same sex pair on the team. What was wrong with me?

"It's okay, sir," Kendra said with a loopy smile. "You don't have to worry about political correctness with me and Jos. Just say guy and girl."

Josie nodded. "But thanks anyway," she added with a little laugh.

"You sure?" I said.

"Of course." Kendra walked over to me and gave my arm a firm pat. "You're a good guy, man."

"Well, thank you, Ma'am. I try." I'm sure my smile came off more crooked and cocky than I'd meant it to. It was my natural grin. In my periphery I could see Arabelle rolling her eyes.

"Okay, anyway, after she does her slow sultry leg lift, the guy turns her around in his arms, by the waist, and she turns to him. He lunges toward her and she lifts her leg up in back, in a pretty arabesque."

"That's a lot of leg lifting. What if not everyone has the same flexibility?" Arabelle said. "Or the same ability to hold the other person?"

She was met with a sea of stares. I'd choreographed something pretty and she wanted to change it. But damn if she wasn't right. It wouldn't look good if everyone's leg was going up at a different angle.

"Fair enough. Let's try it and see how it looks. I extended my hand toward her. At first she looked at it and frowned. Then she came toward me, took my hand. Her palm was a bit wet and there was a kind of vibration in her wrist, but no tremor. I wondered if this was how they began.

"Okay, let's start with the spins. I'll count."

Everyone did the spins out, on beat. The guys all lunged, but since people were different heights, the spacing was a bit off. No biggie, I'd fix it. And the women lifted their legs at different rates of speed, so we'd have to choreograph that to the beats. But happily, once everyone had their leg in the air as far up as possible, it was clear that we had a flexible group. When I directed all the women to put their legs in the air at the same time and arch their backs over the guys' supporting hands, all the legs were at nearly the same height in the air.

"Awesome!" I was a bit shocked, but happily so. There was often someone in the group who couldn't do it exactly as the others did, but that wasn't the case here. When I looked in the mirror, I couldn't help but focus on my gorgeous partner. Her leg was still the longest. *Of course*. But that was okay. Everyone knew we were the pros, and therefore the focal point.

"Okay, now turn your partners around," I said.

This got a little sloppy, understandably. A lot of the guys didn't know how to rotate the woman by the waist. And they weren't supposed to. They were supposed to lead it, then let the girl follow through on her own.

"Okay, we'll have to work on this. Let's just continue. Ladies, lift your right leg back now in arabesque."

At first it was a mess. Everyone went at a different rate of speed and made a different shape.

So I directed the women to arch their backs and just raise their leg a bit off the floor, holding their arms back to look like they were flying. They all did so. This was gorgeous, with everyone raising at the same height now.

"You know what would look so awesomely cool right here?" Kendra piped.

"What?" I asked.

"If the guy, or the leader, you know, would take the woman over his head right here, and she could do that same move, with her arms spread out behind her like a bird but this time off the ground. I've seen it done and it's awesome!"

"You're so right. It is an awesome lift!" Judy squealed.

"The bird is beautiful," I agreed.

"You're not serious." Arabelle put her foot back on the floor and came out of her position, backing away from me.

I nodded, indicating both that I was serious and that I understood what she was freaking out about. Yes, it was hard and dangerous. But yes, it was also gorgeous.

"That's incredibly hard on the lifting student's back. Especially..." Arabelle said, eyeing Kendra.

"Oh come on," Kendra said. "We've already been through this before with the fish dives. I can totally do it!" she said pumping her fist in the air. "Come on, A! Don't be a party pooper!"

"We could do it very quickly. And the follower wouldn't have to go entirely overhead. If the leader just straightened his or her arms for a split second," I said.

"A split second, A!" Kendra echoed me.

Arabelle took a deep breath. "First, I'm not being a party pooper, Kendra. I'm just making sure no one gets hurt. Second..." She seemed to forget what she was going to say. She threw her arms up at me.

What? I thought without saying anything.

"What's the purpose then of putting it in for a split second? Just to show everyone can do a crazy trick. There's no meaning in it then."

I didn't know exactly what she was saying. Yes, it was to show the leaders were strong, the women were flexible and we could do something challenging all in sync. Isn't that what dance competitions were supposed to test? When I expressed as much, she stomped her foot and walked away, fuming.

"Ms. A, come on!" Kendra said, chuckling. "Don't go anywhere. We need you!"

Arabelle circled the room, breathing deeply, before walking back to Kendra.

"Okay, you know, if you say I can't do it, then how about all of us students just hold our partners with their leg on the ground, maybe one slightly lifted off, and you two do that crazy cool lift overhead. That way you can take your time and Jett can hold you up in the air and you can lift your back leg super high, maybe both legs? You can just do anything that is super cool and shows what awesome shapes you can make with your miraculous body, A. And that tells a good story set to this beautiful music!"

Not a bad idea at all. Kendra was a smart girl, a natural born choreographer. I nodded, raising my eyebrows at Arabelle. She glared and shook her head.

"That's an excellent idea!" Samantha said.

"Totally," Judy chimed.

"I third it. Or fourth, wherever we are," Josie said.

I shot Arabelle my cocky, looks-like-you're-outnumbered grin.

"And then, and then—" Kendra cracked me up. She was so on a roll. "And then Jett can slowly stand up with you above him like that! I've seen that and it's *awesome*! And then he can go to one hand only! Holding you all the way up by only one hand!"

That was similar to the lift Arabelle did with Willem, and that I'd done with Belinda at the studio party. I could so do it. And she was so right. It would be an awesome lift. Arabelle's gorgeously flexible body balancing up there on my one hand, me holding her up, showing my all strength.

Arabelle's mouth fell completely open and she rolled her eyes then looked to the ceiling. What was wrong?

"What's your objection, Arabelle?" I said, my voice now sounding beleaguered. It was such an awesome idea.

She harrumphed, and finally spoke after a few beats. "Dance is about art, about storytelling. You're just stringing tricks together."

Ugh. Back to that haughty ballet attitude. *I'm such an artiste, you're just a trickster. Yes, that's exactly how it is; I'm a total phony.* "Well, that's how you win competitions, isn't it?" I said.

She opened her mouth but I was a quick thinker and I knew what she wanted to hear. Before she could say anything, I added, "but you're right, we will make it fit the story line. And here it does, because she is telling her lover not to be afraid in this part. So, that's like me telling you to take a risk, stretch your arms out and lift your legs up and trust me with your weight, your body, so that you look like you're soaring. There's no more perfect move to set those lyrics to, when you think about it."

She thought it over for a few beats. And the more she thought the more she realized I was right about telling a story to the music. Each movement, each sequence, and each lift should tell a story. And this string of movements, or so-called tricks, would do just that. They went along perfectly with the music, with the passions both the music and lyrics evoked.

The class-is-over buzz sounded. We were done for the day. But, she brought her head down and looked me straight in the eye. I could read her thoughts now. She knew I was right. And she was going to give in. She was going to do it. She was going to let me lift her.

Arabelle

"What exactly are you afraid of?" Dr. Marsh asked me. After Alessia had paid me for my first week of working with the team, I had a bit more money to go back to my shrink.

"Afraid?" I shook my head. "I'm not afraid of anything."

"Are you sure about that?" She looked at me straight on, her dark eyes full of seriousness.

"Yes. I'm just really annoyed at him. He has no respect for artistry. He's a…he's a charlatan, a trickster. He only wants to wow the audience, without moving them, without bringing any meaning or emotion to the performance."

"But you told me he thought the lift would be moving because the words were from one lover to the other not to be afraid to trust, to soar."

"Yes, but … he made that up on the spot just to get me to do it. I swear, I could see his beady little eyes thinking, scheming." His eyes were anything but beady though. His eyes were deep brown and full of wonder and depth. Eyes you could get lost in. Damn those eyes.

She smiled and pursed her lips.

"What?" I said.

"Are you afraid, Arabelle? I want you to think seriously about that over the next week. Because I think you are. That's what I'm hearing. I want you to figure out what exactly you're afraid of."

"Please. I've done that same lift and many far more difficult ones a bazillion times. He thinks it's such a hard lift; that one's easy. Please."

"You've done harder ones in prior showcases?"

"Yes, yes, yes. With…" I felt a sting in the back of my eyes.

She nodded, as if acknowledging my pain. But she didn't look away to give me a little peace like others, like Lucia, might have done. I guess that's why I was seeing her. She wouldn't let me off easy. She continued to drill her eyes into mine. "And now you're doing them with another man. Another partner. Is that what you're afraid of? Not the lift itself."

"No. No, no, no. We're not doing the same ones. Maybe a variation or something similar but not as hard. It's not the same. It's totally different. It's totally…he's totally different. Nothing is the same. Nothing." I caught my breath, then inhaled and exhaled deeply a few times.

"Arabelle, I didn't ask you if this man was the same in any way. I know he's not. There's only one Willem. There's only one of each of us. I just asked if the lifts were the same."

I took a few more breaths. She wasn't putting me on the defensive. I was getting way too worked up about a question she didn't ask. "Yes. I mean no, the lifts are different. Different lifts."

She nodded, and gave me a slight smile.

"And, are you scared this man might drop you; that you might fall?"

"No, not at all." I shook my head adamantly.

"Because you trust him not to drop you."

I let the words sink in, then laughed. Trust Jett? Never. "No way. I trust myself to protect myself from him."

"You can do that? I mean if you're high in the air?"

"Most definitely. I know how to fall properly to minimize injury."

She listened, nodding. But she still wore that little smile. And I had to admit, the more I heard myself the more I realized how silly I sounded. If he was standing and I fell, I could get hurt. That just wasn't going to happen. It just wasn't. So I guess I *was* saying I trusted him if I was so sure I wasn't scared of the lifts.

"How is the tremor? I don't see it today."

Sometimes I didn't even notice when it was or wasn't present. I looked down at my hand. "Yeah, it's okay today. At least while I'm not thinking about it." I laughed nervously, not wanting it to come back now that my mind was on it.

She nodded. "What about when you're dancing? Have you noticed it during your team practice?"

I thought about it. Weirdly, not much. Except for the initial time with the rag doll. Unless I just hadn't noticed. I hadn't had any problems with connection. Granted, we'd spent more of our time talking about the routine—okay, fighting about the routine—than actually dancing. I shook my head. "It's mainly when I'm practicing with Drew. Not teaching, and…not working with Jett."

She nodded again. "Good."

Yes, I guess it was. Of course my dancing with Drew was far more important to my dance career, so it would be best if the tremor didn't happen with him. But I needed to take improvements as they came.

* * *

THAT EVENING, I got another call from Alessia asking me to come into her office first thing when I got to the studio the next day.

"What's up?" I asked. She sounded a bit frantic, which was unlike her. She was usually calm and poised and confident.

"I'll tell you tomorrow. I...I think it's going to be okay."

I think? Okay, that worried me.

* * *

JETT WAS ALREADY in her office when I got there. One glance at him through her little office window sent an electric zing up my spine. Stop it, I said to myself, wanting to slap the zing right off of my back. He flashed me a cocky grin as if he knew exactly what had just gone through my mind. Or body, rather. I took a breath, shook him off, and walked in.

"Hi Belle," Alessia said, that same slightly beleaguered sound in her voice that I'd heard last night.

"Is everything okay?" I sat next to Jett.

"Hopefully. Yes, yes, it will be," Alessia said after a deep breath.

"What happened?" Jett said. She apparently hadn't said anything to him yet either.

"This guy named Landon Brantley just opened a new studio. This one in West Hollywood. He's from New York. He had a huge, very successful studio there. In fact, I took lessons with him. That's where I trained." She took another deep breath. "He knows how to run a studio. He knows how to be a big success, and take over a lot of the little people. He did just that in New York."

"You think he's going to take business away?" My voice squeaked with nerves. I was just getting back on my feet

167

financially with the team coaching. I didn't want to have to worry about losing students to a competing studio.

"I know he's taken Xenia and Piotr from another studio to dance there. You know they used to dance here before Sasha and Xenia broke up. Luna's friend has talked her into going there. You know how much money she brought into the studio. Nikolai, an up and coming standard ballroom dancer, just signed on to teach there with his partner, Katusha. He's taking Gloria, this studio's other big spender. And Svetlana has told me he's trying to get her and her partner to go. They're Rising Star champions, you may know."

"What is he giving them?" Jett asked.

Alessia shook her head. "Not sure. I would assume more money. And maybe job security. According to Svetlana, he's trying to make this place look like a sinking ship."

"Yes, but you've got the world champs, Sasha and Rory," I reminded her.

"Yeah, but you know, now with this movie he's making and this documentary he and Rory are doing, he hardly teaches anymore. Rory never taught since she returned to her law practice instead. And now that she's pregnant, they won't be dancing at Blackpool this year. No matter how much publicity they bring to the studio with his fame, it doesn't really matter if they don't teach regularly, do private lessons, take students to competitions, or bring in championship money." I could really hear the worry in her voice now.

"Hopefully, Drew and I will win big at Blackpool. We're established as a top couple since we placed third last year and the top couple isn't competing. And we both teach." But I heard my voice. It totally lacked conviction. I was having so many problems with Drew, with my tremor.

"What can we do to help?" Jett asked.

Arabelle looked back and forth between the two of us. She smiled weakly. "I'm not really sure. Other than work hard on the team. It would be awesome if you guys could do really well at that upcoming Vegas comp. I've heard Landon's bringing a team too."

I snickered. *You've got to be kidding*, I thought. Totally copying us.

"What kind of team?" Jett asked.

"I'm not completely sure but I think it's a Latin formation. I think Piotr and Xenia are the leads. With them being world finalists in Latin, it makes sense that's what the studio's going to be known for." She said this without looking at me. I was a Latin finalist too. But if my problems continued, I wouldn't be anymore.

"That one's in a month. So, we've got a lot of work to do to be ready in time." But Jett didn't sound the least bit worried. He sounded excited by a challenge. "We'd have to speed it up, maybe triple up the sessions, if it's okay with the team. We've got a lot of really good students. And, I really think they're up to the challenge." Jett flashed those large white teeth at me and nodded, as if pleading with me to agree with him.

"What are you guys thinking for your dance style," Alessia asked, a note of hopefulness now coating her words.

"Since we're specialists in showdance, we're doing cabaret with several different music rhythms and dance styles, fast to slow. And of course, lots of fancy theatrical lifts and all," Jett answered immediately, his grin widening.

"That sounds excellent!" She nearly jumped in her seat.

"I mean, you've got as the centerpiece of your team a Las Vegas dancer who's starred in a big, popular theatrical show, and the three times Blackpool showdance champion," he nearly shouted.

"You're so right!" Alessia popped out of her chair and hugged him. *Oh good lord.*

I forced myself to smile as she moved from him to embrace me. But over her shoulder, I caught his eye, gave him my nastiest glare possible. *Fancy theatrical lifts.* He'd agreed to leave out tricks for tricks' sake. I wanted to kill him.

I wanted badly to talk to him as we exited her office. But I was almost late for my coaching with Drew.

"After you," he said, extending his hand toward the stairs.

"I only have a second, but let me make this clear," I said looking at him as I descended the staircase.

"Be careful, that's not the best way to go down a flight of stairs you know—"

"Shut up." I stopped. He stopped. I grabbed his black t-shirt, fisted as much of the material into my hand as I could. The shirt was tight and it was hard not to touch muscle. Serious muscle. Damn, he had an eight pack in there. Okay, focus, Belle. He widened his eyes, his penetrating pupils shooting that electric spark down my spine again. "I am only doing this for Alessia. And for myself, so that I don't lose my job if the studio closes. I am not doing anything more with you than what is required for this team. I am not. And we are going to do this on my terms. No flashy B.S. We are going to tell a beautiful story with our routine and fill the dance with passionate choreography that furthers that goal. No theatrical nonsense. That's not what audiences—at least ballroom audiences—respond to, and I should know, don't you think?"

He nodded, a cocky grin covering his face that I wanted to rip right off. "Yes, ma'am, you're the boss."

"Don't you even dare try to humor me," I spat.

"Believe me, I'd try no such thing. You're the champion. You heard me say that. You are the boss." He still wore that grin. He raised his eyebrows again, creating a pool of hot liquid in my center. He needed to stop doing that. Or, rather, I needed to stop letting him do that to me.

"What's that look on your face about?"

He shook his head and shrugged without removing the grin. "I was just wondering what you meant that you wouldn't do any other kind of dancing with me than what was required by the team? What other kind of dancing would we do?"

I had no idea what he was talking about. What had I said? I remembered saying it. What had I meant? Had I been thinking in the back of my mind that we'd be at Blackpool dancing a showdance together? Had I had that vision? How could I have done that to Willem? I stepped down to get away from Jett and almost lost my footing.

"Careful," he said reaching out for me. He caught me and held me up. I felt heat spread from my feet up through my center to my shoulders. I had to go. I struggled out of his embrace.

"I'm fine." I turned and took the rest of the steps two at a time.

17

Jett

I couldn't believe Arabelle's words to me on the stairs. That she'd never dance anything other than the team dance with me. Had she been thinking of competing in showdance with me, just the two of us, at the professional cabaret competitions? At Blackpool? She couldn't have meant anything else. So, she was at least subconsciously thinking of us as a partnership.

But did *I* want that? I had my Vegas career, which I loved. I could manage both though. I was a master juggler. Hell, yes, I wanted to dance with Arabelle. I knew my Tarzan routine backward and forward—until Veronique wanted me for another show, Belinda and I really needed no practice. I just had to show up at the theater. I had all my free time to devote to competition. I hadn't done comps since I was in ballet school as a kid, and man, did I thrive on them. That's where you could show what you were made of. I was a born competitor. I knew what it took and I'd get us there. We'd kill that damn Latin formation team from the other studio. I just needed Arabelle to let me do my thing. Hopefully she wouldn't fight me too much. We needed the difficult moves. The judges knew what was hardest, and they rewarded you on that. They also rewarded you on what was most compelling to the crowd. Yes, you needed artistry too, but that was secondary. Believe me, I knew. I did a lot of ballet comps.

I had a private lesson with a new student today, Corey. She had little dance training but wanted to learn fouetté turns and pirouettes. She'd apparently seen me doing those earlier in the week. Oh wow. Turns are tough, and for advanced students.

I tried to teach her but it was hard because she had so little dance training. I focused on showing her how to wind up for the pirouettes, doing them two-footed at first.

Drew and Arabelle were in the main room, toward the corner. I couldn't help noticing how bad Arabelle's tremor was while she was working with Drew and the coach. The tremor was worse than I'd ever seen it. They couldn't maintain connection at all. She kept apologizing and was now grabbing her wrist as if that would help. The coach looked more worried than mad and she kept telling Arabelle to stop apologizing, it was unnecessary and a waste of time and breath. I wondered if our conversation with Alessia had made Arabelle more anxious. It was stressful to know the studio was counting on you to win a big comp in order to stay solvent. That's not exactly what Alessia had said, but that was the general takeaway for me—that we needed wins or else.

"I'm getting help for it, I really am," I heard Arabelle say at one point. I wondered what that meant.

Toward the end of the session, Drew tried to whip her around, leading her out into a series of wicked spins, then pulling her back in close to him. But when he went to reach for her arm to pull her in, she was shaking so badly, he unintentionally let go, and she went stumbling several steps before falling.

"Hey, Arabelle, you okay?" I called out. But Drew was already at her side, holding her madly shaking hand. He picked her up.

"I'm fine, I'm fine." She nodded, regaining her footing. "It's okay," she said to Drew, shaking off his hand. He let go, then huddled close to her. The coach joined in and they whispered. I apologized to Corey and returned my full attention to her as she tried without success to make two pirouettes in a row.

"No, it's totally okay. But what's wrong with her?" Corey asked. She'd told me she was new here, but I was still somehow surprised that she didn't know of Arabelle. Plus her tone was laced with judgment, as if Arabelle had a horrible, contagious disease.

"Nothing."

Corey raised her eyebrows. "With all that shaking?"

"Nothing. Seriously," I repeated. "She just had a recent tragedy, followed by a frightening experience. She'll be perfectly fine in no time."

But I was wrong. She transferred her tremulous nerves to me during our team practice. And I was probably partly to blame. At the beginning of class, I ran the comp plans and accompanying schedule by the students. I'd done some research on the best comps that were closest to L.A., and okayed it with Alessia. The first was the big one in Vegas, followed by one in Orange County a month later. The team was absolutely ecstatic about the comps, about working their asses off and increasing class time. I knew they would be. There wasn't a lazy one on the team. I was proud and super psyched. But my excitement may have brought Arabelle's nerves on. Damn, I'd have to be more aware.

She and I demonstrated the opening of the routine, up until the beautiful but significantly modified bird lift she'd finally agreed to do with me. But her tremor was so bad we just couldn't get anywhere. I swung her out and pulled her back in, just as Drew had. But I didn't let go. I held her tightly. The twitch went all the way up her arm, and was beginning to snake up mine as well. But I wasn't letting go.

I released her hand and pulled her body into mine, to go into the rag doll dip. Her entire body was trembling. The tic affected everything, from the way she arched her back, to the way she stood on her legs with no solidity whatsoever, to her inability to let loose and look relaxed. She looked stiff as a robot but with jerking limbs; the antithesis of lyrical and fluid. It was killing me that this was ruining her beautiful lines, her beautiful form.

Then came the overhead lift. She was shaking so badly, she couldn't even lift her arms back birdlike. And the tension throughout her whole body created a heaviness, making it seem like she weighed a good three times more than she did. I began to go from kneeling to standing position with her overhead, but it was too much. I couldn't get a good hold on her center because of her squirming body. Then she must have lost control of her thigh muscles because one of her legs fell out of position, and I nearly got kicked in the face. Okay, that was enough. I wasn't going to drop her.

I slowly let her down.

"I...I...I'm obviously not liking that lift. We have to change it more," she said as soon as she was squarely on her feet and had caught her breath. "I want to keep it with you kneeling the whole time, like we're having the students do. No standing."

Her words were met with a chorus of groans. I clearly wasn't alone in my disappointment. No, that wasn't going to happen. It was far too cool a lift. It totally fit in to our routine and would score us major points to boot. But she was clearly struggling. She was literally shaking now, even though she was solidly on the ground. I wasn't about to insist on keeping the lift in right now.

"Okay," I said after a breath. "I know you can do it. And it's a beautiful lift. But we'll talk it out later."

But she shook her head. "The lift is not beautiful. It's too theatrical. It's too…it's too, just stupid, and it's not…It's ugly because it's just a trick meant to wow. It's meaningless and ugly." She threw up her arms. I'd never seen her so inept with words. But she was wrong. It wasn't stupid and it definitely wasn't ugly.

"It's definitely not ugly or stupid," I said, feeling myself getting defensive. I looked at the students for support. Now they were all silent, either worried about Arabelle or scared she wouldn't budge. But one by one they began to nod. "See, you're outnumbered." I said.

She shook her head, her lips pursed, and her whole body tensed. There was no shaking now, but you could see her muscles visibly flex and tense. She made a fist. She took a deep breath and when she exhaled her nostrils flared. As soon as she unclenched her fist, the tremor began again.

I placed my hand gently on her arm. She looked at my hand. The shaking stopped, at least momentarily. Good, maybe this is what it took. Gentleness, touching, caring. I could do that.

"I need to go get some water. Excuse me," she said, pulling away.

"Okay," I said, unsure whether I should follow her. I couldn't leave the students. They weren't paying for us to run off after each other. So we stood around for a moment. It would be hard to choreograph without her. And I didn't know how long she would be gone. Then, I got an idea.

"You guys go over the opening. Practice makes perfect. I'll

put on the music. I'm going to make a quick call and I'll be back in just a sec."

"Sure thing, J," Kendra said.

I ran out the door and called Belinda.

"Hey, what's up?" she answered.

"Hey, just wondering if you're in Hollywood?"

She was. She was just getting out of ballet class, right up the street. Perfect. I asked her if she could help out, as my regular co-coach wasn't feeling well. I promised to pay her a couple hours work.

"No prob, Jett. Sounds fun!"

By the time we went over the opening sequence once more, Belinda arrived. Arabelle hadn't yet returned.

"Damn that was fast," I said running toward her.

"I was only across the street." She gave me a cheek kiss. "This looks fun!" She eyed the students with a wide grin.

"Guys, as most of you know, I'm a dancer in the 'Look of Love' show currently at the theater up the street. This is Belinda, my partner there, who some of you may have seen me perform with at the student showcase earlier this month. I thought she could help us choreograph until Arabelle feels better so, you know, we don't waste time."

The students initially looked dubious, but leave it to Kendra to warm everyone up to a new idea.

"Cool. We don't have a lot of time until the first comp, so any help we can get would be awesome."

Belinda nodded. "Show me what you guys have."

I saw Arabelle enter the room right as we began going over the routine. She held a large bottle of Evian. Her mouth dropped and she stopped walking. I held a finger up to her indicating I'd explain as soon as we finished the opening sequence. The music was playing and I didn't want to stop it.

"Okay, you walk away and I lunge toward you," I directed Belinda. The students danced alongside us. "Good, now I whip you back and you lean over me, like the students are doing." She looked at Judy and Paolo, nearest to her, and imitated Judy. It felt perfect. I looked in the mirror. She didn't have Arabelle's gorgeous lines or lyricism but she did the step perfectly and the mini-lift felt right. "Okay, now the students are going to hold that position while we do the bird lift. Take your back foot off the floor. I'm going to slowly rise to a standing position, and then go to one hand. That wasn't the modified lift Arabelle had insisted on, but I knew Belinda could do it full out and I wanted to see how it looked in the routine.

"Okay!" One word, full of excitement. Just the way I loved my partners.

I slowly rose, balancing her center in both of my hands. She was heavier than Arabelle but she held her body well and it wasn't hard at all. I looked up at her as I stood all the way, then extended my arms and lifted her all the way up. She arched her back and raised her arms and legs. Loud applause from the students.

"Yes!" Kendra said.

Slowly, as I balanced and tested her weight, I let my right hand do most of the work, then all of the work. And I ever so slowly let go with my left hand, holding her only by the right.

I could feel her core lose a bit of its strength, telling me it was time to let her down into a fish dive.

"Okay," I called out, letting her know.

"Yep," she said.

I released my hand from her center and she dropped. I caught her at my waist. I'd have loved to have rolled her down like I'd seen Willem and Arabelle do, but we'd never done that before. So, I just dropped her straight, catching her in my arms. I whipped her lower body up and to my back. She wrapped her leg around my back and held it there.

"Okay," she said.

I let go of her waist and voilá, we went into a hands-free fish dive.

"Awesome!" Judy said. Applause and hoots echoed throughout the room—the whole room, not only the students. Belinda was getting shaky. She couldn't hold her back up as long as Arabelle could.

As I grabbed her and let her down, I looked out and realized we had a pretty big audience. Everyone in the private lesson room had stopped what they were doing to watch, and the door to the hall was open, with several faces peeking around the corner. The only face I couldn't find was Arabelle's. *Shit, what happened to her?*

"Super fun, awesome routine you guys have!" Belinda trilled.

"I'll be back in a sec." I ran toward the hall, peeked around the corner. No Arabelle. Crap. I ran down the hall, down two flights of stairs to Alessia's office. She wasn't there.

"Everything okay?" asked Alessia seeing my frazzled face.

"Yep," I said, running toward the lobby. Arabelle obviously hadn't come to see her. No Arabelle in the lobby. Well, I couldn't be bothered by this now. I couldn't leave the team hanging. I'd call her as soon as I finished. Hopefully she'd come back later in the rehearsal anyway.

Belinda was chatting with the students back in the private lesson room. They seemed to be discussing further choreography they wanted. She was excitedly explaining various lifts she knew, most of which she'd done with me.

"Arabelle didn't come back, did she?" I interrupted.

Heads shook. "Nope, but I'll totally take over. I mean for today," Belinda said. "Your students are great!"

18

Arabelle

I couldn't believe I left team rehearsal, but I just had to. I was shaking too badly. Jett had momentarily stopped it. But he wanted to do a lift I'd done with Willem—or a version of it anyway. I couldn't. I just couldn't. I'd had a bad session with Drew so I was already in a bad way emotionally. When Jett started to go into the lift, I started to feel light-headed. I felt like I might pass out. I just wanted him to let me down.

As soon as I was on the floor I excused myself and quietly walked out of the private practice room and down the hall, to the ladies locker room. I sat down on the bench, bent over, and put my face in my palms. I still felt weak, and now like I might keel over. I turned to my side and lay down on the bench.

The door opened. I opened my eyes slightly. It was someone I didn't know. I didn't want to be somewhere where I had no privacy. I needed water. I opened my locker, took out my purse, changed into my street shoes and walked outside, down the street to the nearest coffee shop. I ordered a bottle of Evian. I drank half of it, then walked back to the studio. I felt a little better, but not much.

When I walked back into the room and saw Jett dancing our routine with his theater partner, I just kind of lost it. This time I stormed out. I was only gone a few minutes and he couldn't wait? No, he needed to practice that blasted lift all he could. Heaven forbid he lost ten minutes of lift time. Now I felt not only faint, but nauseas too. I walked back to the coffee shop and this time ordered a tall iced mocha with whipped cream. I found a table by the window, where I just gazed out. I don't know how long I sat there. I had so many emotions bubbling up inside me, and I didn't even know what all they were. Jett's calling Belinda made me so mad. So flipping mad. How dare he ask someone to take my place without asking me!

It was obvious I had a problem. I know it was obvious to the students who watched me dance Latin, and now show-dance. But I was fine until Jett insisted on putting that bird lift into the routine. If he just hadn't insisted. Then he was doing the lift—our lift—in a ridiculously drumroll theatrical fashion, with Belinda. It took so long for him to get Belinda up there. She was so slow, it made them late on the music. If he actually performed it with her, they'd have to stop the regular music and literally do some stupid drum-roll sound for the lift to fill in the gap. What a joke. The move needed to blend fluidly with the lyrics, with both the music and chore-ography telling the love story. The dance was a story of love, not thrills. Why couldn't he understand that? I hated this guy. I really did.

And not to sound pompous but Belinda could not really make the proper lines at any point in the choreography, not just with the lift. I could arch my back better. I had a far superior range of motion. My legs were stronger and my thighs and hamstrings more flexible. And when he let her down, she couldn't roll; he had to take her straight down. Did she not know how to roll? And then when they got into the hands-free fish dive, she couldn't hold it for longer than three seconds. She didn't have the requisite strength in her back and leg muscles. She was less practiced on that than even Josie and Judy.

Despite the tremor, it really needed to be me doing that lift, up there in his arms. Simply because it looked way better on me. I should be the one doing the fish dive and the roll down. Because I knew how to do them. Because I was a consummate show dancer. This was *my* dance. It was me. Not Belinda. But there was no way I could do any of those moves if my tremor didn't stop.

My thoughts returned to the way he brushed my arm, caressing me. Jett. He'd been trying to calm me. But in a sensual way. Being touched by another man still seemed so wrong. Logically, it did. But it didn't feel that way. *But it should, right?* I lay my head on the table for a moment, still looking outside. The world kept on going after Willem died. My life kept on going as well.

"Hey, Arabelle?"

Huh? What was going on? I lifted my head and looked up into bright sunshine. It was afternoon, and the sun coming in through the window was in my face. I'd fallen asleep. That touch on my arm...I turned toward the voice. It was Jett.

"Hey," he said again. Those little boy dimples, that warm smile. Those eyes that made my insides heat up. Then it all came back to me. He'd chosen his partner over waiting for me to return from getting water, brought her into our class without even checking with me, did our lifts—my lifts—with her. His smile dissipated as he obviously saw my anger grow.

"Now, just hear me out."

I shook my head. "No." I picked up my iced coffee. It had

soaked through the napkin, the whipped cream had melted all over the table and was now a sticky mess. I reached for my bag. He grabbed it and held on to it. What the heck? Who did this guy think he was? "Are you serious? Give me my bag!"

"Just hear me out for five minutes. Arabelle, I just didn't know what else to do. I couldn't choreograph on my own and I couldn't keep going over the beginning with them. We owed the team members the time, and we had to move on with the choreography. They're paying good money for this, you know. I knew Belinda was probably in Hollywood, since she takes a bunch of dance classes here. I just asked her to finish out the first part of the routine since I didn't know when you were coming back."

I stopped reaching for my bag, sat back and let out a breath. As much as I wanted to fight him, I really couldn't. At least not about his bringing Belinda in. He couldn't waste the students' time. I couldn't just keep walking out of class whenever I got angry at him, or shaky.

"I didn't feel well. I felt faint."

"I know. I'm not blaming you for going to get water. But I just didn't know what else to do."

"You used her to show me up to the students," I said. "To show them your crazy lift that I'm...having...problems doing..." My voice fizzled out and I couldn't finish the sentence.

He snorted. "Arabelle, she didn't show you up. They all know you're better. She did no such thing."

"But you meant for her to."

"Arabelle, don't be ridiculous. You're the best. You know it, I know it, the students know it, everyone knows it. You left me without a choice."

"I'm not the best though." My heart pounded, my stomach dropped. The sad fact was that I left, not only because I was pissed, but because I couldn't do the lift. My hand wouldn't let me. I must have looked at my hand as my thoughts went there because he seemed to know what I was talking about.

"Arabelle, what's wrong?" he said softly. "I know it's not the lift, I know it's not me. I know that because I saw you shaking when you were dancing with Drew. And it didn't happen yesterday when we danced. It doesn't happen all the time, only at certain times."

I so didn't want to go here with him, to let him in. Not him. Not now. I was going to get over this in my own time.

I shook my head and frowned.

"Don't pretend you don't know what I'm talking about. Come on." He still spoke a little above a whisper.

"I don't…it's none of your business," I said.

He touched my arm, the arm of the hand that had trembled first and still trembled the most. But I pulled away.

"Is it maybe because dancing Latin brings back what happened at Blackpool last year?"

How the hell did he know about that? And how dare he try to psychoanalyze me? Who was this guy?

"I was thinking…I know there's so much pressure now to win—"

That was enough. He was not my shrink, thank the Lord. I grabbed my purse from him and stood.

He exhaled audibly. "You gotta stop doing this. Walking away from the problem."

That really got me. The problem? How dare he tell me how to act. How dare he act like my problem is all about him, something that he can solve. Walking away from the problem? I was walking away from him. I finaled at Blackpool in Latin with Drew. We lost partly because someone threw a frigging water bomb onto the floor. Hello? I'd think Latin was my thing if I got that far at the world's biggest competition.

"Okay, okay. Before you leave, at least tell me what you want me to do about Belinda. Should I ask her to come tomorrow to help out again?"

Help out? He made me sound like an invalid. I couldn't think at all. "Tell her she can be your partner permanently," I said.

"Arabelle, don't do that. Just don't."

But I was off.

I got home, picked up the mail, threw my bag on the table in the foyer and collapsed on the couch. My emotions were a mess. I got up and flipped on the TV and DVD player, popped in last year's Blackpool video, and watched myself dance with Drew. I saw myself take that horrible fall, my face all bloody. I threw the DVD jacket at the TV screen.

Poor Arabesque was so scared of me, she darted to the top rung of her cat tree and wouldn't come down. "Oh, I'm sorry girl. I didn't mean to scare you."

I made her a bowl of Fancy Feast and put it on the floor beneath the cat tree. But she just looked at me wide-eyed. *Fine, she'll come down in her own time,* I thought.

I needed a serious glass of wine. I poured myself some Cabernet, walked back to the couch, plopped down, and watched the scene again. And again. And again. Until it all just became a laughable cartoon.

I turned the TV off and went back to the kitchen for more wine. On my way, I glanced at the bar, realizing I hadn't opened the mail. I'd just thrown it down. I usually received mostly junk mail so not a huge deal. But this time I saw the return address on the first envelope. It was from Winter Gardens, in Blackpool. It was from the Blackpool organizers. My breath caught and my heart stopped. I ripped it open.

Dear Ms. Fonseca. Again, we are so sorry for your loss. We hope you are feeling better and have recovered as much as it is possible to recover from a tragic loss. We continue to mourn dear Willem, as he was such a valued member of our community. He will always be dear to our hearts.

"The point of this letter is that we would like to invite you, and a new partner, to compete in the showdance championships at Blackpool. As you know, this is an incredibly prestigious event, and one only open to invitees. Again, as in years past, you are one of them—you and whoever you have chosen as a new partner. If you do not yet have a new partner, you are invited to do an homage dance on your own again. You may not enter the competition alone, but you may perform a dance in honour of Willem, like you did last year, which all of our attendees would love immensely. He was beloved and had so many fans here. Please let me know your decision as soon as possible. We would love to see you grace our floor again. Until then, God Bless you and the spirit of Willem."

I grabbed my glass of wine and collapsed on the couch. I closed my eyes and breathed slowly in and out, in and out. I lay my head back on the back of the couch and continued just to breath. I remembered the last time we danced at the Winter Gardens. I went over it again and again. We were so happy. The routine was beautiful. I was so proud to dance it with him. I had no tremor. I had Willem. I was whole. I inhaled, concentrating on my breath, on getting that air to all parts of my body, as I'd learned in yoga. I sat up on the sofa, criss-crossed my legs and placed my hands in meditation position. Suddenly, I felt a ball of vibrating fur jump into my lap, followed by small but sharp claws kneading straight into my center.

"Arabesque is back! Unafraid now!"

"Mrrreeoww," she responded in a bass purr.

I closed my eyes and remembered our last dance. The pumping of my heart echoed in my ears. I tried to cry, but I had no more tears. I'd cried my heart out too many times. I only had the sound of my heart pumping blood throughout my body, to every organ, to every extremity. I was still alive. Somehow by the end of the dance, I felt a warmth fill me. A happiness and peace over what we'd had. And, for the first, time, I felt a hope at what could be again. Jett was right about one thing—showdance was my soul, not Latin.

19

Jett

I had no idea what to expect for the team the following day. Arabelle was pissed at me—that was clear. I didn't know whether she'd show up, whether she'd told Alessia she'd quit the team, or whether she'd told Alessia she wanted me off the team. I heard nothing from Alessia or Arabelle. So in case Arabelle didn't show, I asked Belinda to help again, and told her I'd pay her again from my own funds.

Belinda arrived to the team meet all chipper. She did love doing this. If Arabelle really wanted a replacement we'd have a good one. She wasn't as gifted as Arabelle but she was a damn good dancer. She was also a dancer who wasn't much into choreographing, who wouldn't counter me on anything I wanted to put into the routine. I had every logical reason to want Belinda to replace Arabelle, to hope Arabelle wanted off the team. Yep, every logical reason.

But Arabelle showed up. She eyed Belinda the moment

she spotted her. She looked around, took a breath, nodded, and walked toward me.

"Belinda offered to help just in case—" I began.

"It's totally okay. It's good for her to be here. She can…she can help you demonstrate the choreography in case…in case I can't. Thank you, Belinda." Arabelle looked down as she spoke, her voice shaky. But her body was not. When she looked up, I noticed smudged mascara under her eyelids, as if she'd been crying.

"You're welcome," Belinda said. "Oh honey, are you okay?" Belinda obviously noticed the mascara too.

Arabelle self-consciously wiped the area below her eyelids with her finger and nodded.

"Hey, Belle!" Kendra shouted on entering the room. "I'm so happy to see you in here! I was worried when I saw you and…well, I'm just…you rock, girl! Let's do this, J!" I'd never heard Kendra's words so jumbled before. She seemed to know something I didn't. She walked straight up to Arabelle and wrapped her arms around her in a big bear hug.

Arabelle laughed. "Thank you, Kendra. Really, thank you." Arabelle's face wasn't visible inside Kendra's embrace but I could hear her crying. What was going on?

"I am so psyched you're here as well," Josie said. "We are really going to rock!" Her tone was more subdued but still genuine.

The other students entered and Kendra released Arabelle from her embrace. Arabelle wiped her eyelids again and nodded at me to begin class.

"Okay, instead of going over what we already have—which is pretty dang good," I started, "let's continue with the choreography. I'd rather get this whole thing mapped out as soon as possible so we have plenty of time to work out any kinks and get it all polished and into our muscle memories. What do you all say?"

A chorus of *yes*'s filled the room.

"That was a pretty resounding affirmative." I laughed. Before going on, I glanced at Arabelle. She looked at Belinda, which I took as an indication to choreograph on her.

I held my arm out to Belinda. "Okay, so give me one, two, three beats to let her down, and then all the ladies will come out of the smaller lifts and we'll go on as a group. Sound good?"

"Sounds awesome, sir," Kendra said.

I played the music again to figure out where we were so I could choreograph to the beats. I closed my eyes and envisioned the steps we should be doing with that section of music. When I opened them, I saw Arabelle standing in the corner of the room, watching. She had her arms folded in front of her. It didn't look like she was trembling at all.

"What's next, what's next, J?" Kendra shouted excitedly.

"Okay, let's do a..." I thought about going into another lift but then decided we needed something lyrical and soft in between. So I decided on a ballroom-esque Waltz spin, where the partners twirl in unison.

"Ooh, pretty," Judy said.

"Very," Charlene echoed.

"They have to be wearing gorgeous, twirl-y dresses," Kendra said.

"Okay, everyone try." I nodded at Kendra's suggestion. Yes, gorgeous dresses were so right. We all tried it to the normal beat of the music. Some students definitely needed practice spotting, especially the men. But I had every belief they'd eventually get it, and felt it better to go on at this point.

"Okay, now, we spin the women out like this," I said demonstrating with Belinda.

"Wait," Arabelle called out. "Aren't you going to work on

spotting with them? They need to know how to spot if they're going to turn like that."

"Yes, definitely. But right now I wanted to go on with the choreography. Work on details later." It initially annoyed me that she was directing me from the back of the class, but I also realized if she cared how the students looked that meant she was staying on the team.

"Okay, okay, go on," she said, holding up a palm. "I'm just watching."

"So then, the music is going to crescendo soon. The ladies will spin out and then they'll look back at us, hold that for, let's say, four beats, and then run toward the man, and jump. We'll do a lift-spin. Once we reach momentum, the lady can take her legs off the ground and slowly extend them into a split. Okay?"

"Better than okay!" Kendra shouted.

I could see Arabelle's eyes widen. But she didn't say anything.

"Okay, here's how it looks." I demoed with Belinda, to expected wicked applause.

"Mr. J., you are so incredibly awesome. You just don't know!" Kendra said.

"Beautiful!" Judy echoed.

"Gorgeous!" Samantha sang.

"Crazy hot!" Paolo added.

"Okay, then, let's do it. First, slowly, without the music," I said. "Opening position. Guy just let the girl down and now we do the dual spin." I demoed with Belinda, watching as the students followed us. "Slowly so no one gets dizzy this time. And then, spin her out like this." No one seemed to have a problem yet. "She stops and looks at the guy for four beats. Okay, excellent. And now she runs toward him and we lift her up—"

"Wait." It was Arabelle again. I put Belinda down. "Just to

make sure no one gets hurt, why don't you do little things to simplify that. Just at first, and then they can see if they can do it the exact same as you."

"We're not going to do any overhead lifts. This is just a small one. The overheads are only for you and me." I said this without even thinking. She looked me straight on, those big beautiful doe eyes penetrating mine. "I mean, me and...my partner," I corrected.

Arabelle blinked then looked at Kendra and the other students. She shook her head as if shaking off a thought. "Okay, now that it's on my mind, there's been something I want to correct, a while back. Do you mind? Just something I noticed that I want to make...a little easier, okay?"

There were murmurs around the room. I knew the students didn't like the word "easier." She was going to have to come up with a different term. I nodded anyway. She walked toward me, into my closed hold embrace. Belinda moved out of her way. I felt no tremor as I held Arabelle.

"Okay, so there's that part where the guys are turning the girls and it gets faster and faster."

"Love that part, and it's all on the ground, Ms. A!" Kendra said.

Arabelle nodded. "I know it is. But I noticed a lot of you are not turning in a straight line. You're veering toward the front of the room. So your partners have to raise their arms high and follow you, and you're all out of line and it looks like everyone's struggling. It's just not a good look. And I think it's happening because you are facing the audience and when you spot during turns, you automatically veer toward the direction you're spotting. It would be easier to keep in line if you all spotted forward, in the direction you're actually going."

I thought about it. I was so used to dancing with all professionals I hadn't even thought that students would have difficulty with something that wasn't very hard. But she was right—it was more natural to spot in the direction you're traveling. It was just cool to have them face the audience. It wasn't that hard. They could learn it. Probably.

"It doesn't seem hard to learn to spot facing another way," Kendra said, echoing my thoughts.

Arabelle sighed. "It's just a lot of practice. It's very advanced. There's no reason why you can't spot the direction you're turning. It's not even going to be a thing that's noticeable to the average audience member. It still looks very cool, because the spins are so fast."

Kendra harrumphed.

I exhaled. "Let's just…let's just try it Arabelle's way and see how it looks."

"Here, let me demonstrate." Arabelle held her arm toward me, inviting me to lead her into the spins.

"Let me turn the music on so we know how it looks to the beats," I said.

"Good idea. Okay, we start slowly," she said as the music began.

I led her in the turns but with her looking down the line instead of out toward the audience. "One, two, three, and then it speeds up, so, four five six-seven-eight-nine-ten."

"Whoa, that's awesome," Josie said.

"I just wish we could all look like that," Judy added, a bit forlornly.

I couldn't have agreed more with Josie and Judy. Arabelle looked gorgeous doing those spins.

"See, I don't think there's any reason you shouldn't do it this way," Arabelle said. "It's totally do-able, and with much less practice than turning with your faces toward the audience."

I saw what Arabelle meant. The students could do this— spin at the speed of light without getting dizzy and risking falling into the audience—but facing another direction would really set them back and make them have to work so much harder.

"I dunno, Ms. A." Kendra said. "I kind of like working hard."

"Yes, of course you do. You all do," Arabelle said. "But it's not about working hard right here, right now. It's about having a certain history of dance in your bones, about having a lifetime of training and experience, to be able to take something a hard-core choreographer dreams up. It's not that you guys can't ever do that; it's just that it's making it all the harder to get that level of expertise down when we only have a limited amount of time. And it's really not necessary."

"I agree," I cut in.

"You do?" Kendra frowned at me.

"You guys are going to rock it this way—Arabelle's way. I know it. I don't know how long it's going to take to look good the other way. It may well not be in time for Vegas. Let's do it Arabelle's way. And if we have time later, we can do little things to make the routine harder. For right now, let's work on looking damn good together."

"Can you guys do it again?" Paolo asked.

"Of course," I said, holding my arm out for Arabelle. This time, I spun her a few extra times. Just for effect. I knew she could go fast, so we kept up with the music, adding spins to the already fast beat.

"Whoa!" Kendra enthused.

"Okay, that's frickin' gorgeous," Paolo said.

"Okay, that's enough. Stop," Arabelle said. And I detected a slight little laugh. I spun her around a few more times for effect. I could tell she wasn't getting dizzy and there was no tremor in sight.

"Now we're just showing off." She giggled.

She was right. We were. But I wanted to show her off,

even if just to let her know she could do it sans tremor. We demoed one more time.

"Absolutely fucking gorgeous," Kendra screamed again. Applause filled the room. I finally stopped and we looked around. The room was nearly full now of onlookers. "Yes, Mr. J. and Ms. A. are back together again!" Kendra pumped her fist in the air. More cheers. Arabelle rolled her eyes, but I could also see a slight smile. Plain as day.

Toward the end of class, Alessia walked through the door, waving at me and Arabelle to get our attention.

"What's up?" I said.

"I need to see you two after class," she said, looking back and forth between Arabelle and me. The way she said it didn't sound good. Her voice was serious business. Arabelle looked equally confused.

We nervously walked into her office. She motioned for us to sit.

"What's up?" I said again.

She took a breath. "I just found out that Landon has now gotten the current world cabaret pros. They're teaching at his studio, and they're heading his team. They won Blackpool last year, and Nationals, and the World's."

"I know them," Arabelle said flatly. "Duke Gozzoli and Natalia Beloserkovskiy. They're…not nice. At least she isn't. Fierce competitors. The last five competitions, we were neck to neck. I mean, the last time I competed. When I danced an homage to Willem at Blackpool last year, I swear I saw her smile. She was happy we were no longer their nemesis. She was glad he died." Arabelle's eyes were black, her eyelids heavy. "Then, they won. They were thrilled. But they live in Florida. What are they doing here?"

"I don't know," Alessia said.

"But now that you and Drew are officially a no-go, I really need the team. We need to outperform them."

Arabelle and Drew were a no-go? What?

I reached over and held Arabelle's hand, lacing my fingers through hers. She wasn't trembling and she didn't flinch. "They're going to be sorry they ever made you feel that way," I said. "And they are going to lose."

Arabelle closed her eyes and breathed deeply. And I swear I felt her fingers squeeze back.

20

Arabelle

J ett looked so sincere when he told me Duke and Natalia would be sorry for the way they made me feel after Willem died. Not only that, he looked angry on my behalf. Earlier this may have made me mad, wondering why he thought he had the right to be angry for me. But now, I didn't feel that way. I was no longer defensive and possessive about my pain over Willem. Jett cared about me. And it felt really nice.

We walked out of Arabelle's office together.

"You okay?" he said under his breath, opening the door for me.

I nodded. I was. I was anxious, but I also felt determined to win over Duke and Natalia. The thought of them brought back memories of Willem, but it also made me mad and made me want to excel and be the best I could be.

Alessia had, of course, been talking about the team—defeating their team at the team comps. But my mind went to the letter from Blackpool, which I hadn't answered yet. Could Jett be my partner there? Was I ready for that?

I think it was actually Jett's anger at Natalia and Duke that made me realize I was angry, too. And his determination to beat them was contagious. Was I really going to do this, go back into this world again? I was going to have to dive in deep to win, to defeat them. Was I up for it? Was Willem up for me being up for it? He was still around. I felt his presence. He was. I felt my muscles throughout my body. They were at ease. No tremor. I think Willem wanted this. He did—and I did.

"Whoa, your mind is in serious overtime! A penny for those thoughts? Just one of them?" Jett chuckled.

I laughed back, and shrugged. "Just brings back memories. Beautiful and horrible. About who I was."

He nodded and looked at his watch. "You want to get some lunch?"

I was hungry. "Sure."

* * *

WE WENT to a little French place in the mall that I liked. I usually ate at the bar, but the waitress took one look at Jett and led us into a back area that was quiet and secluded and quite cozy. She must have thought we were romantically involved. Jett pulled the table out for me and I scooted into the dimly lit booth side.

"So," he said after we ordered. "I definitely don't want to pressure you or anything, but do you want to talk about these memories? I just saw so much going on behind your eyes after we left Alessia's office. Sometimes it helps to talk— if you want?"

His big brown eyes were so piercing, so soul-searching, and so sexy. A bolt of electricity shot down my spine to my belly. I squirmed, trying to rid myself of the feeling of excitement. I wasn't ready for that yet. I was beginning to think I may be soon. But not yet. I smiled and looked off to the side to try to get that sexy, penetrating gaze out of my head. Suddenly, I had no words.

"Like this. What's this about, Arabelle?" He reached out and took my right hand in his palms, covering it, then caressing it with his fingers. I hadn't realized it but the tremor had returned. Briefly. I hadn't even felt it. I guess I wasn't feeling it all the time; it had become such a part of me, such an extension of me. I'd only felt it when I was trying to do something physical, like dance, or hold a glass of expensive champagne. Damn. But when he released my hand, it was no longer shaking. He'd quashed it.

I took a deep breath, shook my head again and looked off to the side. I hadn't wanted to tell anyone outside of the shrink and Lucia but I was beginning to feel he was okay. More than okay. He was worth trusting. "I really don't know. I honestly don't. I'm trying to get to the bottom of it."

"I believe you," he said, making me realize I sounded defensive. "Well, when did it start? I mean, you haven't always had it, right?"

"Of course not." Now I heard the defensiveness in my voice. I took another breath. Something about him right now, about the way he was looking at me, the way he'd stood up for me in Alessia's office... *Okay, calm down, Arabelle. Let him in.* I opened my mouth and the words just started coming. "It was after Willem passed. Not right after. Months later. I tried dancing showdance with another partner. One of Willem's old friends. It began then. At first I was worried it was medical, but a bunch of tests ruled that out. The doctor told me it was due to anxiety. After I knew it wasn't some horrible neurological condition, I didn't focus on it much. My pain and grief of losing Willem were too raw. I felt nauseas, sick, whenever I tried to dance with this guy. I had to stop. Then, I switched to Latin. I first partnered with Sasha, the Latin star. He was extremely serious, intense. It was too much for me. The tremor came back then. I thought it was just Sasha and his perfectionism. I switched partners. Everything was fine with Drew until I had an accident on the dance floor in Blackpool."

He nodded.

I frowned. "You knew?"

"I saw it," he said.

I was confused. "Wait, you were there? You said you weren't into ballroom?" I knew he'd watched videos of me and Willem, but the ones of me and Drew as well? I was now embarrassed. He'd seen me at my worst.

"No, no. I… " His face took on a rosy glow. He was blushing. "Okay, I admit, I was kind of taken by you when I met you. So when I went to that ballroom store for the DVDs of you dancing showdance, the clerk told me about the Latin comp at the last Blackpool. So I picked up that one too." He paused. "I hope you don't think I'm some kind of crazy stalker. I was just intrigued." He looked off to the side, his face getting redder by the second.

It was actually kind of funny. I had found him to be such a pompous jerk when I first met him. So into himself, flirting it up with all those girls, so bombastic about his own dancing, and flashing his money around. And yet he was interested enough in me to go out and buy all of my DVDs.

"I scared you, didn't I?" he said.

I shook my head. "No, it's…it's sweet, actually. Just surprising."

"Why?"

I laughed. "Because I just didn't think you liked me at all."

He laughed too. "To be honest, my first impression was that you were haughty."

"Haughty?"

"Yeah. No. I mean, my first impression was that you were beautiful and you were obviously a dancer because of the way you held yourself, and your overall sophistication and polish and gracefulness. And beauty. My second impression, when you began talking about your ballet background and showdance, was that you were haughty. I didn't think you thought very highly of my style of dance."

I opened my mouth to talk but he kept going.

"And my third impression of you was that you must have been a great dancer from the way everyone talked about you and from your accomplishments, but that you were now... stifled by your..."

"You noticed my tremor back then?"

"I did." He looked down. "I saw you drinking a glass of champagne and your hand began to tremble. I knew with the style of dance you described that would definitely present a problem."

"And it made you feel sorry for me, made you want to help?" I felt a pit in my stomach. I didn't need anyone's pity—certainly not his. And I didn't need him thinking I was a damsel in distress in need of saving.

"No, not at all. I knew nothing of your past then. I just somehow felt you must have been an excellent dancer and I was intrigued and wanted to see, that's all." He spoke softly now. He kept his head down but looked up at me over his eyelids.

"So, what did all of my dance DVDs make you think then?"

"What did I think?" He laughed. "I'm here, aren't I?"

Now it was my turn to feel my face redden.

"Seriously, Arabelle. I think you're a consummate show dancer." He took my palm between his hands, caressing it gently. "I think you're a fine Latin dancer. But I think showdance is your passion, your soul." He was nearly whispering now.

I nodded. He could see through me. "I broke it off with Drew this morning," I blurted out. I hadn't meant to talk about that yet. It was painful.

He raised his eyebrows. "I wondered what was going on. I mean, I saw you hugging people and there were tears in your eyes, and..." A slight blush crept across his face again. He certainly noticed a lot!

I tried to focus on Jett's interest in me and allow myself to be flattered by it. I was still upset about having to break up with Drew and I didn't want to get teary-eyed anymore. "Yeah. It was hard—so hard. But I finally realized it was for the best. He needs a new partner. He deserves to win. And the big comps are coming up, and he's going to need time to find and get up to speed with another person."

He rubbed my hand between his palms again. It was warming, soothing. "It's always hard to end something. Even if it is for the best."

I nodded and closed my eyes, letting the warmth of his caress comfort my entire body.

"Maybe that's what you needed," he said.

"Needed?"

"To get rid of the tremor?"

Suddenly the warm feeling evaporated. I first had the problem when I tried to do showdance with Willem's friend. It likely wasn't gone. I shook my head. "I don't know if it's that simple."

"Yeah, I knew right after I said it that was a dumb thing to say. I mean, nothing's that simple. But hopefully switching back to the dance you're so passionate about may...help."

I nodded. "Hopefully." But I was worried. If I was going to throw myself into this again, I really needed to keep my jitters at bay.

"I want to make a pact with you." Jett began massaging my hand. It really felt good.

"What's that?"

"I want you to let me know when we're dancing whenever you feel it coming on, whenever you feel nervous or anxious, or ill at ease with something. I want you to be honest. I promise I won't get annoyed. Ever."

I smiled. I wasn't always up front with Drew. I tried to hide it. Jett was asking me to do the exact opposite. But he was right.

"Okay. I'm taking you up on that."

"You'll see how good to my word I am, Arabelle." He shot me that cocky grin again and sent shivers down my back. I tried to ignore my silly hormones.

"One thing, Jett, is that I really want to make the dance beautiful. I want to make it about passion and trust and acceptance and l-l-l-love." *Okay, why was I stuttering?* "I-I-I mean, I know how into big tricks you are."

Now he was the one to squirm. He gave my hand one final squeeze then let go. Our food arrived, and we ate for a while in silence.

"I understand," he said after a few bites. "We will do that. Definitely. But in order to win —I mean the team comp— I've researched it, and we have to have a certain amount of lifts and other stunts—or tricks, whatever you want to call them."

Hmm, he'd actually researched the team comps. This guy really wanted to win. And now I did too.

"But the other teams can do the lifts and tricks too," I said. "Especially Duke and Natalia. They are all about them. What made Willem and I special was that ours were about passion and love. The lifts and tricks were not incidental; they were an elaboration of our passion, the story we told through our dance. I know from reading all the reviews that that's what the judges loved about us. We didn't just have athleticism, we had soul."

He nodded. "I know. We'll have both too. I promise." He put down his fork and shot me another wicked grin that made me squirm once again.

After we finished eating, we decided to return to the studio to practice and choreograph the routine. We didn't have the team meet until tomorrow and it would give us a chance to work things out among ourselves, so we could better direct the students. Neither of us had anything that night. The theater was dark for him, and I had no students.

We began at the beginning and went through until the end of the first lift sequence. I had to admit it felt good to be in his arms. He felt very steady and strong. The overhead lift felt wonderful. It felt beautiful. It was like working with a real pro. But there was something extra wonderful about it, though I couldn't explain it. Our bodies just fit together. We didn't even have to work on all the things we usually did to learn each other's body weight and strengths and flexibility. It's like he knew my body before we even began. *Weird*.

"Okay, so I let you down and turn you, and then you can go into a fish. Do you want me to dive you all the way down to the floor, or should we save that for later?" He was so excited. He looked like a wicked cherub.

"Let's listen to the music so we can see if that jibes."

I could tell he felt a little let down. It probably seemed to him I didn't share his enthusiasm for the lifts. I'd been here before. With Willem. He was a lift-happy guy, and I was always trying to rein him in. For a split second, I saw him. I saw Willem's face in place of Jett's. Shock pierced my center.

"Sure." He ran to the bench to get his iPod. His face, momentarily turned away from mine, gave me a little time to recover. What was happening? Why did I see Willem? Because I now remembered we'd had this same fight before.

Clear as day. I mean, not fight. We never fought. But we did. But it didn't seem like a fight. He was always the one to want to do crazy things. But I trusted him. I trusted him with my life. And he would never ever let me get hurt. Never. If I would have been with him on his motorcycle that day, he'd still be alive, because he always looked out for me.

"Okay, here we go." Jett clicked on the music. "Whoa, you okay?" he said, seeing my face, which must have been ghost white. He clicked the music off.

I nodded. "Perfectly. Let's go on." I shouldn't have let my thoughts veer there. There was no point in thinking like that. Willem was gone. I hadn't thought of anything negative in a very long time. Jett gave me a double take, but my expression made clear not to push it.

"Okay, cool," he said, and the music resumed. "Okay, this is where the long lift ends. So, I'd be bringing you down here, and we'd go into the fish...here."

I had a hard time returning to the present after having seen Willem's face on Jett. I tried not to look into his eyes so as not to see it again. I don't even know what happened during the rest of our practice. I just did what he said in an effort to keep focused on him. I let myself be carried away by the movement, let the dance overtake my brain.

At one point I did feel the tremor. But only slightly. He began leading me into a move Willem and I had done, and no one else. I reminded myself he'd seen the tapes. He was probably stealing without even knowing it. Though it was my choreography anyway, so if I was doing it, I wasn't stealing.

"What? Come on, that looks so good—"

Without realizing it, I'd stopped. Jitters had overtaken my body. Jett looked right at my hand. "Okay." He nodded, not sounding angry at all. But his tone was loaded with disappointment.

He was right to be disappointed. It was a beautiful lift. It was perfect for the dance. I imagined Belinda doing the same lift with him, and doing it perfectly. Should she take over? At this point, she was more able than I was. It would be the same as me giving him over to a better partner, like I had with Drew.

No, I belonged in this dance. I was going to do this.

"It's okay," I said. "Let's try it again." Then I got another idea. "Instead of me just running toward you and you taking me into the overhead lift right from there, why don't you first lay me over your back. I'll lift my leg and arch my back over yours. You can then swing me down, I'll do a couple turns in front of you, and then we can go into the lift. We'll build momentum from the spins."

His eyes widened, and a grin slowly began to encompass his face. Yes, I'd just suggested something more complicated, and thus flashier. And, yet, it wasn't the same exact lift I'd done with Willem. It was different. And it actually worked better for this routine. It had fluidity. And it had more air, so it would look more romantic—not that I was thinking of such a thing with him.

"That sounds gorgeous, Belle," he said. "Are you sure? We have to have a stable—I meant Arabelle. Arabelle! Sorry."

I rolled my eyes. I hadn't even noticed, honestly. A lot of people called me Belle now. I was just being difficult earlier. "It's okay for you to call me Belle," I said with a smile.

His dimpled grin returned. "Awesome." But then his gaze went to my wrist. I wasn't shaking now. I'd calmed down. He noticed and nodded.

We tried the lift as I suggested and it felt as gorgeous as it sounded.

"Of course we'll simplify things for the students," Jett said.

Holy crap. I'd totally forgotten about them. I was mentally concentrating on us, choreographing for Blackpool, which I hadn't mentioned to him yet. I couldn't believe my subconscious was so active.

"Yes, of course." I nodded. I couldn't bring up Blackpool right now. I wasn't ready to. If we didn't compete, we'd still use all this in our team routine, simplifying it down.

"You look confused," Jett said.

I shook my head. "I'm fine."

We ended up working late into the night, choreographing the whole way through. It was amazing. It just flowed out of us. And everything looked and felt so perfect, so natural, and so original. Every time something got too close to something Willem and I had done, I altered it slightly so that it wouldn't feel the same. So that it wouldn't be like anyone was replacing anyone else. Unbelievably, the new lifts looked even better and fit us better—our bodies and the music and overall dance story.

"You are a pretty awesome choreographer, Belle," he said.

I giggled. I was. Who would have known I had that talent? Willem and our coach had always done our choreography before.

Amazingly, I didn't feel the tremor all night. Not once.

We filmed ourselves with our phones and went through the whole thing one last time. When I looked at the clock, I couldn't believe it. It was two in the morning.

"Holy crap!"

"I know." He chuckled. "We kind of got lost in...ourselves a little there." I looked at his face. That wicked smile was back—which brought all the blood in my body directly to my face. I felt a little dizzy. But not in a bad way. I fanned myself.

"Okay, um, I guess I'll see you tomorrow..."

"Where do you live? In Hollywood, didn't you tell me?"

"Yeah, it's only a couple short blocks. It's an easy walk from here."

"You think I'm going to let you walk home alone at this hour?"

"Uh, yeah, well…" It would be a little secluded on my street at this time of night. And my neighborhood was safe-ish… but okay, no place in L.A. was entirely risk free.

"Well, I can take an Uber."

"At this time of night there's going to be a crazy surcharge. Why don't I just drive you? It would be so much easier."

Why didn't I want his help? He was totally right.

"Come on," he said, picking up my bag.

"Uh…"

"Don't fight with me, Belle. I have an early morning lesson, and the later you make me, the more you're depriving me of sleep."

Putting me on the defensive now? This guy… But when he turned around and shot me that oh-so-hot loopy grin, I knew he was kidding. He turned back around, but that smile stayed with me, and I felt a bolt of lightning shoot straight up my belly. I shook it off and followed him.

He had a hot little car, of course. A red convertible BMW. Everything about this guy was expensive.

"Okay, this is my building," I said.

"Whoa, look at that—there's actually a spot right in front."

"Oh no, I can make it from here." He was actually parking?

"Nonsense. I'm here. Of course I'll walk you to your door."

"Suit yourself," I said, snappishly. I wasn't that much of a weakling. Though I had to admit it would feel good to have him walk me up to my door. I once encountered a drunk guy sleeping on my stairway. It wasn't a big deal at all; I just stepped around him. But still, you never know.

But when we got to my apartment, something crazy

happened. I didn't want to let him go. I turned to him and leaned against my door. His eyes were so deep brown, you could get lost in them. He had a dreamy look on his face. His smile now was serene, not at all cocky. For a moment, I thought I was going to swoon. For a split second, I just wanted to let him inside, to let him hold me. I even wondered what it would be like to sleep with him. But then I caught myself. *What was I thinking?*

"It's okay, Arabelle," he whispered, as if he read every single thought in my head. And then I felt his fingers caressing my cheek. He traced my skin from the top of my cheekbone to the corner of my mouth. I closed my eyes, letting him. I felt his lips touch the place where his fingers had started, the top of my cheekbone, near my ear. One soft kiss. I wanted more but I didn't. I couldn't. Not now. I opened my eyes.

"You get a good night's sleep. We've got a lot of work tomorrow," he said, his hand gently receding.

I nodded, fumbled with my keys, and unlocked my door. Once inside, all I could think was, what did that kiss mean? A kiss to the cheek. A friendly kiss? Yes, I hoped. No, I hoped it meant more. I didn't know what I hoped.

21

Jett

I was so tired for my group class the next day. All I could think about was Belle, about how much more I wanted to do to her than that one simple kiss to the cheek. What did she think of it? She seemed receptive, but hesitant. Was it still too early? I know it's been almost two years since Willem died. I've never had anyone close to me die before, knock on wood. So, I had no idea how hard that could possibly be. Mandi had told me Lucia thought it was more than time Belle start to live again. So, at least her close friends thought it wasn't too early.

When I walked into the practice room, something was very off. Belle was practicing her part solo. But she wasn't doing the moves full-out. She looked shaky. Another flare-up?

I met Drew's eyes across the room. He was practicing with another woman, maybe a new partner? He seemed to be making a point of getting my attention. He nodded his chin in the direction of another couple, whom I'd never seen before. They were very smooth, and pretty good. The guy whizzed the girl all around him. She could turn. Very flashy. They ended a series of high-speed turns with him hoisting her up high above his head and turning with frigging lightning speed. That was not any kind of ballroom I knew. That was showdance. Who were these people?

I looked back at Drew. Though I wasn't a natural lip reader I could very clearly read his. "Your competitors," he mouthed. I turned my attention to Belle. She concentrated on herself in the mirror, practicing simple rumba walks. She seemed to be paying them no mind; at least, that's how she wanted it to appear.

The guy and girl glanced at me, whispered to each other, and then gave me a glare. She had long, cinnamon-colored hair and bright green eyes that felt like they were burning a hole through me. He was a stocky dark-haired guy with a lot of muscle in his arms and legs. His nasty look echoed hers. *What the hell?* How did they even know who I was? What the hell were they even doing here? Initially I just shrugged, pretending not to care. But then I remembered Belle saying how competitive they'd been, how they seemed happy when Willem died. Bastards. Just as I was about to go over and ask them what their deal was, Belle walked toward me.

"Not now," she whispered when she got close enough. "I don't want to go over our routine and show them what we have. Let's just practice basics."

As much as I wanted to show these a-holes what we were about, she was right. We didn't want to be showing our competition what we had.

"What are they even doing here?" I asked.

"Trying to intimidate us," Arabelle said.

"But Alessia let them in?"

"Alessia probably doesn't know. She doesn't keep track of everyone who rents out lesson space."

"Yeah, but shouldn't we tell her?"

Arabelle nodded. "I'll mention it later. I wasn't going to create a scene now by marching down to her office and letting them know they're getting to me. I'm just pretending they're not here."

I nodded. "Okay." I didn't like it but I understood. I looked around. Several rolls of the eyes and shakes of the head made me realize I wasn't alone in being pissed. Kendra even shook her fist at them.

Arabelle took my hand. Her skin was silky smooth. "Come on. I don't want to get worked up. Let's just practice." I took in her beautiful scent, her quiet energy. I stood behind her, in shadow position, and did a rumba basic, our bodies touching lightly. I placed my hand on her abdomen. It was warm. I reached out with the other arm, and shadowed hers, reaching her hand, where I laced my fingers with hers. She closed her eyes and breathed heavily. I caressed her center and breathed in her sugary scent. Our bodies moved in unison, and, though it was just a basic move, I don't know if I'd ever felt anything so beautiful.

Suddenly the door slammed shut, knocking me out of my reverie. I looked around. The competition had left, apparently pissed about something. The room was suddenly quiet, everyone looked around wide-eyed.

"What the flaming fuck?" Kendra yelled. Good ol' Kendra.

Alessia opened the door. "I'm sorry. Debbie was taking a break and I didn't have anyone to replace her, so they just walked right in."

"Thank God!" Kendra sighed dramatically. "I thought they were teaching here now."

"I can't imagine anyone here would take lessons with them." Alessia laughed. But her smile soon receded. "I guess we can't let our guard down anymore." She looked weary.

She was worried. They were good, I had to admit. But we were better.

For team practice, I took out my iPhone and we showed everyone the routine we'd recorded last night.

"Oh man, it's gorgeous—but we have so much to learn," Josie said with a sigh.

Judy nodded.

"Nonsense. We'll master it all in no time," Kendra shouted. The more I got to know her, the more grateful I was for this girl. We started teaching everyone the new stuff, from where we left off. I knew it would be a lot, but I knew the team was up for it. We ended up getting almost all the way through, which meant we were ahead of target. It would give us plenty of time for going over things and polishing them. At the end of class, I gave everyone a thumb drive of the routine and told them to watch it at least three times every night before going to bed.

"It's only three minutes long, so it's not like reading a novel. It should be easy to do. This way it will be in your brain memory, so we can more easily convert it to muscle memory."

"Totes do-able, sir," Kendra said. That girl would always crack me up.

Afterward, Belle and I practiced. This time we went over the actual routine. When we started I could tell she was still a bit shaken, but not anywhere near as badly as before the team practice. We went through the routine once, slowly. There were several places I wanted to put in more oomph, but I wasn't going to force it right now. Seeing those a-holes again was a lot for her. She was trying to control her trembling. I wasn't about to sabotage anything now. So I forced myself to hold back, to not overdo it. It actually wasn't hard to do at all. It was nice to feel her body, to touch her soft skin as I held her in a close hold, to focus on the romance of the choreography. And it was *very* romantic. As we went through the moves, I felt her energy return to me, maybe even her desire. Maybe. Desire was part of the storyline of the dance, after all. *But was it just in the dance?*

She totally caught me off guard when, before we began the second go-through; she suggested we amp it up. Well, kind of. She looked me in the eye, her pupils large and wanting, the blue of her irises fierce, and with a squeeze of my hand, said, "Let's do it to the max."

And we did exactly that. When we started I felt for her tremor. Totally absent. So I amped up the music, did everything full-out. No holds barred. I lifted her high, dropped her low, spun her fast. Of course I wasn't reckless. I'd never ever allow her to get hurt. I trusted myself. And from our rock solid hold on each other, I knew she trusted me too. Everything was so perfect. She flew on those lifts, whizzed on those spins. We were so on, so together. The students who'd stayed around to watch, along with the other teachers in the room, broke into full out applause when we finished. There were standing ovations with loud cheers all around. As usual, it was hard for me not to suck up all the applause. That's just me. But Arabelle did too. The genuine full-out smile on her face was unforgettable. And, did I say she never once flinched? No tremor whatsoever.

Arabelle

I nailed it. I knew I could. Actually, I hadn't. I hadn't known until I saw Duke and Natalia in the studio. I knew what they were doing. I knew Alessia didn't let them in. She would never. But I didn't dare let on to them that they were getting to me. I was so above their simpleton bullshit. Sorry.

I'll just never forget the look in her eyes when she saw me dancing Latin at Blackpool last year, when she won the showdance crown. There was more to our story than onlookers knew. Natalia had been on the ballroom circuit for many years. And she'd lusted after Willem from the first time she met him. She wanted him as both a partner and lover. But he chose me over her. So when she won, those green eyes that had been the eyes of envy were now the eyes of gloating, of angry triumph. If she couldn't have Willem, she was happy I didn't either.

She'd made a faux sad face at me after I performed my homage to Willem at Blackpool. But immediately after that, she'd smirked. She was happy he was dead—both because he'd rejected her, and because we'd left the championship wide open for her and Duke. It almost made me wonder if she had something to do with Willem's accident. I knew she didn't. But I'd never forgive her for gloating over my pain, my grief.

When I first saw her, of course I felt my stomach drop. Connecting with those horrible green eyes brought back the last Blackpool, then the other Blackpools before. But as soon as Jett strode in, it all went away. I felt warmth. I felt power—even though he had no idea who they were. I now knew what I had to do. I had to write back to the Blackpool organizers and tell them I had a new partner. Jett and I would compete in showdance together.

The routine felt so good, first when we took it gently and slowly, then when we ramped it up and did it full-out. We were both on the same page when we decided which parts to keep soft and lyrical and romantic, and when to unleash our athletic power.

We practiced many times, and I hadn't felt the tremor once. Not once. Nothing felt so good. Well, not since I'd danced with Willem.

"Jett?" We'd finished going through several times, with no flubs, no tremor. We were going to be awesome together at Blackpool. I knew it. But did he have time to train with his job and all? I took a big breath.

He looked at me, eyebrows raised, his smile slowly growing cocky. Did he know what I was going to ask?

"What?" I said.

"What do you mean what?" He grinned. "You called out my name."

Another breath. This was ridiculous. Out with it. "I received a letter from the Blackpool organizers asking me if I wanted to compete in showdance with a new partner."

His grin grew dimpled and boyish, and charm oozed all over his face. I guess I had my answer. "Uh-huh?" he said, motioning for me to go on.

"Jett, do you want to compete with me?"

"You're asking me to be your Blackpool partner?"

I closed my eyes. Was that what I was doing? Yes, yes, it was.

I opened them again.

"Arabelle, I would be honored to be the partner of the reigning queen of Blackpool."

Okay, that was a bit much. I rolled my eyes. "That would be Natalia, actually."

"No, no, it really isn't. We both know she only won last year because there was no you. You let her win."

I giggled self-consciously. "Jett, it's hard work to train. Do you have time with your schedule?"

"You asking me if I can work hard?" He cocked one eyebrow up. *So sexy.* He peered deep into my eyes, nearly penetrating my soul. For a moment I thought he might kiss me, on the lips. That, I wasn't ready for. Or maybe I was? Yes, I think I was.

"Of course, I know you can." I laughed, deflecting his desires—my desires—for the moment anyway.

Jett looked at the clock. "Whoa." He chuckled.

My eyes followed his. Again, it was pretty late.

"At least you don't have any classes till tomorrow afternoon, right? You can sleep in," he said as we gathered our things and walked toward the door.

I nodded. "Fortunately. You can too, right? You don't have private lessons till evening."

He shook his head. "Performance tomorrow is a matinee. So the only time to warm up and rehearse is before lunch."

"Oh no, but you're going to be way too tired."

He shook his head again. "I'll be fine. I'm a trooper. I can take it. I'm just so glad we got so much done."

Suddenly I was angry at myself. He needed his sleep far more than I did. This was his job, and it was a dangerous one.

"Jett, I'm sorry. We've spent a lot of time on choreographing for the team. And you have a serious job…"

He reached for my hand. "What do you mean? This is a job too."

"I know but not your main job. This is just…a student team comp." Suddenly I felt like what we were striving for was very small.

But Jett shook his head. "There's nothing 'just' about it. We have to win for Alessia. And it's not like Blackpool is unimportant in the least. If we use a similar routine, then we worked on that as well."

True. But he wasn't being paid to compete at Blackpool. I mean, there would hopefully be championship money eventually, but I suddenly felt guilty about taking him away from his job.

"We're going to do this, Belle. We're going to beat the assholes who glorified in your misery. We're going to win for Alessia, and we're going to win for us."

He drove me home again, and then walked me to my doorway. When we got there I suddenly felt sick. But not in the way I'd often felt sick since Willem passed. My nerves went all tingly—but not in a bad way. I felt sick with excitement. Yes, we would win for Alessia. I hadn't yet completely processed that I was competing again at Blackpool. And with this man.

"Are you okay?" he asked.

I nodded. Air caught in my throat and I momentarily couldn't speak. I opened my door wide and nodded toward it. "You…you want to come in?" I managed.

He took a breath. "Sure," he said, eyebrows raised, a slight, bemused smile beginning to cross his lips.

He walked in and looked around. I read his eyes. He wasn't sure what to do, why he was here. I wasn't sure why he was here either.

"Um, something to drink?" I asked.

"Ah, sure. What do you have?"

I searched the fridge. Not much. Embarrassingly, I hadn't entertained at all in the past two years. I had a half bottle of cheap Chardonnay, a pitcher of iced tea, about a quarter of a carton of almond milk, and of course, water. I wished I had some beer on hand. Or fancy alcohol. I remembered he'd had a fancy drink in hand at the after-performance party in Vegas, and that he'd ordered the most expensive champagne at the restaurant. Then I became embarrassed, remembering how used to luxury he was. My tiny studio had practically no furniture since I'd downsized. My place was pretty much the antithesis of luxury.

"I'm actually not very thirsty," he said after I went through the choices. Maybe my embarrassment showed on my face all too clearly.

"Water?" I shrugged.

"Yeah, that's good."

I went to grab a glass then realized the hot pink cups with "Crazy Cat Lady" on them were not quite suitable. Since moving, I had mostly bought only things for myself to use. I reached in the back for a clear glass.

I sat next to him on the loveseat. No, I didn't even have a real sofa. As I plopped down I realized it was pretty much covered in white cat hair. His wicked grin indicated he didn't seem to mind. I took a breath, trying not to think about the liquid heat rising in my belly from that devilish smile. I tried not to think about our thighs touching. I tried to think about where Arabesque might be. She was likely hiding in the closet, like she usually did the few times we'd had company over.

And then it happened. The heat of his body just melted into me. And I let it.

He set his cup down on the stand next to the loveseat, and cupped my face with his hands. And I let him. I closed my eyes and felt myself moving my face toward his, lifting my chin, soaking up his caress. And then his lips were on mine, and my mouth was opening and his tongue met mine. I melted into that too, forgetting everything else. And then he was pulling me to him and I was wrapping my leg around his body, my knee rubbing the small of his back. He took his mouth off mine and trailed kisses across my cheek, my chin, down my neck, around my shoulder, breathing heavily at the back of my ear, a cool breeze on wet hot skin, making me shiver.

"Belle, beautiful, beautiful Belle," he whispered.

I opened my eyes, looked into his twinkling, long-lashed brown eyes, half open—the very definition of dreamy bedroom eyes. And I was a goner from there. I tore off his jacket and lifted his t-shirt while he struggled to get his arms out of the jacket's sleeves. He laughed as I basically stripped him naked.

"Hold on there, cowgirl." He laughed.

But no. I couldn't hold on. Once the shirt was off and I was faced with his muscled chest, his eight-pack abdomen, his gorgeously intricate abstract tattoo covering his mid-right side and his chiseled pecs, I felt my mouth literally watering. It had been way too long. I ran my hands up and down his front side, his skin so silky smooth. He reached out to me, but before he could touch me, I was at his pants, unbuttoning him. I couldn't help myself. I really couldn't. I had to have all of him.

"Okay then," he said as he lifted himself off the couch to

let me push the jeans all the way down. All. The. Way. *Oh wow.* He was spectacular; the perfect specimen. Seriously. I couldn't help but stare as he kicked his boots off along with the pants, now down at his ankles. He was enormous. And he was only half erect. I swallowed. I'd never had anyone that big. Well, I'd only ever had one other man, and well... But Willem didn't take over my thoughts now. The thought of Willem didn't even faze me. This was a completely new experience with a new man. A man I'd grown so close to despite my wholehearted attempts not to. I wasn't hurting Willem. I wasn't hurting his memory. I would always have him, and he would always have me. This was something—someone—completely different.

"Um, your turn?" Jett said, holding a hand out to me. I wondered if he could read my thoughts. My thoughts at that point were, *I want you, I want you, I want you.* I rose and backed up toward the curtained bed in the corner of the room. He followed me, growing more erect by the second, leading me to back up more and more quickly. I walked backward through the pink silky curtain, all the way to the bed, which I nearly tripped over because I was going so fast. That was okay. This was right where I wanted to be. I fell backward, onto the bed.

Jett climbed on top of me, wrapping his arms around me, kissing me deeply—very deeply. I wrapped my legs around his waist, feeling his growing erection poke at my panties. My panties. *Why was I still dressed?*

He lifted himself off a couple inches and began trailing kisses down my neck, down my shoulder. He pulled the spaghetti strap of my dress down, lower and lower, kissing every new millimeter of exposed skin. I arched back and closed my eyes, taking in all the sensations. I was small enough not to have to wear a bra all the time and when I'd changed out of my dance clothes and put on the sundress, I didn't bother putting one on. When the dress went down low enough, it was only a second that I felt my nipple exposed to air before he placed his lips around it, licking and tonguing and sucking gently. Then the other strap slipped down, and soon I felt the dress being pulled down over my waist. He was really taking his time to undress me, despite the fact his erection was growing by the nanosecond. I wanted him in me. I pushed my dress down all the way, along with my underwear, then kicked both off. He moved his head down more, trailing kisses down farther and farther. I rolled my fingers in his gloriously thick, soft hair and arched my back more, still closing my eyes as I felt his tongue on my pubic bone, beginning to tickle the front of my clit.

"Jett, I want all of you," I said, trying to pull his body up. I felt the dress and underwear fall off my toes to the floor.

"Mmmmmm," he moaned as I felt his body move back over me. "Delicious. And so, so, so beautiful." I wrapped my legs around his back. He continued to trail kisses, even as I pulled him closer.

"Belle?" he whispered.

"Mmmm hmmm?"

"Do you...you know, have anything?"

I opened my eyes and looked at him. He shrugged, his loopy smile returning.

Oh crap. Condoms! No, of course I didn't. I hadn't even thought about having such a thing since I wasn't sexually active.

I shook my head. "Do you?"

His loopy smile intensified. He nodded. "Just have to get them."

I thought about what that meant. He was carrying condoms around with him.

"Sorry, old, old, *old* habit," he whispered, his thoughts where mine were.

The emphasis on "old" made me giggle. "Go ahead," I said.

He was quick about it, returning to me in with lightning speed. He began the trail of kisses again. I pulled him over me, and soon he was inside of me. He was so gentle, which I appreciated. But I knew why. And I wanted him to be normal —I could take it. I grabbed his ass and pushed him further inside me, stretching my legs all the way into a split. I pulled his face to mine, found his lips and opened my mouth wide. He got the hint and as his tongue met mine, he thrust harder, moving more aggressively.

"Mm-hmmm," I moaned, lifting my leg up toward the ceiling now as I felt his heart beating faster and faster. Or was that my own? I remembered this—feeling two hearts beating so fast, I couldn't tell where his ended and mine began. Perhaps they were the same in that moment. I pulled more on his ass cheeks and he pumped harder and harder, and I arched back farther and farther, until the explosion erupted through my body, and we both collapsed, drenched with sweat and exhausted.

He rolled off me but remained on his side, next to me. He put one arm around me and the other on my stomach, while he kissed my wet forehead.

He opened his mouth and I felt he was going to say something but he stopped. I knew what he was going to do. He was going to ask if I was okay. He'd decided against it, wisely. Because it couldn't have been more obvious that I *so* was.

I was also tired, though. It had been a long day and we'd worked hard. I found myself dozing off to sleep, but in his arms. Before I realized what I was doing I turned my back to him so we could spoon. This is how Willem and I always ended up. But before I could turn back around—Jett must have instinctively known what I wanted—he wrapped his body around me from behind, both arms caressing my belly, his lips on my neck, right behind my ear. I felt his breath get deeper and deeper as if he was falling asleep. Willem didn't spoon quite as close. He didn't wrap his arms around my stomach, but would fall asleep with his hand on my ass, his head above mine.

I laughed to myself at the memory and my initial surprise that Jett was different. Of course he was different.

"Mmm, so perfect," Jett whispered, his voice so light it sounded almost like he hadn't meant for me to hear.

"What is?" I asked.

"Hmmm?" He sounded half asleep.

"Perfect, you said. Yes, for me too," I whispered.

"Oh, I meant this position," he clarified, waking a bit. "Ending in this embrace. I've never been a real cuddler before, but it's so natural." He kissed me on the ear lobe and rested his head over my shoulder, his breaths getting longer and longer, until I could feel his muscles relax and him fall asleep. He remained in the same position after he fell asleep. It *was* natural. I stayed awake a while longer than he did. My mind was alert, even though my body was tired. It was like I was trying to process something that didn't need processing. Jett was amazing, incredible, wonderful, perfect. I still missed Willem, for sure. I always would. But for the first time, I realized that feeling didn't have to rule every aspect of my life. Its existence was its own special part of me, and always would be. And now I had another part of me that had been awakened.

23

Jett

I pretended to fall asleep. But honestly, I couldn't. I'd been waiting for this for so long. And it was kind of unbelievable that it had actually happened, and so fast. Maybe it needed to be so that we'd go through with it—that she'd go through with it, I mean. I wasn't sure what she was thinking. I tried to go slowly. I didn't want to of course; I wanted to rip off her clothes and take her. I made myself go slowly because I knew it would be hard for her. But then she didn't seem to want it that way. Her head was in the exact same place as mine.

I had to keep spooning her, our bodies fitting perfectly together, one in the other. I had to keep her that close to reassure myself that it had really happened, and that it was okay with her. I rested my chin on her shoulder and wrapped my hands more tightly around her tiny, soft, sweet waist, and she cooed.

I did finally get to sleep. I knew this when her white long-haired cat jumped on the bed and scared the living crap out of me. At first I didn't know where I was. But, believe it or not, I was still wrapped around Arabelle. I'd never ever been the spooning type before. Ever. But with her, as I told her, it felt natural.

"Mmmm," Arabelle moaned. I felt her eyes flutter open, and her precious lungs fill with air. I felt her frown and then immediately turn her head toward me, realizing I was still there, remembering the night before. Or rather, the early morning before.

"Oh, oh wow. Arabesque usually wakes me and, I guess nothing's changed about that," she mumbled, followed by a giggle. But she didn't move. And neither did I. Remaining in our spooning position, I kissed the back of her lovely head. She still smelled of strawberry shampoo.

We stayed like that for a while, until Arabelle finally moved my hand. "Hey, what time did you say you had to be at the theater?" she whispered.

Mmm, back to reality. "Eleven," I murmured.

"Jett, you need to get going soon."

I knew as much. The sun was coming in strongly through the white curtained window, so I knew it was mid-morning. A sandpapery lick to the back of my neck made me remember I had to get home to let Ranger out. I hadn't been a bad dog dad until these last couple of nights that I'd spent out late working with Arabelle. This one was the worst, since I hadn't even come home. Poor Ranger. At least he had the grassy disposable indoor dog potty.

Before un-spooning ourselves, I gave her one last, long kiss on the back of her head, then trailed a few kisses to her neck and then cheek for good measure. I didn't really want my mouth to meet hers with my morning breath, although I probably had only been asleep for a couple hours.

"I think your kitty would like some food." I laughed, as I managed to pry myself away from her beautiful body.

"Mmm, I know. Sorry, Bess," she moaned, stretching, just like a sleek, slinky little cat herself.

I washed my face in the bathroom and used a little of her toothpaste to brush my teeth, enough so that I could kiss her on the way out. I couldn't leave without doing that.

"Sorry we have to rush. I wish I could feed you breakfast." She wrapped her arms around my back, her gorgeous blue eyes peering up into mine.

"Me too. But we will have tonight." I held her more closely, kissing her deeply. I thought briefly of calling in late to practice. We had the routine down pat, after all. But something in me told me I couldn't be any more irresponsible than I already had been. I really needed to get home to Ranger anyway.

* * *

IT WAS a good thing I showed up to practice, because Belinda was sick. Pam would be her stand-in. I hadn't worked with Pam before. She was smaller than Belinda, and much shorter than me. Our bodies didn't work together as perfectly as Belinda and me. Things didn't feel as right. When I caught her in mid-air, I nearly missed because her arms were shorter than I was used to. It didn't seem like she noticed, because she didn't show it. I didn't either. I never showed weakness. But it was there, and I knew it.

I was tired. I only got a few hours of sleep and as the practice wore on, it became more noticeable. My head was also wound up in Arabelle, in her soft touch, her beautiful eyes. I wondered how she was feeling. I was the first person she'd slept with since Willem—that much I knew since she looked at me like she'd never heard of a condom before. There had been no tremor whatsoever all last night. Hopefully, now that she was back to showdance and was dancing in my safe arms, that would be a thing of the past.

We finished and I went home for lunch. I thought of stopping by Infectious Rhythm to see Arabelle, but I decided against it. She didn't need me bothering her, and I owed it to Ranger to spend more time with him. *Or else get him a proper walker.* I'd see Arabelle tonight for a rehearsal after my performance.

I walked up Hollywood Boulevard to a burger joint, and ordered a veggie burger made of black beans, a large order of sweet potato fries, and a bottomless Coke. It wasn't the healthiest dinner in the world, but I needed the caffeine, carbs, and sugar to get myself together for the performance tonight.

I drove back to the theater and used the pre-performance time to do some in-place cardio—jumping jacks, running on the treadmill, and stretching at the barre in my changing room. Performance time was called and I put on my costume, feeling much, much better. Almost like my regular self—almost.

But almost, it turned out, wasn't good enough. I remember waiting in the wings in the rafters, the lights off, waiting for my cue to swing out. I remember hearing the cue —the Tarzan call. I swung out, did a back and forth across the stage once, then twice, then the third time I lifted myself up and stood on the bar, holding the sides. The fourth time I lifted my leg in arabesque while doing my macho push-ups on the top bar. I remember the crowd going wild, as they always did. Ladies will always go nuts over pecs.

And then, I saw Pam getting ready for her turn across the stage. It was my last swing. I was supposed to balance on one foot, holding my arms out for balance. It would be a crazy hard trick for a newbie. But it was one, by this point, I could do in my sleep. I lifted my arms, lifted one leg, and sailed half way across the stage gripping the bar with my toes. I remember seeing Pam's face, but thinking of Arabelle, wishing it was her up here with me. I was thinking of flying toward her, reaching out to her, reaching her, and lifting her up all the way until I had her small, delicate little foot in my hand, and propelling her high above my head, standing. It would be the most beautiful lift in the world. Hard as hell, but too beautiful and glorious to be hard-looking. But then I realized that was our competition dance we were rehearsing, and the part I'd wanted her to do. The part that she hadn't yet agreed to do, because of the aforesaid difficulty. If only she'd trust me—just trust me—and let me do it. Those were my last thoughts before I felt the bar below me give, and I flew through the air with no support.

Next thing I knew, I was being lifted onto a stretcher by two men, who were telling everyone, "make way, make way." I was in and out of consciousness.

"Sir, don't move. You've fallen. We're taking you to the hospital," one of them said when he saw my eyes open. At least, I think that's what he said. Then I fell asleep again and didn't wake up until a while later.

2 4

Arabelle

I was in the middle of my private lesson with the dreaded Jones. I looked at the clock, willing the lesson to be over soon. It would be about an hour and a half until Jett showed up. I was trying to teach Jones how to turn me without nearly breaking my wrist. He held on so tightly, as if I might get away from him. My frustration was starting to make my wrist tremble.

"You need to give me the space to turn," I said, stopping him mid-step. I didn't need the tremor back.

"I don't mind if you bump into me, honey!" He laughed.

I shook my head. "That's not what I mean." This guy was insufferable.

Suddenly, Alessia flew through the door and walked quickly toward me. Not like her at all to interrupt a private lesson. She looked right at me, her pupils big and intense. Then the tremble came back big time, snaking its way from my wrist up to my shoulder. I knew what she had to say wasn't good.

"I'm so sorry, I need to interrupt this lesson," she said looking at Jones. "We've had an accident—"

"Oh no, what's wrong with Jett?" I asked.

She looked confused. "How did you—"

"What is it?" I asked again, my whole arm shaking so badly I had to grab and steady it with the other.

* * *

I OPENED the door of the Hollywood Hospital emergency room, Kendra right at my back. I'd run into her on my way out of the studio, apparently with an obviously distressed look covering my face. She took one look at me and insisted on driving me. Belinda had called Alessia since she thought Jett may have lessons tonight that needed canceled. She'd been out sick. I was supposed to find his replacement part-ner, named Pam.

"Pam?" Kendra called out. Yelled out, was more like it. I was thankful she was at my side. I'm not sure I could have handled this alone. The memory of Willem's sister calling me, telling me there'd been an accident, of arriving at the hospital and seeing her distraught face and knowing some-thing horrible had happened, all flooded my mind. I was glad I had Kendra to talk for me.

A young woman with long, ruby-red hair walked quickly toward us.

"Arabelle?" she said, looking at Kendra, then at me.

"Yes," I said. "What happened?" I felt my voice crack. Kendra squeezed my hand.

"He has a broken foot," she said.

I breathed, maybe for the first time since we got in Kendra's car. "A broken...foot?"

It didn't sound so horrible, but the look on her face indicated otherwise. "And a concussion. The doctor is going to talk to you about it all."

I breathed in as much air as I could. "What happened?" I said, exhaling.

"He was flying across stage on the trapeze in our opening routine. I'm not sure what happened, but he was standing, doing the daredevil trick where he's on one leg and no hands, and his eyes got glassy. And…" She took a breath.

"What?" I nearly screamed.

"He fell. Fortunately, he was still on the part of the floor that was covered with the double mat trampoline or it could have been much worse." She reached out to me. I then realized my tremor was back in full force. My hand shook all the way from my pinkie finger to my ear lobe. "He came down on the foot pretty bad. Twisted his ankle and broke a bone. And even though he didn't hit his head on anything hard, he got concussed—probably from the height of the fall, the doctor said. He was out for a while."

"A while?" I could hardly think. Now I felt my head shaking back and forth as well, as if the tremor had climbed all the way to the top of my body.

"A few minutes. The paramedics arrived and he came to then. He was in and out of consciousness on his way to the hospital. But he's conscious now. He's going to be okay, Arabelle." She squeezed my shaking hand.

But I couldn't get her words "could have been much worse" out of my mind.

"When can I see him?"

She looked around. "I don't see the doctor, but I will definitely let you know when he comes back out."

"Come on, honey. Let's sit down," Kendra said, walking me to one of the few empty chairs. I didn't hear anything else she said, though I knew she kept talking. I could only hear the words, "Blunt force trauma…impact…pronounced deceased on arrival..." My eyes stung, my stomach ached, and my head began to throb. Then I felt a liquid ball rising in the pit of my stomach. It was making its way up to my esophagus. I pulled free of Kendra, held a hand up to her as if asking her to excuse me, and ran to the bathroom. I just made it to a stall when I fell to the floor and let everything come up. I felt faint. I put my hands on the toilet seat for support. I breathed deeply, and then retched again—several more times. I didn't know I even had all of that in me.

"Hey, hon, are you okay? Arabelle?" It was Kendra. "You've been in here for a while. That you?" She knocked on my stall.

I nodded, stupidly. Of course she couldn't see me, my face anyway.

"Hon, let me in."

I managed to pull myself up, turn around, and unlatch the door.

"Oh, wow," she said upon seeing my face. She waved her hand about in front of her. I realized I hadn't flushed the toilet. I turned around and kicked the flusher, wobbling on one foot.

"Okay, take it easy," Kendra said, catching my fall. She walked me to the mirror and turned the cold water on. I splashed my face. My skin felt like I was burning up with fever.

"He's going to be all right. You know that, right? Jett is going to be all right." Her words made it clear she knew what was going through my mind.

I nodded. But I couldn't go through this again. I just couldn't. Jett was the type who needed to be free to do dare-devil stunts. I couldn't hamper him. His was a soul that needed to soar. I couldn't stand in his way. I just couldn't. But I also couldn't deal with accidents that could so easily result in tragedies. Pam had made it clear this could have easily been much, much worse. Jett could have ended up like Willem.

Kendra and I walked back out to the lobby.

"Here she is," I heard Pam call out. She was standing with a man with long, dark hair, who seemed way too young to be a doctor.

"You can go in and see him as soon as the other person is finished. We only allow one visitor in the room at a time." When his eyes caught mine, he looked down, seemingly embarrassed for me. I probably had vomit on my lip or something. I'm sure I looked the classic wreck.

"Wait," I said as he began to walk off. "Other person?"

"Yes, his sister, I think."

Sister? I didn't even know Jett had a sister. I guess I didn't know that much about him.

25

Jett

I had a bad headache and was queasy from the pain meds, but when the nurse told me a lady was here to see me, I felt better immediately. Until she walked in. It wasn't my Arabelle. It was Francesca. My sister.

"Oh my God," she dramatized, her arms reaching toward the ceiling, as she ran to my bed.

"What are you doing here?" I asked, bluntly.

"Is that any way...Jett...I...we're all just so horrified over this."

"Was there anyone else out there to see me?" I asked, still confused as to why Francesca was even in L.A., and wondering where Arabelle was.

"What? No. Not that I know of."

My heart sank. Arabelle didn't come? Did she not know? I needed her. I needed to hold her, feel her soft skin on mine. Maybe word never got to the studio. I didn't know exactly how long I had been here. And now that my sister had really made me come to, I realized I didn't know where my cell phone was.

"What are you doing here, Francesca?"

"What do you mean? Jett, I love you. Hello, I'm your sister."

"No, I mean in L.A. Why aren't you in New York?"

"Jett, are you serious? Oh no, do you have memory loss? You do, don't you!" Her gaze widened, making her huge angry eyes bulge even more than normal. I didn't get along well with my sister, to put it mildly.

I shrugged. Maybe I did have memory loss, regarding my sister anyway.

"Oh no." She took a deep, melodramatic breath. "Well, I know I told you, or Dad told you, that I've been doing a reality TV show where we help people find their dream homes."

Right as she said it I remembered Dad mentioning it. I hadn't been paying a lot of attention to that conversation, since it involved—once again—trying to get me take a hand in his business and give up this ridiculously so-called 'girly dance career.' It was a conversation we'd had ad nauseam. *You're such a showoff. Don't you want to be on TV?* I remembered him saying. I'd learned to completely tune him out. "Yeah, now I remember Dad saying something."

She pursed her lips. I knew she wanted to chew me out for not taking greater interest in their business, or in her career. But she couldn't. Not right now. "Oh Jett," she said, regaining control of her facial expression. "The doctor says you could have been killed. You literally fell within an inch of your life."

"Stop being so dramatic—" I began.

She held a hand up. "Don't shush me. Let me speak. This is serious. This job is too risky; you put your life in danger.

Jett, how much money do you make? It's so not worth it. You can make so much more in the company—"

Now I held a hand up. I didn't want to hear it. And I wasn't going to. "No. If you're going to talk like this, you have to leave, Fran. I'm not hearing it."

"Jett, you can be on TV, like me. Don't you realize how awesome that would be? You're so hot. Think of how many girls you'd get having so much more exposure. How can you not want that? You, of all people!"

If she wasn't my sister, and if she wasn't a woman, I'd seriously want to smack her. I mean, I wouldn't. But she just grated on my nerves so. She made my headache so much worse.

"You think I'm a man-whore? I dance just to get girls? That that's all my life is about? I'm an artist, Fran."

She laughed. Loud and hard. It was more like a witch's cackle.

"I'm sorry, but you fly around on a stage in a loincloth—"

This was it. She wasn't insulting me right now. Or ever. I was done with her. I had been done long before, but somehow she'd managed to get herself into my hospital room. "This conversation is over. This visit is over."

"Oh no, Jett, don't do that. I'm sorry, I shouldn't have laughed. I know how seriously you take that…show." She'd had to search her little brain for the last word. And she said it like she'd say 'trash,' with a look of wholehearted disgust overtaking her face.

"Nurse," I yelled.

"Jett, stop it. Talk to me."

"Nurse!" I yelled more loudly.

"Jett, stop." Fran's face was beginning to redden. I was embarrassing her.

Good. "Nurse!" I said more loudly.

There was some commotion outside and then the door

opened. A porcelain-faced, blue-eyed beauty peeked in. My Arabelle. Our eyes connected and she opened her mouth to speak, but no words came out. She looked simultaneously sick with nerves and as beautiful as ever.

"Belle." I held my arm toward her.

"Just a moment, Ma'am." The nurse pulled Arabelle away from the door. "We can only have one visitor at a time," she said, looking between Fran and me.

"She's done," I said, pointing to Fran.

"Jett, no, please," Francesca whined.

"Done, Nurse." I looked at the woman in scrubs, her eyes all serious. I raised my arm toward Arabelle again. "I'm ready for my next visitor."

"Ma'am?" The nurse looked at Fran, extending her arm toward the door.

"This conversation isn't over, Jett. We need to talk about this."

I refused to look at Fran, keeping my gaze firmly on Arabelle, who looked down, the blush sweeping across her beautiful face making her look even more angelic.

Fran sighed and, with a proud lift of her head, walked out. I saw her give Arabelle a once over followed by a little glare on the way out. I snickered and shook my head. Only my sister could fantasize herself superior to someone like Belle.

"Ma'am," the nurse said to Arabelle. She walked in, slowly at first, then hurried toward me. Both arms were shaking. The tremor was worse than I'd ever seen it.

"I'm so sorry. I have no idea what my sister was even doing here. When they told me someone was here, I assumed it was you."

She shook her head. "Not your fault at all. I came right when I heard." Her voice was low and shaky as well. The tremor seemed to have taken over her entire body.

"I'm okay, Belle. It's all going to be okay. It's just a broken foot that will heal in no time. False alarm." I wrapped my hands around hers, trying to stop the trembling. She nodded, but the light was out of her eyes, and she wouldn't look directly at me. I knew she was having flashbacks to Willem. "This is really nothing, Belle. Nothing at all. Nothing at all like...nothing at all." I was a stuttering fool.

She closed her eyes and breathed in deeply. When she opened them again, her beatific blue irises were hard to see through the wetness. She opened her mouth but nothing came out. She simply shook her head.

26

Arabelle

I stayed with Jett for as long as I could. I found it increasingly hard to speak. He kept telling me he was okay, and he was right—he was. For now. I kept seeing Willem lying there, not okay. Not okay at all. And I kept remembering and feeling the mass of extreme emptiness in my core and the knowledge that nothing would ever be the same. The nausea kept returning. I had nothing left to throw up but bile, and I somehow willed even that back down. I couldn't look at Jett. I couldn't look at his beautiful boyish face, his happy, eager, excited smile brimming with life. Just like Willem's had been.

I stopped trying to talk and eventually he stopped trying to make me. I also quit trying to quell the tremor and he followed my lead on that, too. I placed my head on top of his chest and just listened to him breath for a while, until the nurse called me out, ordering him to get some rest.

Jett protested, but I knew my presence was troubling to him. I know he knew what was going through my mind, through my body. I was disturbing him, and he needed his mind to be at ease so his body would heal.

"I'll come back tomorrow morning," I said. "You need sleep."

He shook his head. "But it's too late right now, Belle."

At first I didn't know what he meant. Too late for us? For me to go through this again? Or did he mean literally—that we couldn't compete now because of his injury? No matter, I knew deep in my core he was right. I couldn't take this again.

"I mean, I don't want you walking around Hollywood at this hour," he continued when it was clear I was confused. "It's too late. You don't know who's out there."

"Oh, Kendra can drive me home. She came with me." I smiled. It felt good to have my voice back, if just momentarily.

He slowly grinned. "Oh, that's nice of her to come."

"We were all worried, Jett." My voice started to crack. I cleared my throat and breathed deeply. "We both need rest. Let's make a pact to see each other bright and early tomorrow morning." I kissed his head.

"Okay," he groaned.

I was walking toward Kendra in the lobby when the woman who had been in the room with him—apparently his sister—stopped me.

"Could I please have a word with you?" she said. She was tall, and her gaze was directed down at me. She had a short, dark, asymmetrical bob that swung when she talked. She was like a tall Liza Minelli. But not as sweet and charismatic as the actress. Her thin lips were tightly pursed and her gaze was hardening.

"Excuse me? Who are you?" Kendra said.

"It's okay," I said to Kendra. "Sure."

"Great. In, ah, private?" The woman eyed Kendra, clearly distrusting her.

I nodded.

"Let me know if you need anything. I'm right over here," Kendra said. I smiled at her. Sweet wasn't exactly the right word to describe Kendra, but she was a true friend—always there for you.

The woman pulled me over to the quietest corner in the busy room. "I'm Francesca Ridley, Jett's sister." Her tone made it sound like I should bow to her, like she'd just introduced herself as royalty. Her downward gaze was not just because she was taller; she didn't like me. It was obvious. I wondered how she could dislike me so, without even knowing me.

"I'm Arabelle."

"Arabelle? Hmm, Jett hasn't said anything about you? Is that your real name?" She snickered at the end and I thought, *This is hardly a time to joke around.*

"Yes," I said bluntly, getting annoyed. Jett hadn't said anything about me to her, likely because he rarely talked to her, seeing as how I didn't know he even had siblings. But I didn't say that. He was injured and this was hardly a time for his supporters to be picking fights with each other. But apparently, she didn't feel the same way.

"Well, Arabelle." She fluttered her hand about as if she'd called me Tinkerbell. I internally rolled my eyes, wanting this to be over with. "You're Jett's dance partner, I assume?" I had to think about it for a moment. I knew I couldn't go on like this, with him in this risky career, very possibly getting hurt again. So no, I wouldn't be. Not any longer.

But before I'd had a chance to say anything, she continued. "I'm just wondering what went through your mind as you saw him falling?" Her voice was rising, turning accusatory. "Did you think 'But for the grace of God, there go I?' Did it make you scared at all that the same could happen to you? Are you people so unconcerned about your safety that you'll just do insane stunts like this without thinking?"

"Arabelle?" Kendra asked, off in the distance.

"Oh, oh no, I'm not ..." Suddenly I couldn't remember the names of his work partners. "I, I don't work with him at Beauty in Motion."

"What? Well, where do you work with him then? Who are you?"

"Excuse me, I don't like the way you're speaking to my friend," Kendra boomed, walking up. "Your attitude is very derogatory."

"I teach at a ballroom studio called Infectious Rhythm. I'm just Jett's friend," I said.

The woman shook her head, apparently confused. "What does he have to do with a ballroom studio?" The edges of her mouth curled down, making her look literally like she may puke. "Are you co-teachers? Are you dating?"

"I don't know that it's any of your business. Jett obviously kept you out of his life for a reason, lady," Kendra said.

The woman literally took a step back at this. After she caught her breath, she unfortunately resumed speaking, rather loudly. "Listen, Jett almost died today. We're told that one inch over and he wouldn't have hit that mat. As it is, his foot is shattered. He may never dance again."

This was news to me. He'd told me it was only broken. My heart completely stopped beating for a moment. Did this mean his dance career was over? Not that I was happy with him doing daredevil stunts—but it was his life, his passion.

"We've been trying for ages to get him out of this ridiculous line of business and get him into the real estate business. That's the family business, and we do quite well, thank you very much. But it wasn't flashy enough for him. He needed to be in Las Vegas, hooking up with a different girl every five seconds."

Was that him? I thought back to when we'd first met. Yes, that was very much him. Or it had been. It didn't seem to be him here in L.A. though.

"Well, now I have a flashier career than he does. I'm on television, starring in a reality show about buying your dream home." She smirked, as if I was him and she were competing with me. "He could have been me. He still can be. And I don't have to risk my life for a living. Daddy's pissed he won't go into the family business. He's threatened to cut off Jett's trust fund. And he's serious. Jett relies on his money but isn't taking Daddy seriously at all. I tried to talk sense into him in his room here. He wouldn't listen; he never does. Maybe you have more sense than he does, especially if you're not stupid enough to work for Beauty in Motion."

So, I'd found out where all Jett's money came from. His father.

"He has a degree from Harvard, you know that?" Francesca continued. "And he's using it on this." She shook her head and laughed. "I don't know if he'll ever dance again. But I don't know if he'll want to come back and work for Daddy's company either. He might do something ridiculous and teach ballroom or something just to spite us. But he can have it so much better. He can have all the flash he wants. Just look at him. He could get all the girls he wants just by being on TV. He'd be a celebrity. He'd be in heaven. But, seriously, he wants to kill himself on a stage?" By this point she wasn't even looking at me. It was like she was talking to herself, or the air, but not to me.

But one thing was becoming clearer and clearer to me. Jett was a ladies man. He was a daredevil. These were his true essences. He wasn't right for me and never would be. I was stifling him, trying to focus our routine on storylines, on poetry. Maybe that's why whatever happened in the theater happened. He was tired from the night before, sure—partly my fault, of course. But perhaps I was turning him into something he was not, and he was internally rebelling against it by taking even more risks with Beauty in Motion than he otherwise would have.

"You know this isn't the first time he's hurt himself, right?" Francesca said.

What? My breath stopped. I shook my head.

"No, you don't know him that well. Just as I thought." She smirked again.

"What happened?" I asked, my voice shaking beyond control.

"What hasn't?" She scoffed, shaking her head. "Broken shoulder, broken arm, broken leg, torn rotator cuff, torn meniscus. Two concussions." She looked up, as if searching her memory for any others. "He might as well be a stuntman for the movies. He'd make a hell of a lot more money, and be compensated for his continuous injuries."

I felt sick all over again, felt the bile literally rising. He'd never told me about any of this. Of course, I'd never asked.

"He's injured himself this way just dancing?" I asked.

She laughed a short, shrieking laugh. "Of course. How else did you think?"

I had to excuse myself; the bile was definitely on its way up. Okay, now I knew for sure. This was him, who he was, a stuntman by nature. I couldn't control that. And I shouldn't. Who is anyone to tell someone else what to do? But I couldn't tolerate his stunts. I just couldn't, no matter how engrained in his nature they were or how much he lived for them. Losing Willem was the most horrifying thing that had ever happened to me and that I ever could imagine. If Jett had injured himself so many times before, it was only a matter of time. No, I couldn't go through it again.

* * *

I GOT HOME to a letter in my mail box from the organizers of the Blackpool Dance Festival. It confirmed my registration as a showcase competitor with my new partner, Jett. I breathed hard. I had to withdraw. Shattered foot or not, we could no longer dance together. Our partnership was over.

27

Jett

"**G**ood news. Everything looks good with your brain scan," the doctor said, his tone upbeat. "Your concussion was minor, and temporary. And your foot's all set. So I see no reason why we can't release you this afternoon."

"Awesome!" I wanted to high five him. But he was too far away.

"But Jett, remember what I said. You need to take it easy. Absolutely no dancing and no walking on the foot without crutches, for minimum of six weeks. Then you come back and we'll remove the cast, and re-assess—the key word being re-assess. So, you're not necessarily home free after six weeks."

I nodded, but I knew I healed quickly. I'd be back on the foot in less time than that. I had to be. The team competition was only weeks away and Blackpool loomed shortly after that. There was no way I could be out of commission for that long. And I wouldn't be. As I said, I was a quick healer. I'd been here before. Not with the foot, but with a few other things. All minor, like this.

"Jett, I'm serious." He seemed to read my thoughts.

"Anything you say. You're the doctor."

He shot me a dubious frown and left.

* * *

I WAS THRILLED to relay the doc's news to Arabelle when she showed up. My whole body warmed when I spied her radiant, angelic face peeking through my door window.

"Hey, gorgeous!" I reached out to her. "I'm getting out today!"

I could tell right away something wasn't right. She smiled but her smile was way too fast and big to be anything but phony. There was definitely something going on in the back of that beautiful mind of hers.

"What's up?" I asked.

"I—I'm really happy you're healing so quickly," she said with a forced laugh.

"Yeah, of course. It was only a small break and a baby bump on the head."

She frowned and shook her head.

"What?" I said.

"I just thought it was more. The break, I mean."

"No, where'd you hear that? Did the doctor talk to you? It's really not that bad, Belle. Doc says it will heal in no time."

She looked out the window, continuing to shake her head.

"Seriously, who told you it was more serious?" I didn't think the doctor would talk to her without my authorization, and the only thing the doc would have said that I hadn't was about the six weeks' recovery. Maybe because of Willem, Arabelle was simply prone to worry.

"Jett." She glanced at me, took a breath, and looked out the window again.

"Seriously, Belle. This is really not a big deal."

When she looked at me again, tears began to pool in her eyes.

"Babe, I'm okay. I am!" I reached out to her.

She shook her head. "You very easily could have died, Jett. And now your bone is shattered."

"Shattered? It's just a break. Who said anything about shattered?"

She shook her head. "Well, I must have heard wrong."

"From who?"

She shook her head again. "That's not important, Jett. What's important is that you very well could have died. You're not valuing your life. And I—I can't take that. I can't take it again." Her voice cut off at the end and the tears began to flow. She put a hand—a very trembling hand—over her face and turned away from me.

"What do you mean? Of course I value my life."

"Then how did this happen?"

"Belle, I'm a theater dancer. There are inherent risks. It's very rare that anyone…"

She shook her head. "I'm a dancer too and I've never risked my life."

"What do you mean? You risk your life whenever you do a crazy one-handed overhead lift, whenever you do a swan dive. Hell, you risk your life when to get on the plane to go to Blackpool every year."

"Don't be ridiculous. Jett…" She locked her shaking hands in a clasp behind her back. Crap, it looked like the tremor was back, big time. "Maybe I am taking too big a risk with all those tricks in the routine. You know, maybe I am. Especially because of who I'm doing them with—someone who has no respect for his own life. So how can he have any respect for mine?"

I opened my mouth but couldn't form the words because I was in shock. I would never let her fall. I'd take better care of her than myself. She knew that.

"I can't do this, Jett. I just can't. I have to go. I just have to —" And she was out the door, before I could even respond. I'd never had anyone accuse me of that before, of not taking care of the girl. I'd never ever let a girl down. Ever. I've saved a lot of women, before they took a spill by catching them. How could she not trust me?

And can't do what? Have a relationship, or a partnership? Neither? I wanted badly to run after her, but there was no way I could.

I reached for my phone, called her. Left several messages. "What did you mean, you can't do this? Belle, you owe me more than that, especially since I can't run after you. Belle, please call me back and talk to me about this. We've gone too far to turn back now."

But she didn't return my calls.

Fortunately the injury was to my left foot, so I could still drive, although it wasn't easy. The first place I went, before even going to my house, was Infectious Rhythm. Belinda had taken Ranger to her apartment so I didn't need to worry about him right now. I had to get to Belle and work things out with her. But I couldn't find her in the practice room or the teachers' lounge.

So I went to talk to Alessia about continuing my teaching job. And that's where I found Belle.

"Speak of the devil himself," Alessia said as I gave Belle a weak, pleading smile. Of course it came as no surprise they were talking about me. "Jett, sit down." Alessia extended a hand to the empty chair beside Belle. "So, what's the prognosis? I have to say, you look a lot better than I was expecting by the sound of things."

"Yeah, I'm taking some pain meds, but I feel fine, really." I looked at Arabelle, who was avoiding my gaze. "Doctor says I can still teach, I just can't dance for a few weeks, until it's completely healed. But I'd definitely like to stay on to teach. Now that I'm out of commission for the theater, I have all the more time to help the team. And, by competition time, I should be able to dance."

"The competition is in less than a month," Arabelle said.

"I'm a quick healer, Arabelle. Besides, there are other competitions, future ones. And Blackpool is more than six weeks away. That one, I will really be ready for. But I may seriously be able to dance in the upcoming team comp. I heal very quickly. Always have, always will."

Arabelle continued looking away but Alessia nodded at me.

"Well, you're a good teacher and team coach and I will definitely keep you on in that capacity."

"You got it!"

"But, Jett." Alessia's tone took an audible downward turn. "Arabelle has expressed to me that she doesn't want to partner with you. She'd rather either do a solo dance both with the team and at Blackpool, or partner with someone else." Alessia looked at me with raised eyebrows. She knew I was going to be pissed at this.

"Another partner? Who?"

"My question as well," Alessia said, extending her arm to Arabelle, for commentary. "Drew?"

"I actually don't know. I just said that without really thinking." She looked at the floor. "I probably don't want another partner. I just can't partner with Jett anymore. Despite the fact that he's injured and is currently out of commission, we just don't see eye to eye about things and...I just...no."

"Belle, please. I would never let you fall. I would guard you way, way more carefully than I take care of myself. It's how I've always been."

"I've thought a lot about it, Jett. The Blackpool Dance Festival asked me if I'd like to do another solo this year. Not for competition, just for fun. And...and I think I'm going to say yes. And I'll use the team to practice the solo, putting it in the middle where our solo was."

"Are you serious?" I said. "This is a ballroom competition. Everyone else is dancing in pairs. It would look ridiculous if the lead danced by herself."

Alessia nodded, but Belle couldn't see her. She was still focused on the floor.

"Well, maybe not then. Maybe we'll just have it all be students," Belle said. "Maybe Judy and Paolo can be the leads. They're the best. Or maybe Kendra and Josie. I don't know."

"But the competitors are having a pro teacher pair, right?" I said.

Alessia nodded.

"So we wouldn't be very competitive without a pro couple."

"I don't want to do this." Arabelle's voice was rising, as was her arm. Her very trembling arm. "I don't. I want you to respect the decision I've made, and not fight me on it."

I exhaled deeply. She finally looked at me. Pain combined with exhaustion shone in her eyes. I reached over and rubbed her shoulder. I had to stop. For now. But I'd win her back. I would. I'd show her she needed to dance with me.

28

Arabelle

To be honest, I expected more of a fight from him. I didn't want to make the decision I did. But I felt it was the only one. The team would look stupid with a pro dancer doing a solo. And it would be hard to do a solo again at Blackpool. It was hell working myself up to it mentally last year. Plus, people were probably tired of my sadness. I remembered the mood in the room when I danced last year. I wanted Willem to live on in their memories as an exciting dancer who filled people with joy, not sorrow. It would be much better to dance with a new partner. But it wasn't going to be Jett, and I wasn't ready to train with anyone else.

The whole team clapped wildly when Jett hobbled in on his crutches.

He chuckled and gave a good natured nod. "You guys are the best. So, if Alessia didn't already tell you, I'm still going to coach, but, ah, Arabelle and I are no longer going to dance the leads."

The room filled with a chorus of *booo*s. "I know. I know. But we're still going to make this team absolutely awesome—the best."

"But why aren't you guys still dancing? That will heal in a few weeks," Kendra said.

"Well, we're going to work on the routine as it is now and perfect it. Maybe in the future…"

I knew it. I knew he would do this, tell people whatever he wanted to happen, with no regard to me.

"But we just don't know yet. Let's focus on you guys. The judges already know the pros can dance. It's your dancing the judges are going to be concentrating on for the marks."

I nodded. He was right to put the focus on them.

We started over with the routine again, from the beginning. It was hard for Jett not to jump around when he corrected someone or demonstrated the proper way to do something. Several times he reached out to me, but I shook my head. We were not going to dance together, even if it meant he remained stationary and tried to show the move on me. His foot needed to heal, and I needed to be free of him. This wasn't easy though. Seeing how much he wanted to move, and seeing him restricted—even though it wasn't permanent—was heartbreaking. It made me wonder how horrid it would be if he became paralyzed permanently.

"Hey, earth to Arabelle," Kendra called out. "This feels a little off." She was in the middle of the lift we'd rehearsed and she was doing it all wrong. Yes, right. I had to snap out of it.

"Wait, put her down," I ordered. "You need to have Josie put her arm around you and push down to help her hold herself up and take some of the burden off you, like I told you," I said.

"I know, but then Jett was saying it doesn't look as cool as letting her have both arms out so she can look like a bird."

"No!" We'd been here before. Had he really said that? I looked at him and he could only shrug.

"It would look better."

"But it's too hard for them."

"Belle, we can do it. We really can," Kendra piped up.

Why did he have to make this harder? He'd put a thought in her brain and now it wouldn't leave. He would never change. And I guess I wouldn't either.

"Not getting hurt is far more important. It's number one. Because if you hurt your back, then you're out for a long time, possibly forever. Back injuries are serious, Kendra."

"I know, but I have ways to protect—"

"No!" I shouted. "We're doing it my way." The room was still. Everyone looked at me. I don't know if I'd ever shouted in this studio. I inhaled deeply. "There's another reason you want to do it my way," I said, much more softly. "If Josie's arm is around you, she can look into your eyes as you carry her. That's romance, that's poetry, and that tells a story. She doesn't need to look like a bird. Why do you need to carry around a bird? That's too abstract."

"Because she's setting her free—" Jett began.

"She doesn't need to set anyone free!" I yelled again. "They're both human. They're in love. I just...argh!" I threw my hands up.

It was becoming clear to me that now he didn't care about opposing me since we weren't dancing together anymore, and my demand that we seek compromise had been predicated on our partnership. With that off, our deal was dead too? Compromise! Ha! Us? What a joke. We would never see eye to eye. Never.

Jett thought about it, then nodded. "I understand. But the judges reward a lift that they know is harder—"

"The judges value artistry—"

He held his palm to me. "I agree with you. I do, Belle. This makes sense. It works. We're doing it Belle's way, Kendra, you guys."

Was he really giving in? Or was it a ruse? Now I felt like I should compromise. "We can always use speed as our strength. We can use quick, complicated footwork to wow the judges. We're good at that."

Jett nodded. "There are some upbeat sections. That's true." But I could tell he was a little let down.

He turned the music on softly and counted out the beats and everyone did the steps as he called them out. The lifts really looked beautiful. Of course two of the couples—who were not romantic partners—laughed when he told them to look longingly into each others' eyes, but Kendra and Josie and Judy and Paulo did it with meaning, and it was so sweet. And the guys—and Kendra since she was doing the guy's role —looked much stronger since they weren't struggling as much.

Jett nodded. "It looks...okay, it looks pretty good." I couldn't tell whether he was just humoring me or whether he really thought so, but something—the way his eyebrows raised in surprise maybe—made me think it was the latter.

29

Jett

I had to admit when I really opened my mind I was beginning to see things Arabelle's way. It did tell a little story about the characters in the dance by having the girl wrap her arm around the guy as he twirled her around, and have them look into each other's eyes. It wasn't as difficult as having the girls spread their arms about bird-like, but audiences didn't know that. And who knew really what these judges would reward or not? I'd done ballet comps ad nauseam but I didn't really know that much about ballroom judges. Arabelle had a lot more experience there than I did, so I'd have to trust that she knew her stuff.

I was getting excited about how beautiful the choreography actually was when we focused more on the emotion and lyricism. Damn, I wanted to dance with Arabelle. But every time I got up and put pressure on that foot with that blasted awkward cast, I caught her glare, and remembered doctor's warning. If I was going to heal, I needed to stay off of it. But man, how I wanted to do the lift Belle's way, to let her wrap her arm around me and gaze into my eyes as I carried her around. It would actually be easier on my foot if we did the lift her way. Maybe I could talk her into doing it while I still had the cast. But those penetrating glares she threw my way whenever I got up made me realize that plea would have to wait for another day. For now I had to be happy she was still co-coaching.

3 0

Arabelle

It really kind of amazed me how Jett was letting me have my way and agreeing to focus on the art of the dance, rather than the stunts. Sure, he was pretty much out of commission with his broken foot, but he could have still fought me. I knew he was trying. He'd give me these puppy dog eyes and tell me how now that we were making things easier on the guy maybe he could lift me with the cast still on. I'd shoot him my *No way, Jose* look. He'd do the puppy dog eyes and I'd do the *No way* look, again. And again. I wondered how he'd be when he healed though. Part of me wanted to think he would see things my way—that he would focus on art and not on stunt work. Part of me wanted badly to think that. But I knew I was just kidding myself. I knew men like him. I'd been married to one.

Sometimes, after team workout, he'd walk beside me, brush his arm against mine, and ask me to dinner. I'd shake my head. According to his contract with Beauty in Motion, he would be returning to the show after his injury healed. No way could I be a part of his life, either as a dance or a romantic partner. I just couldn't. I had to say no to both.

I wrote back to the Blackpool organizers, telling them I was sorry for the late notice but my partner and I would need to withdraw. I blamed it on his injury. I was heartbroken as I typed. This would be my first year missing Blackpool in almost a decade. It had been part of my life for my entire adulthood.

* * *

THE DAY of the team competition arrived. I was quite proud of the team. We looked good and solid. We'd worked crazy hard and we were ready. We'd decided that I wouldn't dance solo. So, since Jett wasn't dancing, there wouldn't be a professional lead. It would be all about the students. The students looked great, so I felt confident the judges would like us, and hopefully even favor us.

Though we were in Vegas, Jett didn't want to see any of his friends or his boss. He shot by his house to check up on things, but spent the rest of the time with us. Said he would rather focus on the team right now, not his "old life." Interesting choice of words. I didn't ask him to elaborate on whether he meant old life for the time being or whether he was thinking of permanently relocating. It didn't matter since we were no longer a partnership. He was just a friend now. His life was not mine to ponder, to get my hopes up for, or worry myself over. He would always be a friend, wherever he spent his life. Sweet Mandi showed up to cheer us on, as did Lucia.

We arrived early and did a couple warm-ups on the floor. I always liked the team to dance twice on the actual floor to get their bearings. You never knew when something would be slightly different from the studio's performance space and throw someone off.

During the second run-through I spotted Natalia and her team setting up across the dance floor. She had a couple students on her team that had left our studio earlier in the year. A woman named Cheryl who'd had a crush on Sasha, and was angry when he'd chosen Rory over her. And Luna, Cheryl's friend, whom no one liked and was always throwing her money around, demanding things be her way. *Good riddance to both of them*, I thought.

It made me a little nervous while Natalia, along with Luna and Cheryl, watched our team. A glare in Natalia's eye seemed to be getting angrier by the second. After we were done rehearsing, we sat around our table and took a well-deserved breather. I made sure we had plenty of water and snacks.

Before we went on, I gave everyone a final pep talk. "You guys looked so great out there. Seriously. Keep it up. Don't let any pressure hold you back, make you nervous." As I said the last word, I realized I hadn't felt the tremor in weeks, since soon after Jett got out of the hospital. He must have thought the same thing because I caught him looking at my hand right then.

And then, our positive little exchange was interrupted by Kendra's "uh-oh."

What? I looked up to see Natalia approaching.

"Arabelle," she said, lifting her heavily drawn-in eyebrows. She stood above me, so she looked down.

I stood up so as to be level with her.

"Nice to see you again, Natalia," I lied.

She laughed. Cackled was more like it. "Yes, I'm sure it is. Anyway, your team looks pretty good. I wanted to tell you."

"Thank you," I said, wondering what she was up to.

"But I did notice that you and uh…" She motioned toward Jett, who seemed to be paying her no mind.

"Jett," I said.

"Yes, him. The not-Willem."

At first a chill went through my entire body, but then I realized what she was doing. She was trying to shake me. And I wouldn't let her.

"Yes, Willem passed away. This is Jett." My voice was angry but still low. I wasn't going to let this get out of control.

"Yes, I realize that. My memory isn't that bad. And I remember how special he was to you, and I thought I even remember you saying you wouldn't dance with another man, as he was so special."

I wanted to wring her neck. I had said that, to several dance journalists, right after Willem died, not knowing how I'd ever go on. I could feel some shaking returning to my arm, but it wasn't the same kind of tremor as before. Not at all. It was based in anger, not fear or anxiety.

"But that's not even what I came over to say."

Like hell it wasn't, I thought.

"I was just going to say that I noticed that you two are not dancing with the team, as the central leads. I do see that he's injured." She peered down at Jett's foot, making a faux sad face.

"What's your point?" I said bluntly, wanting her to leave us alone.

"Well, I just wondered if that's a good idea. Wouldn't the right thing to do for the students have been to have another pair, like Sasha and Rory, take over? I mean, I'm pretty sure every other team has a pro pair leading. I'd hate to think you were letting your team lose by not taking responsibility."

"Rory's like, nine months pregnant right now. And Arabelle is more than responsible, you donut-head," Kendra barked. "Now get out of here and leave us alone, or I'm going to report you to the authorities for harassment."

"Yes, I'm sure they'd listen to you, of all people," Natalia said under her breath but loud enough for all of us to hear, as she walked away. I didn't know Natalia had known since she wasn't living in California last year, but Kendra had had a run-in with Luna at a similar competition last year managed by the same organizers. Josie had worn the same costume as Luna. Of course Josie was far more beautiful and a much better dancer, and thus showed off the costume much better. This, of course, infuriated Luna, who got the pair booted from the competition. She'd claimed that Kendra and Jackie stole Luna's idea after seeing her try on the dress in the ladies' locker room. It's forbidden in the rules for a pro dancer to steal another professional's creative ideas, which include costume design, but there's nothing in the rules about amateurs. But since Luna contributes quite a bit of money to the competition organizers, she got her way. Since Kendra was now on a team and dancing in a different competition, the organizers had let her back in. One look at Luna glaring at us from across the ballroom made me realize how word of that ridiculous incident from a year ago got around.

I noticed Kendra was shaking too. Out of anger as well. "That b—"

"Luna, who's now on Natalia's team, got us in trouble last year and got us banned from the Latin competition," Josie said, nearly in tears, "over something ridiculously stupid that she totally lied about."

"Okay, ladies, come on," Jett said. "This is exactly what they meant to do—rile us up right before we go on. Neither of you have anything to feel the least bit badly about. We're better than they are and she knows it, which is why she had to come over here and try to sabotage us by screwing with us mentally. We have this in the bag. We do."

I somehow found myself laughing.

"What's so funny?" Jett asked, though he must have known since he started chuckling with me.

"This type of thing always seems to happen at ballroom competitions. I mean in ballet there's jealousy and competition for the best parts, but not these ridiculous cat fights where people are trying to get each other in trouble by making stuff up to the competition organizers. It's all so childish. I can't imagine this happening in your world." I thought for a moment of what it must be like to be part of his world. For a split second, I wondered what my life would have been like had I kept dancing ballet and not gone off to ballroom all those years ago.

He thought for a moment. "Yeah, there's definitely fierce competition for leading roles and all, but the person with the best charisma and dance ability wins since we have audiences to please. You can't just give a bad dancer top position because they have money. That's unique to ballroom, I think."

Jett's pep talk, along with our laughter at the childishness of it all, defused the situation. Everyone on the team nodded and snickered, like this was all par for the course. We had a team of almost-pros, and we could rise above this. We would not let Natalia's bitter words get to us.

We were scheduled to go on near the end of the competition, which was good because the judges wouldn't feel compelled to mark down so as to leave room for better performances, and because the students got to see most of the other teams. Jett and I had watched most of the other teams rehearse and we knew we were a good, solid team in comparison, as did the students. We'd rehearsed hard, and, even without the tricks, our footwork was swifter and more complicated, the choreography was more challenging, and our routine told a sweet little romantic story between each partnership. With the other teams, the pro leads were way better than the students. The other teams seemed to have relied on the pros. If I were a judge, I wouldn't take that into consideration, because then it would be a competition of pros and not the students who'd paid for the performance training and for the chance to be competitors in their own right.

Before the team went on, we formed a circle and locked hands. "Let's kill it!" Jett said.

Our music began, and I could tell from the get go it was going to be as perfect as possible. Sometimes you can just tell whether it's going to go smoothly and be awesome, or there's going to be trouble. I could tell it was going to be the first— and I was right. No flubs. Kendra and Josie looked into each other's eyes during the lift, which they could do easily now after all the practice and after we'd simplified it, and it was so sweet. I saw Jett look at me out of the corner of my eye. I didn't return his gaze, but I smiled.

"You were right," he whispered.

"Thank you," I mouthed back.

The audience went wild after it was over and I could tell on the judges' faces that we'd won. If no one else was better that is. Natalia's team occupied the coveted last position.

When their music started, I knew it was going to be a mess. I'd actually kind of known that when Natalia harassed us earlier. You wouldn't do that unless you needed to. And, watching us nail our routine put them off their game even more. Their performance was pockmarked with screw-ups. They were small ones, but I could see the judges notice them. They did exactly what Jett had tried to do. They did tricks full-out. And the pros—Duke and Natalia—handled them very well of course, but they were too advanced for the students, and the lifts were wobbly. At one point, I worried the guy partnering Luna would drop her when she was well over his head, his arms extended fully above him. Despite her bitchiness, it made me cringe. No one wanted to see anyone get hurt. Natalia and Duke had definitely focused on themselves, to the exclusion of their amateur students.

Nevertheless, they came in second place, likely for difficulty and effort. We came in first! The team went wild when our names were called, obviously. Jett and I hugged each student in turn. Jett went to hug me, and at first I thought twice about it, but then gave in. It was cause for celebration, and we'd done a good job together. I hated to admit, but it felt good to be in his warm embrace again. Jett and I took a bow with the team, Jett hobbling to the dance floor. We'd done Alessia proud. This was hopefully one solid step in saving the studio and its reputation.

On my way of the ballroom, I felt a firm hand pull my dress from behind. What the hell? I turned to see Natalia's angry face.

"You cheated," she spit. Her lips were twisted into a nasty grimace and she looked like she was about to spew venom. I couldn't believe this had upset her so. It was just a team competition, primarily for the students. She was acting like this was a pro comp of the highest order. She acted like this was Blackpool—which she now probably had in the bag— though I didn't know if she knew we'd withdrawn.

"Um, no we didn't?" I said, confused as to what she was talking about.

"I told you before. You were supposed to have a pro lead dance."

"That's not part of the rules. That's just a convention that teams often follow, but not a solid rule."

"We'll see about that. We're contesting it."

And then I saw Luna's beady little eyes several feet behind

her. She glared. Of course it would be this way. Luna had made up rules in the past, then argued that Josie and Kendra broke them. Same old, same old.

I felt anger bubbling up, and I felt my hand begin to shake.

"Hey, what's up?" Jett said, walking up behind me and putting his hand gently on my shoulder. "I thought you were right behind me."

"We'll see," I said, through clenched teeth.

"And you also cheated by not allowing us to see you. You got to see us. We didn't get to see you. That wasn't playing fair."

"What are you talking about? You did see us rehearse. You might have walked in during it, but you had the opportunity to see."

"Not the team. You and him." She pointed her long, bony finger at Jett.

What? "But we didn't dance with the team. He's injured. Of course we didn't do a rehearsal for a dance we didn't perform. If there's no rule we have to perform, there's certainly no rule we had to rehearse a performance we weren't doing!" I was beginning to question this woman's connection to reality. She made no sense.

"I wasn't saying that was a rule violation. You misunderstand." She was literally spitting in my face as she talked. "I am suggesting you didn't want us to see you because you know how bad you are. Especially with him, like…" She motioned to Jett's foot, a look of complete disgust on her face. Her eyes were so large they were nearly popping out of her head, and her contorted jaw and downward-turned mouth made her look almost comical.

I just shook my head, not even knowing what to say. It seemed impossible to have a logical conversation with her.

"Nice seeing you again, as always Natalia," Jett said, his

tone seething with sarcasm. "Now, if you'll excuse us, we have lives."

"We'll see what you're made of at Blackpool—or not!" Natalia called out as we left. So, she didn't yet know I'd withdrawn us. Her words also made me want to turn around and reinstate us.

"Forget her, she's just a sore loser." Jett held my trembling hand. He didn't address the Blackpool issue, making me wonder if he'd heard her. He hadn't heard the entire conversation.

I opened my mouth to tell him about Natalia's threat to contest our winning with the judges, but the whole team was now within earshot and I didn't want to do anything to burst our well-deserved bubble. It may be creating undue worries anyway. Hopefully that was all it was—a threat.

I took a deep breath, but simply nodded, and gave him my best smile. "I will. Thank you." He squeezed my hand and gave me a nice kiss on the cheek. It felt nice, I had to admit.

Jett

I wanted to punch my hand straight through the glass of Alessia's office window when she told Belle and me our team had been disqualified because there were no pros on it.

"What the major fuck?" I yelled, unable to control my mouth. "I couldn't dance because of an injury that nearly killed me. What we were supposed to do?" Arabelle had been looking down, but when I said the second sentence, she looked right at me, her big blue eyes dead serious.

"And I thought this wasn't even a real rule? It shouldn't be. If the students are good enough on their own, why can't they dance on their own? Isn't that the better outcome anyway, for the students to train to succeed on their own and have their moment in the spotlight as pro dancers?"

I spotted a slight smile cross Arabelle's face. "Yes," she whispered. "It *is* the better outcome."

Both women looked at each other, with knowing eyes.

"So then, what happened?" I repeated.

Alessia sighed. "There was no rule. It's just a custom. But Luna being Luna and realizing she has an ally in Natalia, convinced Nat to go before the judges and argue that it's a custom important enough to be considered a rule."

"What's so all important about it?"

Arabelle snorted. "It's an all-important rule because Luna wants it to be. Because Luna's money wants to it be."

"You know about last year, right? When she got Kendra and Josie disqualified for another non-rule?" Alessia added.

"So they really let her buy the competition?" I was actually pretty shocked. Yeah, people kind of bought their way into big shows in Vegas. But only at the lower levels where it didn't matter that much. You wouldn't be able to buy yourself into a star role, or it could seriously hurt the entire production. Winning the whole competition was kind of the equivalent of a starring role. At least, I'd think it was.

"The comp organizers don't like to see it that way, but basically, she's able to find loopholes. Like any good lawyer, I guess—which her husband is."

I got up and paced around the room. I usually worked out my anger by punching something inanimate, but there didn't seem to be anything in here. I had to control myself anyway. I just clenched my fists and kicked at the air. "So what do we do now? The students were on such a high."

"I'll tell them," Arabelle said. "Kendra, unfortunately, probably won't be that surprised."

"Yeah, but we really needed this win for the studio." I looked at Alessia's heavily furrowed brow. It was clear she was worried about the studio's future now. "Are we completely disqualified, like not even second place? As if we never even competed?"

Alessia nodded. "Yep, as if we'd never competed."

"She's got to be stopped."

Both women just took deep breaths, swallowing their

disappointment. But I wasn't the type to do that, and I didn't think Arabelle was either. She was a fierce competitor, a winner. I knew that and she did too.

"Does Blackpool have the same problem with crooked judges?" I asked.

Arabelle's eyes widened and she shifted in her seat. She slowly looked up at Alessia, then me.

"There's far too many competitors there, from all over the world. Luna couldn't even compete there; they don't have student comps," Alessia answered.

"So, it's a fair competition," I said.

Arabelle took a breath, her gaze now concentrated on something out the window. "More fair than here, certainly."

I looked at Alessia, who began to grin, knowing what I was up to. She looked at Arabelle. We both waited for Arabelle to look at me. I knew she would eventually.

When her eyes finally connected with mine, I said, "Well, then that's where we're going to beat the shit out of them."

Belle's eyes closed but the edges of her lips began to curl up.

Arabelle

W e could *so* beat the shit out of them. And I was ready to. Nothing would make me more satisfied. Nothing.

Jett had come around to seeing things my way. I could tell by the way he argued to Alessia that the professionals shouldn't have to dance, since the comp was meant to showcase the students and let them have their moment in the spotlight. Jett was advocating that someone other than him should have center stage. I was proud of him. I really was. It's not easy letting someone else have the attention, especially for someone like him.

And after the performance, he'd also agreed with me I was right about simplifying the lift and making it more about the romance than the thrill. I knew it from the way he squeezed my hand afterward, the way he looked at me, the way his entire face lit up. He'd seen it in the way the team members all looked together—particularly Kendra and Josie —and he'd seen that the judges rewarded that over Duke and

Natalia's team creating lifts that only the pros could do properly. I knew the judges would reward us. Now he did too.

Okay, I could compete with Jett alone at Blackpool in showdance. I could do it for Alessia, and for the sake of art triumphing over drumroll stunts. I should do it. I could and I should, so I would.

The doctor had taken the cast off and told Jett to go easy. He had promised he would, not dancing full out until very close to the competition. I trusted him.

I called the Blackpool organizer and explained our situation: that Jett had an injury but that it had healed and that we would like to be reinstated. The organizer said she was delighted to hear it, and would place us back on the roster immediately.

I apologized again for all the confusion and changes she'd likely have to make to the program, judging, etc.

She laughed. "Arabelle, I don't care. You make this competition, dear. Blackpool would never be the same without you. You *are* this competition."

Wow.

So, fine, for now, we were back on as a partnership. But a dance partnership only. I kept hearing Jett's admission to Alessia that he nearly died when he got injured. *I almost died. What were we supposed to do?* He'd insisted to me in the hospital that it was a run-of-the-mill accident. Of course I knew better, and now I knew he did too. He'd lied to me. I couldn't accept that in a relationship.

Yes, I would dance with Jett for Blackpool. But this relationship had to remain platonic. This was only about winning for Alessia. After he healed, he'd return to Beauty in Motion, even knowing it could kill him. I wouldn't be lied to again, and I wouldn't be devastated by death again.

* * *

THE TEAM WAS inconsolable when we told them about being disqualified, as I knew they would be.

"I want to punch that bitch right upside the head," Kendra said, punching her hand instead.

"I know. Believe me, I know how you feel," I said.

"This is the second time. She has too much power. Way too much. Something needs to be done, Ms. A!"

I nodded.

"Don't worry; we're going to beat the hell out of them at the next competition. By the time Orange County rolls around, my foot will be well-healed, so you'll have pro partners. I mean...I don't know, who exactly..." Jett's voice petered out. I hadn't told him yet I would return to being his dance partner. I was going to do that today. "But anyway, we won't have any stupid non-rule violations, and the championship will go to the true winners," Jett said firmly.

Josie looked down. "You don't understand. If we win again, they'll come up with another rule we broke."

"She's a B like no other," Judy added.

"Ow," Kendra said, still punching her hand.

"Hey, honey, stop that. We don't need our star dancer getting hurt now," Paulina called out from the barre. She hadn't joined the team but she liked to watch rehearsals. Kendra finally broke a smile. "You ladies do know, a curse from that one eventually ends up a blessing."

Kendra and I both frowned at Paulina.

"Who won Blackpool last year? Latin division, I mean?" Paulina asked.

"Rory and Sasha," Kendra said.

Paulina nodded. "And that was after Luna and her cohort Cheryl tried all that sabotaging, following poor Rory all around, intimidating her and saying nasty things."

"Really?" Kendra said.

"Oh sugar, you don't know. They wanted their woman—Xenia—to win, of course. Sasha's ex."

"She came all the way in fourth!" Kendra chuckled.

"Yep, and their enemy won—the person I think we can all agree was the most deserving," Paulina chirped.

"Yeah, but nobody from our studio is competing in Blackpool this year," Josie said. "So they'll win there too."

"Hmm, got a point there, girl," Paulina said.

I felt Jett's eyes on me. I looked at the floor, feeling my face get redder and redder by the second.

"Wait, what's that blush about, A?" Kendra shouted.

Leave it to Kendra to figure everything out. I closed my eyes and shook my head. But I couldn't help but smile.

"Yes! Someone from our studio *is* competing at Blackpool! I knew it, I knew it, I knew it! Wooo hooooo!"

Nothing like announcing your plans to the entire building via Kendra.

* * *

"WHEN IS your next follow up with the doctor?" I asked Jett, choosing not to respond right now to what I knew he was trying to ask me, judging by the loopy smile taking over his entire face.

"Actually I have a check-up tomorrow morning. Why?"

"I want to come with you."

He chuckled. "Okay, sure. Can I ask why?"

"I want to know how long it's going to take to finally heal." I eyed his foot.

"What, you don't trust me to convey accurate info from the doc?" But the loopy smile remained. He knew his weakness, that he had a tendency to overstate things, namely his injury-healing progress. And he knew that I was onto him. And he was letting me be. He was letting me in.

33

Jett

Obviously Arabelle didn't trust me when it came to assessing my own health. At first I felt a twinge of resentment, but I realized almost immediately thereafter that I had no grounds to be pissed. I'd injured myself a lot. I was always so gung-ho to recover quickly and get on with my dancing, I had to admit, I hadn't always taken the best care of myself.

I was starting to see myself through her eyes. My mind took me to the day I was in the hospital seeing the look on her face when she saw me. I remembered her beautiful tribute to Willem at last year's Blackpool, watched that horrible tremor return in her Latin dance, then saw it again in my hospital room after my injury. Of course after what happened to her first true love, she was devastated by my injury. More than I was. I suddenly I saw myself as she did. I was seriously careless. I had to be more responsible. For her sake, as much as for mine.

* * *

"It's looking pretty good," the doctor said. "It has healed nicely. I still want you to keep everything light. No heavy lifting, no tricks, no crazy footwork. You can work on it, but keep it light."

"And how long before I can dance full out?" I hadn't wanted to ask that question at all because then I'd have a timeline from a professional, but I knew Arabelle was going to ask if I didn't.

"Hmm, give it a couple more weeks. Of course, I'm inclined to say never return to the crazy tricks and stunts you all do. They're just not good for a body. But I'm a doctor. I know you all aren't going to listen to me."

I looked at Arabelle. Her face was turned toward the window but I detected a slight smile. She was included in that "you all" and she knew it.

But when we got in the car, her mood darkened.

"Hey, you okay?" I asked.

She took a breath. "Yes. I just realized that now that you're healed—or almost healed—you're going to be returning to Beauty in Motion. I'm just...I'm just getting worried about how much time we've lost preparing for Blackpool, and how little time we have left..." Her voice trailed off.

I hadn't even thought about my job. That surprised me. I guess I hadn't missed it all that much.

"And what I'm really scared of..." she continued. "What if you get hurt again? Then we won't be able to compete. And I..." Her words faded again. I was about to speak when she caught her breath and began again. "I know it's your life. I told myself that, and it is, and you're completely entitled to return to your regular job whenever you like. But right now I have a stake in your life too since we're partners. Dance partners of course. And…maybe this wasn't such a good idea." She looked away.

"Okay. Look, I'll speak to Veronique about it. The doctor said I shouldn't dance full out for another two weeks, at least. That'll bide me some time. And by then, I think there will only be one or two more weeks of the tour here. I'd only agreed to go to L.A." I was thinking out loud. "Audiences are now used to my fill-ins, both here and in Vegas…I'll—I'll ask her to let me stay out until we're done with Blackpool."

"But what if she won't let you?"

I shrugged. I honestly hadn't thought about it. "I'll make her let me." And I knew I could. She wouldn't let me go.

For the first time in this conversation—for the first time I think Beauty in Motion had ever been a topic in our conversation—the corners of Arabelle's beautiful lips curled up into a very slight smile. "You'd do that," she said more than asked, as if she knew I would.

Arabelle

For the next few weeks, Jett and I practiced our team solo and mapped out our Blackpool routine. He remained true to his word to the doctor about keeping things light. We marked the routine only, not dancing full out. And I trusted that he'd talk to Veronique and make her agree to release him from his contract until after Blackpool.

I knew he'd eventually return to his company, to all the risks. And that's why I knew we'd never be more than dance partners. And the dance partnership was only for now, for the immediate purposes of winning Blackpool for Alessia and for the school. We'd never be more. I'd accepted that he wasn't going to change for me, or for anyone, and I was at peace with it.

We made our team solo a shortened, much easier version of our Blackpool showdance, which meant we were able to get a lot of choreography done in the short amount of time we had to get our routine down solid. We also got a huge amount done without Jett having to do his performances every night. I hadn't realized how much those took out of me —not even so much the actual time he was away at the theater, but the worry I had if something were to happen to him. I now realized how much of that trepidation I had always carried around with me, long before he was actually injured.

Amazingly, we argued very little, only having minor disagreements. Jett agreed to let me have my way—to trust me about focusing on the lyricism and poetry of the relationship we depicted, and not do tricks for tricks' sake. Of course, it may have been somewhat easy to agree with me at this point since it was all in theory, as we weren't yet dancing full out.

But, unbelievably, wonderfully, nothing changed after we did begin dancing our routine in full. He didn't try to fight me and make the lifts or tricks flashier or more risky than they had to be. Maybe he trusted me now, since we won our first team competition without all the flash.

Honestly, he'd kind of amazed me when he agreed to let me come with him to his doctor appointments. Initially, I'd told myself I wanted to go because I didn't fully trust him. I needed to know for myself what the doctor's orders were, so I, along with Alessia—whom I'd report back to—could prevent him from further injuring himself. But at that appointment, I realized that wasn't at all why I'd really gone.

I'd gone because I actually cared about the man. The realization kind of hit me all at once. I saw the doctor examining his foot and Jett's range of motion, and the look on Jett's face when the doctor pronounced it healed. His dimpled smile oozed that boyish energy, his youthful elation at the world, which I'd so fallen for. His sheer happiness, his joy of just being, was palpable and contagious. I felt it travel as a heat wave throughout my entire body, warming me from the crown of my head to the tips of my toes. Then his devilishly dreamy brown eyes connected with mine. And a tingle went through my body. A different kind of warmth. I forced myself to push that feeling away immediately. No, I wasn't going there again with him. But I would enjoy his dance partnership. That, I would fully embrace.

3 5

Jett

Finally, I could dance full out again. Nothing felt so good as to be able to lift Belle high above my head, hold her in my arms, and whisk her around the floor till she felt a good kind of dizzy. Amazingly, everything went perfectly the very first time we went through the routine completely. Not a step out of place. And it all felt so right.

"Wow," Arabelle said, as I released her from our ending hands-free fish dive, the beautiful and difficult trick we decided to end our routine with.

"Wow, what?" I was slightly out of breath. But only slightly.

"I'm just surprised you remembered it all."

"Now you're accusing me of having memory problems?" I laughed, knowing what she meant.

"No, I just mean since we never danced full out before, you never had a chance to solidify everything into your muscle memory."

"I could never forget such a beautiful dance. It doesn't have to be only in my muscles."

She blinked and looked away, a slight smile crossing her lips, one she seemed not to want me to see.

Of course there were a few places where I wanted to go further than we had—but just a few. In our initial lift, I managed to convince her to let me carry her onstage without her wrapping her arm around my shoulder to lift herself. This made it look as if I were cocooning her. It looked equally as beautiful as when we'd wrapped our arms around each other, but now the difficulty was back. The judges might or might not notice.

"Okay, I'm letting you win this one because it's not necessary for my arm to be wrapped around you; it looks just as nice your way," she'd said.

"I wouldn't have suggested it for any other reason," I maintained.

"But I don't want to do that in the team comp. Let's do it my way there, so we're the same as the students."

I nodded. We had won that competition as far as I was concerned, so the judges were very happy with the team's level of difficulty. They didn't want us to make it harder for the students, nor did we. And we would have looked off if we did something other than what the students did.

The other place I wanted to make a change was where the music swelled, and the lift I wanted to do would—yes—be flashier, but it would also go along with the music. If she didn't go for it, though, I was prepared to let her win.

"When the music crescendos right here, I think I should lift you higher, like they do in Russian ballets. I'll hold you by your lower calf while you reach up as if you're touching the stars." Right now I was just holding her at the waist and turning it into an overhead bird lift. This would be far better, and more original.

She took a deep breath and thought about it. I could see by the raise of her brows and the intensity in her gaze that she knew it would be beautiful. But then the edges of her lips took a turn for the south. Her eyes took on a glassy haze and she stared off far into the distance. As she folded her arms in front of her, I saw the very beginnings of a tremor in her right wrist.

"What's going on?" I reached out to her, gently brushing her tremor ridden arm. "Come on, tell me, let me in."

She shook her head, then uncrossed her arms and shook her hands from the wrist. "It's nothing. It's just…"

Her eyes filled with water, but only for a split second. Then she blinked and they were dry again.

"What? It's just what? Come on, I'm here for you. Not to pressure you. Just talk to me."

She nodded. "I know. It's just that Willem and I were thinking of that. We'd seen a new version of *The Nutcracker* and they did that lift in the end, where Clara dances with the Prince, and it was so beautiful. But then we never got to it."

I exhaled, deflated. I couldn't take his idea. It might be like taking his place, which could of course never happen except symbolically in her mind.

"Oh, wow. I see." I thought a moment. "Okay, then we'll modify it. We'll just…" I thought, trying to come up with something just as majestic-looking without it being exactly the same.

"No, it's okay," she said. "I mean, it's really not that. It's not like anyone's taking anything from Willem. It's just that if I get the shaking, then it's going to be hard for me to maintain a shape and for you to keep hold of me." She spoke quickly, which made me think she knew what she wanted to say but just had a hard time saying it. Her eyes were darting all around. She took a deep breath. "Let's just try," she said. That was my usual line.

Awesome. She wasn't thinking of anyone replacing Willem. It was just about the tremor, which we could cure. I knew we could. "I won't let you fall, Belle. If you start to shake, I'll let you down immediately."

She held out her arm. The tremor was gone, at least momentarily. She smiled, looking down, like it was like a smile meant for herself and no one else. She blushed and put her head down, wrapping her arms around the back of her neck. She was going through something, something good, something positive, and well worth my wait. I wasn't about to invade her thoughts. I let her have her time. Finally, she brought her head up again, the smile having grown even larger, and nodded.

"I'm ready!" She threw her hands up.

We did it. I felt the strength in her body. She was solid but light all at once. I lifted her easily. And held her by the foot. I stood with my feet apart, looking up at her. She stood in my open palms, gingerly lifting one leg up in arabesque, both arms to the sky, her head following. Not a tremor in her entire body, from head to foot. I wrapped my hands around her feet. I was prepared to reach out and let her fall into my arms, if she had to. But she never did.

"I gotcha," I said.

"I know." Her words were almost a whisper. But I heard.

"Okay?" she said, calling down, but with her head still lifted toward the sun. As if the words came from somewhere else.

"Ready."

She brought her other leg down, placing both feet in my hands again, then lowered her arms parallel to her body.

"Okay, fall and I'll catch," I said.

And she did just that. I caught her in my arms, swung her around, turning around and around, raising her up and down with each turn. She laughed. Soon, she said, "Wait, wait."

I slowed my swinging, and then stopped. I had no idea why I had done that. The music had ended and this move didn't go along with it. It just felt right.

"I don't know what I'm doing. I'm just so happy you went for that and it was so gorgeous and you did it so expertly and…I'm just happy. Dancing for joy, I guess." I laughed.

"You know, in a weird way, that works," she said once I let her down. "I mean, swinging me around like that, turning for more beats than the music. Like we're not done just because the music is—like we have so much more. I mean, sometimes extending beats, or not doing things exactly to the music works well."

I thought about it. She was right. We could totally make my spontaneous choreography, derived from sheer elation, work for us.

As we were walking out of the practice room, something came over me. I couldn't help it, but I pulled her toward me and kissed her. It was quick, very, very quick. And it was only one small peck. But it was on the lips. I couldn't help it. "Sorry," I said immediately. "I don't know what came over me. Well, I do, actually. It was the dance." I looked into her eyes. They were alight. She said nothing. I didn't give her much of a chance, I guess. I did it again. And then I rushed out the door, wanting to kick my heels up like Gene Kelly.

36

Arabelle

This was going to work—Jett and me and Blackpool and the team. It was. He—Willem—had told me. I know that sounds ridiculous, but it's not. When Jett told me of the lift he was thinking of, I was thinking the exact same thing. Like we were on the same wavelength. Willem and I had been choreographing to completely different music, but with him I'd thought of it at the same time he did, too. For a moment my mind turned fully on Willem and the thought of him brought chills, and the tremor.

Initially, I cursed myself. I could never two-time Willem like that. And then, I swear, the most amazing, incredible thing happened. I felt a warmth spread throughout my body at the thought first of Willem and me doing the lift, then of Jett and me. My whole body became warm and strong. No chill. And no tremor. No cold, no shaking in my toes or in my fingers, no madly coursing blood. Everything was comforting, like I was cocooned in a diaphanous shell. And I felt Willem saying, "Go ahead. Do this. It's right." I felt it so strongly, I almost heard it. I sensed it through vibrations rippling through my body.

Thankfully, Jett gave me plenty time to think it all out and have that mental experience. When I looked into his eyes again, I knew it was right. I felt the warmth again, the soothing vibrations. And then we did it, and it was so, so special. We were inside, in a building with a ceiling, but I felt like I was right under the sun when I was at my highest during the lift. I felt my foot solid in Jett's hands, and I felt my entire body, warm and strong. I lifted my hands and face up to the sky and realized this was the absolute perfect tribute to Willem. I felt the sun on my face—his warmth—from Heaven.

When Jett let me down and began swinging me around in his arms—it's funny, but even though it didn't at all go with the music—it was like we were on the same wavelength again. He was perfectly expressing my joy at connecting with Willem, as he twirled me around and around. Jett felt happiness too, for his own reasons, in his own way. And he expressed it exactly the way I wanted him to. Major meeting of the minds, of the souls.

* * *

I NEVER ASKED and Jett never told me, but I assumed Veronique gave him the time off for Blackpool because he didn't return to his job. We spent the next several weeks practicing hard, both as a partnership and with the team. And practice made perfect as can be. We looked good, solid. We were ready.

* * *

BLACKPOOL HAD FINALLY ARRIVED. Jett had taken to kissing me every time we finished the routine. But the kisses were always short and sweet. It was clear—to both of us I think— that our relationship was platonic. I loved being with him, practicing, working on something we both wanted so badly, working towards a common goal. We had twin goals of making art and performing it on a world stage for everyone to see, and winning a big competition—both for Alessia's studio, and for ourselves. I was beginning to see I wanted to win not only for the sake of Infectious Rhythm and the team, but for myself, for Willem's memory, and now for Jett too. He was worth working for, winning for, even if he was just a good friend and dance partner, and always would be. Friend-ships and dance partnerships were just as important as romantic partnerships. Who ever said they weren't?

As Blackpool neared, I realized this was the first time I'd be there competing in the same competition Willem and I had, without Willem. I knew it was going to be difficult for me, to put it mildly. But I also knew Jett was going to make it okay.

We arrived a couple of days before our competition. Blackpool lasted for a week and was so much fun for ball-room people. It boasts the world's largest collection of dance costumes and paraphernalia, dance music CDs and DVDs, shoes, bags, makeup artists, and hair stylists. It's a mecca for ballroom enthusiasts. And everyone goes—professional dancers, students, and fans. I knew I'd see all my old friends there. I was worried I'd have to deal with everyone's looks of sympathy and sadness, and that I might have a hard time holding up. But Lucia convinced me that it had been long enough since Willem's death that people would be over it by now, and they would know I needed to move on as well. "They'll be thrilled to see you dancing with a new partner," she'd insisted.

Our competition was the second to the last night. Willem and I had always gone for the whole week anyway, just to revel in the glory of being ballroom dancers. But I didn't want to overwhelm myself. Last year was rough, mainly because I'd made the mistake of trying to commit myself too fast to a new dance style that I now admitted didn't fit me. Being so overwhelmed last year weakened me, which may have been partly why I hadn't seen that water bomb coming until it was too late.

Anyway, bygones are bygones, and I knew the same wouldn't happen again. In terms of the water bomb, I mean. But I also didn't want to weaken myself by getting too emotional, and that could easily happen right now. This year, we'd arrive two days before we danced, giving ourselves just enough time to unwind from the long flight, get our energy back, and practice a few times in the actual ballroom. I'd go for the full week next year—if there was a next year.

I booked us a hotel that was a little out of the way, not the hotel Willem and I and many of the other competitors stayed at. It was an idea that had good results, because we didn't run into anyone checking in, and the owners of the hotel didn't know me. It was nice to be anonymous for a while. Plus, I didn't want Jett getting bombarded with questions and looks the way newcomer Rory did last year when she went with Sasha, the star. Jett would be able to handle it for sure; he's a seasoned performer, and knows how to act like a star even if no one knows him. That's an art, I was beginning to realize. It was more that the attention given to us might enervate me. I didn't need to take any chances right now; chances would be for later.

After we checked in—blissfully, sans fanfare—I showed Jett around the little seaside town. I took him to my favorite little pub, far enough away from the Winter Gardens, which housed the ballroom, that we didn't run into anyone. We walked to the farmers' market and loaded up on some snacks, walked around the perimeter of the little mall, and then on the boardwalk by the sea. The night air in late May was chilly, but we dressed for it. I wrapped my heavy sweater around my shoulders and Jett wrapped his arms around my entire body. We walked side by side. I had to admit, it felt good being cocooned in his arms. Jett got a kick out the Ferris wheel and little amusement park down the boardwalk, the constant onslaught of advertisements for casinos and Vegas-style shows that were so not-Vegas, and the loads and loads of pinball machines.

"I know, cheesy. But, seriously, wait till you see the ballroom." I giggled.

"Are you kidding? No one knows cheese better than me. I lived in its capital." He laughed.

I laughed with him, agreeing that Las Vegas was, indeed, the cheesiest place on earth. But then it hit me what he'd just said. He "lived," as in past tense. Had I heard him properly? The Los Angeles tour was only for the spring. It would be ending very soon. We hadn't talked about the future—and we didn't need to since Blackpool was the only reason for our partnership, and it was happening now. I'd assumed he'd be going back to Las Vegas to work with Beauty in Motion. Unless he was going on tour again? Well, I wasn't going to broach it now. We needed to get through this first.

Of course a huge part of me didn't want him going back —either to that style of dance with all the risks, or to another city away from me. But why did I feel that way? We were friends. Our friendship wouldn't be hampered by miles. I thought about him performing with Beauty in Motion again, and my pulse momentarily stopped. But why? He wasn't mine and never would be. I couldn't worry about him. And I wouldn't, as long as we were only friends. I'd been so focused on Blackpool for the past several weeks I hadn't thought at all about the future, but I began to feel shivers making their way down my spine. I could feel tingling in the nerve endings in my wrist and fingers. No, I couldn't let this happen. No tremor, no thinking about Jett and Beauty in Motion, no thinking about the future. Only the here and now.

"Hey, you okay?" He probably felt the slight tremor.

"Yes, I'm fine." I laughed, shaking it off.

* * *

THE FOLLOWING night was the professional Latin competition. This was the comp most of my friends danced in, and generally the most popular comp among Blackpool fans. And it was the one I got hurt in last year. We had one more night until the showdance championship. At first I hadn't wanted to go to Latin night, but once I took Jett to see the immense ballroom, I knew I had to. The energy lit the place on fire. And so many of my friends were there. I had to cheer them on—particularly Drew and his new partner. Yes, I would be his loudest, greatest support.

"Whoa, this gives the word ballroom a new meaning." Jett looked around, taking it all in. "And grandiose, too." He laughed, shaking his head.

"Yep," I agreed.

I wore all black—long-sleeved black top, pants, and high boots. And I pulled my hair back. It wasn't that I didn't want to be seen; I didn't want to make it about me by dressing fancy, like so many other past champions did. Greta—my former coach and a Blackpool champ for ten years in a row before she retired—wore this floor-length red gown with a high collar that rose halfway to the back of her head. The whole thing was beaded with Swarovski crystals. She looked like Queen Elizabeth I. Everyone applauded like crazy when she entered. No matter who won tonight, she was still the star. On second thought, the star might have been Imelda—the champion throughout the entire eighties into the mid-nineties—who had her hair piled into a crown on the top of her head, her immaculate bun likewise beaded with diamonds. She wore an emerald gown with a several-foot long train. She got a standing ovation when she entered.

"This is a hoot!" Jett chuckled. "I mean, I watched all those Blackpool DVDs, but there's so much they don't show."

"You haven't been to Blackpool until you've literally been to Blackpool," I agreed.

"Hey, isn't that your old coach?" He pointed to Greta.

"Sure is!"

"She looks...like I've never seen her!"

Luna and Cheryl were here. I hadn't seen them yet, but I could sense them. They always came. Those women were toxic, and that toxicity just permeated the air. I felt it, I swear.

"Okay, I understand why the former champs are dressed to the nines, but why are *they* so dressed up?"

"Who?" I asked, but didn't have to. I knew he'd seen them.

He pointed to two women standing in an aisle about three rows down from us. "They look like nominees for an Academy Award." He cackled. I followed his finger to see he was totally point on. Luna wore a long gold dress with a short train, studded with sparkly things—probably actual diamonds, knowing her. She stood next to her cohort, Cheryl, who donned a red full-length satin number that was so tight it looked like she might suffocate. *Yes, they totally looked like they were at the Oscars*. Fans and students didn't dress like that—that look was reserved for ballroom royalty. They both looked ridiculous. I watched as people glanced at them, thinking they were someone famous, only to look away in confusion upon seeing an unrecognizable face peeking out of the top of the gown.

"They mistakenly think they own the place," I said, and right then caught Luna's beady eye. "Let's go to the other side. I think Drew may be over there."

"Whatever you say, sweet. You're the queen here." Jett kissed the crown of my head.

"Arabelle, is that you?" called out a voice I recognized but couldn't place at first. I looked over. It was Trudy Glenn, a former showdance champion from England. She was eighty now, and she looked gorgeous. She was definitely my model for aging. She always had the sweetest, most genuine smile. She was dressed in a skirt and blouse now. Tomorrow night would be her night to glam it up. "It *is* you!" she rushed toward me with open arms.

"Ms. Glenn!" I walked quickly toward her, equally open-armed.

"You look really beautiful, dear. I'm so glad you're back. They told me you might not be here this year, and I was just heartbroken. I thought, 'She has to come back and dance something, even another solo.' You're just too beautiful a dancer to miss." She patted me on the back as I tried hard to hold back the tears. The past champions were the sweetest, most endearing people. They were done with their competition careers, secure in their legacies, and could see only the beauty in the current crop. Their vision was completely uncorrupted by jealousy or competitiveness.

"Thank you so much. You don't know what it means to me to hear you say that, Ms. Glenn."

She held my shoulders and looked me straight in the eye. She opened her mouth to speak but then closed it. I could tell she wanted to ask me how it was going, how I was doing. But maybe she saw the hint of a tear in my eye and thought the better of it. She'd lost her husband years ago and she knew what it was like. That it wasn't something you ever got over or recovered from. It doesn't mean you don't go on living your life, of course. But the question 'how are you' after something like that is just too loaded.

She brushed her fingers along the bottom of my chin. "Well, I'm delighted you're here. It just wouldn't be Blackpool without you."

I closed my eyes to blink the tears away. She squeezed my hand.

"You are so kind," I said.

"And honest," she said.

I glimpsed her eyeing Jett. "Oh, this is my partner, Jett. Jett, this is Trudy Glenn, showdance champion for the entire 70s!"

She gave him a polite nod and took his hand in hers.

"Such an honor to meet you," he said, giving her a magnanimous little bow. Yes, Jett could be quite the charmer, which in this instance, made me proud.

"Now, I haven't seen what you can do yet, young man, but if Arabelle Fonseca has chosen you, you are clearly the best male show dancer out there." The way she said it, so bluntly and as if it was the objective truth and there couldn't possibly be any contradiction, made me giggle. His boyish smile brightened his entire face and shot a bolt of lightning down my spine. Ugh, that was going to happen again?

"Thank you so much, Miss," he said, a little blush now crawling across his cheeks. I loved how he called her 'miss.'

Ms. Glenn's very presence, her kind words to me and to Jett, her understanding look at me, and her decision not to ask if I was 'okay,' all made me just that—okay. More than okay. I was here, at Blackpool, now, and with Jett. We were about to dance, just like Trudy had once danced, and just as I had once danced with Willem. Time all blends together and the past is not really past.

Trudy kissed me on the cheek and squeezed my hand once more, before bidding Jett and me adieu in her elegant English way until tomorrow night.

I heard whispers, giggles begin. People had heard us greet each other, heard our names. I saw heads turning all around me.

"There she is!"

"She's here!"

"Is she dancing with that guy?"

"He's hot!"

"She looks awesome!"

I was shocked, but delightfully so. I heard no one saying, "Remember what happened last year? It's so sad. Remember Willem? It's so sad what happened to him." I heard none of the tragic, I heard only the happy chatter. I felt like thanking each and every one of them. Instead, I just smiled to myself, gave a few nods and pleasant grins, and reached for Jett's hand, pulling him to the other side of the ballroom to find Drew.

"That was fun." Jett kissed my head. "I'm clearly with the biggest celebrity here."

"Hardly." I laughed. "Especially tonight. Wait until the competition actually begins."

With that, the emcee announced the beginning of the first heat. The room went completely silent. I spotted Drew and his new partner, Carolina.

"There!" I squealed, pointing. I was suddenly very excited. The lights in the seating area dimmed and the crowd began to roar.

The emcee started announcing the numbers of the competitors. Thankfully, there were enough heats that we had plenty of time to work our way around the ballroom, to the standing area nearest Drew. Michaela and Jonathan, last year's second place finalists, were announced and the crowd went completely wild. They were the contestants most likely to win tonight, since Sasha and Rory were out due to Rory's pregnancy.

"See!" I shouted to Jett.

He laughed. "Yeah, I do. Again, it's so different being here. You definitely don't get the full effect on tape!"

When Drew's number was called, I screamed as loudly as I could. There were some roars, but not as loud as those for Michaela and Jonathan. He wasn't as well known, being a newer contender.

"Andrew, Carolina, go, go, go!" I screamed, pounding the air. Jett echoed me, hooting and whistling.

"Oh yeah, that's the guy who danced with Arabelle last year. And they almost won!" I heard someone say.

"Yeah, he placed third. Keep your eye on them, they're going to be finalists!" Another voice said.

"Is that Arabelle?" I could feel fingers pointing, but they were pointing in a good way. Soon, there was so much screaming and roaring that, with the music bellowing, I couldn't think. There was no contemplation about the past, about what I was doing here, just that I was. With Jett. He squeezed my hand right then, as if he could read my thoughts. I squeezed back.

About a quarter of the way through the competition, I led him outside to get some air and a bite to eat. There wasn't a huge food choice in Blackpool. There were a few good restaurants inside the Gardens, but everyone went there. A few blocks away, there was a little Italian bistro. It was by far the best place food- and atmosphere-wise, and it wasn't frequented by as many competitors as the Japanese place, also nearby. Still not wanting to run into too many people yet, I took Jett there.

"Sweet," he said as the waitress took us to a rather romantic, candlelit table in the back.

Don't get any ideas, I thought. "The food is very good. And it's away from the maddening crowd," I said, perhaps sounding more defensive than I'd intended to.

"I know, I know," he said. But then he flashed me those dimples, and my insides melted.

And then, it had to happen. The door opened, and in she whizzed—Natalia, dressed in a body-hugging crimson dress with the highest patent leather black pumps I think I'd ever seen. She fixed her eyes right on me. It was like she knew I was here before she came in. She was with only Duke, no Cheryl or Luna. At least, not right now.

"What is it?" Jett turned around to follow my gaze. "Oh shit. Pay her no mind, Arabelle."

"Of all the places to go for dinner. And so early. I brought us far from the ballroom and well before dinner time specifically to avoid something like this," I murmured, more to myself than to Jett. In all the years Willem and I had come here, I'd never seen her in here. She'd followed us; I was sure of it.

The waitress went to seat her and Duke on the opposite side of the restaurant. *Oh good*, I thought. But the fact that she plopped her bag on her seat, held a finger up to the waitress, and walked in our direction made it more than clear to me that she was here to harass us. Ugh.

"Just wanted to say hello, Arabelle." Her voice was high-pitched and squeaky, as if she was trying to be cute.

"Hello and goodbye," Jett said, not turning around.

"Well, that wasn't very nice at all." She acted aghast. "I'm just trying to be the big person here and congratulate you on showing up."

I frowned. What did she mean? Jett was buttering his bread, completely ignoring her.

"Showing up?" I shouldn't have encouraged her, I knew it.

"Yes, I mean, your injury was serious." She looked at Jett,

who was still focused on his bread, ignoring her. "I doubt you are actually at your top form now. But that's how some people just are…"

"Mmm, bread is pretty good. Soft and warm," Jett said to me. It made me giggle. But Natalia wasn't getting the hint. She wasn't leaving.

"And I know how hard it must be for you here. This is your first year without Willem. Well, your second I guess, but the first where you are actually competing with someone else in the same competition. That must be hard, trying to over-come his memory to be able to dance adequately with his replacement. In fact, it must be so hard to think of replacing him." Her words sounded completely rehearsed. "But, I saw you earlier today and you look so happy to be here. Getting over Willem must not have been as hard as I thought. Not as hard as it would have been for me, anyway…"

She kept going on but her words weren't registering anymore. Hearing her say Willem's name produced a slow coldness dripping down my spine, beginning in my chest then getting heavier as it made its way to my stomach, flooding every internal organ along the way. The words "memory," "replacement," and "overcome" struck my soul like an icepick, piercing my center and shocking every nerve. I began to tremble, but not just my hands. My entire being, beginning in my core, and emanating everywhere.

Jett saw what was happening to me and pushed his chair back so quickly and with such force that he ran right into her. The back of his chair hit her in the crotch and she nearly fell backward.

"Oh my god, what are you doing? You—" She stumbled, having to back away quickly or he would have accidentally run over her foot.

"What the hell were you doing there? You were on top of us," he roared. "I actually got some of your spit on my face."

His voice bellowed so loudly, she actually did stumble over her heel and fell backward.

"Now, get back to your little boy over there and stop harassing us. You are not to approach her again. Do you hear me?"

There was nothing but silence in the restaurant. Everyone was looking. Now Natalia was the one trembling. She tried to get up but couldn't seem to. So, she scooted on her hands and heels as quickly as she could back to her table. She looked like a crab. Duke remained glued to his chair, open-mouthed. I don't know if he was too scared to get up, but he did nothing to help her. Then I saw Cheryl and Luna peering into the restaurant through the window. They were both open-mouthed, but their faces looked like they were feigning shock.

Jett sat back down. He grabbed my hands across the table, his palms surrounding mine, his thumbs caressing my wrists. "Belle, you can't let her get to you. You know she's only trying to sabotage us by getting to you mentally. They know we can beat them and they're stopping at nothing to try to win."

"You, you twisted my ankle. If I can't dance, it's because of you," Natalia shrieked.

"Stop making stupid excuses for yourself," Jett said without looking back.

She continued to shriek and moan.

I nodded. He was right, and I knew it. But I still couldn't stop shaking.

Jett

If Natalia wasn't a woman, I'd have punched her right in her obnoxious little face. Yeah, I know, violence isn't the answer, but sometimes you just have to shut someone up. And now she'd gone and screwed with Arabelle's mind, which was far worse than screwing with her physically. She knew she couldn't beat us. So she took the only route she could—a low, low blow.

But she wasn't going to win. No way. I tried to calm Belle down over dinner, but every time I saw that fork rise from her plate of lasagna to her beautiful lips shaking like it was possessed, I had to calm myself down.

"You're not seriously taking in anything she said, right? I mean, you know her words are worthless. She's only trying to do whatever she can to screw us up. She's a low life. We're so far above her, it's not even funny." I didn't know what else to say. I didn't know what to say about Willem and our partnership having nothing to do with disrespecting his memory.

I was afraid I'd screw it up, so I just focused on Natalia being a total coward.

Arabelle nodded. "I know that. Of course I do." She looked out the window. "Her words about Willem initially stung, and then I forced them aside. I don't feel guilty for dancing with you after Willem. Willem wants that. I don't know how to explain how I know that, but I do."

I put down my fork and wrapped my hand around hers. She smiled, still looking out the window.

"But then I started remembering the accident. My accident, I mean. Seeing Natalia fall actually brought back those memories from last year of the Latin competition, of when I fell. And then I saw the faces of Luna and Cheryl peering through the front window and I just—"

"Yeah, I saw them too."

"It makes me think they're up to something, which unnerves me."

"Belle, they're harmless here. That's what you and Alessia said, right? That they have no power here."

She nodded. "Yes, that's true."

"Belle, we can't let them get to us. That's what they want. They want you to shake, they want us to wobble. We have to be strong and solid and impenetrable."

She already seemed to know that. She was smiling and I felt her hand starting to lose some of its jitteriness. Not all, but some. I knew we could do it. "That's my girl." I drew her hand toward me and gave it a big kiss.

"Jett, I don't know...I don't know that the tremor was ever about Willem. He knows I'm here, and I don't know how to explain it, but I feel that he's happy I'm here, that *we're* here. It's nothing tangible, but I can sense it."

"Senses are so much more profound than physicality, Arabelle. Of course he's happy that you're here doing what you love, what your passion is, what you were put on this earth to do. How could he not be? He loves you."

She closed her eyes and smiled.

We finished our dinner without talking about or looking at Natalia and company. Coven was more like it. We walked out, hand in hand. And Arabelle's hand wasn't shaking one bit.

Arabelle wanted to go back and watch Drew. The ballroom was packed, and completely alive. There were practically no free spaces, even for standing. The crowd was raucous, everyone cheering for their hero and heroine. The band was on fire, the dancers exploding with energy; it was like how I imagined the Olympics to be. It was so different from the crowds at a concert dance performance, where everyone's generally pretty quiet until the end. This was a very different world from mine. It was, in a word, thrilling.

Arabelle somehow found us some space with a decent view. We watched all the way through to the finals. I had to admit, Arabelle's ex-partner was pretty awesome. And the judges thought so too, as he and his new partner came in second—a step up from his and Belle's rank last year. They placed right after last year's second place champs, Michaela and Jonathan.

"This is enormous for him!" Belle squealed. "Even though everyone knows when Sasha and Rory return they're going to take first again, and Michaela and Jonathan may well take second, it's still huge. They could be the champs someday." She cheered louder than everyone. I wondered how she'd be able to talk the next day.

After she hugged Drew, we took a cab back to our hotel, since we were staying so far out of the way. We could have walked, but we decided to save all of our energy for our rehearsal and performance tomorrow night.

We woke up early, had a nice big breakfast at the quiet little hotel, showered, and were off for practice. The ballroom had a rehearsal area in back. We went over the routine a couple times, first marking it out, then dancing it full out. Then we did the same thing in the ballroom before it opened to the public, wanting to mark everything in the space where we'd perform it so there'd be no surprises. Fortunately and surprisingly, we didn't run into you-know-who and her people. I was thinking they might show up to harass us more, but they didn't. I have to say we danced the routine as perfectly as possible. There were no flubs, no missteps. And no tremor. We were perfectly in time to the music, and perfectly in character. Everything felt so right. Everything felt so beautiful.

"That was simply awesome," I said, after I let her down at the end of the last lift.

"You are the antithesis of crazy, demanding Sasha in a wonderful, wonderful way," she said, giggling. I wasn't sure exactly what she meant and had a hard time taking it as a compliment given he was a world champion and all. But her giggles were priceless, as was the kiss she planted on my lips right after she said it, ever so briefly but ever so certainly, and so non-platonically. Hmm. I tried not to focus on how that made me feel—like I'd shot straight to the moon.

And that's when the coven made its pathetic entrance. I heard a "tsk, tsk, tsk," coming from the side of the room. We both turned to see Natalia standing in the corner, shaking both her head and wickedly long-nailed index finger at us as if she'd caught us red-handed doing something we should be very ashamed of. Luna and Cheryl stood on either side of her with twin expressions, hands on hips, nasty glares in their beady little eyes. Another big difference between this world and concert dance—the degree of sabotage attempts.

"Get lives, psycho ladies," I whispered to Arabelle, leading her away, before Natalia could say anything. We heard only harrumphing as we went. At first I'd thought we should stay and watch our competition, since we were allowed to. But when I'd mentioned it to Arabelle, she'd shaken her head.

"Why bother? It's not like we're going to be wowed by anything and change our routine last minute. Too risky to change at this point."

I actually agreed with her, which wasn't like me at all. Risky had been my middle name. But she was right. If we changed last minute a new trick wouldn't be in our muscle memory well enough and we might flub it. Plus it probably wouldn't be in the character of the dance. Our routine couldn't rock any better than it already did; I was sure of it.

So we went back to the hotel, relaxed, ate a good meal, and took a nap. We were on at eight o'clock sharp. Best to get a good rest in.

When the alarm woke us up, I was spooning Arabelle, cradling her closely in my arms. Interesting, because we hadn't fallen asleep that way. She smiled and I could see her trying to cover a little blush with her hand while she made her way to the bathroom to wash up. When she turned toward me just before shutting the bathroom door, we made eye contact and I raised my eyebrows. She squinted playfully at me. "Okay, enough goofing. It's show time," she said, and shut the door.

Arabelle

What was the man trying to do to me? It was just a couple of hours before the most important dance of our careers, and he was being all flirty! The bolt of electricity that cocky raised eyebrow had shot through my core, to my womb, to my thighs, kept me warm through my entire shower.

Fortunately, he managed to behave himself the entire time we were getting ready. I had the makeup artist I usually used come to the hotel and help us prepare. I was more of a homebody than many of the other dancers, who all seemed to love getting ready either in the tents in the pavilion near the ballroom or in the ballroom changing areas with the other dancers. I needed to be alone, especially before a competition. It had always been a point of contention between Willem and me. He'd thrived on being the center of attention, clowning with the others until it was time for us to go on. He'd been so uncompetitive, and more the kind of guy who was easily everyone's friend. He had been far more comfortable in crowds than I was.

Here, at Blackpool, I could really see the differences between Willem and Jett. Jett was more competitive, and actually, contrary to what I'd originally thought when I met him in Vegas, did not have a need to be in the center of things. Not offstage, anyway. He had a greater need to prepare for the challenge ahead than to play the crowd. He didn't put up any fight whatsoever when I asked him if he minded getting ready in the hotel room instead of in the ballroom, like the others.

"I can't imagine doing it any other way," he said.

We arrived at the hotel an hour and a half early, which was perfect. It gave us time to stretch, do a bit of in-place cardio, greet fans and friends, and mentally prepare again, now with the crowd surrounding us.

Now that I was in show dancer mode and dress, everyone recognized me, and, happily, only had encouraging things to say.

"So glad to see you back, Arabelle," said a fan I didn't personally know.

"Can't wait to see what the two of you can do together," chirped another, eyeing Jett.

"The start of a lovely new partnership," pronounced a sweet, white-haired British lady.

"Arabelle, you look breathtaking, as always," said Letitia, a show dancer I'd known for a few years who, with her partner, usually placed near the bottom of the finalists.

Natalia seemed to be the only one fixated on Willem. Thinking of last night momentarily made me shudder—but only momentarily. *No thinking nasty thoughts, no letting her get to you*, I told myself. This ended up not being tremendously hard, given that she still hadn't shown up with only minutes before the competition was set to begin. I wondered where she was. I think we all did, judging by the confused looks and noise from the ballroom floor once the emcee took the microphone to announce the showdance comp. There was some whispering among the dancers and judges, and the emcee put the mic down again.

"Do we know where they are?" he said, perturbed.

More chatter. The audience seemed to be getting restless as well.

"I wonder what's up," I said to Jett.

"I dunno. Some drama. Doesn't surprise me, actually."

"She hasn't done this before."

"What's the protocol—" a judge began, but then stopped. "Oh, never mind."

I followed his gaze. Natalia and Duke had just walked through the corner door. She was wearing a purple mesh costume with cut outs strategically darkening certain places, like nipples and her crotch. The rest of the costume was completely see-through. It was a beautiful costume, I had to admit. I'd be too nervous to wear it for showdance, where you're basically doing air acrobatics, but it would be lovely for staying put on the ground and not being so afraid of costume malfunctions. I felt Jett's hand squeezing mine. Right, I was paying her no mind. I started to look away, right when I sensed her piercing eyes trying to penetrate me.

From the corner of my eye it looked like she was trying to come up with something to say to me, perhaps some snide remark about how I was cheating on Willem or some kind of threat. She wasn't very far from me. But then I felt Jett's lips press warmly against my left cheek, the side of my face from which I could glimpse Natalia in my periphery. He was preventing me from looking at her.

"Ladies and gentlemen," the emcee began. "This is one of our most prestigious competitions, as dancers have to be specially invited to compete by our judging panel. These, ladies and gentlemen, are thereby the best show dancers in the world today." The audience went wild with applause.

"Arabelle!" I heard. Then chants began. "Arabelle, Arabelle, Arabelle, Belle, Arabelle!" They were accompanied by clapping, which soon grew to be in rhythm. Jett smiled, and put his arm around my waist, doing a little side hug. He then kissed my temple. The audience went wilder. And I heard several, "Awwws." No one seemed to mind that Jett was not Willem. They were happy that I was here to dance with a new partner.

There were no chants for Natalia, but it was almost worse that way; I could really sense the heat of her anger. She was only two couples down from me and I could literally feel ire radiating from her body.

The emcee graciously waited a few moments for the chants and applause to stop, then laughed and said, "Okay, okay now, let's get to the issue at hand." He called the names of the ten contestants and in the order we would dance. Natalia and Duke were second to last; we were last. More crazy applause when our names were called—and more heat from Natalia. I heard her speaking in Russian, either to Duke or to another couple. I didn't know what she was saying but they were angry words. She was not happy to be dancing second to last. It was always worst to dance first since the judges couldn't give you top scores; they had to reserve room for better performances. It was best to dance last, but close to last wasn't bad either. They could give Natalia and Duke almost perfect scores and if we weren't perfect, then we wouldn't win. It was that simple. It actually put pressure on us, if you looked at it that way—which she, it seemed, wasn't.

"Come on," Jett said, leading me off the floor so the first couple could begin. I actually didn't like to watch other performances until I'd gone. Early on in my career, when Willem and I had danced first or closer to first, I'd watch everyone after I'd gone. I loved watching the other dancers because I still had so much to learn from them. But when we started doing well and began winning and the judges placed us farther to the end, I didn't want to watch until we'd danced. Instead, I'd get whatever learning I needed by watching the videos afterward.

"You want to go into the practice room?" Jett asked me. It seemed he already knew how I felt, though I hadn't remembered telling him.

"You read my mind," I said.

"Of course I did. I've been doing that for a while now." He laughed.

Hmm, was that true? I wondered.

"Just as long as you-know-who doesn't show up here," he added as we walked into the empty room.

"She's usually a watcher," I said. And I was right. She didn't show up to torment us.

We did basic dance moves to keep us warmed up, along with a bit of stretching. Soon, the judge's assistant popped his head in and told us to start making our way out to the deck; there were only two couples ahead of us. It always surprised me how quickly these dances went. We were limited to three minutes of music, so, allowing for audience applause and sweeps of the floor in between each dance, the whole comp lasted under an hour.

The bad thing about Natalia and Duke going right ahead of us meant we had to be in the ballroom and ready to go on deck during their routine.

"We'll stay in back, keep focused on the deck, and go over when it clears," Jett said, again reading my mind. I nodded. We walked into the ballroom, where it was quite warm due to all the bodies and all the excitement. Several heads turned when we came through the door.

Natalia and Duke's music began. Fortunately, we were in the back and couldn't see the dance floor over all the heads.

"Belle, Arabelle," one man said, giving me a little wave. I smiled and waved back. A few other heads turned and several people clapped in our direction and waved.

"Good to see you back, Belle Arabelle," someone said. It was a little embarrassing given Natalia and Duke's dance had begun, but I smiled at everyone. Jett squeezed my hand.

"Shhh," someone else whispered.

Suddenly, a chorus of *ohhhhhhh*s took over the room. Something happened on the floor. It didn't sound good. I could see Leticia and her partner from where we stood. They were watching as well. She covered her mouth; her partner was open-mouthed. Something had happened to Natalia and Duke. A bolt went through my body. They'd messed up. But were they hurt? I didn't want to know this right now. I didn't want to be out here right now. Someone else screwing up and possibly getting hurt, even if they were my adversaries, made me very uneasy. Jett squeezed my hand more. I looked up at him. He shook his head and shrugged his shoulders. He couldn't see anything either.

"You want me to go look?"

I shook my head.

There was a strained silence followed by clapping. The music swelled to its crescendo and there was silence. The audience seemed nervous. The music ended and the applause began.

There were a few moments where there seemed to be chaos. Chatter, angry words spoken by someone in Russian. There were lots of Russians here—both competitors and audience members—so I didn't know who said what. Natalia and Duke had exited on the other side of the ballroom. I still couldn't see what was going on, and I didn't want to see. I continued squeezing Jett's hand.

After they exited the commotion continued. I heard more angry words spoken in Russian, a few yells, and some chatter. I still didn't look out on the floor. As long as the floor was safe from water bombs—I'm pretty sure it was, or there would be a little more chaos than this—I was okay with remaining in the dark about things in the moments before we performed.

Finally, we were announced. The angry words were overtaken by applause and "Belle Arabelle" chants. Jett gave my hand one final squeeze, shot me one final charmingly dimpled smile, and led me to the center of the ballroom floor.

As usual, the lights on the audience dimmed and the spotlight centered on us. Once we were out there, I couldn't see anything or anyone but Jett.

"Okay," the emcee said, indicating he would start the music in a couple seconds.

Jett gave me a nod and a smile, then took me in his arms for our beginning pose.

The crowd filled with *awwwws* and applause as he wrapped his arms around me and slowly began to lift me.

The music began, slowly, and we started our cradle lift that would turn into the overhead bird lift. The crowd was right there with us, already cheering before we'd hardly even begun to dance. He lifted me higher and I turned my face up, to the heavens. Something happened at that point. A light began to shine down, but it was a soft light. Like it wasn't real in the sense that anyone else could see it. It flooded my whole body with warmth, producing a comfort that told me no matter what happened, it was all okay. Everything was good. Everyone was happy and at peace. My life would be full of peace. I almost couldn't even feel Jett underneath me, but the music told me we were right where we were supposed to be. I knew it was another of Willem's blessings from above, and at the most important time. It was a blessing that made it all worth it to come here, to have found Jett, to be alive.

The music changed to a faster tempo and I was back with Jett, right on point, right on the beat, being lowered in his arms into our fish dive, before being placed on the floor. I was grounded again. The crowd went wild for our opening lift sequence, which felt perfect.

I brought my eyes back to Jett as he whipped me around into a series of turns. The cheering grew louder as we danced faster. We both knew the steps backward and forward; they were so totally in our muscle memories—or muscle memory, singular, since it seemed to be a collective one. I hadn't felt that for a while, not since Willem. Jett and I were dancing as one, just as Willem and I did.

As we went into a slower part and began another lift sequence, I felt Jett guiding me, taking care of me. I knew what I was doing, of course, but I felt so secure in his arms. I knew he would take care of anything that got in my way, any outside attempts to sabotage, like a water bomb. I'd thought of what had happened last year to Drew and me before we went on, but forced myself to banish it from my mind. But now it was as if I didn't even care. Nothing could hurt me because I was dancing with Jett.

The music swelled and the lyrics about the woman following the man wherever he went, even into eternity, began. I loved these words, and knew them so well. They were like a favorite poem to me. I'd loved this song since I heard it over a decade ago, I think. But Willem had always wanted to dance to faster music. Funny but it hit me only now that Jett and I were finally doing the dance I'd envisioned for so long.

We did a snazzy quickstep sequence and I felt like I was gliding on air; it was all so smooth. Jett really was an amazing

mover. He could do smooth ballroom, rhythmic Latin ballroom, and ballet and lyrical dance with equal amounts of
ease and charisma. He could make anything look flashy. I
could tell by the way the crowds went wild over our Viennese Waltz portion, where we did lightning fast turns though
our feet never left the ground.

We were nearing the end, with our most challenging lift
sequence. This is where my tremor, if it happened, would
really kill us. I concentrated on balancing, on strengthening
my core, and helping Jett get me into the air. But his arms
were so strong. I knew he could hold me up completely.
Somehow his strength told me, without him having to say it,
that it didn't even matter if my tremor happened. We'd be
okay; he'd make sure of it.

He lifted me to his waist, then chest, then up over his
head. I soared as the music hit a crescendo and the two souls
declared their undying love for each other. Jett spun me
around and around in the air. I kept my eyes tightly closed so
I wouldn't get dizzy. He suddenly stopped, gazed up at me.
He gingerly removed one hand, holding his palm open. I
stepped onto it with one leg, slowing extending the other
back in arabesque. His palm was so large and so steady and
secure that I balanced easily on it as I reached up for the
heavens, arching my back even more. I slowly brought my
hands together, in a prayer. The audience seemed stunned
silent. This was an extremely hard move and if I trembled at
all, it would never have worked. I needed all the concentration I could to maintain my balance. They knew that as well.
This was an audience mainly of dancers or watchers who
knew dance so well, they understood exactly how every lift
worked, and what everything required. And they honored
that, allowing us our concentration.

Just as the thought entered my mind that Natalia or her
cohorts may try to sabotage us by doing something to ruin

my concentration, that same feeling I'd had at the beginning of the dance overtook me. That feeling of light shining down on me and lifting the psychic burdens I'd been carrying without fully realizing it. I looked to the heavens with my hands clasped together, raised high above my head. And I felt it. Willem was not going to let any evil come to us. Nor was Jett. And, most importantly, Willem gave me his blessing to do what I was doing, to dance with Jett. I actually heard a sound in the distance—a rumbling—and some angry words. But it was all in the background. I was protected by the light, by wonder, by those I loved and who loved me, and I was able to completely ignore it.

Slowly I began to hear cheers as Jett reached back to me with his other hand, holding me two-handed now. As soon as he had me in a secure position the audience erupted with cheers. And I smiled. I knew Jett was in his element, thrilling the crowd, while creating an evocative, memorably beautiful image with me.

As the music came to its end, Jett let me down, rolling me into a waist-high fish dive.

As soon as we were steady and ready with my leg wrapped firmly around his back, he let go of me with both hands, my body wrapped around his through the strength of my leg. The music sounded its final beat and we held the pose for several seconds. It was hard as hell to hold myself up for so long but it was worth it to hear the roar of the crowd, who knew how difficult it was. Jett lived for the thrill, for this kind of wowing the audience, and I did it in large part for him. He'd held me up, helped me to get rid of that horrible tremor, and I owed it to him to keep the audience cheering for as long as I could. I owed it to myself as well. It felt good to use my muscles in a way that they hadn't been used in so long—in too long.

The emcee announced our names once again, not

needing to say "let's give a round of applause." Jett put his arms around my waist, and brought me back onto my feet. We took our bows to a deafening chorus of "Belle Arabelle" chants. Jett twirled me around to face a different section of the audience, and we took bows again, as was customary, until we'd completed all four directions. At the end, he twirled me into him. When he stopped me, he wrapped his arms around me and looked deeply into my eyes. His gaze was so intense. I actually had to catch my breath, not from our movement but from his soul-piercing eyes.

"I love you," he mouthed, before placing his lips softly on mine. It was a sweet, light kiss, but given the words he'd uttered before it, it was everything. The audience went even wilder with their chants, and I realized that no one was thinking any less of me for having another partner now, least of all Willem. The whole room was filled with a radiance even brighter than when we were dancing. He was giving us his blessing. And I was taking it. I was in love with Jett, and I was going to be with him.

"Ah, now I know why we were last!" Jett laughed. At first I didn't know what he meant but then I felt something fall at my feet. I looked down to see a beautiful bouquet of flowers. Soon, bouquets came flying at us from all directions. Jett caught some of them. I laughed too. This had happened the last time Willem and I performed, when we were on last. I laughed so hard I nearly began to cry. Then Jett bent down on one knee, and presented me with one of the bouquets he'd caught, one bearing all red roses. I laughed more, tears now in my eyes. He didn't say anything but I understood what he was asking—could we go back to being more than just dance partners? And the answer was yes, even if he was going to return to his Vegas job. I loved him and I couldn't help it. Sometimes you just can't help who you fall in love with. I nodded tearfully. The crowd screamed.

The emcee gave us our moment, then announced that the floor needed to be cleared so the judges could present the awards. Jett walked around picking up as many bouquets as he could, and I followed his lead, doing the same. Drew actually skipped onto the ballroom floor and helped us.

"Oh, it's you! Thank you!" I said.

"You did it!" He wrapped his arms around me, full though they were of flowers.

"So did you!" I squealed.

He laughed. "I am so proud of you, girl!"

"Me too! Me too!" And I meant I was proud of both him and myself. I'd performed the whole dance completely sans tremor.

All couples took the floor and the judges announced the winners in reverse order. Natalia and Duke came in second, and we won. It almost felt unnecessary for the emcee to make the announcement. It was not so much because the crowd's eruption made it clear we were their favorite, but because I'd already knew I'd won. I'd won because I'd returned to the dance that was my life's passion, I'd done so with a new man and a man I loved, and I'd overcome my evil tremor.

I was so secure in knowing I'd won so many things tonight that it didn't even faze me when the commotion began—commotion I knew in my heart of hearts was coming. Because the ballroom world, wonderful as it was, included people like Natalia.

Just as the presenter was about to place the gold medal around my neck, there were loud, angry words. And they were hers. I'd realized it was her voice that I'd heard during the most difficult part of our routine. It hadn't fazed me then, and it wasn't going to do so now, even as the emcee told the presenter to stop. She mouthed "I'm sorry," and took the medal from my neck, holding it. There was apparently a contention that needed to be addressed.

Now Jett had a tremor. Not the same kind as mine, not at all. He was downright shaking—with anger. His hand made a fist, as if he were about to haul off and hit someone. I forced his hand open and squeezed his palm. Whatever ridiculousness was going on, he didn't need to become a part of it.

39

Jett

I really felt like hauling off and hitting Duke. Of course it wasn't his fault; he wasn't responsible for his partner. But I'd never physically hurt a woman. But beautiful Belle stopped me with her sweet caress.

I'd never felt better about any performance in my life as I did now. We more than nailed the steps. We gave the most moving, transcendent performance of our careers—or at least, of mine. We killed the tricks and wowed the audience, but we created a beautiful dance that was full of meaning and poetry and love. And I was so in love with this woman. I was never more proud of anyone in my life than of Arabelle. And myself, actually. She had no tremor whatsoever, and I did everything she wanted, making no demands of my own for once. Because my demands were silly. Her vision and her ideas were everything. They were perfect for me, for us. I needed to be with Arabelle. We were meant to be partners, in dance and in life. She brought out the best in me, and made me full, to make a massively clichéd understatement.

But now Natalia was trying to take our medal away, shaking her boney finger at me repeatedly and screaming something between Russian and English to all the judges, who'd gathered around.

From what I could understand of her English anyway, she was saying, "He cheated. He tried to maim me. My foot. He hurt me so I fall." We hadn't seen her and Duke perform but I pieced together that she must have fallen during her routine and was blaming it on what had happened at the restaurant yesterday when I'd backed up my chair and her foot was there.

I shook my head. I didn't really know what to say because I didn't understand all of what she said. She wasn't letting me get a word in edgewise, anyway. The judges looked back and forth between us. It nearly killed me when the judge directed the presenter to take Arabelle's medal. I grew so angry my whole body started shaking. I felt a fist forming in my right palm. I was so angry this woman wanted to take away what we had worked so hard for, and won. And that's when Arabelle unwrapped my fist, caressing my palm, squeezing it.

"Don't give in to her," she whispered.

I breathed deeply, trying to calm myself.

"Let's go into the back," the head judge said. "Natalia, Arabelle, Duke, and Jett. Come on." He motioned for us to follow him. The emcee began explaining to the audience that there was to be a brief hearing before resuming. The ballroom echoed with the loudest *boooo*s I'd ever heard. Damn right it should. I turned around, looked into the audience, and punched the air, letting everyone know I was going to fight this to the nail. They went wild and soon a chorus of "Jett, go!" overtook the boos. Arabelle giggled and wrapped her arm around me.

We got to the back, to the practice room, and the head judge told everyone to find a seat. All of the judges sat up front, while Arabelle and I sat at one table, with Duke and Natalia at another. Duke's face was bright red. I didn't know if it was because of anger or embarrassment, or just the pressure of partnering with this woman.

There was some commotion at the door. We all turned around to see Luna and Cheryl walking in.

"No, no, no. This is private," the head judge said.

"But we are witnesses," Luna said, not stopping.

"I said no. You will have your time when we call you," the judge insisted. He texted something on his phone and two security guards walked in.

"Escort them out, please," he said to them, motioning to the women. "I will let you know when they are needed, if they are needed, and you can escort them back in."

Luna and Cheryl looked at each other, their mouths open, aghast. Cheryl harrumphed. Luna began to protest. Apparently they'd never heard the word 'no' directed at them before.

After the door closed behind them, the judge addressed me. "Natalia is saying that you harassed her and wounded her foot yesterday in an attempt to sabotage them." He seemed to roll his eyes as he spoke, making me wonder if she often made such accusations when she didn't win. "This despite the fact that she still placed second, after a serious mistake, which she says occurred because of the wounded foot. I would like you to tell me your side of the story, sir."

I nodded. "Yes, sir." I told him exactly what had happened, emphasizing how Natalia had tried to get to Arabelle mentally, how Arabelle had begun shaking and how I had backed up to get out of my chair to stand and ask her to leave. I had no control over the fact that her foot was right behind my chair, and I hadn't know it was, and hadn't meant to bump into her.

The judge nodded. "Do you have anything to add?" he asked Arabelle.

"Judge, my version of the events is the same. We asked her to leave us alone and she would not. I was sitting across from Jett and he merely backed his chair out to get up. I didn't know Natalia was so close behind him partly because she'd made me upset and I was looking down as he backed out. But before, when I'd looked straight at her, I had noticed she was kind of gutting herself over his chair to stare me down. But I wasn't thinking of it when I looked down. He had no way of knowing she was on top of him. And he never touched her again. She backed away and he had words with her but he didn't touch her."

The judge nodded again. "We have a few witnesses. Bring them in," he shouted toward the door. "One at a time."

Cheryl testified that she and Luna were watching through the window and saw me back up my chair. Right before I backed up I glanced over my shoulder to make sure that my chair leg would go right over her foot.

I shook my head, feeling my anger return. Arabelle patted me on the arm.

Cheryl continued, claiming that after I made sure I hurt Natalia's foot, I threw the chair aside and began walking over her.

"He walked over her?" the judge asked, dubious.

"Yes." Cheryl nodded.

"How exactly did he do that?"

"Well, she was down on the floor since he'd run over her with the chair, and then he walked right on top of her."

"On top of her body?"

"Yes, on top of her body!" Cheryl rolled her eyes, as if the judge was an idiot.

The judge raised his eyebrows. It was probably not a good

idea to ridicule the judge as she seemed to be doing. "Which parts of her body did he walk over?"

Cheryl harrumphed.

"Her arms, her legs, her torso, her pelvis?" the judge asked.

"Yes!" Cheryl shouted.

"All of them?" The judge frowned.

"Yes! That's what I'm telling you!"

The judge looked dubiously at the other judges before returning his attention to Cheryl. "Well, he didn't seem to hurt any of her other body parts as he literally stepped his entire weight all over her body."

"I don't know. She was hurting pretty badly," Cheryl said.

Luna said the exact same thing, including the walking all over her. They'd clearly rehearsed the ludicrous lie.

"Did he step on her hands, thighs, stomach?" the judge asked. "Where exactly did he walk?"

"Just all over her, like I said!" Luna seemed equally annoyed by the specificity of his questions.

During their testimony, two judges had actually gone to the restaurant and returned with two employees to testify— our waitress and a bartender. At first I was worried Natalia had paid them off or something, because it was weird they were ready to testify. But fortunately, they told the truth. The waitress said she hadn't noticed anything was going on until Natalia started screaming that I'd hurt her. She couldn't tell how Natalia had been hurt, since by that time I was standing several inches from her and she was far away from the chair. She hadn't seen me move the chair and she'd never seen me touch Natalia.

The bartender saw me back up the chair. He said he was surprised because it looked like Natalia saw me backing up and, though she had plenty of room behind her, made no effort to get out of the way. "I know this is strange, but it actually looked like she wanted to get hurt," he said.

Thank you, dude, I thought.

The head judge told us all to go out to the ballroom while they made their decision. The other couples were still out on the floor. The audience began cheering. Belle and I paced up and down the narrow hallway area separating the dance floor from first row of seats. She stopped me, grabbed my hand, and held it. I looked down into her eyes. There was a shine in her eyes, almost diamond-like, and her eyes lit up her whole face. They lit up the whole friggin' room.

"I want to win, Jett. Obviously. For Alessia, for us. But, honestly, whatever happens, I'm so happy. We won in my heart. I didn't have the tremor, and we worked out this routine together, each of us with equal input. This was *our* dance—our perfect dance. I don't care what the judges say. We won."

I smiled down at her. I went to cup her chin in my hand but she beat me. Her lips were on mine before I knew it. The kiss was long, serious, and full of intent—full of non-platonic intent, that is. I went to pick her up and kiss her more deeply, but the emcee's voice interrupted us.

"Ladies and gentlemen, the judges have made a decision. All the competitors out on the floor, please."

We all walked out to the floor as the "Belle Arabelle!" and "Go Jett!" chants began.

"I'm sorry, but I need it quiet please," the emcee said. *Uh-oh*, I thought. Given that they were cheering us on, this may be a serious upset to the audience. I held Arabelle's hand, squeezing her palm.

When the chanting stopped, the emcee continued, "There has been a contesting of the results due to cheating. The new results are as follows." He went through the results again, but starting at ninth place instead of tenth. Chatter in the ballroom abounded. Belle and I looked at each other, frowning. All the couples looked at each other. What was going on? Why did they start at ninth place? Had someone been disqualified?

Natalia was the only one whose eyes weren't darting around. She looked rather smug, in fact. Duke looked down. All the results up to second place were the same, with each couple having advanced one notch. Now he was up to first place. Natalia and Duke and Belle and I were all still standing. One of the couples had clearly been eliminated and didn't place. Confused chatter overtook the ballroom.

"The first place winners, ladies and gentlemen... Arabelle Fonseca and Jett Ridley!" The confused chatter turned to cheers. Arabelle simply shrugged and said, "See, they agree with me." I didn't have time to bask in the glory of our win because the judge continued.

"Ladies and gentlemen, there's been a disqualification." The room was completely silent. "This committee takes its job very seriously. We absolutely will not condone frivolous allegations. We find that Natalia Beloserkovskiy and Duke Gozzoli have done that with their charges. We find not only that they have no merit, but that they were frivolously raised only to change the results and were based upon untruths. We hereby disqualify the aforementioned couple from this year's competition. Again, your winners, ladies and gentlemen," he said, extending his hand to us.

The audience went wild with applause again, which soon became deafening. *Now* was the time for basking in our glory. I picked Arabelle up, raised her high above my head, then brought her down to eye level—well, mouth level. And I planted a big, very serious one on her.

EPILOGUE

Arabelle

The studio was packed. Jett and I had decided to give an encore performance at the big midsummer studio party. It was a couple of months after Blackpool, and we'd basically recovered all the students who'd left Infectious Rhythm for Natalia's studio, and then some. Well, besides the coven—Cheryl and Luna—thankfully. Most people over there were not happy with the fact that Natalia had been disqualified from the world's most prestigious showdance championship because she'd lied to organizers in order to get her competition disqualified. She'd single-handedly given the studio a bad reputation. To save face—and her job—she'd turned around and blamed it on Cheryl and Luna, and said it was their hairbrained idea since it had worked in the regional U.S. competition earlier. I actually felt a bit sorry for the owner; you couldn't blame him for wanting to hire such star dancers and it wasn't his fault they'd gone behind his back and behaved so badly. He tried to save his studio by firing them. It was anyone's guess where they'd show up next. They were certainly banned from Infectious Rhythm over the problems they'd repeatedly caused us in both competitions.

Sasha and Rory showed up at the celebration. "We have two Blackpool champions at IR now!" Alessia hooted. Rory and Sasha were hugely popular the world over. I loved that we shared the same studio. They didn't dance; she was very pregnant, her face glowing. The students wanted an update on their lives.

"Well, I guess you can kind of tell what we've been up to." She laughed, pointing at her enormous belly. "Other than that, I've been preparing for the baby, doing work on the trial I'd worked on before I came here, and peeking in on Sasha's filming! As you may remember, after Blackpool last year Sasha was cast in both a movie and a documentary. The film wrapped last month. It's in editing and is scheduled to premiere in April. They've given me their word you will all be invited to the Hollywood screening!" Everyone screamed. "As for upcoming plans, we will continue work on the documentary later this year, after we acclimate to life as a threesome. And, next year, we plan to tour with Jett's new company!"

Now I squealed with delight.

In the past two months since Blackpool, Jett had made me so, so happy by deciding not to return to Beauty in Motion. He explained that now that he'd worked with me and we'd done so well together that he no longer believed in the thrill aspect of dance alone. He didn't want to subject himself to danger just for big audience-wowing stunts. There had to be art involved. But since Blackpool only came around once a year, and there were no more prestigious championships than that, he didn't think he would be satisfied only doing the competition circuit. He was a performer, and now a choreographer, with lots more stories to tell through movement.

So, he decided to follow in his father's entrepreneurial footsteps after all, albeit not in real estate, but as founder of his own dance company. He named it Moving Through Space and Time, and planned to focus on different dance styles, what they had meant as an art form, and how they'd evolved throughout American history. He'd hire a corps of dancers, but would also include stars to do cameos. Who better to start with on that front than Sasha and Rory?

Unbelievably, his father was tremendously pleased with his decision, delighted that his son was now the owner of his own business. His father even lent him a good deal of startup money.

Eventually, we'd probably leave Alessia's studio, but for now we were still teaching our old students. She'd already attracted several more top local dancers to teach, due largely to our Blackpool win and notoriety.

Jett talked to the crowd a little about his new venture, and said the company's first performance would be in this very studio—only for Infectious Rhythm students—before moving on to larger venues in Los Angeles and then going on tour. He said everyone was invited to the premiere later this year at the big Hollywood theater where he'd once performed as a member of Beauty in Motion. The crowd went crazy with applause. I was so proud of him.

When he'd told me about his initial thoughts for the company, I'd liked the idea of touring. L.A. would always be our base, our place to come home to. But I'd always wanted to see more of the world than the few showdance competitions I competed at year after year allowed for. I longed for new places, new experiences. This would give me the chance.

After all the chatting and catching up, we performed for the studio. We hadn't danced our routine since Blackpool and it felt like magic all over again. Every time Jett lifted me in that absolutely beatific one-legged lift, I felt the bliss all over again. I felt Willem in the room, looking down on me, telling me it was all good. Better than good. He was happy, he was at peace, and he was loving his ability to watch me live my life.

After Jett brought me down and lowered me into our ending fish dive, the crowd went crazy wild, as expected. Not to sound obnoxious of course. But what was not expected was that, just like Blackpool, they started tossing bouquets onstage. I laughed. Our studio never did this. Jett reached out and caught one big one. He caught it just like a football player would catch a football, grabbing it right out of the air and claiming it as his own.

"Wow, this one is gorgeous," he said. It was.

This time he bent down on one knee to present it to me. I laughed and reached out to take it. But then I noticed there was something shiny secured to the stem. It was so lucent it almost blinded me momentarily.

"Wait, what's that?" I said, feeling for it.

"Lights, please, lights!" Jett called out.

All of the studio's lights flashed on and I could see much better. Oh my gosh, it was…it was a ring. And the ring had diamonds on it.

"Arabelle, I love you. You are my everything. You made me the person I was always meant to be. I didn't see it until we came into each other's lives. I hope you'll say yes to becoming one forever."

I felt tears well in my eyes and I looked down at him. Here was the man who thrilled me, who set my passions aflame, but who also listened to me and trusted me to know the best way not only to wow a crowd but to create poetry and beauty. He was the man who helped guide me back from the edge of despair, who helped me to see what my true life's passions were, and helped me to overcome the horrible thing that was thwarting me from being who I was meant to be. That bolt of light shone down on me again, the one that happened every time I pressed my palms together in prayer. I received Willem's blessing, just as I knew I would.

"Yes," I said, tears filling my eyes. "Of course!"

Jett wrapped his arms around me and I held the bouquet with the ring still attached to the stem up high above our heads, my hand not trembling one bit.

The End

A NOTE FROM THE AUTHOR

Thank you to Rebecca Kimmel, my excellent editor, Marisa-rose Wesley, my wonderful cover designer, and all of my inspiring co-writers in the Los Angeles and Arizona chapters of Romance Writers of America for their generous advice, encouragement and words of wisdom. Thank you to my parents for their never-ending support.

But mostly, thank you to you, dear reader. To an indie author, reader support is absolutely everything. There are so very many books out there and I am so beyond grateful that you chose to read mine. I would love it if you would leave a brief review on Goodreads or wherever you purchased this book. And please do connect with me on Facebook, Goodreads, or my website at *www.tonyaplank.com*!

ABOUT THE AUTHOR

After working for many years as an attorney in New York and Los Angeles, Tonya Plank returned to Southern Arizona, where she grew up. A former amateur ballroom dancer, she wrote the dance blog, "Swan Lake Samba Girl." Her first novel, *Swallow*, won several awards, including gold medals in the Independent Publisher and the Living Now Book Awards, and was a finalist in ForeWord's Book of the Year and the National Indie Excellence Awards. She is also the author of the *Fever: A Ballroom Romance* trilogy and *Sasha*, a duet, both part of the *Infectious Rhythm* dance romance series.

When she's not hard at work on her next novel, she enjoys taking road trips with her rescue dogs, Sofia and Irina, cuddling up with her cat, Katusha, and a good book, and of course watching dance performances of any kind.